Archer of the Heathland

Book Two

Betrayal

D1528636

J.W. Elliot

Bent Bow
Publishing

Copyright © 2018 J.W. Elliot

Bent Bow Publishing
P.O. Box 1426
Middleboro, MA 02346

ISBN-13: 9781718150461

Cover Design by Brandi Doane McCann

If you enjoy this book, please consider leaving an honest review on Amazon and sharing on your social media sites.

Please sign up for my newsletter where you can get a free short story and more free content at: **www.jwelliot.com**

TO MY CHILDREN

Book Two

Betrayal

MAP OF
FREI-OCK ISLES

Chapter 1
The Bloody Parchment

Killian peered at the blood-spattered message. "They're missing, Your Grace," he said.

Killian watched as the Duke of Saylen revolved on the spot and resumed pacing the velvet carpet that covered the floor of his tent. Fine incense glowed red in the brass burner, letting off the rich, pungent smell of exotic resins from the continent. The Duke never had liked the stench of an army encampment.

He was a powerful man with broad shoulders and an angular jaw. His sandy-brown hair was beginning to thin. Killian glanced down at the document in his hands. The message had been scrawled in a hurried script and the ink had smeared. Flecks of mud and dark, red splotches of blood speckled the paper.

"We'll be surrounded in a few days," the Duke said.

"Yes, My Lord." Killian noted the streak of mud on his own sleeve. He withdrew the red, silk handkerchief from his pocket and scrubbed the spot away. Even in an army camp, it wouldn't do to appear too casual.

The Duke fell into the leather-covered chair before his writing desk and placed his head in his hands.

"And the messengers?" the Duke asked.

"Dead, My Lord."

The Duke slammed his fist onto the table, causing the inkwell to jump off onto the velvet carpet. Killian sighed. That stain would never come out. But the Duke didn't care. He was a passionate man, and Killian often had to step in to check him. Of late, he had become even more agitated. Seeing the Duke's restless tension and nervous fidgeting, Killian concluded that now was not a good time to

1

mention the ruined carpet.

"Do you understand what this means, Killian?" the Duke said.

"I believe I do, My Lord." Killian had served the Duke of Saylen since the Duke was a boy. And Killian had grown old in his service. There was nothing that Killian didn't know about him or what he had done and how the past haunted him. He pitied the man and admired him at the same time.

How many people could stand by while their entire extended family was murdered? And how many could have navigated the dangerous post-coup years to become one of the most powerful men in the entire Kingdom of Coll, even though he was tainted with the blood of the old royal family of Hassani? The last of the family line—well, except for his sons and the lost prince who had disappeared into the vast heathland without a trace.

The Duke had made himself invaluable to King Geric as a soldier, as a statesmen, and as a legitimizing force for the usurper line that ruled Coll. As the nephew of King Edward, the last Hassani king to sit on the throne, the Duke's support of King Geric had been crucial in allowing Geric to secure his rule. That was the Duke's genius, but would it be enough to see him through this last test of his craftiness and determination?

"Who can I trust?" the Duke said. He raised his head to stare at Killian as if he expected his old steward to have some occult knowledge of other men's intentions. Sometimes, even the Duke could look like a lost child. He passed a weary hand over his head.

"Your son, My Lord?" Killian said.

The Duke didn't stir. He stared over Killian's shoulder with a faraway expression. "My son," he whispered. Then he turned his gaze back to Killian, his lips pinched tight in anguish. "I may have to kill him myself," the Duke said.

Chapter 2
The Old Midwife

What does one do when he is awaiting the clash of armies? When one holds the key that could unleash a torrent of blood, a secret for which men were prepared to kill and to die? What does one do when he finds himself adrift in a storm of uncertainty about the most basic questions of existence—like one's own identity?

"You wait," Brion of Wexford said to himself as he gazed out over the open prairie from the back of his Salassani war pony, Misty. She swished her tail at the biting flies that hovered over the prairie grass, seeking an easy meal. The grasses brushed against Brion's legs as they rode toward the large outcrop in the distance. The clean air tasted of cedar and fresh-cut straw.

Brion didn't like waiting. It had already been several days since he had ridden into Wexford after rescuing his sister, Brigid, and his sweetheart, Finola, from slavery.

Secrets existed to be uncovered, and he was going to dig as deep as he could to find out the truth. The big questions might be beyond his reach for the moment, but the old midwife knew more than she had said.

"What?" Finola edged her horse up next to Misty. The horse nibbled at Misty's ears, and Misty jerked her head away with an irritated grunt.

Brion glanced at Finola. She wore her blonde hair pulled back, like she always did. And she still wore the loose shirt and trousers that she and Brigid had been given by the Salassani. They were the only clothes they had since Finola's house had been burned and Brion's and Brigid's cabin had been ransacked. But Finola and Brigid agreed that they were less bothersome than a dress and more comfortable. Finola gave him that devilish smile that made him want to laugh.

"You trained that horse to pick at Misty, didn't you?" he said.

Finola grinned. "You hear that, Brigid? Now he's accusing me of corrupting a horse."

"He's always been afraid of women," Brigid said. Brion cast her an annoyed smirk. Brigid's fiery-red hair played about her shoulders in the warm breeze. She was smiling.

The sudden memory of the words the old midwife had spoken to them that first day they had returned from the heathland made Brion frown.

"Your father comes for the ring, the papers, and the son he gave into Weyland's keeping," she had said.

Weyland and Rosland had been Brion's parents his entire life. Brigid had been his sister. Now, he couldn't be sure who any of them were. The midwife had insisted that Weyland's and Rosland's real son lay buried in a grave in the woods.

Brion reached up to touch the golden ring that hung from a strap of leather around his neck. The ring bore the tiny image of the coat of arms of the Duke of Saylen—a stag in a teardrop shield. The midwife had said that his mother had been wearing the ring when she died.

Finola must have seen his frown and the way he fingered the ring because she stopped smiling.

"Do you think she'll talk?" Finola asked.

"She's crazy," Brigid said. "She's lived alone in that dirty cave for at least twenty years."

"If you think she's crazy," Brion said, "why did you insist on talking to her?"

"Because you're never going to give this up until she admits that she made up that whole story about the four babies." Brigid slapped a large, biting fly that landed on her arm.

"I don't know," Finola said. "She didn't sound crazy to me."

"So you think Brion should run off into the heathland again looking for some lost prince?" Brigid asked with an angry wave of her hand.

Finola winked at Brigid. "Admit it," she said. "You're just grumpy because Emyr hasn't come rushing back to your arms." Finola gave her a wicked grin. "Maybe he came across some fancy, city girl in Dunfermine that he likes better."

Brigid grunted and kicked her horse into a canter, leaving Finola and Brion behind.

Brion laughed and glanced up at the mid-summer sun that now rode high in a clear, blue sky. It warmed his face. The wind tousled his hair. Despite the uncertainty and the worry, it was good to be out on the land again, riding through the tall, prairie grass—to feel it brush against his legs, to hear it sigh and rustle as the horses passed through it, to smell the warm earth and the dry grass.

Their wild dash through the heathland pursued by Salassani and Dunkeldi now seemed like a distant memory, maybe just a horrible nightmare. Brion flexed his right hand. The injury he had received to his sword arm still ached occasionally. A few days of resting, setting the vandalized cabin in order, and waiting for Neahl to return or for Redmond and Emyr to come from the city of Dunfermine had restored their strength. But Brion was getting anxious. He needed to do something.

The rocky outcrop where the old midwife lived stood out of the rolling landscape to peer over the scraggly oak and beech trees that huddled close about its base. Brigid reined her horse to a stop and waited for them to catch up.

"Her cave is around here somewhere," Brion said. They dismounted and plunged into the shadows of the trees on foot. Brion's sword slapped against this leg. The scent of wood smoke filled the air.

"Hello," Brion yelled. The trees swallowed the sound.

"Over here," Brigid called. She stood on a narrow trail, waving to them. They stumbled down the path over the rocks and roots. The constant smell of wood smoke told them they were near. They passed under a rock overhang, and there it was. A dark hole yawned in the black rock. Little rivulets of water slicked over the stone, leaving shiny trails. A thin cloud of white smoke drifted leisurely through the opening to disappear into the leafy canopy.

"Hello," Brion called again.

No one answered.

"I don't think she's home," Finola said.

Brigid stepped past them. "I'm going in," she said.

"Hang on," Brion said.

Brigid spun to face him. "I want answers, and I want them now," she said.

"Brigid—" he began.

"I'm going in." Brigid spun and disappeared into the cave. Brion and Finola followed.

The cave smelled of human filth and something else that made Brion wrinkle his nose. He found Brigid standing in the half-light of the cave beside the smoking embers of a fire. Pots, pans, and moldy, wooden boxes were stacked all about in no apparent order. The old woman seemed to be reclining on a pile of rags. Her bare feet poked out from under the ragged cloak and skirt, stark white against the dark earth. Her cracked and holey boots stood beside the pile of rags as if she had just taken them off to massage her feet. But her head dropped forward at an awkward, unnatural angle.

"Is she . . ." Finola breathed into Brion's ear.

Then Brion saw the wet stain that soaked her front. He recognized the smell that had bothered him when they first entered. It was death.

Brion drew his sword and pushed Finola behind him. "Brigid!" he said. His voice carried a note of warning.

Brigid drew her knife. The cave wasn't large, but they couldn't be sure that the murderer wasn't lurking in the shadows. Brion stepped forward to search the cave. He found a small chamber at the back that apparently served as the old lady's sleeping chamber.

"No one's here," he said.

"She hasn't been dead long," Brigid said.

"That's why we need to get clear of here," Brion said, trying to shepherd them toward the entrance.

"Wait." Brigid bent and retrieved a slip of charred paper that had fallen from the fire. She held it up.

"Anything on it?" Brion asked.

Brigid peered at it. "It's part of a ledger," she said. "Whoa." She glanced at Brion with wide eyes. "It says the Duke paid her 'thirty gold coins for delivery and 'burial.'" That's a fortune."

"Whose burial?" Finola asked.

"Can't tell," Brigid said. "That part is burned."

"Okay, bring it with you," Brion said, still anxious to get far away from the cave. He had come looking for answers, not a fight. And he didn't want to get trapped in the cave. Brion motioned for the girls to wait while he inspected the ground in front of the cave. He bent to examine a set of footprints.

"Boots," he said. "New and probably expensive. No one around here wears boots like this."

"How do you figure that?" Finola asked.

"Sharp edge to the sole and no wear on the heel," he said. "The shape is weird, and they have a complicated stitching pattern. Not normal." Brion stood. "Let's get out of here."

There might be only one set of bootprints at the mouth of the cave, but for all he knew, there could be an entire band of men watching them.

"Should we tell the headman?" Finola asked as they rode side-by-side back toward the cabin.

Brion considered. "How do we prove that we didn't do it?"

"Nobody will care anyway," Brigid said. "To them she's just a crazy, old woman."

"Midwives learn secrets," Brion said. "She tried to burn that page for a reason. Maybe whoever has been trying to have us all killed found out about her."

"It was Seamus," Finola said.

Brion gave Finola a surprised glance. "What?"

"Seamus heard what she said to us in the village," Finola said.

"He wouldn't do something like that," Brion said.

Seamus had been his friend since they had run around naked on hot, summer days in their little, bare feet. The midwife had always been a fixture of the village. She seldom drew attention to herself— just haunted the margins of whatever was going on. People tolerated her because they needed her. She was good at what she did, and she had a special skill with herbs. No one local would have hurt her.

"I'm just saying," Finola said, "that he's the only one who knew what she said to us."

"Which would mean that as long as we stay here, we're making it easy for whoever is after us," Brigid said.

"It's the Duke," Brion whispered as the sudden realization hit him. "He wants the ring and the papers. He's searching for them. If the

King found out what he did, he'd be executed."

"You think the Duke had her killed?" Finola asked.

"Who else would know about her?"

This realization sobered them. The bright sky seemed to darken. Brion had wanted to forget that they were being hunted, that Weyland had left him a secret about a lost prince who had survived the coup eighteen years ago, that Brion had promised Weyland to see it through.

"Why did she put quotation marks around the word 'burial?'" Brigid asked.

"Did she?" Finola said.

"Yep."

"No idea," Brion said.

"Well, what do we do now?" Finola asked.

Brion glanced at each of them and patted Misty's neck. "There's always the grave," he said.

"No." Brigid's voice was sharp, and Brion twisted in the saddle to stare at her.

"I thought you didn't believe her," he said.

Brigid pursed her lips and furrowed her brow. "You can't just dig up a baby's grave," she said.

Brion shrugged. "It's the only way to find out if she was telling the truth," he said.

Finola scowled. "I'm with Brigid on this one. I've seen enough dead bodies to last me a lifetime. I don't want to have nightmares about a baby skeleton."

Brion checked the sarcastic reply that came to his lips. He knew how sensitive Finola was about little children and how adults treated them. He didn't want to unleash her fury.

"I'll go by myself then," he said.

Chapter 3
Reunion

ara stood up from the washbasin over which she bent. Twice before she had experienced that sudden knowledge that the world was going to shift under her feet. It came to her the day she discovered that Redmond, the man she loved, had left the island and abandoned her and their unborn child. She felt it again that day beside the river hours before the Taurini attacked, leaving her for dead while they carried away her only child, Evan, into slavery or death.

Lara stretched her back to ease the knotted muscles and listened to the sounds of her nieces and nephews playing somewhere in the house. She draped the dripping shirt over the scrub board, wiped her hands on her apron, and strode through the adjoining room into the hallway to the front door. She pulled it open and stepped out into the street.

The afternoon noises and sharp smells of Dunfermine came to her on the little breeze that stirred her long skirt and tickled the strands of blonde hair that fell around her face. The heavy smell of burning coal from the blacksmith shop down the street mixed with the warm aroma of horse manure and the stench of human waste from the nighttime chamber pots. Nothing unusual about any of that. Lara returned to her laundry, trying to shake the feeling. She didn't have time for it.

Her younger sister, Morwyn was still confined to her bed from her recent childbirth. It was her sixth. So Lara had to pick up the work of two. She hadn't even had time to make the fine lace that she sold to the local shops. She had become the spinster who cared for the sister lucky enough to find a good man rather than the useless, sots

9

who preyed upon Lara after her disgrace.

Lara finished the washing and checked the large pot of boiling stew hanging on a hook over the fireplace in the kitchen and the bread baking in the oven. She glanced up as her father, Kurk, shuffled through the door. His shirt and trousers seemed to sag around his bent frame as he leaned on his crutch.

"How was the shop today?" Lara asked as she filled her father's bowl. The children started to filter in, making so much racket that she couldn't hear his reply. His crutch leaned against the table. He bent his silver head to the spoon of hot broth.

Lara paused to examine Kurk's gnarled hand that quivered as it raised the spoon. The rheumatism made his cobbler work difficult, but he never complained. Lara rubbed warm oil on his hands every night, which eased the discomfort some, but they were getting worse.

She served the children and took a slice of bread and bowl of steaming soup up to Morwyn. She found her nursing the baby. Lara caressed the soft head. The touch brought back the longing for her own little Evan. Sometimes her arms still ached to hold him.

A muffled knock on the door below created pandemonium in the kitchen as the children scrambled to see who would reach the door first. Lara descended the stairs to find that the house had become quiet. This puzzled her. She couldn't remember a time when a visitor made the children more quiet. It usually made them even more excited and rambunctious.

She stepped into the hallway to the sound of low voices. Men were speaking to her father. She paused in the doorway to the kitchen. A man in his mid-forties stood grasping her father's hand in his. He was tall and thin with a grizzled beard. His clothes were dirty and travel-worn. Beside him stood a tall, handsome young man, perhaps in his early twenties. This young man was dressed in the earth-colored Salassani clothes that had the closed neckline and long sleeves that tightened on the wrist, but he didn't have the same dark hair and eyes. His hair was sandy-brown and his eyes the color of honey. He had scars on his face and a long, purple line on his right hand. Lara hesitated at the door, uncertain whether she should intrude, but concerned for her father's safety.

The young man noticed her movement in the doorway and their gaze met. The recognition in his face puzzled her. He touched the older man with the grizzled beard standing next to him. When the older man raised his head, shock swept through her. She would have recognized that expression anywhere. She had seen it a million times while growing up in Comrie and then hundreds of times after that. It was the expectant look of one who wished to please, but who feared rejection.

Lara's lips moved. She whispered his name. Her father, turned to look at her but she could not take her gaze from the man. "Redmond?" she said aloud.

"I . . ." he began as he stepped toward her and then stopped. "Lara, I'm sorry. I've come home."

Lara swallowed. She blinked rapidly. What was she supposed to feel? For years, she had hoped and waited and waited and hoped. She had endured scorn and poverty, and now he returned and told her that he had come home? That he was sorry?

She opened her mouth to speak, but could find no words. She left the room, climbed the stairs to her bedroom, closed the door softly, and sat on the edge of her bed. Why had he come? What did he want from her?

Redmond watched Lara walk away with a despair he could not describe. She still had that delicate, kindly face with deep-brown eyes. She wore her blonde hair shorter than he had remembered, but it still had the soft, yellow glow. She hadn't recognized him at first, and, when she had, she hadn't seemed happy to see him.

He hadn't expected her to throw her arms around his neck as if nothing had happened. But the stony silence was difficult to experience. He glanced back at Emyr who simply shrugged, but his face betrayed his emotions. Lara had not recognized her own son. Redmond reached out and squeezed Emyr's arm in reassurance, though he felt none himself.

Redmond looked down at Lara's father, Kurk, who peered up at him expectantly. Redmond remembered him as a soft spoken, gentle man, but one who was not afraid to be direct when necessary. Redmond blinked at the sting in his eyes. He didn't know what to say.

"I think you gave her quite the shock just now," Kurk said as he waved to the table where the crowd of children stared at them in silence. "Sit down and eat with us. Lara is still a good cook."

Redmond hesitated, then nodded his acceptance. The children made room for him and Emyr. The oldest girl arose after a command from her grandfather to serve them a bowl of soup and a slice of bread.

"Are these Lara's children?" Redmond asked.

Kurk smiled. "No, no, my boy. They are all Morwyn's rascals, every one." He reached over and pinched the cheek of the boy nearest him.

"Derrick should be home shortly."

"Derrick?" Redmond asked.

"The children's father," Kurk said. "Good man, Derrick. He took us in when we first came to Dunfermine. Hard worker, that boy." The old man paused. "Now tell me lad, where have you been these long years?"

Redmond swallowed his mouthful of bread. It was warm with the sharp taste of rye. "I've been in the southlands beyond the sea. I sold the skills I learned in the Heath War as I wandered about."

"So you've been a wandering warrior, have you now? Seen many great battles?"

Redmond nodded. "Too many, I'm afraid."

"Lots of southern women too, no doubt," Kurk said with a mischievous grin.

Redmond shook his head. "No, sir. I never took a wife." How could he explain to this man what his life had been like for the last eighteen years?

Kurk studied Redmond for a long moment. "You know she waited for you," he said.

Redmond nodded. "I know."

"You broke her heart, boy." It wasn't spoken as a rebuke, only a statement of fact.

"I know." Redmond bowed his head. The bitterness of his wasted years pressed down upon him.

"So why come back now? What do you want?"

Redmond blinked as he struggled to keep his emotions in check. He had known this would be difficult, but he was finding it more of a challenge than he had expected. How could he explain? "I didn't know about the baby," he said. "Or I never would have left."

"The Taurini got him," Kurk said quietly. "That's when they ruined my leg." He reached a hand down under the table. "They left us for dead, you know. Lara nearly drowned in the river, and I would have bled to death if that Carpentini man hadn't found me. He saved my leg, but, well…" Kurk trailed off.

"I've brought him home," Redmond said. He cleared his throat and blinked rapidly, trying to control the raw emotions that tightened his throat.

Kurk raised his head slowly. His gaze swiveled toward Emyr. For the first time, he took a long, hard look at him. Emyr sat still, watching.

Kurk swallowed. "Is it you, Evan?"

Emyr nodded.

Kurk turned his gaze back to Redmond.

"How?" Kurk said.

"It's a long tale, and you've just sat down to your dinner." Redmond paused. "I think Lara should hear it."

Kurk nodded. "It won't be easy for her." He examined Redmond. "What are you going to ask of her? She has suffered enough."

"I'll ask for nothing. I only want to explain."

Kurk nodded and motioned to the oldest girl to fetch Lara.

"Come over by the fire where it's more comfortable," he said. "These old bones like the warmth of a fire."

Lara entered the room with a passive face. She had now had time to absorb the shock a bit, and she was ready to hear what Redmond had to say. Redmond stood and offered her his seat, but she shook her head.

"I'm sorry to disturb you," Redmond said. "I hardly know where to begin." He paused as if deciding something important. Then he motioned toward the young man. "This is Emyr, Lara. He is our son."

The warmth drained from Lara's face. She stepped forward involuntarily as Emyr rose to his feet. His brow was wrinkled the way her Evan used to wrinkle his when he was worried. His golden brown eyes watched her, excited, anxious. He stepped toward her.

"Mother," he said as he clasped her hands in his. She gazed into his face. There behind the scars, the dirt, and the whiskers was her little boy.

A sob escaped her throat as she pulled him into a fierce embrace. He smelled of sweat, and dirt, and heather. It was a wild smell—the smell of the open heathland he had so loved as a child. Her boy. Her little boy had come home.

Lara's mind seemed to freeze for a long moment as she struggled to comprehend how this could be. She could form no clear thoughts or words as she sobbed into the dirty, smelly shoulder of her boy who now called himself Emyr.

No one spoke. The quiet popping of the fire competed with Lara's sobs as she clung desperately to this strange, young man who had returned to her as if from the grave. Fifteen years of heartbreak burst from her in a torrent.

When she had regained some control of her herself, Lara pulled away and wiped at her tears. Emyr left his tears to glisten on his cheeks.

Lara sniffled. "You're a man now," she said. Then she glanced at Redmond. "How did you find him?"

Redmond shrugged. "He found me. It's a long tale if you would like to hear it."

Lara nodded. She scooped one of the children from the chair behind her and sat cradling him in her lap. Redmond and Emyr resumed their seats.

"First, I want you to understand why I left," Redmond said.

Lara bowed her head to stare at the floor. She didn't know if she could bear to hear it. "Neahl already told me," she said.

"Neahl didn't know," Redmond said. "He thought I was a coward who had abandoned him to a desperate fight. But that wasn't true."

The earnestness in his voice caused Lara to look up.

"I would have stayed and, if necessary, died with them." Redmond clasped his hands in front of him and stared at a spot on the floor. "But my horse was shot by an arrow, and he bolted. My boot was caught in the stirrup so I couldn't dismount. By the time I regained control and made my way back to them, they were gone."

Redmond raised his gaze again. "I had to fight my way through the Dunkeldi, but I kept hearing how Neahl and Weyland were boasting that they would kill me on sight for being a coward. I knew they would, too. I felt betrayed."

"That's a pretty lame excuse for leaving me with a child," Lara said. She didn't care that pain flicked across Redmond's face. He deserved it after all she had suffered because of him.

"If I hadn't left," Redmond said. "Neahl would have kept going until we were all dead. You know how stubborn he is. I realized that I had to kill him or leave him. I couldn't kill my own brother. But things were worse than you know. On my way south, I discovered that I was being trailed by assassins. I couldn't lead them to you. So I lured them off the island and killed them. I couldn't come back after that."

"Why not?"

"Because I was being followed. The only way to keep you safe was to stay away."

"Weyland managed," she said, though she suppressed a twinge of guilt. She hadn't told Redmond about the baby. It had been her choice to remain silent. She had wanted him to come back to her because he loved her, not because he felt an obligation to his child. She had believed he would come back. But she had been wrong. He hadn't loved her enough.

Redmond shook his head. "Neahl protected them for years. But in the end, Weyland's enemies got to him."

Kurk poked an iron into the fire, and Redmond sat forward, his face alight with an earnestness she had seldom seen. Lara glanced down at the floor again.

"I know I betrayed your trust," he said, "and I am sorry. But if I had known that you were with child, I would have taken you with me. I never would have left you alone with a child, no matter what the risk."

Silence filled the room again, but Lara refused to look at him.

"I don't expect you to forgive me," he said. "But I wanted you to know the truth." He paused. "All these years I imagined that you would already have a family of your own. I didn't know."

He paused to wipe at a tear and to clear his throat.

Lara lifted her gaze from the floor. She had no reason to doubt his word. In fact, she had never known him to lie, except for the promise he made to come back to her. That betrayal had been the source of all of her suffering. In some ways, it might have been better had he died on the heathland. At least then she would not have had to suffer all the years of doubt and wasted hope.

"Do you have any idea what I have been through?" Her voice was even and low.

Redmond shook his head. "I can only imagine," he said. "I would take it back if I could."

"No, I don't think you can imagine." Lara let the bitterness fill her words. "I don't think you have any idea what it has been like to be spurned and mocked and hated and ridiculed all because you chose to run off and leave me." Her back was up, and she would give him a piece of her mind. "I don't think you have any idea what it was like to have my child, my fatherless child, torn from my arms because his father wasn't there to protect him like he should have been."

"Lara," Kurk tried to cut in but she talked over him.

"I lost my child to the Taurini whom his father had spent half of his life fighting because he insisted on following his selfish brother."

By the time she finished, she was shouting. Her chest heaved and burned. She glared at Redmond, daring him to contradict her.

Redmond had bowed his head under the assault. This act of submission fueled her anger. He should defend himself, give her some reason to keep shouting, tell her that she was partly to blame for not telling him about the child. Tears of bitterness and anger trickled down Lara's cheeks to drip onto the child in her lap who wiped at them and peered up at her with a frightened gaze. Lara squeezed him reassuringly and tried to smile.

The uncomfortable silence settled over the room like a damp blanket.

Emyr sat forward. "Mother," he said with that expression he had when he wanted to please. "You asked how Father found me."

Lara nodded.

"I remembered the stories you used to tell me about my father and Neahl and Weyland." Emyr shifted, and his face became troubled. "I captured a girl named Brigid on a raid only to discover that she was Weyland's daughter. Her brother Brion, Neahl, and Redmond came to rescue her and another of their friends. Eventually I realized who they were, and we came to find you together."

Lara wiped at the new tears. "But what happened to you after they took you? Where have you been?"

The child in Lara's lap wiggled, and she let him down.

"I was sold up north to the Taurini," Emyr continued, "where I lived for a few years. Then a Salassani warrior bought me and raised me as his son."

Emyr glanced at Redmond. "His name was Mortegai. He had met Redmond years before when Redmond had killed his son in battle and then spared Mortegai's life."

"Neahl never forgave me for sparing him," Redmond said, "for what he called my 'weakness.'"

"But because you spared him," Emyr said, "he was there to raise me as his son."

Redmond bowed his head to contemplate the dirt floor.

"Mortegai died in a raid a year ago," Emyr said, "and his mother recently passed away, as well, so I came south."

"I don't understand," Lara said to Redmond. "Why did you come back at all?"

Redmond held up his hands. "I heard rumors that the entire island would be engulfed in war. I wanted to come home to see if you were all safe. But the day I found Neahl over in Wexford, I found out that Weyland had been killed by the Salassani that very morning, and they had taken Weyland's daughter."

"Weyland is dead?" Lara asked.

Redmond nodded. "The assassins finally found him," he said. "They killed Rosland, too. Their son, Brion, and Neahl and I went into the heathland to find their daughter, Brigid, and two other village girls. That's how we found Emyr."

Lara blinked at Emyr. "You did it?" Lara's stomach tighten.

Emyr nodded. "I was the leader."

"You've become just like them then." Lara couldn't keep the bitterness from her voice. Her own son had become a murderer and raider just like the ones that had stripped Evan from her arms.

Emyr shook his head as a pained expression swept across his face.

"No, but I had to survive, Mother. I was a child. I could barely remember anything else."

Lara persisted. "But you've been raiding and enslaving all these years?"

"No, I haven't. When I raided I only took horses or property. I never took slaves. I only killed when I had no choice, and I never raided in Coll except that one time."

"Lara," Redmond began, but she silenced him with a glance.

"It's hard," she said as if to herself. "It's just hard."

Redmond watched Lara before turning to Kurk. "Sir, we need to get you and your family out of Dunfermine," he said.

Kurk blinked at him. "We can't up and leave, my boy," he said.

"The Dunkeldi and Taurini are surrounding the city," Redmond said. "You'll be trapped."

Chapter 4
A Child's Grave

The wind haunted the hollow, swirling about the tiny group as they bent over the pile of stones. Despite their protestations, Finola and Brigid wouldn't let Brion go alone. The full moon peeked through the leafy canopy, casting a dappled light on the grave.

"This is it," Brion said as he straightened.

"It's creepy," Finola said. "What do you think you're going to find?" She kicked at one of the stones with her boot.

Brion glanced at her. Her linen shirt rippled in the breeze. She was always so beautiful, even dressed in the pants and shirt of a Salassani slave girl.

"Answers," Brion said.

Brion glanced at Brigid, who stood tight-lipped with her arms folded. Her hair blew across her eyes, and she brushed it away. She had her loose-fitting shirt tied at her waist with a belt and her trousers tucked into her boots like Finola. Brigid wasn't pleased with this idea.

She had been moody ever since the old woman had told them that Brigid's real older brother had died as an infant. Brion didn't want to believe that his whole life had been lie, that he was the son of the Duke of Saylen, anymore than Brigid did. Weyland and Rosland had raised him, and he had loved them. Still, he couldn't help but wonder what the Duke was like.

Brion contemplated the pile of stones. He was determined to search the grave where the old woman said Weyland's real son lay buried. He wouldn't believe her until he saw the body with his own eyes. But it *was* a grave.

Brion tossed the stones aside before he lifted the spade and plunged it into the earth. The wind picked up the fragrance of age and decay and flung it around them until the entire hollow seemed to fill with sadness. Trees moaned and creaked. A cloud passed over the moon.

"Would you hurry up?" Finola said. She cast a furtive glance over her shoulder as another tree groaned. "I don't see why we had to do this in the dark."

"I didn't want to be followed," Brion said. "The last time I was here, someone tried to kill me."

Brion drove the spade into the earth again. Finola jumped as a thud echoed in the hollow. The grave wasn't deep. Hadn't they been worried about wolves and coyotes digging up the body?

Brion bent to scoop away the rest of the dirt that covered a slab of wood. He worked around the edges until he could grasp them. He gave a tug and the nails ripped through the rotted wood. Brion glanced up at Brigid who had bent close. The three of them stooped low, peering into the black hole.

Something ghostly-white lay in the bottom of the box.

"Oh no," Finola said.

Brion tore away the rest of the lid. They stared at the little form enfolded in a white shawl.

"I don't think you should touch it," Finola said.

Brion hesitated. Did he have the right to desecrate this tiny child's grave?

"Move over," Brigid said. She knelt beside the grave and tenderly lifted the bundle.

"Something isn't right," she said.

They gathered around Brigid as she lifted the edge of the shawl. They stared in dumb silence.

"I don't understand," Brion said. He had expected to see the hollow eyes of a baby skeleton staring up at him. Not an empty shawl. Where was the skeleton?

Brigid peeled away the rest of the shawl, searching for something. Under the first fold, something dark and shriveled was caught up by the wind. Brion caught it. He held it up to examine it.

"It looks like a dried flower," he said.

Finola snatched it from him. "I think it's a tulip," she said.

Betrayal

They all exchanged curious glances, and Brion reached to peel back another fold of linen. He uncovered a little book. Brigid slid the book from the linen. She turned it around and lifted the cover. The pages fluttered and snapped. Brigid caught the first page and pulled the book close. A ray of moonlight lit the words.

"I'm so afraid," she read. Brigid gazed around at them with wide eyes.

"What does it mean?" she asked.

Finola lifted the book from Brigid's hands and thumbed through the pages.

"It's Rosland's diary," she said.

Chapter 5
The Call to Duty

he rumor of war spread like wildfire when it caught in the dry grasses of the Oban Plain. Couriers pounded up and down the roads at all times of day and night. Long lines of wagons and people on foot filed south passing through Wexford or off to the east to larger cities, such as Mailag and Brechin. The south road became a veritable highway as people scrambled to get out of the way of the clashing armies.

No one could say they had seen a single Dunkeldi warrior, but that didn't seem to matter. Even with all the traffic, no one had heard any word from Dunfermine. It was as if the Dunkeldi had enclosed the entire city in a tight noose. Nothing and no one went in or came out.

"I can't stand not knowing," Finola said as another company of wagons trundled down the south road. "What if Redmond and Emyr didn't make it to Dunfermine?"

Finola, Brigid, and Brion had learned on their return from the heathland several days ago that Finola's parents, Paiden and Shavon, had been driven out of town by those who had blamed Brion and Neahl for starting a war with the Dunkeldi.

"I don't understand why we haven't had news of a Dunkeldi attack," Brion said.

Finola faced Brion. "Let's practice now," she said. "I need to focus on something else."

They had kept with their routine of keeping watch at night, caring for their gear, and practicing fighting. Given the uncertainty of their situation, it seemed like the only reasonable thing to do. But waiting for Neahl to return from his trip to Chullish was wearing on their nerves. It was the inaction that picked at Brion. It was like having an itch he couldn't scratch.

"I won't be carried away like a sack of potatoes again, Brion," Finola said. "Not for any man."

Brion grinned. "You would make a cute sack of potatoes," he said.

Finola slapped his arm and pulled the wooden practice knife from her belt. "Don't play with me." She held up the wooden knife.

Brion raised his hands.

"All right. Why don't you and Brigid go over what we covered yesterday?"

The two girls circled and began their drills. Brion watched absent-mindedly. They had both become very good with knives, and Brion had them practice the drills that Neahl and Redmond had taught him.

But his mind was still preoccupied. He gazed out over the fields, enjoying the cool breeze that cast up the scents of the earth and the forest. He knew that their time at the cabin couldn't last. War was coming, and Wexford was exposed. It was too near the heathland. He was anxious for Finola's parents and worried that Redmond and Emyr hadn't made it to Dunfermine or that they had made it and had been trapped inside. And what was taking Neahl so long to return from Chullish?

"Don't move," Finola said.

Brion glanced back to the girls again to find Finola holding Brigid tight with the wooden knife to her throat.

"You're a natural," Brion said.

Finola wiped the sweat from her eyes and wiggled her eyebrows at him. "I guess it pays to be ornery," she said.

Before Finola finished speaking, the sound of pounding hooves broke from the trees behind the cabin. Brion scrambled for his bow as the girls did the same. He ran around the smokehouse to peer over the back pasture, now thick with weeds. A blonde head bent low over the back of a galloping horse.

"Seamus?" Brion said.

"He looks like he's got a burr under his saddle," Finola said.

"This can't be good," Brigid said.

Brion waited until Seamus yanked the horse to a stop and leapt to the ground.

"He's coming," Seamus panted.

"Who?"

"The Sheriff, and he has men with him."

Brion exchanged glances with Finola and Brigid.

"I think you should go," Seamus said.

"Why?" Brion asked.

"They're accusing you of murdering the old midwife," Seamus said. "The headman has been in a fury ever since you returned, but he's too much of a coward to do anything himself. I think they're coming to arrest you."

"We didn't kill her," Brion snapped. The anger and frustration he had been suppressing for weeks began to rise to the surface.

"I don't think anyone is going to care much whether you did it," Seamus said. "They're out for blood."

Brion cursed. "Are we packed?"

"We're always packed," Finola said.

"Thanks, Seamus," Brion said. Once again, his friend had been there for him, and once again, he was going to leave him behind.

"You had better hurry," Seamus said.

Brion and Seamus saddled the horses while Brigid and Finola brought their gear out of the cabin.

"Where are you going to go?" Seamus asked.

Brion shrugged. "Into the woods, I guess. Tell Neahl when he comes that we went to the place where Weyland killed the wildcat a few years ago. He'll know what I mean."

"Brion!" Brigid called.

Brion ducked under Misty's neck to see Brigid and Finola facing the road. A line of horsemen appeared on the crest of the hill.

"Let's go," Brion said. "Hurry."

Brigid and Finola ran to their horses and climbed into the saddles.

"Goodbye," Brion said to Seamus. "And thanks."

Seamus nodded to him.

Brion kicked Misty into a gallop at the same moment that Brigid cried out.

"Neahl," she yelled.

Brion reined Misty around to find Neahl leading five horsemen down the hill. Sheriff Cluny rode at Neahl's side. Two more rode behind them, and a short, round man, slouching in his saddle, dawdled at the rear.

Brigid kicked her horse toward them.

"Wait," Brion called after her.

But Brigid had already reached Neahl's side. He pulled her from the saddle into a hug before letting her down and dismounting himself. Neahl favored his right leg as he dismounted. The arrow wound in his hip that he had received while shielding Finola as they had escaped the Salassani encampment at the Great Keldi had almost killed him. He survived because of Redmond's care and his own stubbornness.

Brion chuckled and shook his head. It was good to see Neahl again. Somehow the big, burly man with the grizzled hair exuded confidence. He made Brion feel safe. Brion and Finola slipped from their saddles as Neahl gestured toward them.

"Lord Sheriff," Neahl said, "you already know Brion."

Cluny inclined his head in Brion's direction and dismounted. His long sword swung awkwardly, and his polished, mail shirt caught the morning light. His gray, speckled beard did not hide the long, lean face.

"This is Brigid, Weyland's daughter," Neahl continued, "and Finola."

The two young women stood awkwardly, uncertain how to greet a lord sheriff. Maybe it was that neither of them wore dresses now that they had discovered the freedom that breeches gave them. Or maybe it was because they were covered in dirt and sweat from their knife fighting practice.

"It's a pleasure," Cluny said. He faced Brigid. "I was sorry to hear about your parents, and I'm happy that you both made it home safely." Brion noted that Cluny's eyes shifted and his gaze slid over them without pausing long enough to meet their eyes.

Then Cluny gestured toward the men behind him. Two of them had dismounted. One wore rich clothing and expensive weapons. The other two were more shabby and travel-worn. The wealthy young man kept his gaze on the girls while the other two men watched Brion.

"Let me introduce young master Hayden," Cluny said. "His father was sword master to the King."

Hayden bowed slightly with a glance at Brion before focusing his attention back to the young women. He had sandy-brown hair and a sharp, angular face. Brion guessed that women might find him attractive. Hayden was taller than Brion by several inches, but Brion noted that most of his height was in his legs. He let himself consider for a moment how best to defeat a man of this build.

"And this," Cluny said, stabbing a hand toward the stocky, dark-haired man standing beside Neahl, "is Jaxon."

Brion's gaze paused on Jaxon for a moment because where his right eye should have been was a shriveled, blackened socket. A shock of jet-black hair dangled partway in front of the empty socket. Jaxon's good eye studied Brion, and his expression was one of detached interest. An involuntary shiver swept over Brion. Jaxon was probably the creepiest person he had ever seen.

"And the one who can't seem to find his way down from his horse," Cluny continued, casting an annoyed glance at the balding man who lounged in the saddle, "is Tyg."

Tyg inclined his head, but made no move to dismount. His hands rested on the pommel. His hair was uncombed and disheveled. His eyelids sagged, and he seemed disinterested in the entire conversation. At his ample waist, several sheaths held a variety of knives and one short sword. Brion decided that Tyg was the most dangerous man of the three because it would be easy to underestimate him.

After the introductions, Neahl gestured to the cabin, and Brion invited them in. He glanced at Seamus where he still stood by the smokehouse with his horse's reins in his hand. Brion nodded for Seamus to follow, but Seamus shook his head. Brion wondered if Seamus was just being shy, but he left Seamus to himself and followed the others inside the cabin. The men gathered around the small table, while Brigid and Finola huddled in a far corner, trying not to be noticed.

Without any ceremony, Neahl handed Brion a folded piece of parchment sealed with red wax bearing the royal coat of arms—a boar with crossed swords underneath. Brion had only seen the coat of arms a few times, but he recognized it.

"What is it?" Brion asked. Considering that he had been at least partly responsible for starting a war and that Seamus had just told him that they were being blamed for the old midwife's death, Brion wasn't sure he wanted to open the letter.

Neahl nodded to the letter, gesturing impatiently. "Just open it."

Brion broke the seal and unfolded it. It crackled as writing powder spilled onto the table. He scanned the first line then looked up, first at Neahl and then at Cluny.

"Is this a joke?" he asked.

"No joke. You've got one week," Neahl said.

"Neahl—" Brion began.

"Don't even start with the excuses," Neahl said. "It's not a request. It's a command from the King himself."

"Me?" Brion was sure that Neahl had messed something up somewhere. He glanced at the Sheriff, who wore a fatherly smile that Brion found annoying. Hayden, who stood behind the Sheriff, smirked. Tyg and Jaxon didn't look directly at him.

"That's what it says," Neahl replied. "You've got one week to form a company of not less than five men and not more than ten. Your orders are to penetrate the heathland, to harass the enemy at every opportunity, cut supply lines, and gather intelligence."

Brion stared at Neahl. "What do you mean, *my* orders? Aren't you coming with me?"

Neahl shook his head. "I'll be leading my own company over in Laro Forest, my old stomping grounds."

"What about Redmond and Emyr?"

Neahl glanced at the Sheriff, who cleared his throat.

"Ah, well, that has become a difficult question," Cluny said.

Brion waited for him to continue.

"Redmond has been, uh, how do you say, gone an awful long time," Cluny said. "No one knows where his loyalties lie."

Brion gaped at Cluny. "But you've fought with him," he said. He turned to Neahl. "And he's *your* brother."

Neahl scowled. "I never said I didn't trust him." He gave Cluny a meaningful glance. "But the King says he's been in the southland too long and can't be trusted."

"And he has a son who's a Salassani," Cluny added.

"Emyr was kidnapped." Brion protested. He couldn't believe the stupidity. Of all the men to suspect of treason, Redmond and Emyr were the last.

Brion glanced at Jaxon. Jaxon was clearly a Salassani. Why was Cluny riding around with a Salassani if none of them could be trusted? Cluny saw the direction of his gaze and raised his hands to head off Brion's question.

"You're arguing with the wrong people here, Brion. The King has given his orders, and that's the end of it. Will you accept the commission or not?"

Brion glared at Neahl. He had expected an arrest warrant or something like that, not this. And he didn't like being forced to make a decision without talking it over with Finola and Brigid.

"Besides Redmond and I," Neahl said, "you know that part of the heathlands better than any southerner alive."

"Can I talk to you in private?" Brion said to Neahl. Neahl glanced at Cluny and stepped out to the front of the cabin to stand beside Weyland's and Rosland's grave. Seamus still lurked by the side of the cabin as if he had been listening. But Brion didn't have time to worry about Seamus.

"I know," Brion said.

"What?" Neahl eyed him suspiciously.

"I know that I may not be Weyland's son."

Neahl's mouth opened in surprise, and he stared at Brion. Then he bowed his head. "I'm sorry, Brion," he said. "I should have told you."

"How long have you known?" Brion asked, struggling to control his rising frustration that Neahl would keep something this important from him.

"Not long," Neahl said. "There was a letter in Airic's papers."

Airic was the trader they rescued from the jaws of a bear on the heathland. He had helped them until he had been murdered on their way back to Wexford by two Taurini warriors.

"He had a note," Neahl continued, "from the Duke of Saylen that told him to look out for you because you were his son."

Now Brion remembered that strange look of surprise and shock that Neahl had given him that day as Airic lay dead at their feet.

"Why didn't you tell me?" Brion asked.

Neahl raised his hands in a helpless gesture. "How could I tell you something like that when we were trying to save Brigid and Finola?"

"But this changes everything," Brion said.

"What does it change?" Neahl countered. "Where was the Duke when you needed a home? Who raised you and loved you?"

Neahl's face grew red and his gaze grew hard. Brion knew that

Neahl was right, of course. But Neahl didn't know about the hidden prince. Brion glanced at the cabin. Cluny stood in the doorway, watching them. Brion grabbed Neahl's elbow and stepped several more paces away from the door.

"Look," Brion said. "I've got papers and a ring Papa left me. I have to tell you about them before I can agree to this. It explains why we've been tracked and hunted." He glanced back at Cluny again. "Someone is trying to kill us to keep us quiet. But I promised Papa I would see it through. I think I am going to have to go find the Duke."

Neahl tried to interrupt, but Brion plowed ahead.

"And we have to find out what happened to Paiden and Shavon. I can't just take off into the heathland without knowing where they are. Besides, I don't think I want to fight for King Geric. Redmond was right. I don't want to die so he can keep a throne he murdered people to get."

Neahl grabbed Brion's arm. His grip was tight and his eyes hard.

"You're not fighting for some soft noble," he growled. "You're fighting for your homeland. The nobles can sort out their own problems for all I care. But these are *our* people, Brion. If we don't use the skills we've developed, our people will die."

Brion shook Neahl's hand loose and then leaned in close to Neahl.

"Weyland helped them rescue the real prince during the coup," he whispered. "The prince is alive. I saw him at the Great Keldi."

Neahl stared at him with his mouth hanging open. Then he glanced back at Cluny. The hardness evaporated from his face.

"Don't say that again while they're here." Neahl said. He rubbed the stubble on his chin. "Well, that does change a few things," he said. "You can't refuse the King's orders, Brion. Cluny will arrest you and take you to Mailag. You won't have the chance to talk to the Duke." Neahl shook his head and rubbed his beard. "I don't know how long this will take," he said. "The war could last for years or a few weeks. But we'll only be able to operate for a few weeks before it gets too dangerous. Then you can find the Du . . . your father."

"What if things don't go well?" Brion asked. "What if I mess things up?"

"You won't," Neahl said. "I trained you."

"Yeah," Brion said with a laugh. "You beat me until I was black and blue and made me sit out all night freezing in the pouring rain."

Neahl grinned and slapped Brion on the back. "Best training you'll ever get," he said. "Are you ready to give Cluny an answer?"

Brion nodded, and they returned to the cabin where Cluny waited with his gloves in one hand slapping them into the other.

"Can we get on with this?" Cluny demanded.

Brion still didn't like the man. He came across as pompous and domineering. "I'll only accept if Redmond and Emyr come with me," Brion said.

Cluny shook his head. "That's not possible."

"That's my condition."

"Brion, the King doesn't—"

"He didn't say who I could choose for my company, did he?"

"Well, no, but—"

"Then they come with me, or I don't go."

"Cluny." Neahl said, giving him an exasperated expression.

"Oh, all right." Cluny gestured to the other men with his gloves. "Hayden, Jaxon, and Tyg will go with you. That would give you a team of five."

Brion considered protesting, but a look from Neahl silenced him. He inspected the men more carefully now that he knew his life could depend on them and their skills.

Hayden wore the arrogant smirk of a bully. Jaxon was more serious. And it wasn't just because of the creepy eye. He had a solid build for a Salassani and a deeply tanned face. He carried himself like an experienced fighter, and his dark eye seemed to hold little empathy. He was a hard man. That was plain enough. But why would Cluny be riding with a Salassani on the eve of a major war with most of the Salassani tribes? And why would he make such a fuss about Emyr being raised as a Salassani when Jaxon actually was one? It didn't make any sense.

Tyg looked like he would be more comfortable with a barrel of honey mead and a loaf of bread than with a bow or a sword. This apparent ease made Brion suspicious. He studied Tyg. Tyg's eyes kept moving. He was wary and alert despite his façade of unconcern.

Brion regarded Cluny. "I thought I could choose my own company."

Cluny raised his eyebrows.

"I chose these two for you," Neahl said with a casual wave at Jaxon and Tyg. "The King sent Hayden."

Brion examined Jaxon and Tyg more carefully. If Neahl chose them, then they had some special quality Neahl valued and trusted. Brion nodded.

"So long as I get Redmond and Emyr," he said.

"Done," Cluny said. "Have you heard from them yet?"

Brion shook his head. "They went to warn Dunfermine. The Dunkeldi and Taurini have surrounded it."

"So they have," Cluny said. "Well, you have a week to collect them. You had better consider alternatives in case they don't appear."

He said this as if he didn't expect Redmond and Emyr to show up. Brion had long nursed a healthy distrust of Cluny, ever since he wouldn't meet his gaze after Weyland and Rosland had been murdered. He still didn't like him.

Cluny slapped the gloves in his hand again. "Well, I'll be on my way. Brion. Ladies. Neahl."

The other three men followed him out of the cabin with curt nods to Brion and mounted their horses. Seamus still loitered by the shed.

Cluny waved to Jaxon, Hayden, and Tyg. "They'll be staying in town until you're ready." Cluny mounted his horse and rode off at a canter. The other three followed.

Brion watched them go with a furrowed brow.

"You could've warned me," he said to Neahl as they disappeared over the rise.

Neahl shook his head. "King's orders. Had to be secret."

"I've never led men before, Neahl," Brion said, "and operating behind Dunkeldi lines is a suicide mission."

Neahl poked a finger at Brion. "Look, there are only three, well, maybe four men in the entire kingdom of Coll that could pull it off, and you're one of them. Take it as a compliment and quit complaining."

Finola and Brigid exchanged glances but didn't say anything. Brion was too preoccupied to give it a second thought, but Neahl frowned.

"And don't you ladies get any silly ideas into your heads."

Finola opened her hands submissively in front of her, looking around in shock. "What did we do?" she asked.

"Don't try to pull that on me," Neahl said.

"What does this mean?" Brigid interrupted. "What are we supposed to do while you and Brion are off fighting Salassani again?"

Neahl shrugged. "You can't stay in Wexford. It's likely to get overrun. Actually, I was thinking of sending you south. I have a friend there—"

But a chorus of protest from Finola and Brigid overwhelmed his words.

"Look," he said, waving his hands at them as if he hoped to swat away their objections. "Come inside, and we can talk this over while you make me a nice, hot meal."

Finola scowled. "You expect us to cook for you after what you've just said?"

Neahl smirked and shook his head. "I'll cook for myself, then."

"I'm not eating what you cook," Finola replied. She stomped off into the cabin. Brigid followed.

"That one's too headstrong for her own good," Neahl said.

Brion turned to follow Neahl into the cabin when he saw Seamus still standing by the smokehouse with the horse's reins in his hand. His expression told Brion that he had something on his mind.

"Seamus?" Brion said.

"I want to come with you," Seamus said.

Brion didn't know what to say.

Apparently, Seamus had been listening to the entire conversation. "I can use a bow and a knife. And I'm the best grappler in Wexford."

"I know Seamus, but this is the real thing. We could all get killed."

"Well, I'm not staying here," Seamus said. "If you won't take me, I'm going to Mailag to join the army."

"What about the tannery and your parents?"

"My father said he would go if he could. My mother, well, she's Momma." He said this with a shrug. "Either way, I'm going to fight."

Brion sighed. Seamus had been his friend as long as he could remember. Seamus had remained loyal even though his loyalty had placed him in danger. And Seamus was a good fighter, but he hadn't been trained the way Brion had. Still, he knew he could trust Seamus, and that was something he had grown to value in the last few months. "All right Seamus," he said. "But you have to do what I say."

Seamus grinned. "I'll be back tomorrow with my gear." He climbed into the saddle and galloped away.

Chapter 6
The Eagle's Cry

hodri squinted into the setting sun to watch the eagle bank and turn on the wind. It soared over the crystal waters of the lake, banked again, then folded its wings and dropped. The eagle pulled up before it plunged into the water. Its great wings sent up a spray as it rose into the air with the fish twisting in its talons.

Rhodri lifted his right hand to examine the tiny brand of melted skin. The eagle-shaped brand formed the same curving arch of the eagle's wings as it had lifted the fish from the water. He had been branded at his mother's bedside seconds after birth—the mark of the prince. As he watched the eagle alight on the limb of a gnarled, old tree and begin to shred its prey, he wondered if he was more like the eagle or the fish.

Rhodri hefted the deer onto his shoulders and trudged up the rocky bluff. The musky scent of the deer filled his nostrils. The soft fur was warm on his neck. The day had been hot, but now a cool breeze filtered its way through the junipers and rustled the little clumps of blue and white heather that dotted the hillsides. The breeze played with his sweat-soaked tunic.

It had been more than a month since he had seen the young warrior at the market of the Great Keldi trying to hide behind a mask of paint and Salassani clothes that didn't fit him. He had found the eagle face paint the young man had worn strangely appropriate, but he doubted that the young man understood it. The young warrior had no idea who Rhodri was or why he had helped him escape the tall Salassani that had pursued them.

Maybe it didn't matter. The Dunkeldi were going to war and dragging all the other tribes with them. The young man didn't even know that he was being used to start that war and that someone very powerful in Coll wanted him dead. But Rhodri knew who the young man was because Finn maintained a complicated network of spies, and Rhodri had tried to warn him. Rhodri had given him the golden eagle for the Duke of Saylen just in case he survived.

Still, he and Finn had escaped the slaughter at the Great Keldi that followed the boy's daring rescue of his sister. Tristan, the king of the Dunkeldi, had chosen to use that rescue as an excuse to inflame anti-Alamani sentiment and to stir up the northern tribes for war.

Rhodri crested the ridge, pausing to catch his breath before working his way down into the valley on the other side. His time was coming. He sensed it like he could sense the smell of the rain on the wind. He expected a messenger from the Duke any day to set the plan in motion. In fact, he had expected this some time ago. He couldn't understand why the Duke delayed.

The sun settled behind the Aveen Mountains as Rhodri descended into the shadowed valley. The aroma of wood smoke drifted through the stand of pines and junipers, drawing him toward the encampment.

Rhodri stopped and sniffed at the air. Something wasn't right. That smoke had a greasy scent and feel to it. He dropped the deer on the blanket of pine-needles that covered the ground and placed an arrow on the string of his short, recurve bow. Dusk had fallen and the shadows were deepening. Rhodri crept toward the encampment until he peered into the clearing from the cover of the trees. Yellow and orange tongues of flame licked at the smoking remains of the Carpentini shelters. Bodies littered the ground. A few blackened corpses lay in the ruin of collapsed lean-tos.

A sudden dread filled him, hot and tense. Where was Finn? The old steward had rescued him as an infant and fled with him into the heathland to the far northern end of the island to hide him among the Taurini. Rhodri had lived the outward life of a slave while Finn had trained him in secret for the moment when he would return and reclaim his family's throne. Finn was his mentor, his savior, his friend.

Ignoring his better judgment, Rhodri hurried into the collection of smoking shelters, searching every corpse he passed. The shelter he and Finn had been using lay in a tumbled heap. Finn was nowhere to be seen. Rhodri kicked at a smoking pole. All of his gear had been in the tent. But that would have to wait.

He continued his search when a rustle in the undergrowth on the edge of the clearing sent him dashing for cover. He drew the bow and trained the arrow on the spot where the serviceberry leaves shook.

Finn stumbled into the clearing. The left side of his face was bathed in blood, and his left arm dangled at his side. Blood dripped from his fingers.

"Finn!" Rhodri rushed to him and helped him lie down. Rhodri drew his knife and cut away Finn's sleeve. Finn's arm lay open to the bone and was gushing blood. Ripping Finn's sleeve free, Rhodri tied it around the wound. Then he held it tight, trying to stop the bleeding. The head wound had already stopped bleeding and was starting to clot. Finn blinked up at Rhodri with his somber, blue eyes. The gray hair matted to his head.

"They came for you," Finn said.

"Who?"

"I don't know. But they were looking for the 'slave boy.'" Finn swallowed.

"How could anyone know?" Rhodri asked. "We've never told anyone."

"Someone in Coll must suspect. At least two of them were Alamani, from Chullish by their accent."

"But how could they connect us to anything in Chullish, and how would they know we were here with the Carpentini?"

Finn rolled his head from side to side. "I don't know." He tried to lick his lips.

Blood continued to seep from between Rhodri's fingers. Why wouldn't Finn's arm stop bleeding? If he didn't do something, Finn would bleed to death. Rhodri searched the burning huts in desperation until his gaze fell upon the blackened hilt of a sword poking from under a still-flaming log.

"Hold on," he said as he jumped to his feet and snatched the sword from the flames. Its tip glowed a dull red. Rhodri knelt beside Finn.

"I'm sorry, but this will hurt," he said. He straddled Finn's body, pinning his arms to his side, and pulled aside the bandage. He placed a hand over Finn's mouth so his cry wouldn't attract any attention and touched the hot metal to the flesh. It sizzled. The blood boiled. Finn screamed and bucked before he fainted away. The reek of burning flesh stung Rhodri's nostrils. Rhodri moved the tip of the sword around to cauterize as much as he could before the metal grew cold. When he was done, he washed the wound with water, made sure the bleeding had stopped, and went in search of sphagnum moss. He collected enough to last for several days.

After washing the moss clean in the little creek, he applied it to the wound. He knew that the moss would protect against infection and that it would absorb any blood or discharge from the wound. He wrapped everything tightly in strips from Finn's shirt. That was all he could do. The moss would keep the wound moist and clean and hopefully prevent an infection.

Finn didn't awake until late in the night. Rhodri had carried him to the shelter of a rock overhang and gone to find any of their gear that hadn't been destroyed in the fires. He found that Finn had saved most of it, which meant they were in a much better position than he had feared.

Finn opened his eyes and swallowed as Rhodri dropped the gear beside him.

"How do you feel?" Rhodri asked.

Finn blinked. "Listen to me," he said. "You have to leave me and go in search of the Duke."

"I won't leave you."

"Rhodri, there's something you need to know, in case I don't make it." Finn swallowed. "There was another boy, a baby."

"Another prince?"

"No, but they gave me another baby to put in your place. I thought he was dead already, but now I can't be sure."

"You mean there might be another boy my age with a brand on his hand who thinks he's the prince?"

Finn nodded. "I didn't think so, but I've heard whispers. I just don't know anymore. You need to be careful."

Rhodri sat back on his haunches and stared into the fire. All his life Finn had told him that he was the prince, had forced him to learn the names of all the noble families in Coll, to study statecraft and warfare. Finn had told him stories about his father and mother and how his mother had died trying to save him. Now Finn was telling him that some other young man might be out there with someone telling him the same things.

"How do I know that I'm the real prince then, Finn?" he asked.

Chapter 7
Farewells

"I feel like a noose is tightening around my neck," Brion said as they bent over the steaming bowls of savory stew Finola and Brigid had cooked. The cooking herbs had filled the cabin with a delicious aroma. "We need to find out who paid Emyr to attack us, who sent the assassin, who ransacked our cabin, who betrayed us to the Salassani, and who killed the old midwife."

"Midwife?" Neahl asked.

"She was stabbed to death in her cave," Finola said.

"Days after she told us that Brion was the Duke's son," Brigid said. "We found this." Brigid handed him the diary. "It was in the grave that was supposed to hold a baby's bones."

Neahl flipped through the diary. "I knew Rosland was a crafty lady that first time I met her riding Weyland's horse," he said. "But I had no idea she and Weyland were this entangled with the Duke."

Neahl sat back in his chair and ran a hand over his graying head. "I thought I knew Weyland," he said.

"Yeah, well, someone has it in for us," Brion said.

"Or two someones," Finola said. "If the Duke only wants the papers, the ring, and Brion, he wouldn't need to pay Emyr to have us killed. But if the King knows about it, he would."

"You mean the King would hire Salassani to do his dirty work," Brigid said.

"If I was King, I would," Finola said.

Neahl pushed his empty bowl away. "You two sure know how to make a nice stew," he said. "You cook a lot better than Brion or Redmond."

"I should hope so," Finola said.

Neahl stretched. "Well, Brion," he said. "I knew Weyland and Rosland were up to something when we first met Rosland, but I didn't know Weyland was involved in this. If what you say is true, the Duke might want us all silenced, just to cover his back. And there's one thing you all need to remember." Neahl folded his hands on the table. "To the nobility, we don't mean anything. In their minds, we only exist to serve them. If we get in their way, they'll kill us without a second thought."

Brion knew that neither Redmond nor Neahl had much respect for the nobility, but now that he was probably the child of a nobleman, he didn't know how to take Neahl's words. He had no intention of becoming a nobleman himself. The Duke could do what he liked, but Brion wasn't going to live in some fancy castle. He needed to be close to the land.

"Well that makes me feel good about myself," Finola said.

"You haven't had to deal with them out here," Neahl said. "Not like you would if you lived on their land. Don't trust them—ever."

When Brion raised his eyebrows, Neahl continued.

"I've seen men whipped for stealing a crumb of bread from a nobleman's floor. I've seen women raped by nobles, and, when the nobles found out the women were pregnant, they either killed them or abandoned them to raise the children alone. Why do you think the Duke has never bothered to claim you as his son?" Neahl gave Brion a moment to answer and then answered for him. "Because he has a legitimate son."

Silence settled over them. Finola watched Brion. He tried not to show his shame, but he knew she saw it.

"But what does this have to do with my brother," Brigid said, "the one that was supposed to be buried in that grave. Where's his body?"

Brion awoke before the sun, stirred to wakefulness by the persistent doubt that he had made the wrong decision. He collected his archery equipment and stood in the doorway, watching the faint glow begin to appear on the eastern horizon. He had spent most of his life roaming the woods before the sun was up. In the winter, he and Weyland had trapped weasels, otters, beaver—any animal with a thick coat that would fetch a gold coin in Mailag. In the summer, they trapped rabbit and opossum to sell in the village. He and Weyland had planted barley and rye in the fields around the cabin. It had been a life of labor, but it had been a good life. And now it was gone. He was being dragged into things he didn't understand.

The morning was cool with a breath of warm air that promised a hot day. Brion's mind was not easy as he gazed around at his boyhood home. Everything had been so simple then. Now he didn't even know who he was, and he probably wasn't going to get the chance to find out. Brion stepped toward the field where he had tied a bale of hay to act as an archery target. He needed time to relax and think.

He hadn't taken more than three steps when he stopped. The hair stood up on the back of his neck. He glanced over at the corral where Misty stood. Her head was up, but she had not given an alarm.

Brion ducked and sprinted for the cover of the trees. As he ran, he nocked an arrow on his string. He leapt over the low lying snowberry bushes and dropped into the shadows of an oak tree. He waited, forcing himself to breathe slowly, quietly. Someone was out there, and after all the weeks of running and being hunted, Brion wasn't taking any chances. He scanned the tall grasses along the edge of the road and the hillside that rose up beyond the cabin as he absorbed the sounds of the waking forest, searching for any clue that might tell where the enemy was and how many there were. A bird called once, then twice. Brion jumped up.

"Would you knock that off and get over here?" Brion called.

A tall, slim figure rose from the thick grass along the road. He strode forward with long, confident strides. Brion jogged to meet him.

"Where've you been?" Brion asked.

Emyr raised his eyebrows and gave an exaggerated sigh. The morning breeze drifted a strand of his sandy brown hair into his eyes.

"Long story," Emyr said. "Once we got into Dunfermine, the Dunkeldi and Taurini tried to lock us in. It took a bit of work to get out."

Brion peered up the road. "Where's Redmond?"

"He'll be along in another hour or two. I was sent ahead to warn you that you were going to have company."

Brion stopped. "You mean you found Lara?"

Now Emyr grinned and nodded.

"Brigid will be glad to see you," Brion said as he turned toward the cabin. "How did you get out of Dunfermine?" he asked as they walked.

"Ah, about that," Emyr said. "Redmond told me Neahl would worry me to tears trying to get the story out of me, but he wanted to tell it."

Brigid appeared in the doorway. Her red hair fell around her shoulders, and her face lit with an intensity Brion had never seen. Finola peered over Brigid's shoulder. A little smile tugged at her mouth.

Brigid waited, wide-eyed and breathless, while the two approached, but she had eyes for no one but Emyr. Brion and Emyr stopped, and an awkward silence seemed to blow in on the warm breeze. Brigid's gaze flicked to Brion. Then she threw herself into Emyr's arms. He caught her as he stumbled backward. Then he held her.

"It's nice to see you, too," Emyr said.

Brion gave Finola a helpless shrug before he stepped to her and clasped her hand in his.

"We better start cooking if we've got guests for breakfast," Finola said. Brigid released Emyr and followed Finola into the cabin with Emyr's hand in hers.

"I hope you have a well-stocked larder," Emyr said.

Finola stopped and faced him with a guarded expression.

"Why?"

"Well, my mother and her family are coming, along with a couple of others."

The way he said this made Brion suspicious that Emyr was hiding something. An hour later, he found out that he had been right.

Redmond appeared with a small caravan. He strode beside his horse, while children trudged along behind him or rode, cradled in the arms of two women. An old man sat astride a lop-eared donkey, followed by a short, muscular man wearing a pack and carrying a child on his shoulders. Several hammers dangled from his belt. Brion was surprised to see Paiden and Shavon, Finola's parents, bringing up the rear. Now he knew why Emyr had been so cagey. He had wanted to surprise Finola.

Redmond greeted them with a raised hand and a big grin. But his words were cut off by Finola's cry of delight. She dashed past him and flung herself into her parents' arms, sobbing into their shoulders. Tears glistened in Shavon's gray eyes as she stroked Finola's hair. The two could have been sisters they were so much alike. Paiden patted Finola's back and grinned as he blinked back the tears.

A burden lifted from Brion's shoulders. That was one less thing he had to worry about. Finola would be with her parents. They could go south like Neahl had suggested. They could be safe.

"You've been dawdling again," Neahl called to Redmond. "Emyr got here hours ago."

Breakfast was the noisiest thing Brion had heard since the market at the Great Keldi. He counted five children scurrying about, but it felt like twenty. They never stopped moving. Finola took it all in stride with the help of her mother, Lara, Morwyn, and Brigid. The men tried to stay inside, but finally gave up and escaped to the front of the cabin. They leaned on the rails of the fence to talk.

"Okay, Redmond," Neahl said, once the chaos of the kitchen was behind them. "Spill the beans." Neahl plucked a blade of grass and began to chew on it.

Redmond grinned at Emyr. "Threatened to beat it out of you, didn't he?"

"Well," Emyr said. "Not quite, but he did pester me to tears."

Neahl glared until Redmond laughed. "I'm going to let Derrick explain," Redmond said. "He's the one who figured it out."

For the first time, Brion studied Derrick. He was a short man with broad shoulders and massive forearms. But he had a kind face and seemed embarrassed to be the center of attention.

Derrick draped his arms over the wooden rail. "I'm a stone mason," he said. "About a week ago, we uncovered a narrow cleft in the rock near the base of the castle where we were reinforcing some of the older walls. A few of us checked it out and found that it opened into an ancient tunnel that led down to the Bowman River, south of the city." He shrugged. "It seemed the best way out."

"It would have been easy," Redmond said, "if the Dunkeldi hadn't camped out on the river bank."

"We waited until dark," Emyr said, "and then we slipped past them." He poked a thumb at Derrick. "Derrick here is pretty good with his hammers. He wields them better than I do my sword."

Brion knew Emyr was exaggerating because he was a very good swordsman. "You had to fight your way out?" Brion asked.

Redmond nodded. "A little. The Dunkeldi had had a bit too much to drink, so they didn't give us too much trouble."

"What about Finola's parents?"

Emyr smiled. "We found them hiding in the woods and invited them to come back with us."

"Hmm," Neahl said. "How many men did the Dunkeldi bring to Dunfermine?" He spit out his blade of grass and plucked up another one.

Redmond shrugged and glanced at Emyr.

"I estimated about three thousand in the army north of Dunfermine," Emyr said, "and about a thousand Taurini south."

Neahl whistled. "How many men will defend Dunfermine?"

Redmond and Emyr both turned to Derrick.

"We have five hundred or so in the active militia," Derrick said, "with another six hundred in reserves. The Duke brought another thousand."

"Outnumbered almost two to one," Neahl said. "Cluny needs to know."

"I already wrote to him," Redmond said. "He should have the letter by now."

"Wait," Neahl said. "When did you send it?"

"We met a courier, what, five days ago?" Redmond said.

Derrick and Emyr nodded. "Cluny should have received the letter at least by the day before yesterday. The courier was from the Duke of Saylen and riding hard."

Neahl scowled and folded his arms. "We met that courier in Mailag. Cluny didn't say anything."

Brion knew that Neahl was thinking the same thing he was. Cluny was up to something. Yesterday he had acted as if he had no idea where Redmond and Emyr were, when he had known all along. Could it be that Cluny didn't want them to go with Brion because the King didn't trust them? Or was there something else going on?

"Did you come through Wexford?" Brion asked, wondering suddenly why they didn't know that Cluny had paid them a visit.

Redmond shook his head. "We didn't take the road."

"Well," Neahl said as he contemplated the blade of grass between his fingers. "As you can see, we made it out of the heathland alive."

"I figured as much," Redmond said.

Neahl then told them about their desperate flight down the river and the nearly disastrous ambush and how Finola and Brigid had successfully fought off four men including the holy man and the man with the burned face all by themselves. Then he filled them in on Brion's assignment to harass the Dunkeldi army.

"Will you come with me?" Brion asked. He knew he was asking a lot of them, especially after they had just found Lara. But he couldn't go back into the heathland without them. He would die for sure.

Emyr smiled. "We wouldn't let you have all the fun," he said.

"What about you, Derrick?" Neahl asked.

Derrick raised his hands and looked at them. "I'm strong and willing," he said, "but I'm no warrior."

"Good," Redmond said, "because we'll need someone to look after the women and children."

Neahl nodded. "Any ideas what to do with them? They can't stay here. This place will be overrun in a matter of weeks."

"I've got family down on the Oban Plain near Taber Wood," Derrick said. "They're tenants of the Duke. We can go there."

Neahl considered, then nodded. "That should do nicely," he said.

A line of horsemen appeared on the ridge. Neahl straightened and tossed his blade of grass to the dirt. To Brion's surprise, it was Cluny, Hayden, Tyg, and Jaxon.

"Well, well," Neahl said. "Something has changed."

When the riders entered the yard, they all dismounted, save Cluny. He rested both hands on the pommel of his saddle and pursed his lips as if deciding how to begin. Then his gaze fell upon Redmond. His manner shifted. Cluny hadn't expected to find Redmond there. But he recovered quickly and nodded to him.

"Glad to see you made it out," he said.

Redmond nodded in return, but didn't answer.

"I've got some bad news," Cluny said. "Turns out you don't have a week. You have a few hours. The Dunkeldi have attacked Dunfermine and an army is assembling near the old village of Comrie to march on Mailag. I just received word, and I am on my way back to Mailag. We need you out there doing as much damage as you can right now."

After what Redmond had told him, Brion wasn't too ready to believe Cluny.

"Neahl," Cluny continued, "the King wants you in Laro Forest."

Brion could tell that Neahl had other matters on his mind at the moment by the way he studied Cluny, but Neahl nodded.

"Brion," Neahl said and waved at him to follow him into the cabin. Neahl pulled Brion into the back room and closed the door.

"We don't have much time, so just listen," he said. "Cluny is up to something. I think he thought to come here this morning to force you to leave without Redmond and Emyr. He knew they were on their way. This was all planned. I think Hayden is in on whatever they're doing. Don't let your guard down. You can trust Jaxon and Tyg. Keep them and Redmond and Emyr informed of everything, but be careful what you tell Hayden—only on a need-to-know basis. Understand?"

Brion nodded, working to keep the butterflies from turning his stomach sour.

Neahl continued. "As a leader, you have to be decisive, but not bullheaded." Brion thought this was rich coming from Neahl, the most bullheaded man he knew. But he didn't say anything.

"Let the men have their say and listen carefully to them. All of them but that snot-nosed courtier have more experience than you. Trust them, but don't ever go against your own better judgment—even if you have to use force to get them to follow you. Remember that you're in command. You are responsible for everything, especially the failures. Understand?"

Brion nodded again.

Neahl grabbed his shoulders, looked him in the eyes, and then hugged him tight.

"Remember what I told you at the ambush," Neahl said. "You have more potential than you realize. Don't underestimate yourself. I've got to go. Now that Redmond's here, you don't need me."

"Okay," Brion said.

"No need to agree so quickly on that," Neahl scolded.

At first, Brion didn't understand that Neahl was joking. Brion shook his head. "That was a bad joke," he said. "I wish you were coming with us."

"So do I," Neahl replied. "I don't feel good about any of this. But I can't see a way out just yet."

Neahl bent over and picked up his saddlebags. Brion noted that they were already packed. Neahl had planned on leaving today all along. Brion shook his head. He would never be able to anticipate what Neahl was up to.

Seamus arrived as they were saddling the horses. Hayden, Tyg, and Jaxon had come with a trail of three ponies with enough supplies to keep them fed for several weeks.

Brion fidgeted around with Misty's tackle waiting for Finola to come out and say goodbye. But she didn't come. He finally stepped into the cabin and found her sitting by the fire.

"It's time," he said.

Finola didn't move.

"I have to go."

"Then you had better do it," she said.

"Finola don't be like this."

"Like what? You want me to fawn over you when you're leaving me behind and shipping me off like baggage?"

"You have your ma and pa to care for," Brion said.

"They don't need me to care for them."

"At least say goodbye."

Finola was silent. Brion threw up his hands and spun to retreat.

"Brion!" Finola almost shouted his name. He turned and she threw herself into his arms. She smelled of woodsmoke and herbs. "Don't leave me," she whispered.

Brion's eyes burned. "I can't take you back out there," he said. "Not after everything that's happened. What if something happened to you?"

"I'm not worried about myself," Finola said.

"But I am," Brion said.

"Please," Finola begged.

Brion swallowed the lump in his throat. "I'll be back," he said.

Finola pushed him away. "Like Redmond?" she accused.

"No."

Finola stared at him. "You'll need us," she said. "Just like you did

46

after the Great Keldi. "We're a team. You can't leave us behind."

"I don't have a choice." Brion said in exasperation. "It's only for a few weeks."

Finola nodded. "Okay," she said. "Goodbye, then."

"I'm sorry," Brion said. How did he get her to understand that he didn't want to do this job?

"I know," she said. She took his hand and squeezed it. "Come back to me," she whispered. Then she kissed him. Her lips were warm and soft. Brion almost gave in and let her come. But he knew he couldn't do it. He couldn't risk Brigid's and Finola's safety, not after all it had cost him and Neahl and Redmond to bring them out of the heathland.

Brion found Brigid and Emyr saying their goodbyes. Lara didn't hug Redmond, but it was obvious that they were both unwilling to part again. Brion hadn't known Lara more than a few hours, but she possessed something that reminded him of his mother. It was an inner strength, a quiet determination. Brion stepped up to Brigid and hugged her. Then he handed her Rosland's diary.

"We haven't had much time to see what's in it," he said. "You keep it and maybe while you're down south, you might be able to hear other news that we don't know about. Keep your ears open."

Brigid nodded.

"We should be back in few weeks," Brion said. "I'll try to come south for a visit then."

Brigid nodded again, but the way she pursed her lips and knit her brow told Brion that she was biting her tongue. This angered him. What did she and Finola expect him to do?

"Keep an eye on Finola," Brion said. "Don't let her do anything stupid and . . ." he paused. "Don't do anything stupid yourself."

Brigid gave him a pretty smile that didn't fool him. She was angry. "We'll be safe," she said.

Brion jumped onto Misty's back, waved a hand at the small crowd in front of the cabin, and kicked her into a canter. Misty, at least, was glad to be on the trail again.

Chapter 8
Return to the Heathland

The Leetwater River whispered through the birch and willows that lined its banks, while the evening insects buzzed and whined around Brion's head. He breathed in the scent of the river. The dark of evening began to settle into the little vale where they had encamped beside the rubble of a burned out farmhouse.

Saying goodbye had not been easy. But Brion had not been able to suppress the rising sense of excitement at being on the trail again. He hadn't noticed it at first, but, as they worked their way up the Leetwater, it seemed to rise in him the way water filled a jug. He realized how much he loved the freedom of the trail and the thrill of danger. The heathland grasses had faded to a dull brown in the warm, summer heat. But the heather still sported the little purple flowers as if in defiance of the summer sun and warm, south wind. The only things missing were Finola, Brigid, and Neahl.

Brion had to force himself to remember that he was riding out to attack a Dunkeldi army with six men. It was an insane plan. The King had to be desperate. But Neahl believed he could do it. So Brion was going to try.

"Well," Brion said as his company gathered in the shadow of the one remaining stone wall of the farmhouse. "Since we didn't have time to get organized this morning, here's what we're going to do." Brion wanted to sound decisive. "We'll split the night into four watches and rotate them so that every four days we each get two full nights' sleep. When we travel, we'll avoid open areas and keep scouts on each side, in front and behind. We sleep with our weapons. Those who have bows will have one braced and beside them during the night."

Brion surveyed his men. "Any questions?"

The crickets chirped in the quiet that followed as all the men watched him.

"Okay," Brion continued, "every man will have a say in all major decisions, but the final decision is mine."

He surveyed them again, trying to appear confident, though his insides were churning. He hoped he was doing it right. He glanced at Redmond, who nodded encouragement.

Hayden stirred and sheathed the knife he had just oiled. "And what if we think you've made a wrong decision?" he said.

Brion considered for a moment. "If you think I'm making a wrong decision, I expect you to tell me and to explain your reasons. Since I was given responsibility for this mission, I'll take responsibility for any decisions I make that are wrong."

"That's nice to hear," Hayden said, "but we might be dead." He slammed the knife back into its sheath.

Brion nodded, struggling to keep his anger down. Hayden was baiting him. He was testing him.

"Then you had better give me good advice," he said.

Redmond tried to hide a smile. Seamus turned his head away. Hayden mumbled something, but Brion decided to ignore it rather than force a confrontation.

"Now," Brion continued, "since we're going to be spending a lot of time together and relying on each other, I think we should get to know one another a little better." He looked around to see if anyone was going to argue with him over this idea. No one did.

"I'll start," Brion said. Then Brion told them how his father and mother had been killed in a raid and how Neahl and Redmond had trained him before they set off to rescue the girls. Redmond and Emyr followed his example, though neither of them mentioned their time among the Salassani. Brion noted Jaxon's interest when Emyr spoke. Jaxon's one, good eye narrowed as he studied Emyr.

Tyg shifted in his seat and twirled a small, throwing knife between his fingers. Brion assumed that was why Tyg had so many scars on his hands and fingers.

"I live alone," Tyg said, "and I work alone because I don't play well with others."

He slipped the knife into a hidden sheath and drew another one. His movements were fluid, almost careless, and Brion found Tyg rising in his estimation. The man looked like a sot, but he had skill.

"I sell my skill to the highest bidder," Tyg continued, "and I always finish any job I begin. What else do you want to know?"

Brion considered. "Why did you come with us?"

Tyg blinked and began twirling the knife again. "Because Neahl asked me, and the King paid me."

Brion nodded. "Fair enough," he said. He watched the nimble fingers flip the blade with admiration. Tyg was keeping his past a secret for a reason.

Jaxon kept his good eye fixed on the dancing flames. Brion was about to skip to Hayden when Jaxon spoke. "I was born Salassani, but my people turned on me," he said. "I live now only to seek revenge."

Jaxon spit in the dirt and ground it in with the toe of his boot. "I only came to do one thing. Kill Salassani."

"How did they betray you?" Emyr asked. The way he said it made Brion think that Emyr suspected something. Of all of them, Emyr knew the Salassani the best.

Jaxon studied him. "They killed my boy," he said.

Great, Brion thought. *Neahl sends me a potential turncoat and a fanatic bent on revenge.* But he didn't say anything. Not yet. He decided that neither of them could be fully trusted. Brion shifted his attention to Hayden.

Hayden hesitated. His gaze passed over Brion as if he were uncertain what to say. But his characteristic swagger soon returned.

"I'm here," Hayden said, "because I had no choice. The King needs someone he can trust out here." Hayden's cocked head and curled lip expressed the disdain he felt for his companions as much as his words had done.

When Hayden offered no more, Seamus shifted where he sat. The gathering shadows cast his face in darkness. "I'm just a tanner," he said, "but I'm good with blades and a bow, and I'm willing to learn."

"You mean you've never seen battle?" Hayden said.

"Have you?" Seamus replied.

Hayden averted his gaze. "At least I've been trained for it."

"That's comforting," Brion said. "You have the first watch."

Brion crawled up the rise on his belly. The sharp scent of the heather filled his nostrils. The little line of smoke from a campfire still lifted into the sky. He had seen the smoke while scouting the back-trail as the rest of the company made for the foothills of the Aveen Mountains, where the Dunkeldi army was supposed to be massing. He couldn't let them be discovered by Dunkeldi scouts before they had even had a chance to strike. So he had circled back to check it out. Whoever it was should have known better than to light a fire when the smoke could be seen, which made him suspicious. The fire could have been meant to attract the attention of anyone passing. It could be a trap.

Brion slipped an arrow onto the string of his bow. He had left his quiver hanging from Misty's saddle so that he could maintain a low profile as he crawled to the top of the ridge. He clutched three arrows and his bow in the same hand. A horse whinnied. Brion checked the wind and was sure the horse couldn't have caught his scent. Then he peeked over the rise. Two figures squatted beside a small cooking fire. A third was saddling the horses. Brion's heart rose into his throat as he realized what he was seeing.

Brigid's red hair glimmered against her brown jacket. Finola's hair bobbed as she stepped to the horses. And Lara's slender frame bent over the baggage. Brion rose and strode down the hill. Brigid came up with a bow in her hands. The arrow leapt toward him. Brion jumped to the side and rolled. He heard the quiet scream of the fletchings and the loud smack as the arrow buried itself into a juniper.

When he came to his feet, he found Finola standing with a short sword in one hand and knife in the other. Brigid had another arrow on the string. Lara stood beside the horses as if she expected to mount up and ride away. She had exchanged her dress for a pair of trousers like Finola and Brigid.

"What do you think you're doing?" Brion demanded.

The girls exchanged glances and relaxed.

"Next time," Finola said, "you should give us some warning before you jump out at us."

But Brion was in no mood to listen.

"What do you think you're doing?" he demanded again.

"We're coming with you."

Finola's face was set and her brow furrowed. Brion had seen this expression before. Sometimes Finola was so stubborn she could be foolish. This was one of those times.

"Are you trying to get us all killed?" he said. "We can't be worrying about you while we're fighting the Dunkeldi. I have a job to do."

"We're here to fight with you," Brigid said.

Brion threw up his hands.

"I thought you two had better sense. I thought you had learned something. You're not just endangering your own lives here, you're endangering the lives of every man with us."

"We're coming with you." Finola said again.

Brion stared at them. Of all the crazy tricks they could have pulled, this was the worst. And they had brought Lara with them.

"You just refuse to get it, don't you?" he said.

Finola glared at him for a moment and then stepped up to him. She tried to take his hand, but he jerked it away.

"No, you're the one who just won't get it," Finola said in the cold, quiet way she had when she was angry. "You're not going to leave me behind to grow old like Redmond did to Lara."

She glanced back at Lara, who had bowed her head.

"You're not going to leave me to wonder the rest of my life what happened to you when some Salassani sticks an arrow through your heart and you die alone in the heather. If you die, I'm going to be there."

"That's not the point," Brion said, now desperate to convince her. "*You* could die. *Brigid* could die. *Lara* could die."

They were silent for a moment. Finola raised her hand to touch Brion's cheek.

"I have stared death in the face so many times in the last few months," Finola said, "that I no longer fear it. What I do fear is an empty life imprisoned by memories of what might have been if I had only had the courage to do what my heart told me was right."

"But—" Brion tried again.

"The King said you could take ten men with you," Brigid said.

"That's not what he meant, and you know it."

Finola grinned. "Brigid and I are worth two men each."

Betrayal

Brion smiled despite himself.

"It's dangerous."

"I'll do the cooking," Finola said, batting her eyelids at him.

"Oh, let them come lad," a voice called from behind him. "The day's wastin' away."

Brion spun to find Tyg lounging in his saddle on the top of the hill. Tyg gestured with his head.

"You might want to know that a troop of Dunkeldi just crossed the river and are comin' this way."

Chapter 9
Fire and Sword

Lara stood behind the girls, holding her horse's reins loosely in her hand. She smoothed her tunic and brushed a strand of hair from her face, supremely conscious that she probably smelled of horse and sweat. She had never felt so painfully awkward and unsure as the men gathered around them.

She had seen the shock in Redmond's gaze before he turned away when they had first joined the rest of the group. What must he think of her? She wasn't some lovesick, teenage girl anymore. But that hadn't stopped her. The thought of losing Redmond and Emyr again had been more than she could stand.

When she found Brigid and Finola preparing to follow their men, a fire erupted in her chest, and she joined them on an impulse. Now the furrowed brows and hard expressions of the men made her wish she had considered more carefully.

"You're not seriously considering letting them tag along?" Hayden stood defiantly with his finger pointing at the three women.

"What do you propose?" Brion said.

"Send them back."

"That's a good idea," Brion retorted with sarcastic casualness. "Send them back right into the Dunkeldi patrol we just left behind."

Hayden smirked. "We didn't ask them to come along, and we don't need them getting in the way." Lara watched as Brion struggled to keep his calm. A muscle twitched in his jaw. He seemed like a confident, young man, but she didn't know how he would react to a challenge to his authority. If he was anything like Weyland and Neahl, this would not end pleasantly.

"They know the heathland and the Salassani better than *you*," Brion said. "And they've been in real combat. They'll be of more use than you will on the trail."

Hayden stepped forward. His cheeks flushed. His lips lifted in a snarl.

"Looks like it's time we taught this little farm boy who pretends to be a man that it takes more than famous friends and a big stick with a string to make a warrior."

Hayden swung his fist at Brion's head, but Brion was already on top of him. Brion stepped inside the punch, gave Hayden an elbow to the face and then sent him flying head over heels onto the rocky ground. When Hayden landed with a rush of air, Brion wrapped Hayden's arm in a grip that made him writhe in pain.

"This little farm boy happens to be in charge," Brion said. "You either accept that now, or you leave."

Hayden struggled and arched his back trying to avoid the pain, but Brion held him.

"All right," Hayden choked. "Let go."

Brion stood and backed away beyond the reach of Hayden's legs. Hayden climbed to his feet. "Don't blame me when they get themselves killed," he said as stalked to his horse. "I warned you."

Lara watched Hayden go and wondered why Hayden seemed so intent on testing Brion. She had seen the way he studied Brion as if he were trying to work something out. There was something more to Hayden than he let on, and he had some reason to behave toward Brion the way he did. It wasn't simple arrogance. Of that Lara was sure.

"That was entertaining," Tyg said. "Nice throw. Haven't seen that one before."

"Let's go," Brion said as he leapt onto his horse's back.

The smile twitched at the edge of Redmond's lips. He exchanged a knowing glance with Emyr. When Redmond found Lara watching him, he froze. Their gaze met. Lara waited breathless, trying to read the expression on his face. Redmond stepped toward her as if he meant to say something. Lara braced herself. But Brion called them all to mount up, and Redmond turned away.

Lara let out her breath in a rush and watched as Redmond mounted his horse. She wondered if it could ever work. They had grown so different over the years. Could she ever forgive him? Why should she? And if she did, would he even want her? She wasn't the slim, young woman Redmond had left behind. Not anymore.

She also couldn't ignore the nagging doubt that she was partly to blame. She hadn't told Redmond about the child. She had never imagined he would run off and leave the island. There had been no need to tell him. In their last, hurried goodbye, there had been no time.

"We're caught in the middle of something," Brion said.

They had followed the Leetwater as it wiggled its way into the foothills of the Aveen Mountains. The rotting hulks of old farmhouses, stone walls, and overgrown fields dotted the landscape—mournful testaments to lives shattered by war. And war was coming again. To Brion, it seemed so senseless, so wasteful.

Brion had sent Tyg, Hayden, and Jaxon off to scout so that he could be alone with his friends. It might have been a petty move, but it worked. Neahl had advised him to keep his friends close, and he intended to do just that. As they traveled, Brion filled them in on what Neahl had told him about their companions.

"Cluny is a crafty, old buzzard," Redmond said. "And Neahl is right. There are so few of us that we aren't going to be able to do much damage to the entire Dunkeldi army. If we had a dozen groups out harassing them, we might stand a chance of disrupting Dunkeldi plans, but two?"

"Cluny's been pretty tight with the new headman since the raid," Seamus said. "That's when all the trouble began."

"You think he's behind it?" Brion asked.

"No," Seamus said. "But I think he's carrying out somebody's orders."

"The King?" Finola asked.

Seamus shrugged. "I don't know much about what happens outside of Wexford."

"So why send Hayden?" Emyr said.

"To spy on us?" Finola ventured.

Emyr twisted in his saddle to see her better.

"I don't trust him either," Brigid said. "He gives me a creepy feeling when he looks at me."

"Creepy?" Brion said. This wasn't the word he would have used.

Brigid patted her horse's neck. "Well, he does. The last young man who looked at me that way had the same ideas."

Emyr cast her a dark glance, and Brion knew what he was thinking. Emyr had already killed two men who had wanted to harm Brigid, and he would kill any man that did.

"What about Jaxon and Tyg?" Brion asked.

"I don't really know Tyg," Redmond said, "and I only met Jaxon once before. But Neahl is careful who he trusts."

"I don't like it," Brion said. "Why would Neahl agree to this?"

"Do you have to ask?" Redmond said. "He's been itching to do something grand again. He probably jumped at the chance. It might even have been his idea."

"He's insane," Finola said.

"He always was," Lara added.

These were the first words Lara had spoken all day, and Brion craned his head around to look at her. She didn't tie her blonde hair up the way Finola did, so it fell around her shoulders. She sat in the saddle with comfortable ease as if she was accustomed to it, not something he would have expected from a woman who had spent most of her adult life in a city.

Her face was kindly, and Brion thought she would have been quite pretty as a younger woman. She had a way of returning his gaze that revealed an inner determination and fortitude that reminded him of Rosland, the woman he had spent his whole life thinking of as his mother. Rosland had liked to be in the thick of things, and, when the Salassani had come for her, she hadn't run. She had picked up a knife and fought. Brion smiled. Lara was right. Neahl was crazy. That's why he liked him.

"Bide your time," Emyr said. "We know bigger plans are in motion, something is going to break eventually."

"That's what worries me," Brion said.

"Just don't let it be your head that gets broken," Redmond said.

Brion then told them about the ring and the papers because he had decided that he needed his friends if he was going to survive and unravel the riddle of Weyland's secret—if he was going to fulfill his promise. As he finished, Jaxon galloped up in a cloud of dust with Hayden and Tyg behind him.

"There's a large band of Dunkeldi moving along the old river road," Jaxon said. "They have wagons and horses loaded with baggage."

"Already? How many men?" Brion asked.

"I counted about two hundred."

Brion glanced around at his friends, frustrated that he hadn't been able to get their opinions on the ring and papers. "Well, let's check it out," he said.

Brion found the wagon train spread out along a winding road that paralleled the Leetwater. He peered down on the long line from a rocky crag. Two flankers working their way ahead of the column told him that the Dunkeldi were prepared for trouble.

"This far west," Redmond said, "they must be heading to Dunfermine with supplies."

"Well, looks like we have a job to do," Brion said.

Brion set out with Tyg at his side into the gathering gloom and the rolling fog that drifted down off the high mountains. He had sent Redmond and Emyr to one flank of the small army, and Jaxon and Hayden to the other. He and Tyg took the middle. Seamus waited with the women, though he had protested the idea.

"You'll get your chance," Brion told him. "You don't speak Salassani, you're not a trained warrior, and you're blonde. You'd stick out like a fox among the hens. Besides, I need someone I can trust back here to guard the women and the horses."

Seamus hadn't liked it, but he had stayed. The fires of the Dunkeldi encampment leapt about in the darkness, casting weird, monstrous shadows in the thickening fog. The black hulks of the wagons that encircled the camp sat among the heather like somber, hulking beasts. Brion wrestled with his doubts and fears. What if he had made the wrong decision? If Brion had learned anything in his dash across the heathland, it was that something always went wrong with even the best laid plans.

Tyg slipped ahead of him to clear the way, carrying only his knives. When Brion had suggested that he at least take a short sword, Tyg had simply smiled. As Brion advanced through the heather, ghosting from shadow to shadow, he found comfort in the concealing cloak of the mist. He came across the dead bodies of the sentries who had died without making a sound. Tyg was certainly thorough.

Eventually, Brion crouched in the shadow of a juniper on the lip of a ravine several dozen paces from the circle of wagons. The fog was becoming thicker. He wondered why Tyg had not been waiting for him in the ravine. The smoke of dozens of fires spilled from the camp, bringing with it the sweet scent of roasting meat.

Brion tried to wet his lips, but his tongue was dry, and he couldn't stop the trembling in his hands. It had been easy to be brave when half a mile had separated them from the Dunkeldi army; but now, staring into the shadows that shifted and twisted in the eerie light and contemplating strolling right into their midst, their plan seemed foolhardy, crazy. But there was nothing for it. He was committed now.

Brion stood and strode toward the circle of wagons as if he belonged, as if he were a sentry coming in to make a report. He relied on the face paint Redmond had applied and on his own bravado to camouflage his identity.

When Brion reached the wagon, he glanced around before ducking into the shadows. The smell of greased axles and straw filled his nostrils. He worked his way around to the rear of the wagon and climbed inside. It was warm and stuffy with little space. The wagon was piled high with boxes and bags that smelled strongly of apples.

Brion withdrew from his satchel the small nest of grasses and powders that Redmond had so carefully prepared and nestled it between the wooden floor of the wagon and a pile of bags and straw. He struck his steel striker against the flint and caught an orange spark on the char cloth. He blew gently on it to ensure that it was well-lit before pushing it down into the bundle. He blew on it again to make sure it remained lit. Then he placed several pieces of birch bark and a few sticks over the top to help the flame along. The job done, Brion hurried to the next wagon.

He knew he had ten minutes before the first bundle would ignite, so he rushed to the next wagon and then the next. Brion had placed his eighth bundle and climbed out of the wagon when the sound of approaching footsteps made him freeze in place. He could smell the smoldering tinder bundle and knew that the evening breeze would soon carry it to the Dunkeldi who paced the circle of wagons.

"You there."

Brion straightened and faced the guard as he approached to peer at him through the cloud of mist.

"What are you doing?"

"Just checking my wagon." Brion tried to say it in his best Salassani, but he knew he had an accent.

The man stepped closer. "You're not—"

Brion's knife flashed as he leapt upon the man, seeking to close off his cry so that he could not give the alarm. The lives of his men depended on surprise. But even as his blade sliced across the man's throat and his hand clamped on his mouth, a gurgling cry escaped. Someone in the camp yelled, and men ran toward him. At that moment, a cry rose up in the encampment.

"Fire! Fire!"

The men rushing toward Brion paused, and Brion sprinted into the darkness, letting the mist swallow him as the first wagon burst into flames. The camp descended into chaos. Brion crouched at the rendezvous point to catch his breath and to survey his handiwork. Bright, orange flames blossomed all along the circle of wagons as if they struggled to push back the fog. Some were snuffed out, but others sprouted orange tongues of flame. Soon, two dozen wagons were ablaze all around the encampment, sending great, leaping columns of red-orange flame boiling into the sky, causing the mist to swirl and gyrate in the heat. It was an impressive sight. As food supplies succumbed to the flames, the air took on the odd aroma of a tavern during mealtime, laced with the acrid smell of burning grease from the axles.

Brion jumped as Tyg appeared at his side, silent as a shadow.

"Would you mind letting me know before you do that?"

Tyg grinned, his white teeth showing in the darkness. "That would be the last thing you would hear," he said.

"Where have you been?"

"Hunting sentries."

"Why?"

"Dead sentries tell no tales," Tyg said, "and if all the sentries are dead, it's impossible to know where to look for us."

Brion had to admit that Tyg made sense.

Brion watched as a dark figure bent over the guard Brion had

Betrayal

killed. The mist swirled about the man and the dazzling light of the blazing wagons lit the fog with a ghostly light. Soon a group of twenty or so men set out from the encampment bearing torches.

"Time to disappear," Tyg said.

"The others haven't arrived yet." Brion couldn't abandon them.

"Unless you want to fight two dozen Dunkeldi by yourself lad, you might consider changing your plans." Tyg disappeared into the enveloping mist.

Brion waited until the Dunkeldi reached the dead sentry before following Tyg into the heather. He hoped he hadn't already made a huge mistake. What if the others came to the rendezvous and were ambushed by Dunkeldi? But they should have arrived by now.

Brion worked his way through the fog, struggling to keep the uncertainty at bay. Something had gone wrong. He scrambled up the broken slope of the rocky outcrop where he had left Seamus and the women. They had been carefully concealed in the remains of an old watchtower. When he reached the top, no one was there. His heart sank. Brion jumped over the rubble to the area where they had left the horses. Misty bobbed her head at him. The horses were all there, still saddled and packed for their escape. This confused him. Why would they abandon the ruins and leave their horses? Where was Tyg?

The crash and cries of fighting reached him on the night breeze. Brion ran to the edge of the outcrop searching for the location of the fighting. It came from the creek below the hill. Brion grabbed his bow and a quiver of arrows and sprinted down the hillside as the rushing panic gripped his throat. Why would they leave the protection of the rocks?

Brion followed the cries and clashes of metal, cursing the fog and the uneven ground that slowed him down. He slid down a gravel embankment into the creek bed and sprinted. The mist hadn't yet settled into the low area, and Brion increased his speed as his feet slapped the few inches of water that bubbled in the creek. The moon had risen high in the sky, peering through the churning mist overhead. Little tendrils of mist crept between the trees as if it sought to close his way.

The creek wiggled around the contours of the land as Brion forced his way through the undergrowth. The cries of battle seemed to be moving farther away from him. A sudden panic constricted Brion's throat as he approached a body lying in the creek. The shaft of an arrow protruded from it. Brion almost paused, but the clothes told him it was a Dunkeldi. Brion redoubled his speed and passed several more dead or dying Dunkeldi as he ducked under overhanging branches and scrambled through thick undergrowth that tore at his skin and clothes. He rounded a large boulder and slid to a stop. The scene that spread before him caught the breath in his throat.

The moon penetrated the mist to cast a silver light that sparkled in the waters of the creek. Tyg stood with his back to a large overhang, a sword in one hand and knife in the other. Brion didn't know where he had acquired the sword, but he sorely needed it now. Seven or eight Dunkeldi pressed him with flashing steel. Behind him crouched Brigid, Finola, and Lara. Seamus lay sprawled in front of them half in and half out of the water. Finola raised her bow, seeking a shot around Tyg's body. Brigid's quiver was empty.

Brion began drawing and releasing as fast as could. He had practiced this so often with Neahl and Redmond that the movements came instinctively to him. He was free to concentrate on his targets. Five arrows found their marks before the Dunkeldi discovered where the arrows were coming from. Two of them charged him. Brion dropped one more Dunkeldi before he was forced to draw his sword.

The Dunkeldi was clumsy and overconfident. Brion finished him in a few seconds and splashed to Tyg's aid. The last Dunkeldi heard his approach, broke off his attack and sprinted for the opposite bank. Tyg flipped the knife over in his hand, waited, as if judging the distance, and then threw. The flash of the spinning blade disappeared into the darkness. The man threw up his hands with a cry and tumbled into the water. Brion stared in surprise for a moment. He had never seen anyone who could handle a knife like that. Then he turned to the women in the cutaway.

"Are you all right?" he asked.

They all nodded. But Brigid laid a hand on Seamus.

"He took a sword stroke to the head," she said.

Brion bent his ear to Seamus's chest. The heartbeat was strong. Then he examined the wound.

"It was a glancing blow," he said. "But he's lost half an ear and part of his scalp."

Finola pulled a kerchief from around her neck and wrapped it around Seamus's head.

"What happened?" Brion asked.

"Not here, lad," Tyg said. "Let's get them back to camp. We may have more company soon."

Brion collected his spent arrows, while Finola and Brigid collected theirs. Then he hefted Seamus over his shoulder and struggled up the hillside to the ruins. By the time they reached it, Brion's muscles burned with the effort and his breath tore at his throat. Sweat soaked his tunic. Brion let Seamus down gently and stretched while he tried to catch his breath. The camp was empty. The mist had slipped down into the valley below, and they were now standing above it. In the distance, the scattered light of torches cut through the fog as they advanced from the circle of blazing wagons.

"That's not good," Tyg said.

Seamus groaned, and Brigid bent to help him sit up.

"They're not acting like they were surprised," Lara said.

Brion glanced at her.

"No," Tyg said. "They expected us."

"Why do you say that?" Brion asked.

Tyg placed a hand on his round belly and assumed an annoyed expression. "Why was a band of Dunkeldi hunting the foothills beyond the line of sentries in the middle of the night?" he said.

"What?" Brion expected something to go wrong, but he hadn't expected treachery—not yet.

"They were searching for us," Brigid said. "Seamus led us down to a more concealed spot, but they tracked us."

Seamus blinked and nodded, still dazed, but coming around quickly. "Sorry," he mumbled.

"Good thing I didn't sit around at the rendezvous point," Tyg said. He appraised the ladies. "Uncommon women you've brought along," he said. "If they hadn't kept their heads, we'd be talking over their dead bodies."

"I know," Brion nodded. He had never doubted their courage. "I've got to find the others."

"They'll find you, lad. Sit and wait a bit."

Sure enough, within fifteen minutes, Redmond and Emyr scrambled up the hillside toward them, followed ten minutes later by Jaxon and Hayden.

"Time to ride," Jaxon said. "They're hot on our trail."

They wasted no time in mounting their horses and riding over the rise and down into the mist-draped heathland. Morning found them exhausted and many miles from the army. Brion had led them north and west, hoping that the Dunkeldi would not expect them to retreat deeper into their territory.

Brigid and Finola fixed a warm breakfast over a smokeless fire, while the men cleaned and cared for their weapons. Lara tended Seamus's wound.

Brion had been nursing a cold rage all night. He was sick and tired of being the pawn in someone else's game.

He addressed Tyg, Jaxon, and Hayden. "I want to know what you're not telling me," he said.

They all stopped what they were doing to gape at him, but no one spoke. Redmond exchanged glances with Emyr. They both shifted so that their weapons were accessible and their hands free.

"I want to know why those Dunkeldi knew we were coming," Brion demanded.

Hayden bristled. "Are you suggesting that one of us told them?"

Brion raised his eyebrows at him. "I'm suggesting that you all know more than you've said."

"I told you," Tyg said. "I work for myself."

As Brion tried to sort out what that was supposed to mean, Jaxon fixed him with his one good eye.

"Don't insult us, boy," Jaxon said. "None of us have any love for the Dunkeldi." He pointed at his missing eye.

"How do you explain that they had parties ready to pursue us," Brion demanded, "and that one party was already searching the hills for us? If it hadn't been for Tyg, we would have lost four of our company."

Out of the corner of his eye, he saw Seamus raise a hand to the wound Lara had just finished cleaning and rebandaging.

"I don't explain it," Jaxon said, "because I don't know."

Hayden appraised Jaxon with a wrinkled brow. Hayden knew something. Brion was sure of it.

"Look," Hayden said. "We were together the entire time except when we were lighting the wagons on fire." He glanced at Jaxon again with a note of suspicion. "None of us had time to tell the Dunkeldi anything. When we tried to get to the rendezvous, we found Dunkeldi swarming all over the place. That's what took us so long to get back."

Jaxon nodded in agreement. "Neahl asked me to come," he said, "so I came. But if you're determined to distrust me, I will happily join Neahl instead. It doesn't matter to me, so long as I have Salassani to kill."

Brion tried to keep his rising anger from showing in his face. "You've all avoided answering the question I asked," Brion said. "So I'll repeat it. What do you know that you're not telling me?"

"All right," Hayden said. "I'll tell you." His lips lifted in a sneer. "Nobody at court thinks any of you can be trusted, and everyone blames you for starting this war with your little raid at the Great Keldi. So I doubt anyone will be overly saddened if we don't make it out of the heathland alive."

The words should have shocked Brion, but he found that he was not surprised. He had known it all along.

"We're not meant to survive then? Is that it?" Brion said.

Hayden shrugged like he didn't care. "I plan on surviving, with or without you, but I'm not such a scoundrel that I would break faith with men who depend on me, even if I don't like them."

He stared at Brion with a steady, belligerent gaze. Somehow, Hayden's bravado seemed fake to Brion. It was too overdone. Hayden was still trying to cover something up.

"Neahl warned me that we might be betrayed," Jaxon said. "Question is, what do we do now?"

Brion was sure that none of them had told him the entire truth, but without forcing a serious confrontation that might get people killed, he couldn't figure out how to get it out of them. He also had little inclination to continue this charade. Someone in Coll had either planned the entire escapade to get rid of them, or they had found out about it and warned the Dunkeldi.

"All right," Brion said. "We have to trust each other. What do you all recommend?"

Redmond stirred. "There's no point trying to harass an army that's expecting us," he said. "But if we go back too soon, we will be accused of treason."

No one spoke. It seemed that they had no real options left.

Jaxon broke the silence. "That's probably true, but since we're here, we might as well see what the Dunkeldi are preparing at Comrie."

Brion inspected them each in turn. "Well, what do you say?" he said.

When all the men had agreed, Brion turned to the women. "Ladies?"

Brigid, Finola, and Lara exchanged surprised glances.

"You're asking the women?" Hayden said. He gaped at Brion as if he had just suggested that the whole company strip naked and dance around the fire.

Brion suppressed the desire to beat Hayden over the head with a rock.

"They're part of this company," Brion said. "They fought last night like the rest of us. They have a say." Brion turned again to the women. "Well?"

They all nodded.

"It's settled," Brion said. "We rest here tonight. Tomorrow we head for Comrie."

Chapter 10
The Arrow of Truth

S o, where did you learn to use blades like you do?" Brion asked Tyg as they sat together, leaning against a juniper. The rough bark poked into his back. The sharp scent of the tree made the air smell fresh and clean. Brion's bow lay across his legs with an arrow on the string. Darkness had settled over the heathland, and Tyg had come to sit with Brion while Brion was on watch.

Brion figured that Tyg had something to say, so he had decided to break the silence to see if he could get him talking. Maybe Tyg knew more than he let on, and Brion was anxious for any information that would help him get his friends out of the heathland alive. Brion had kept his voice low so that it wouldn't carry. He heard Tyg shift.

"My father was a blacksmith," Tyg said, "who believed that you had to know how to use the weapons you made before you could perfect your craft."

"Did he teach you to disappear, too?"

There was a pause.

"He disappeared all right, when I found him with a blade of his own making in his back."

"I—" Brion began, but Tyg kept speaking.

"I learned to hunt by killing everyone who had a hand in his death. I find it useful to be invisible before and after you strike."

"I guess you would," Brion said. "So, how did you meet Neahl?"

Tyg gave an airy laugh.

"I saved his life once, and he returned the favor. Then he twisted my arm to get me to come along on this little adventure. Now I really do owe him."

"Thanks for saving Seamus and the girls," Brion said.

"That boy fought well," Tyg said. "He made up in bravery what he lacked in experience. And those girls are something else. Brigid shoots a bow better than most men I know, and Finola is tough. I've never seen anything like them."

"Some people call Finola ornery," Brion said. "You never did get the chance to tell me what happened."

"The Dunkeldi headed straight for the ruins on the outcrop, so Seamus tried to evade them. He ran into another group circling around behind."

Brion shook his head in frustration.

"So they had more than a general knowledge of us. They knew exactly where we were."

"Looks like it," Tyg said.

Brion studied the ground. What was he going to do? One of them had told the Dunkeldi. It could be only Tyg, Hayden, or Jaxon. Even though he was inclined to believe it was Hayden, he couldn't rule out any of them. Even Tyg had been off by himself for a while. He could have orchestrated the entire thing.

"You know," Tyg said. "I've never seen a man handle a bow and a sword like you do."

Brion realized that Tyg was complimenting him. He didn't know what to say.

"It's usually one or the other that a man excels at," Tyg continued. "Never both."

"Thanks," Brion said. "I had good trainers."

"Neahl is a hard taskmaster," Tyg said. "But he said that you were special."

Brion's throat tightened. He hadn't realized how much he missed Neahl until that moment.

"Neahl is like a father to me," Brion said.

They sat in silence for a long while until Tyg stirred and stood. "Well, I guess I'll go get my beauty rest. The ancients know that I need it."

"Wait," Brion blurted.

Tyg glanced at him.

"How do you know Jaxon?" Brion asked.

Tyg considered Brion. "He and I were scouts for Neahl back in the

Laro Forest during the Heath Wars," he said. "Jaxon had been punished by his village for stealing a horse. That's how he lost his eye."

Brion grunted. "Doesn't like to talk about it much," he said.

"Well," Tyg said, "he still insists that he didn't do it. But after he was banished, his wife married another man, and Jaxon fled south. His son followed a few years later to tell him that his wife's new husband had beaten her to death." Tyg ran a hand over his belly. "Jaxon turned real bitter after that. He's been hunting Salassani ever since."

"But he said the Salassani killed his boy," Brion said.

Tyg nodded. "They did. We were following a patrol that had burned a village just outside of Chullish when we were ambushed. Jaxon had been scouting ahead. It was a massacre. We lost half our party—including Jaxon's son."

"I guess that would explain his hatred of his own people," Brion said.

"I think he blames himself," Tyg said. He stretched. "Well, I'm gonna roll up in my blankets and get some shut-eye."

"Thanks," Brion said.

Tyg nodded and walked away. Brion followed Tyg's barrel shape as it merged with the darkness. Tyg was a difficult man to understand. Either he was a good actor, or he was honest. Brion couldn't decide which. But, in the very least, he needed to keep a closer watch on those three and see that they were never alone together again.

Neahl peered from beneath the foliage into the clearing where Alec, the young nobleman assigned to his band, waited in the shadows of a large maple. Alec's horse cropped grass close by. Neahl had followed Alec that morning, drawn by the half-formed suspicion that something wasn't right. It had been more than a week since he had left Brion in Wexford. He had harassed the Dunkeldi at every opportunity—even leading a large company around for a flanking attack that forced the Dunkeldi to withdraw from Chullish. Now his men were resting while they probed the new Dunkeldi positions.

Neahl had sent Alec out to scout that morning, but something about the way Alec averted his gaze when he received the order reignited Neahl's smoldering suspicions. He had not forgotten the way Cluny had rushed their departure, and how the King had insisted on having a personal representative in each of the bands. Nor had he forgotten that Alec had not been with them during the last wild dash to flank the Dunkeldi and Bracari. He had been scouting down the River Tilt, or so he had said.

Alec's horse raised its head and whinnied. An answering whinny sounded moments before a horse and rider appeared in the clearing. Neahl recognized the rider as a man-at-arms he had seen at court, but he couldn't remember to whom he was attached. Alec shifted his footing and looked around nervously as the rider dismounted.

"He wants to know why your man is still alive," the rider said without any preliminary greeting. The man-at-arms wore glittering chain mail and had thick, dark hair.

Alec snorted. "He's not that easy to kill or to deceive."

"He wants it done *now*."

"Why? Why not wait until the war is over? Do you have any idea how many Dunkeldi we've killed? We need him."

"We need him dead. The boy's next, but your man has to be out of the way first."

Alec sighed. "I'll see what I can do."

"Don't just see what you can do. Do it."

Neahl fitted the nock to the string. He now understood. He rose to his feet at the same instant that the arrow flew. The rider fell with a cry that was cut off by a gurgling sound as the arrow passed through his throat. Neahl's next arrow slammed into Alec's chest. He toppled backwards into the low-lying huckleberries. Neahl sprang into the clearing. He grabbed Alec by the hair and pulled his face up to his own.

"Who has ordered my execution?" he demanded.

Alec coughed up blood.

"The Duke ordered," he whispered.

"The Duke of Saylen wants me dead?"

Alec shook his head and struggled for breath. His eyes grew wide. "Protect," Alec stammered. "Assassin." Alec continued gasping for air. "Don't want to die." Neahl had seen the terror of death many times before. He had even allowed himself to wonder if one ever accepted it before the end.

Alec stopped struggling to breathe, and Neahl let his head fall to the ground. He stood glaring down at the two young men. The sud-

Betrayal

den rage at learning he had been double-crossed gave way to fear. Brion had to be warned. Neahl rummaged through the young men's pockets and saddlebags before hurrying back to camp. An hour later, he was riding hard across the heathland. Brion had an assassin in his group of men, and Neahl was certain he knew which one it was.

Chapter 11
Blood on the Stones

ara awoke to the sound of voices. The gray light of dawn was pushing the night away. Redmond and Brion stood beside Hayden. They had camped in a circle of boulders on a little rise. The weary group had run all day, and Lara had gratefully collapsed into her sleeping roll. Her backside was reminding her that she hadn't spent much time in the saddle in recent years.

"I saw them for just a second," Hayden panted, "but they're following our trail."

"Get them up," Brion ordered.

Soon all of the company were awake and packing their gear. Lara was glad Brion had made them saddle the horses and pack everything they wouldn't need during the night. In a few minutes, they were ready to go.

Seamus stepped off to the side of the camp to relieve himself when he shouted and sprinted back to them as he struggled to yank his trousers back up.

"Brion," he yelled again before he stumbled and sprawled on his face. A black feathered shaft protruded from between his shoulder blades. Emyr loosed an arrow in the direction from which Seamus had come. A cry sounded.

"Let's go," Brion cried.

Lara scrambled into her saddle, wondering how anyone could grow accustomed to this kind of life. She admired Redmond's and Emyr's skills now more than ever, but this was no way to live—constantly on the run and desperate to stay alive while others hunted you like rabbits. She was beginning to see why Redmond had left the island.

Brion grabbed Seamus and dragged him to Misty's side. Redmond

Betrayal

helped Brion heave Seamus over Misty's neck, but they were too late. The Dunkeldi burst into the clearing. Lara jumped from the saddle and joined Brigid and Finola, who had retreated to the safety of a boulder, while the men rushed to meet the threat. For the second time in as many days, Lara crouched in terror knowing that, if the others weren't there to defend her, she would have perished under a Dunkeldi blade.

"Give me a knife," she said to Brigid.

Brigid glanced at her, withdrew a knife from her boot, and handed it to her.

"Doesn't take long," Finola said, "before you recognize the value in knowing how to fight, does it?

Lara shook her head, but she couldn't speak-—not with the terror for her safety choking her throat and the horror that two of the men she loved most in the world might die before her eyes without her being able to do anything to stop it.

The battle whirled around her. An arrow buried itself into Jaxon's thigh, but he kept fighting with cool precision. Tyg was grinning as his knives flew and his sword slashed. Emyr and Redmond engaged two Dunkeldi each. Hayden's sword flashed between three attackers.

Brion cut down two Dunkeldi quickly before a third engaged him. Finola shuffled sideways and raised her bow. It seemed as if Finola intended to shoot Hayden, but when her arrow flew, it passed under Hayden's arm to bury itself in the belly of one of the Taurini. Hayden never paused. As one attacker fell, he shifted his energy to the ones that remained. Brigid followed Finola's example, and two more Dunkeldi fell to their arrows.

Lara had become so engaged in the battle that she did not notice the man's presence until a hand grabbed her by the hair and yanked her off her feet. She let out a startled yelp as she was dragged toward the horses. She slashed wildly with the knife in her hand. It bit into flesh and the man released her. She tumbled to the ground and tried to scramble away. An arm encircled her waist and dragged her to her feet. Brigid and Finola stood with their bows drawn at the man that held her. Lara tried the swallow the fear in her throat. The man kept moving backward.

Redmond broke away from the man he was fighting and sprinted toward her. But when Lara's captor placed a blade to her throat.

Redmond skidded to a stop.

Redmond said something in Salassani that she didn't understand. The man laughed and began backing up again. Lara understood that he probably meant to kill her anyway, and he was using her as a shield. Then she realized that she still clutched the knife in her hand.

If she was going to die, she might as well die fighting. She drove the knife upward blindly towards his head. Her stomach lurched as the knife connected with bone. The man jerked and his knife slid across her throat as he stumbled away. Two arrows zipped past Lara's head as she collapsed to her knees, clutching at the gash in her throat. Redmond roared and swept past her, swinging his sword. There was a terrible, sickening crunch, and then Lara vomited.

"I'm sick to death of being betrayed at every turn," Brion said to Redmond as they rode side-by-side up the creek bed they had been following for an hour. The memory of the mad dash from the clearing with Seamus's dead body bouncing over Misty's back in front of him and Lara being held in the saddle by Redmond, was still fresh in his mind. The lump in his throat wouldn't go away. The guilt burned his chest.

"I'm not playing this game anymore," Brion tried to swallow the uncomfortable lump. Seamus, his friend since childhood, was dead. And it was Brion's fault. He never should have let him come. How would he explain to Seamus's parents that Seamus hadn't even lasted two weeks under Brion's leadership? Brion had left his body beneath a hastily gathered pile of stones. How many more would die before he untangled himself from this web of intrigue and deceit?

"He was my best friend," Brion said.

Redmond didn't look at him. "I know," he said.

Brion blinked rapidly and clenched his jaw to keep from crying out in rage and anguish. He couldn't let the others see that he was struggling. He was supposed to be their leader.

Brion glanced over his shoulder at Lara. Her face was still pearly-white and the blood-stained bandage clung to her throat. But she was holding her own. The cut had not been deep, but it had been dangerous. Any deeper and she would have bled to death from a severed artery. Jaxon and Hayden followed in the rear.

Betrayal

"One of them is leaving some sign behind for the Dunkeldi to follow," Brion said quietly. "Should we kill them and be done with it?" He didn't expect Redmond to agree, but that seemed like the easiest way to solve their immediate problem.

Redmond studied Brion. "You're starting to sound like Neahl," he said. "If only one is guilty, you would murder two innocent men. That would make us no better than the men who are trying to kill us."

"Is this why the good men usually lose?" Brion asked.

Redmond clicked his tongue. "They don't always lose," he said, "but, when they do, they at least lose knowing they died as good, honest, honorable men."

Brion grunted and gazed up at the pines that grew on the crest of the hill above them. "I'm not sure I wouldn't rather just stay alive."

"Well," Redmond said, "we're almost to Comrie. We should turn west up closer to the mountains and then swing south again to come around in the high ground above Comrie." Redmond glanced back at the company that trailed them. "I don't know about you," he said, "but I'm a bit disappointed that we turned out to be the rabbits when we were supposed to be the wolves."

Brion nodded. "Looks like we'll be spending a lot of time running and hiding before this is over. I'll tell everyone tonight the change in plans."

Redmond shifted in the saddle. "I wouldn't do that," Redmond said. "We don't know yet if one of them is giving us away. I've tried to watch them, but I don't see it in any of them."

"Tyg is the most dangerous one," Brion said. "And he only works for himself. He could probably be paid to sell us out to the Dunkeldi."

"Maybe," Redmond said, "but Jaxon keeps to himself more, and Hayden doesn't like any of us. It could be any of them or none of them."

"Did you know about Jaxon's son?" Brion asked.

"No," Redmond replied.

"With that kind of hatred of the Salassani," Brion said, "I can't see him betraying us to the Dunkeldi."

"You never know," Redmond said.

They climbed out of the creek bed, rode over a rise, and dropped down into the river valley where more burned-out buildings nestled against the hill. It was hard not to pause and just enjoy the quiet, somber beauty of this land. Even in the scorching heat of the August sun, the heathland seemed alive and awake in a way the Oban Plain never had. If Brion hadn't just lost his best friend, he might have been able to enjoy the scenes they passed through. But the memory of Seamus's waxen face and cold body would not let him. The pain was still too close and too troubling. He had failed his best friend.

They crossed the river and worked their way up a canyon to an easily defensible position amid a pile of huge boulders that both concealed them from unwanted eyes and gave them a wide view of the area around them. Brion and Redmond went back to cover their tracks and to leave false trails. Brion rigged several snares in the valley. If they had to fight again, they weren't going to find better ground to fight on, and they would need every advantage they could get.

Worry lined Redmond's face as Lara let him unwrap the bandage from her throat. The softness in his eyes touched her. He hadn't looked at her like that in twenty years. She winced as she swallowed. Redmond misjudged the tears brimming in her eyes for pain.

"I know it hurts," he said. He rifled through his saddlebags and withdrew a wooden box. He pulled the lid off and dipped his finger into a salve. "This will help ease the pain a bit," he said.

The salve was cold and refreshing, but Lara trembled at the touch of his fingers on her throat.

"I'm sorry," Redmond said. "I—"

Lara grabbed his hand. It was warm and calloused, covered in little ridges from the many scars that laced his hands and fingers.

"No," she said. "I'm sorry for putting you in this position. I should have stayed back, but I . . ." How could she explain the sudden pain in her heart that had made her follow him.

"I'm glad you're here," Redmond said. "It's good to have you close to me again."

Lara swallowed and blinked. Redmond gave her hand a gentle squeeze and withdrew to tend to the horses. Lara rose to her feet and walked to where Tyg was unwrapping his arm wound.

"Let me," she said. Lara had spent years caring for sick and injured children, and she had treated plenty of battle wounds in her time. As she knelt beside Tyg, she heard Finola offer to help Jaxon with his wounded leg. She glanced up to see Jaxon push Finola roughly away.

"I can care for myself," he growled.

"Don't care too well," Finola snapped. She cast him a sickly smile and whirled away. Jaxon would receive no such offer of assistance from Finola again.

Lara wondered at how men could be so similar, yet so different. Jaxon and Redmond were both men of war, but one was filled with hatred while the other was prone to kindness and trust.

Lara dressed Tyg's arm, and he thanked her. Then she withdrew to help Brigid arrange the packs.

Lara watched and listened as Finola returned to check on the bubbling pot that hung over the smokeless fire. Hayden lounged on the ground beside it. Lara had seen how the boy watched Finola.

"Thanks," he said to Finola.

Finola glanced over at him. Lara wondered if this tall, handsome, young man would have some effect on Finola. Hayden's gaze passed over Finola, and she deliberately turned her back on him without a word.

"I never saw a woman shoot like you and Brigid," he said.

"You've never known a woman who had to fight to stay alive either, have you?"

Hayden appraised her, then shook his head.

"No, I can't say that I have," he said. "Most women at court are experts with the needle and thread or maybe the paintbrush or the lute. Some have tongues as sharp as swords, but I never met one who could wield a real sword or a bow."

He bent toward the stew and breathed it in. "And none of them could cook to save their lives."

Finola stirred the stew. Lara wondered if Finola understood that this young man was a fast mover and a user of women. Enough of those men had tried to use her in the long years she waited for Redmond. She didn't trust him, and she made a note to warn Finola and Brigid about him.

"What was she like?" Lara asked Emyr. She had fallen back to ride beside Emyr and Brigid as the line of horses worked their way up the rocky gully. She had longed to ask Emyr about his childhood, those lost years she could never recover. She needed to understand how her little boy had grown to be the quiet, confident, young man that rode beside her. As a child, he had been busy and loud, constantly underfoot, and into everything. Now he possessed the stern bearing of one who was accustomed to making decisions.

Emyr glanced at her. "Who?" he said.

Lara thought the question should be obvious. "The woman that raised you," she said.

Emyr glanced at Brigid, who bowed her head. This confused Lara. Why would Brigid not want to discuss this woman? Lara also noted the brief expression of sadness that swept across Emyr's face, and she felt a sudden pang of jealousy. Emyr had loved that woman. It was plain.

"Dealla was a strong woman," Emyr said, "and very strict."

"Was she cruel?" The words burst out before Lara considered them. Part of her wanted to believe that that woman couldn't have been as loving a mother as she would have been.

"No," Emyr said. "As a former slave herself, she understood how unfair and uncompromising life could be. She tried to prepare me for it. That's all."

"She was a slave?" Somehow, Lara had never considered that possibility.

"She was Alamani from a village in Laro Forest," Emyr said.

"But she raised you to be Salassani anyway?" Lara couldn't understand how an Alamani woman robbed of her freedom could inflict the savage Salassani life on an innocent child.

Emyr glanced at Brigid again as if they had already had this discussion.

"She had to survive, Mother," he said. "If a slave wasn't a better Salassani than the rest of them, they didn't last long."

Lara's cheeks burned as the shame filled her chest. "Oh," she said.

What had she expected? It was easy to imagine that one could resist the pressure to conform, but then, had she resisted becoming the old spinster others thought she was? No, she hadn't. She had refused all advances by men and had spent her energies raising her sister's children and caring for her ailing father. Lara decided to change the subject.

"Did you ever try to escape?" she said.

Emyr reached down to pat his horse's neck. "When Mortegai purchased me," he said. "I was only about seven or eight years old. By the time I had the knowledge and skill to survive on my own, I was already free and had little memory of my childhood."

Lara had known this, of course, but to hear her son say it still hurt. In the secret corners of her heart, she had always hoped that her son was out there thinking of her the way she had constantly thought of him.

"I'm sorry I wasn't there for you," she said.

Emyr wrinkled his brow the way he used to when he was a small boy. "Mother," he said. "I'm going to tell you what I told Father. I had a good life. I was loved and accepted. I know I missed much without you and Father, but I was raised by good people who did the best they could. You can't blame yourself for things you couldn't control."

But Lara *did* blame herself. She had spent those long, lonely years second-guessing every move she had made that fateful day when the Taurini had torn her child from her grasp.

Emyr slipped a silver chain from around his neck and held it out to her. A round pendant of woven silver with a delicate star on the inside dangled on the chain. Lara sucked in her breath in surprise. It was her pendant—the one Redmond had given her the last time they had spoken before he had fled the island.

"I kept it with me always," Emyr said. "Here." He placed a hand over his heart. "I never forgot you."

Tears blossomed in Lara's eyes, and she blinked rapidly to keep them from spilling down her cheeks. Of all the things he had said or done, this act affected her the most. To know that he had kept the pendant as a memento of his lost mother touched her more than she could say.

"What happened to those people?" she said with a thick voice. She blinked rapidly, hoping Emyr didn't notice her moment of weakness.

Emyr glanced at Brigid again. "Dealla was trampled to death at the

Great Keldi," he said, "when they came to rescue Brigid and Finola."

Brigid dropped her gaze, and now Lara understood. Brigid clearly blamed herself for Dealla's death.

"Oh," Lara said. "I'm sorry."

"It wasn't anyone's fault," Emyr said.

"And the man, what did you call him?"

"Mortegai," Emyr said. "The Taurini killed him in an ambush a little over a year ago."

"But why would the Taurini attack a fellow Salassani?" Lara knew that the different Salassani tribes raided each other, but she had been told that they seldom killed each other for fear of starting a blood feud.

Emyr raised his eyebrows at her. "Because he refused to blindly follow King Tristan, the Dunkeldi king."

"You mean Tristan had him murdered?"

"I think so," Emyr said.

"Now I understand," Brigid blurted. She glanced around at them, turning red in the face. "Oh, sorry," she said. She swept a strand of hair from before her eyes. "I've just realized why everyone in the village seemed to think you would be the next headman."

Emyr cocked his head as he waited for her to continue.

"Well, Mortegai had been the headman until he was murdered, hadn't he? And the Salassani always resented the Dunkeldi. They would have wanted someone like Mortegai again, wouldn't they?"

Emyr nodded. "That's why I was sent to lead the raid on your family," he said. "It was a test of my leadership and my willingness to defy Tristan's orders not to raid inside Coll."

"Headman?" Lara said. "But you're not even twenty."

"Age isn't as important as skill and success to the Salassani," Emyr said.

"But you left all that behind you?" Lara asked.

Emyr nodded and patted his horse's neck again. "Some things are more important than power," he said. He glanced meaningfully at Brigid. "Besides, Tristan wouldn't have liked me much."

Lara considered her son. He was so like Redmond—wise beyond his years and unwilling to be controlled by other men.

Chapter 12
The Enemy on the Doorstep

hodri paused to wipe at the sweat trickling down his face as he surveyed the wide, blue lake that stretched out below him almost as far as he could see to the south. A great landslide spilled into its western edge. What appeared to be buildings perched on the far eastern shore. Beyond, the rising heath-covered hills rose up on either side.

He and Finn had remained under the rock overhang where they had first hidden for three days until Rhodri spied several sets of tracks down by the burned shelters.

"They've come back," Finn had said. "You must go."

"I already told you," Rhodri said. "I'm not leaving you behind." Rhodri understood Finn's anxiety, but was a kingdom really worth a friend's life? And he hadn't forgotten what Finn had told him. There was probably another young man his age who believed he was the lost prince. Finn had insisted that Rhodri was the real thing, but in the chaos of a coup, who could be certain of anything? Brands could be faked, as Finn had said. Babies could be switched.

Still, his only hope was to find the Duke of Saylen and find out what exactly he had planned. So Rhodri had rigged an awkward pack that he could use to hoist Finn onto his back. The raiders had taken all of the horses. He set off along the game trail that circled around the lake, over the landslide, and into the wooded ravine beyond. If he worked his way far enough south, he might find some Carpentini band driven into the mountains by the Bracari who would care for Finn. Then Rhodri would be free to seek out the Duke himself.

With Finn in such bad condition, Rhodri was tempted to drop down into the valley, where it would be easier to travel. But with so many Dunkeldi, Bracari, and Taurini moving south to the war, he knew that would be foolish. So he struggled along the steep, mountain slopes, slowly making his way south. But it was taking so much time. What if Coll fell before he could even find the Duke?

Rhodri struggled for the rest of the day to reach the ravine. Finn kept drifting into unconsciousness. It was surprising how a person who was awake and lucid was so much lighter than one that was unconscious. Rhodri decided to camp under the trees, where they were sheltered from view by a circle of junipers and pines. He was bone-tired, but he couldn't rest until he had scouted the area to ensure they would be safe from unwanted visitors.

When darkness fell, he left Finn to his delirium and climbed the hill until he could gaze out over the heathland. He had expected to see nothing but the great vault of the starry sky sweeping up over a shadowed world. Instead, he found the heathland ablaze with light. What had appeared to be a village on the other side of the lake had turned into a large encampment with maybe two hundred fires. To the southwest, a long line of torches bobbed in and out of the trees and up and over the rolling hills.

Why would the army be moving at night? He could think of two possible conclusions. Either they were rushing to the battlefront or they were hunting someone. That thought gave him pause, and he hurried back to Finn's side. He didn't sleep much that night, disturbed by every falling branch or fluttering bird.

In the morning, he scrambled back to his vantage point on the upper edge of the ravine. The entire valley was moving, and, off to the southwest, the dust of a column of horses and wagons kicked up to drift on the still, morning air. A line of horsemen rode far out in front and to the side, heading deeper into the foothills of the Aveen Mountains. He couldn't understand it. Those men couldn't be giving cover to the wagons. They weren't even on the same trail. Something else was afoot. Who else could the Dunkeldi army be hunting but him and Finn?

Rhodri had never quite understood why Finn hadn't simply taken him to live with Tristan, the King of the Dunkeldi. As the sworn enemy of Coll, Tristan would have given them sanctuary. But Finn had always insisted on absolute secrecy and seemed convinced that Tristan would kill Rhodri at the first opportunity. Now it seemed as

Betrayal

if Finn had been correct. Tristan had grander plans. Rhodri would have simply been in his way.

Chapter 13
Betrayal

rion's party scattered into the heather as they each set out to draw the Dunkeldi into a confrontation. Emyr had returned early that morning with word that another band of Dunkeldi were following them.

"Do we run or do we ambush them?" Brion had asked his group.

"Running only delays the inevitable," Jaxon said. "I say we ambush them. Make them think twice about harassing us."

Everyone agreed, so Brion took them back to where he had set the snares. The rocky bluff above the snares would give them cover from which to shoot, and the rolling hill behind them gave them an easy escape route. The Dunkeldi would be pinned down in the open valley with nothing but the heather and a few junipers for cover.

Redmond and Jaxon swung around to the other side of the canyon to eliminate any flankers that might give the Dunkeldi warning. Then they were to come up behind the Dunkeldi at the far end of the valley.

Hayden and Emyr disappeared out the northern end of the valley to lure the Dunkeldi in with fresh tracks. Brion and Tyg waited for the trap to be sprung, while Brigid, Finola, and Lara occupied the high ground among the rocks, where they could rain arrows down among the Dunkeldi while being safe from attack themselves. Brion had been careful not to let Hayden, Jaxon, or Tyg work together unsupervised—especially not when their lives depended on secrecy.

If everything developed according to plan, all three prongs of Brion's trap would spring shut about the same time. They would hit hard and then withdraw—making the Dunkeldi reconsider pursuing them.

Betrayal

But Brion watched his party depart with considerable unease. He glanced over to where Tyg waited, though he could not see him, and then up to the rocks where the ladies lay concealed. He had forgotten or overlooked something. He was sure of it. He reviewed their plans in his mind, but everything seemed to be in order. Still, the long hours of waiting were an agony of doubt.

The first cloud of dust lifted slowly above the nearest rise, drifting up on the gentle, late-morning breeze that brought the sweet scent of heather with it. The day was bright and clear and already beginning to warm. Brion adjusted his position and grasped his bow. He glanced up at the rocks again. Something was wrong. He felt it in his gut.

But he couldn't call the ambush off. It was in motion. He had to see it through. He placed an arrow on the string. Sweat beaded on his forehead. His mouth went dry. He heard the horse's hooves pounding the hard earth and was surprised to see Hayden riding far ahead of Jaxon who was being trailed by a band of Dunkeldi right behind him. Where were Redmond and Emyr? Jaxon and Hayden rode low over their horses' necks, urging them on to greater speed. Brion prepared himself to pick off the riders closest to Jaxon, when Hayden yelled something.

Brion cursed. The fool had given away their position in his terror. Brion had known that the puffed-up pretty-boy in all his fancy clothes would be a liability. Now he might cost them all their lives. Brion waved a hand at Finola, Brigid, and Lara to flee. They knew what to do and where to go. A movement from where Tyg had been stationed told him that he too had abandoned the ambush.

Brion aimed, let out his breath slowly, and released the string. The arrow leapt from the bow and tumbled the rider nearest to Jaxon from his saddle. Another Dunkeldi tripped one of Brion's snares and fell. Brion shot another rider before a larger band of Dunkeldi and Taurini burst into the valley. There were too many.

As Hayden drew near, Brion could make out what Hayden was screaming.

"Kill him! Kill him!"

Brion was stunned. Hayden had betrayed them. Not only had Hayden told the Dunkeldi where they were, he was even calling for Brion's blood. Brion cursed and ducked behind a boulder. He scrambled up to where Misty stood waiting. He wasn't about to risk his life to save Hayden after this.

He leapt onto Misty's back and reined her toward the rocks above, when two arrows arced through the sky and to fall among the oncoming Dunkeldi. Two horses fell, disrupting the group of riders. Brion squinted up the hill to see Brigid duck behind a boulder. He kicked Misty savagely, desperate to get to them and make them understand that the ambush had failed. It was time to leave. Two more arrows arced toward the Dunkeldi, strangely magnified against the clear, blue sky. Brion heard the shouting below, but ignored it.

"Run," he yelled as he neared the rock. "Run."

Arrows hissed as they sailed over his head to clatter amid the boulders behind him. The Dunkeldi had seen him.

Brion found the ladies preparing to mount when he came around the boulder.

"Let's go," he yelled.

As they climbed into their saddles, he chanced a glance back, and his heart leapt into his throat. Hayden and Jaxon were riding directly into the path he had planned to follow. The Dunkeldi would block his escape. Down below, more Dunkeldi were scrambling up the rocky hillside, some on foot, some on horseback. A single wagon even trundled into the valley. Brion shot the nearest Dunkeldi before he turned to Brigid, Finola, and Lara.

Brigid's eyes were wide, and Finola's face was solemn. Lara sat grim and defiant. They all knew that their situation was perilous. Brion set his jaw.

"It's no good going back the way we planned," he said. "We'll head for the cave. Ride."

The girls kicked their mounts up the hill while Brion faced the approaching Dunkeldi. An arrow whistled over his head. He brought the archer down and then another before he raced after the girls. He heard the rumble of the boulder as someone tripped the wire he had set, followed by the crashing of wood and the cries of the injured. Maybe a crushed wagon would slow them down.

His mind churned as he tried to understand what had happened—trying to understand where Redmond and Emyr had gone and why Hayden had sold them all to the Dunkeldi. Jaxon must have been trying to stop him. But Brion didn't have time to consider. A cry from

Finola brought the terror into his chest like a hammer on an anvil. A Taurini sat astride his horse on the crest of the hill.

"North," he called. "Ride north."

The ladies must have heard him as they picked their way along the slope to the northern end of the valley. Brion was gaining on them, but he was still too far to be of any use when the first Taurini galloped down the hill directly into their path. Brion couldn't shoot with the girls between him and the Taurini. The memory of Neahl's confession that he had shot his own wife rushed through Brion's mind. He cursed. He couldn't risk it.

But Brigid raised her bow, canted it sideways and loosed. The man was too close to avoid the shot. The arrow plunged over his horse's ear and punched into his belly. He screamed, clutching at the shaft with one hand while swinging his blade wildly as his horse reared and the girls clambered past him. Then another Taurini appeared and another. Brion shot the first, but the second dodged behind a boulder and reappeared at Finola's side. His horse rammed her horse, causing it to stumble and fall. Finola tumbled to the ground amid the stones and flailing hooves. Brigid's horse reared, slipped, and fell. Lara galloped on for a few more paces before she reined her horse around.

"Run," Brion screamed in desperate panic.

The last thing he saw before being ripped from his saddle was Brigid laying sprawled among the stones, her red hair splayed out around her, her horse thrashing its way back to its feet and Finola fighting with the Taurini who had grasped her hair to drag her to his horse.

Neahl pushed his mount as far and as fast as he could, driven by the terror that he would be too late and the fury that they had been so brashly double-crossed by the very men they served. If ever he met Cluny again, it would be the last time. These nobles were all alike, no matter how much they liked to pretend otherwise. Weyland had always said this, even as he did favors for the Duke. Now look where his trust of a noble had landed him. To nobles, men like Neahl, Redmond, Emyr, and Brion were mere pawns on their little gameboards to be used and discarded at will. It had always been so.

Neahl had known this all his life. But he had let his desire to be back in the thick of things cloud his judgment. He should have seen through the sham. He should have understood that two small bands would not be able to make much more than token attacks. But he had wanted it so badly. He had wanted to be seen as a real man again. Not some useless cripple. Now his brother and friends were going to pay for his pride and carelessness.

Three days of hard riding brought him up to the hills around Comrie. He had swung wide around the army and by luck and craft had managed to avoid being seen by any patrols. Now he had to locate Brion. It was late in the afternoon of the fourth day that the black column of smoke lifted into the sky to the north and west of his position. It could only be Brion. There were no villages for the Dunkeldi to raid and only the greased axles of wagons would let off that kind of black smoke this far into the heathland. He was near.

The big man crashed into Brion from the rocks above, tearing him from the saddle. Brion landed on his bow. It cracked under his weight. Then he was struggling for his life while Finola's screams filled his ears. The stench of onions and rotten eggs filled his nostrils. The Taurini tried to use his weight advantage to pin Brion to the ground while he drove his knife home. But Brion had spent far too many hours with Neahl on top of him to be intimidated by this.

He grasped the man's knife-hand as it descended with one hand while he drove his fist into the Taurini's throat with all the power he could muster. The man opened his mouth in a spasmodic cough as he flung his head backward. Brion spun, swinging his leg up and over the man's head, driving his heel down as he pivoted, throwing the man to the ground. He heard the man's face crack against the stone. The man went limp. Brion yanked the knife free of the man's grasp and drove it to his heart before he untangled himself from the man's body.

Brion scrambled over the boulders, drawing his sword as he rushed toward the sounds of fighting. The terror raged in his chest, making it hard to breathe. He couldn't lose them again—not again. Brion came around the boulder as a Taurini dragged Brigid's limp body onto his saddle. Brion gave a battle cry and charged them. The man jerked his head up, and their gaze met for a brief moment. Brion recognized him. He had seen him at the Great Keldi. He had been the one watching Brion from the tents. The man grinned and kicked his horse into a gallop.

Brion gave chase for a few steps until Finola's cries brought him around. She was still fighting. A Taurini was trying to drag her to his horse. He had a hold of her hair with one hand and her wrist with the other trying to keep the bloody knife away from his body. Brion jumped after them with a cry of rage. His sword stroke nearly cut the man in two. Finola pounced on the body driving her knife home again and again until Brion pulled her free. She fell to her knees sobbing.

Brion searched for any more attackers and wondered where Lara and Misty had gone. He was desperate to find Misty so that he could go after Brigid. Three men lay dead or dying among the boulders. One had Brion's arrow in his chest, the other two had terrible wounds about their necks. He glanced at Finola and her bloody knife. She hadn't lied. She would rather die than be taken again, and she had proven it.

Brion tried to calm his ragged breathing and to clear his head. He couldn't let the past repeat itself—not when he had the training and the power to stop it. Finola's horse stood close by, and Misty trotted up to him as if she had known that he needed her.

Brion helped Finola to her feet.

"Are you hurt?" he asked.

She shook her head. He hugged her desperately before helping her up onto her horse. He collected Brigid's horse and tied its reigns to the Misty's saddle. Brion yanked his spare bow from its case and braced it before leaping onto Misty's back. He glanced back at the broken bow Neahl had given him so many months ago. He had loved the beautiful weapon, and it had saved his life so many times. But now it was just a broken stick. He nodded to Finola, and they rode off after Brigid. They didn't say anything. They both knew what they had to do.

A half-mile on, they found Lara. She limped toward them with her knife in her hand.

"What happened?" Brion asked as Lara climbed up on Brigid's horse.

"They chased me," she said as if that explained everything.

"How did you get away?" Finola asked.

"I jumped off my horse into a thicket, and they rode past."

That explained the scratches on her face and the twigs and leaves trapped in her hair. Brion shook his head in disbelief. "You ladies are always full of surprises. Now, let's go get Brigid."

Despite the danger of riding into an area that would probably be crawling with Dunkeldi and Taurini, Neahl kicked his weary horse toward the column of smoke. He had to find Brion before it was too late. The black smoke lifted his spirits in a way little else might have done. That at least was evidence that Brion was still alive—that he was still fighting.

Neahl's cautious approach brought him to a rise where he could peer down into the valley as the sun was reaching its apex. He had expected to see the wreckage of an ambush, but instead he found a circle of Dunkeldi wagons gathered around a great bonfire. A few dead horses lay in the valley while Dunkeldi crawled over the opposite hill as if searching for something. From the lay of the land, Neahl decided that Brion had chosen those rocks from which to carry out his ambush. But if the Dunkeldi were still here, then the ambush must not have gone well. Neahl scowled down on the scene. Maybe he was too late. But he couldn't believe that. He had to believe that Brion had escaped. That he was leading his band to safety.

Neahl crawled back away from the crest before mounting to swing wide around the valley.

Rhodri surveyed the column of black smoke that lifted into the air and the lines of Dunkeldi horsemen converging on the spot. Apparently, they had found what they were searching for. He glanced at Finn. He leaned against the boulder under the large, twisted juniper where Rhodri had left him. Rhodri had had no choice but to keep moving until he could find a secure spot near some water where he could let Finn rest and recover. He had noted the smell coming from Finn's arm and had tried washing it as best he could. But he had refused to entertain that nagging doubt that Finn might not recover. It wasn't an option. He needed Finn. And to keep Finn alive, he needed to know what the Dunkeldi were doing.

Rhodri climbed down to Finn. "I'm going to scout ahead," he said. Finn nodded.

"Here's some water, food, and a knife. Keep them close. I'll be back in a couple of hours."

Finn grabbed Rhodri's arm. "Be careful, lad. You're all they have left."

Neahl crept into the trees, keeping a vigilant eye for any sign of a trail as he worked his way higher onto the flank of the Aveen Mountains. He had a good idea which way Brion would run. On a high shoulder covered in a bunch of stunted junipers, his persistence was rewarded. He came across the tracks of four horses. That would account for Brion's party—minus the scouts that Brion was sure to have out. With his heart a little lighter, Neahl followed the trail into the fading light.

Hours later when he spied the light of the fire twinkling amid the trees, he stopped. Brion would never allow himself to be so easily spotted. Neahl slipped from his horse's back and disappeared into the trees. The breeze whispered in the heather around him. An owl hooted somewhere. But the night was quiet. The smell of heather mingled with burning wood. Only a fool or someone who wanted to attract attention would have lit a fire in the open, at night, in time of war.

Neahl ghosted through the shadows, alert to any sound. When he peered into the clearing, he found two Taurini seated around a fire and one more wrapped in a blanket beside it. Four horses were tethered nearby. But Neahl could not see where the Taurini had posted their guard. The crunch of a boot sounded. Neahl crouched, sword in hand—not even daring to breathe.

A shadow stirred as if by a breath of wind. Something about the shape and gait of the shadow seemed familiar to him. He waited—tense and ready to spring as he tried to puzzle out why this man seemed familiar. It wasn't Brion or Redmond. He was sure of that. The shadow passed him by, heading away from the fire. The Taurini in the clearing had settled down for the night. Neahl considered sneaking into the camp and slitting all their throats just because he could. But he decided against it.

Instead, he picked his way slowly back to his horse and rode on up into the canyon. The Taurini party puzzled him. Either they were overconfident fools, or they had been expecting the visitor Neahl had seen skulking in the shadows. Neahl was sick at heart. The tracks he had been following were not Brion's. He had wasted so much time. And that was the one thing he did not have.

Rhodri lay on his belly to peek over the rock face into the valley below. The Dunkeldi and Taurini had gathered over a hundred men on horseback, and they were preparing to ride out of the valley. Again, Rhodri wondered who they could be after. They were at least a week's ride from Mailag and a week and a half from Dunfermine. No Alamani in his right mind would be this far north. But Rhodri could see the dead horses and the bodies of at least ten men lying side by side near the bonfire that belched black smoke. Rhodri couldn't allow himself to hope that the Dunkeldi weren't searching for him and Finn.

Something shifted on the far ridgeline. Rhodri tried to melt into the stone and hold perfectly still. If the Dunkeldi had sentries on the other ridge, they might have seen him. He waited and watched until his patience was rewarded with another brief glimpse of movement, then nothing more—someone had been watching the Dunkeldi. Maybe it was the long awaited messengers from the Duke.

Hope filled Rhodri's, chest, and for one brief moment, he considered going after whoever had been on the ridge. But then he reconsidered. He couldn't leave Finn alone that long, and, for all he knew, the Duke's messengers had been killed. Or maybe the Duke had decided to abandon him to die alone and unaided at the hands of the Dunkeldi. Maybe the Duke had sent the assassins in the first place.

It seemed clear that the best thing to do was to lay low with Finn and hope he would recover as Rhodri searched for a clear route southward to find the Duke or, at the very least, escape the heathland alive.

Another movement below him caught Rhodri's attention. Two men crouched behind a boulder, surveying the valley where the

Betrayal

Dunkeldi and Taurini gathered. Then they began studying the ground. The taller one with the grizzled hair favored his leg, while the younger one kept a hand on his ribs. Rhodri guessed they had seen fighting, and, by the way they skulked around the Dunkeldi, it didn't take much imagination to guess that these might be the ones the Dunkeldi were hunting.

Rhodri made a sudden decision. He would talk to them. He needed news, and these two were clearly no friends of the Dunkeldi. Rhodri scooted back off the boulder and circled around to warn them. In his haste, he failed to notice the bent branches and scuffed rocks until it was too late. Pain exploded on the side of his head, and he tumbled into emptiness.

Chapter 14
The Rescue

arkness smothered the heathland as Brion, Finola, and Lara rode on into the night. The overcast sky had snuffed out the light of the stars, but Brion pressed on anyway. He sensed that he was close on the trail of his prey. The signs he had been following were barely a few hours old. If he could just push on, he could overtake them before morning. But a quick glance at Finola and Lara told him that they were exhausted and fading fast. Finola swayed in the saddle. Lara simply drooped.

Brion reluctantly called them to a halt in a little dip in the land encircled by thick patches of mountain mahogany and heather. After they had dismounted and eaten, Brion sat beside Finola and put an arm around her shoulders.

"Are you all right?" he asked.

Finola's face was still pale and her expression grim.

"I couldn't bear it again," she said. "I was ready to die before I let them take me."

"I know."

"The blood," she said, glancing down at the stains on her clothes.

Brion hugged her.

"You did what you had to do," he said. "We're going to find Brigid."

She nodded.

Brion found Lara watching them. "How are you holding up?" he asked.

Lara sat calmly with her hands in her lap as if she hadn't just fled for her life and jumped off a galloping horse into a thicket of bushes. Brion admired her quiet grit and determination.

"I'm okay," she said. "Did you see Redmond or Emyr?"

Brion shook his head. "Those two know how to take care of themselves."

"I know, but . . ." She didn't finish the thought.

Brion wanted to believe that they were still alive and not stretched out somewhere in a pool of their own blood—murdered by Hayden or Jaxon. He busied himself by making the ladies as comfortable as he could. Then he assumed the first watch while they slept. He sat with his back to a tree with his spare bow strung and laying across his lap. If Redmond and Emyr were still alive, why hadn't they found them by now? And there was something else he did not understand. How had the Taurini known to come around behind the rocky hillside? Why had Jaxon and Hayden galloped directly toward their position and then cut off Brion's escape?

Jaxon had been following close behind Hayden as if he were chasing him, but what if they were both traitors and had intentionally cut off the escape route to drive them back into the Taurini that were circling around behind them?

It seemed as if he had been played falsely on all fronts. Hayden's cry had alerted the Dunkeldi to their position. And Tyg had simply disappeared before the battle had even begun. Brion was sure that this is what Cluny had planned all along. And Neahl was either dead by now or fighting his own battle to stay alive. If Brion hadn't lost Brigid, he could have crossed the heathland to the Laro Forest to warn Neahl that their raiding parties were nothing more than an elaborate scheme to get them out of the way, as they had guessed. Together, they could go after Cluny.

Brion shifted in his seat, enjoying the cool evening air after the stifling heat of the day. He decided not to wake Finola to take the next watch. They all needed their rest. He had them well-concealed far back from the trail, and he had left false trails to confuse anyone tracking them. He could afford to catch a few hours of sleep himself, since he knew they would need to ride hard the next day.

He closed his eyes and thought of his broken bow. He had left it behind, cracked and twisted amid the boulders. It had been his first, real, war bow. He remembered the pride he had felt when Neahl had given it to him the day his parents had died.

Without realizing it, Brion had come to see it as the thing that had pulled him away from the bitterness and pain of his parents' death and into his new life as a warrior. He had trusted it, relied upon it, and now it was gone. It might be silly to mourn the loss of simple piece of wood, but he couldn't help it. The bow had become a part of him. Now it was gone, like Seamus. What else was he going to lose before this was all over?

Dawn found Neahl perched atop a large outcrop that commanded a view of the pass through the foothills that he knew curved south toward Dunfermine. He figured the Taurini he had seen the night before might try to take this pass, and, from here, he could see if Brion was moving about in this area as he had guessed.

He didn't have to wait long before a party of Taurini horsemen entered the pass. Shock and dismay drove him to his feet. Even from this distance, Neahl recognized the bright, redhead that rode in front of a Dunkeldi warrior in the center of the five horsemen. How had Brigid come to be here? What did this mean? Why wasn't she safe in the southland with Lara and her family? Neahl scrambled down to his horse and urged it down the rise and into the junipers and pines. Brion might be beyond his help for the moment, but Brigid was not. Neahl had already risked everything to save Weyland's child. He could not let her go now. He would not.

Brion jerked his eyes open to find the gray of dawn creeping back into the world. Something was wrong. He still sat with his back to the tree where he had allowed himself to fall asleep. He had misjudged. He had fooled himself into thinking that he was doing the hunting. Misty shuffled her feet. Brion's fingers found the string of his bow and the arrow. He pulled on the string, ready to draw and shoot.

"It's me." The voice was low, but familiar.

"Tyg?" Brion stood up as Tyg arose from the bushes and led his horse into the little opening where Brion, Finola, and Lara huddled. Finola stirred and sat up, her knife in her hand.

Brion kept tension on the string. He had not forgotten that Tyg had abandoned them the day before. Tyg looked as unkempt as always, but Brion noted the new light of anger and intensity in his gaze.

"How did you find us?"

"I didn't," Tyg said. "You found me."

"I don't understand."

Tyg sat down as if he didn't have a care in the world.

"You're following Brigid," he said, "and I'm following Hayden. They both came this way."

"Hayden? Why?"

Tyg scowled up at Brion. "You can relax," he said.

Brion hesitated, and Tyg smiled wryly.

"No one betrays Tyg and lives to tell about it," he said. "Relax."

Brion lowered his bow. "You think he broke faith with us?"

Tyg shrugged. "Jaxon warned me that Hayden was behaving strangely while they were scouting. Did you hear what he yelled as they rode into the valley?"

Brion had, but he shook his head anyway.

"He said, 'Kill them.'"

That wasn't how Brion remembered it, but, in the heat of the moment, he might have misunderstood.

"And you think he meant us?" he asked.

"Then he cut off our escape route," Tyg said without answering Brion's question.

"But what about Jaxon?"

"He's still trailing Hayden, I think."

"Why?" Brion asked. He sat down again and leaned against the juniper. "They weren't even supposed to be together. Where are Redmond and Emyr?"

"I don't know," Tyg said. "But no one betrays me and my friends and lives to tell about it."

Brion nodded. "Well, let's go after them then," he said.

Rhodri groaned at the throbbing pain in his head and a burning thirst. He blinked up at the darkness that enfolded him. The shadows of men danced on the walls of the tent. The sounds of Dunkeldi singing filled the air. When he tried to relieve the pain in his limbs, he found that his hands and feet were stretched wide and tied to stakes driven into the ground. He jerked against the bindings.

"Finn?" he mumbled.

A shuffle sounded behind him, and he craned his head around to see the tent flap open and a tall figure duck inside. The man stood over him, his face shrouded in shadow.

"Where have the others gone?" he said in perfect Alamani.

"Water," Rhodri said in Salassani. "I need water." He had to stall for time until he understood who these people were and who they thought he was.

The man kicked dirt onto Rhodri's face. Rhodri tasted the strong flavor of the heather as he tried to spit the grit from his mouth.

"Please," Rhodri said.

"Tell us where your friends are hiding." The man switched to Salassani, but he had an accent.

"What friends?"

Rhodri struggled to remember how they had captured him. He had come off the rock, intending to go ask the two men he had seen skulking amid the boulders for information, when something had slammed into his head from behind.

The man kicked Rhodri in the head. Rhodri gasped at the flash of pain and jerked against the ropes.

"I'm a slave from Dalm Heath," Rhodri lied. "We were traveling with the Carpentini when we were attacked by Alamani. My master was killed, so I ran away."

"Don't lie to me, Alamani swine." The man gave him another savage kick.

"Please," Rhodri said. "You can check for yourself. Our camp was four days north from here . . . from where I was when you attacked me. They burned everything."

"Where are your companions? I will not ask again."

"I told you," Rhodri said. "I'm alone." He understood that this man was asking about the men he had seen at the ambush, and he decided it would be best to distance himself from anyone the Dunkeldi were hunting.

"So be it." The man said and left the tent.

Rhodri listened as his footsteps faded into the noise of the camp. As much as he had hated acting the part of a slave all of his life, he began to wonder if being the lost prince wasn't more trouble than it was worth.

Neahl fidgeted against the sharp stones that pressed into his backside. From his perch amid the boulder-strewn hillside, he could peer over the patch of twisted junipers to the gap through which the trail ran. He couldn't understand how Brigid had come to be here. He struggled against the terror in his gut that told him something had happened to Brion and the others. Maybe the assassins had already found them. But that couldn't explain Brigid. Did that mean that Finola had ventured into the heathland with her? Neahl wouldn't put it past the headstrong, young women to refuse the safe course and choose a foolhardy one. After all he and Brion and Redmond had suffered to get them clear of the heathland, why would they throw it all away?

Or was he misjudging the girls? Maybe Cluny had sent someone after them, and they had escaped into the heathland. Maybe Lara and her entire family had been imprisoned or killed. Neahl scolded himself for a fool. He should have told Brion to run as far and as fast he could from this tangle of lies and deceit—king or no king. Why had he been so blind?

Three Dunkeldi riders appeared in a gap on the trail below. He waited until they had entered the clearing to his left. The first Dunkeldi held Brigid in the saddle in front of him. Neahl hesitated, uncertain. Years ago, Neahl had taken a shot much like this one, and it still haunted him. The anguish of that failure had never faded. Neahl ground his teeth in frustration and raised the bow. His arrow tore completely through the rider's head with a sickening crack. The man fell sideways without a sound as a surprised Brigid whirled around grasping at the saddle horn for balance.

"Run!" Neahl shouted to Brigid. She hesitated in confusion for just an instant before she leaned forward over the horse's neck and urged the horse up the trail. Neahl's second arrow took the next rider in the chest. But the third Dunkeldi already had his bow drawn. The arrow narrowly missed Neahl as he dodged behind a tree. A fourth Dunkeldi appeared to Neahl's right, and he cursed himself for being twice the fool. He should have waited until he knew where all of the Taurini were. His anxiety at seeing Brigid a captive again had made him reckless.

The man was too close for the bow to be of any use. Neahl dropped it. He yanked his sword from its sheath to meet the man's rush. The battle was short and intense. Neahl's blade slashed the Taurini's sword arm before sweeping across his throat. Neahl spun away from the man as he fell. The clatter of hooves rattled through the trees. The rush of air made Neahl duck to avoid the arrow that grazed his ear.

He spun to find that the Taurini who had just shot at him lay on his back with a lance protruding from his chest. Brigid leaned over the saddle, trying to jerk it free.

"Leave it," Neahl yelled to her as he snatched up his own bow and zigzagged among the boulders to where his horse waited. He burst from the undergrowth and skidded to a halt. Jaxon stood beside Neahl's horse, sword in hand.

"Where's Brion?" Neahl asked. He suddenly realized that the shadow he had seen skulking away from the Taurini camp the night before had been Jaxon. A cold dread began to fill Neahl's chest. Jaxon was a traitor.

Jaxon shrugged. "Dead by now, with any luck."

Neahl pulled an arrow from his quiver and placed it on the string. If he had to kill Jaxon, he would. A bowstring slapped behind him. Neahl leapt to the side, spinning to release his own arrow, which leapt from the string, but had been too slow. The Taurini's arrow ripped through the inside of his left bicep and tore into his chest. He lost all feeling in his arm. His bow slipped from his grasp. But Neahl's arrow flew true, and the Taurini slid from his saddle with Neahl's arrow in his throat. Neahl faced Jaxon.

"Getting slow," Jaxon said as he approached Neahl with a swish of his sword.

Neahl snapped the shaft of the arrow that protruded from his chest and drew his own sword. "I trusted you," he said. A sharp pain stabbed his chest as he tried to breath. The arrow had pierced a lung. A sick knot formed in Neahl's belly. If he didn't get help soon, his wound would be mortal. And he had misjudged again. He thought he understood Jaxon. He thought Jaxon was a friend and an ally.

Jaxon sneered. "That was always the problem of your kind. Too trusting."

Jaxon lunged. Neahl countered the blow and retreated. He needed a better position, and the wound in his arm was bleeding profusely. The arrow must have sliced across the artery as it ripped through the muscle. Time was not on his side.

They exchanged several more blows, each seeking an entry point through the other's defenses. Neahl knew that Jaxon was an accomplished swordsman, but he also knew that Jaxon had a habit of being overconfident, and he favored his left leg. Still, Neahl's mind raced to understand why Jaxon was doing this. They had been comrades in many a struggle.

"Why did you lie to me?" Neahl asked as they paused between exchanges.

"We had a job that needed doing," Jaxon said, "and you were so anxious to help."

Jaxon came in with a flurry of blows. Neahl backed up, but his blade found a small opening and sliced across Jaxon's forearm.

"Too bad," Jaxon said. "You were one of the best warriors in Coll in your time. You should have chosen your friends at court more wisely."

Horse hooves crashed against the stone. Neahl resisted the urge to look. He knew if he did that Jaxon would run him through.

"Neahl!" Brigid screamed.

Neahl flicked his gaze involuntarily to where Brigid struggled with an injured Taurini who was trying to drag her from the saddle. Her knife flashed down into the man's neck. Neahl didn't understand why she had screamed his name until Hayden broke from the surrounding junipers astride his horse not twenty paces away. Neahl understood. Cluny had sent both Jaxon and Hayden to murder them.

Jaxon swept in for the kill.

Brion heard Brigid's scream echo down the canyon. Heedless of the danger, he kicked Misty into a gallop, leaving Finola, Lara, and Tyg behind. Brion thundered past the bodies of the Taurini amid the twisted junipers and then followed the sound of the clashing steel.

Chapter 15
To Die Upon a Friend's Sword

Neahl parried the blow, but Jaxon was in too close for him to exploit the rush with his own blade, though he did land a solid blow with the pommel of his sword against Jaxon's head. Jaxon staggered backwards. Neahl swept his sword up, but he was too slow, too weak. His mind and muscles were becoming sluggish.

Jaxon recovered in time to block the deadly strike. Neahl struggled to keep track of Hayden as Jaxon renewed his efforts to penetrate Neahl's defenses. Sweat dripped into Neahl's eyes. His head felt light and unbalanced. Every breath burned his punctured lung. He was losing too much blood. He needed to end this soon.

Hayden dismounted and stood behind Jaxon, facing Neahl with his blade drawn. Brigid struggled to untie the Taurini bow that had been strapped to the back of the saddle.

"Jaxon!" Hayden yelled.

Neahl slipped on a loose stone as he backed away from Jaxon's attack. He fell to one knee, and Jaxon drove his blade into Neahl's belly.

Brion burst into the clearing with the sound of Brigid's shriek of anguish ringing in his ears to see Neahl slump to his side. Jaxon yanked his sword free of Neahl's body. It dripped blood. Brion drew and released. The arrow drove through Jaxon's shoulder blade and erupted from his chest. Jaxon spun and stumbled into the junipers and tangle of mahogany with a quick glance at Hayden.

Brion drew his bow on Hayden, who dropped his sword and raised his hands in surrender.

"Let's talk," Hayden said.

An arrow flew past Brion's head so close that he flinched aside. It buried itself in Hayden's thigh. Hayden yelled in surprise, grasping at the shaft as he fell to his knees. Finola galloped past Brion, reined her horse to stop by Neahl, and leapt from the saddle. Lara galloped after her and dropped to the ground behind her.

Brion kicked Hayden in the face, sending him sprawling into the dirt. He was desperate to reach Neahl's side, but he couldn't leave Hayden free. He leapt off Misty's back as Brigid gave a cry of triumph. She jerked a bow free from where it had been tied to her horse and kicked her horse into the brush where Jaxon had disappeared. Tyg hesitated and then followed.

Tyg drove his horse into the mahogany scrub brush, following the clatter and crashing of Brigid's horse. A cold hatred had blossomed in his chest at the site of Jaxon running his blade through Neahl. It wasn't so much that Neahl would die, though he regretted that he would. It was the cold, calculated betrayal that infuriated him. Treachery of any sort had angered him ever since he had found his father facedown in the mud with a knife in his back. Double-crossing one of Tyg's friends was just as bad as betraying Tyg himself.

Tyg came upon Brigid in time to see her launch an arrow into Jaxon's retreating back. Jaxon fell to his knees.

"Brigid," Tyg called. She glanced back at him. Tears coursed down her dust-covered cheeks.

"Leave him to me," he said.

Brigid hesitated.

"Go back to Neahl before . . . ." Tyg didn't finish, but he didn't need to.

Brigid glanced at Jaxon one more time, then wheeled her horse and crashed back the way she had come.

Brion kicked Hayden's sword out of reach and yanked Hayden's sheath knife and boot knives free, tossing them to the ground. He tied Hayden's hands behind his back and left him lying in the dirt.

"Don't move," he said. Then he rushed to Neahl's side.

Moments later, Brigid reappeared, leapt from her horse, and joined them.

Brion tore away Neahl's shirt and tried to staunch the flow of blood gushing from his stomach. The strong smell of severed bowels brought the nausea into his throat. Lara shoved a wad of cloth into Brion's hand and pressed another against the jagged end of the arrow shaft that protruded from Neahl's chest. Neahl watched them for a moment before grabbing Brion's arm.

"It's no use, Brion," he said.

Neahl's other hand clutched at Brion's sleeve.

Tears sprang to Brion's eyes, and he shook his head. He kept trying to staunch the flow of blood and bile that leaked from the gaping wound. Finola pressed a wad of cloth into the wound in Neahl's bicep and began wrapping it in a strip of cloth torn from her shirt. Brigid knelt next to him and lifted Neahl's hand from Brion's sleeve into hers.

"Listen to me," Neahl said, swatting weakly at Brion's hands. "In my saddlebags, you'll find an order signed by Cluny to have the four of us killed."

"Four?"

"Redmond and Emyr were included."

Lara gasped.

"But why?" Brion said.

"There's going to be trouble at court," Neahl said. "I think there's a coup brewing."

"What has that got to do with us?"

"They know about you. The Duke may even be involved."

"But—"

"Just listen." Neahl coughed and grimaced. "You don't have any choice but to find him and figure out what he wants—if anything. But don't trust him. Don't trust anyone. Then you have to get out of Coll."

"Where can we go?"

"North."

"To the Salassani?"

Neahl nodded. "The Carpentini might hide you. You can't go back to Wexford."

Neahl scanned their faces. "Where's Tyg?" he asked.

"He went after Jaxon," Brigid said. "I rode Jaxon down and shot him once, but Tyg told me to let him deal with him, so I came back here."

A sudden suspicion sprouted in Brion's mind. Neahl recognized Brion's expression.

"I don't know anymore," Neahl said. "I thought Jaxon could be trusted. Be careful with Tyg. He's a dangerous enemy. I thought you could trust him, but I just don't know anymore."

He paused.

"I'm thirsty." A shuddering breath rattled from his lungs. Lara helped him take a drink from her waterskin, but most of it spilled onto his chest.

He blinked at her. "Why are you here?" he asked.

Lara shrugged and looked miserable.

"I'm sorry about Redmond," Neahl said. "I never meant for him to leave you."

"I know," Lara mumbled.

Neahl reached a hand toward Brigid and touched her wet cheeks. "My little firebrand," he said. "I'm sorry." His face went slack. His hand fell. His eyes lost focus and stared into nothingness.

Jaxon staggered to his feet and stumbled around to face Tyg. His face had drained of color. Blood dripped from the gash in his arm. Brion's arrow had come out just below the ribs, and Brigid's arrow still quivered in his back.

Tyg dismounted. The two men watched each other for a long moment. Jaxon's chest spasmed as he tried to suck air into his lungs. Tyg had seen it before. Jaxon was a dead man walking. It was only a matter of time.

"Just decided to kill your old friend?" Tyg asked.

"He made powerful enemies," Jaxon replied.

"No doubt, so have you," Tyg snapped. "Who paid you?"

Jaxon sneered and swayed on his feet. "I didn't ask for any payment."

Tyg raised his arm to throw the knife, but hesitated.

"Give me a reason not to end your miserable, backstabbing life,"

Tyg said.

Jaxon gasped for air. "He led us into an ambush."

"What?" This wasn't what Tyg had expected.

"You were there," Jaxon said. "He led us right into that Salassani ambush."

Tyg remembered the hot, August day late in the war when they had been following a Salassani patrol and had ridden right into an ambush in a little vale with a pond and a copse of trees. They had lost over half of their men before they could get away. Tyg's frown deepened and his jaw muscles twitched.

"You were the lead scout that day, Jaxon. *You* led us into that ambush."

"He killed my son," Jaxon persisted.

Now Tyg understood. "You're pathetic. You couldn't forgive him for saving your life from your own stupidity while your son died for it. That's it. Isn't it?"

Jaxon tried to raise the sword that dangled in his grasp.

"Coward," Tyg said. His arm flashed and the knife blossomed in Jaxon's chest. Jaxon's face showed surprise and then anger. He tried to sweep his sword up but his movements were sluggish. Another blade appeared in Jaxon's shoulder. He blinked and shuddered with the impact. The sword slipped from his grasp. He staggered forward to clutch at Tyg's knees, but Tyg backed up and let him fall facedown among the broken rock.

Then Tyg knelt on Jaxon's back, grabbed a handful of hair and pulled Jaxon's head back.

"Who else double-crossed us?" Tyg said. "Was Hayden part of your plan?"

Jaxon's lips curled, but he remained silent.

"No one betrays my friends," Tyg said. Then he swept his knife across Jaxon's throat and watched him die with a sense of grim satisfaction. He had grown sick of killing in recent years, but Jaxon deserved to die. Traitors and cowards like Jaxon always found ways to injure innocent people. The world was better off without them. Tyg rummaged through Jaxon's pockets before cleaning his knives on Jaxon's clothing and returning to the others.

Betrayal

Brion dragged his gaze away from Neahl's body. Tears clouded his vision as he reached a hand to touch Brigid's arm. He had to keep his wits about him. He had to make sure the rest of them were safe.

"Brigid," he said.

She glanced up at him with a stricken face. Tears dripped from her chin, leaving dirty trails on her cheeks.

"Were there any more Taurini?" he asked.

She shook her head, unable to speak.

Brion glanced up as Tyg entered the clearing. Brion lifted his sword and stood to face him.

Tyg slipped from his saddled and raised his hands. "I don't double-cross my friends," he said.

"Where's Jaxon?" Brion asked.

Tyg gestured with his head. "He's dead."

"How do I know?"

Tyg shrugged. "You don't."

Brion appraised Tyg, struggling through his anguish and shock to make the right decision. Everything depended on him now. Redmond and Emyr had disappeared, maybe ambushed themselves. Neahl was dead, and here stood one of the most dangerous men Brion had ever known. Could he trust him? Should he?

Tyg lowered his hands. "I'm no threat to you, Brion," he said. "I'll help you bury him."

"We check Jaxon first," Brion said. Tyg nodded and led Brion into the bushes.

Chapter 16
The Diary and the Stranger

Brion stared at the pile of stones that covered Neahl's body. Everything inside him had grown cold—desperately cold. Brigid laid a bundle of wildflowers on the rock mound. A breeze stirred the dust around them. It brought with it the rich, sweet scent of the heather and the sharp aroma of the cedar. It was as if Neahl had come to bid them farewell.

No one spoke. What was there to say? What was there to do? Brion roused himself and stepped to Misty's side. He dragged himself up into the saddle and waited while the others did the same. He reined her up the hillside toward Dunfermine. His decision was made. He would do as Neahl had instructed. He would find the Duke and then figure out his next move.

Brion struggled against the dull ache in his chest, the empty panic that tried to choke him. Leaving Neahl's broken body behind on a barren hillside was almost more than he could stand. He had leaned on Neahl, relied on him for his strength, his courage, and his judgment. Losing Neahl was like losing his right arm. How could he go on? Why should he even bother?

He hadn't spoken to Hayden yet. He couldn't make himself do it without wanting to grasp his throat and squeeze the life out of him. He had let Tyg tend to Hayden's wound, but nothing more. Brion had tied Hayden to his saddle.

Hayden had become as docile as a lamb, which made Brion all the more suspicious. Everything had gone wrong, and Hayden knew what was going on. Brion knew it. But he wanted to put some distance between any possible pursuers and the site of Neahl's last battle. He couldn't stay on the rocky hillside. Not with the memories of

Betrayal

Neahl's final words still lingering in the air.

Brigid rode up to Brion's side.

"What about Emyr and Redmond?" she said.

Lara came up on the other side of him.

Brion didn't look at either of them.

"We can't leave them," Brigid said.

Now Brion glared at Brigid in frustration. "What choice do we have?" he snapped.

"I don't know," she said, "but after everything they've done for us, we have to . . . we . . ."

Brion shook his head. "I want to find them as much as you do Brigid, but . . ." he paused. "If they can, they'll follow."

"But what if they can't? What if they're waiting for us to come back for them? What if something has happened?" Tears spilled down Brigid's cheeks.

Brion yanked Misty to a stop. His eyes burned and his stomach felt hollow.

"If they were here now, what would they tell you to do?"

Brigid bowed her head. Lara blinked and looked up at the peaks of the Aveen towering above them. Neither one answered because they knew what Redmond and Emyr would tell them. They would tell them to go on—to find the Duke and then get off the island.

Brion kicked Misty into a walk. They traveled in silence all that day up the narrow pass that the Taurini had been following. The trail angled south and west as it hugged the foothills of the Aveen. The mountains loomed over them in a way that Brion found comforting. They were strong and defiant, like Neahl. The wild land around him seemed to understand what he was suffering. Even the calls of the birds had become unusually muted in the heat of the August sun. Brion wanted to question Brigid to see if she could explain what had happened. But his emotions were too raw, too painful.

Tyg served as their scout, leaving Brion and the ladies with their own thoughts and grief. Brion was grateful to him. He didn't know if he could have made himself care enough to be a useful scout.

"There's something I don't understand," Finola whispered.

Brion grunted without diverting his gaze from the pile of ashes left over from their tiny cooking fire. They had climbed ever deeper into the southern canyons of the Aveen, where the junipers began to mingle with the towering pines, working their way toward Dunfermine. The landscape here had become even more broken and covered in stands of juniper and bunches of purple heather on the ridges. Pines and birch huddled in the hollows or crawled up the mountain sides, reaching for the snowcapped peaks.

On the ridges, Brion could see far out over the rolling hills before they disappeared into the purple haze. Brion hadn't decided what to do beyond the general idea that he needed to find the Duke at Dunfermine.

Brion poked a stick into the ashes and stirred them about. They had put the fire out to keep the smell or the sight of the red coals from attracting any unwanted attention. Brigid and Lara had already fallen asleep in the little gully where they had encamped. Hayden was tied to a tree on the other side of the camp. Tyg sat on stone a few feet away from Hayden to guard him, while he sharpened his knives. Tyg was going to take the first watch, but Brion hadn't been able settle down yet.

"Where were Jaxon and Hayden taking Brigid?" Finola said.

Now Brion turned to face her.

"What do you mean?"

"If they were working with Cluny," she said, "they would have headed toward Mailag, right? If they were working for the King or some noble at court, they would have headed toward Chullish. If they were working with the Salassani, they would have headed north. So why did they take the pass towards Dunfermine?"

A chill ran through Brion's heart. He hadn't considered this before.

"Were they going to the Duke of Saylen at Dunfermine?" Finola asked, "or were they going to meet the Dunkeldi and Taurini army?"

Brion ran his hand through his hair. "I don't know," he said. The frustration burned in his chest. Whoever was trying to kill them was still out there, plotting, planning.

"I'll tell you what I think," Finola said. "I think Hayden recruited Jaxon to do something else. Hayden was supposed to kill you all, but, when we showed up, Hayden changed his plans. That's why they waited so long. Jaxon had to organize that ambush. Hayden couldn't have done it because he doesn't speak Salassani."

"But—" Brion tried to interrupt.

"Just listen." Finola talked over him. "I've been thinking about this all day. Hayden wasn't sure he could get all of you killed, so he wanted one of us to bargain with and maybe even to act as bait. I think he was going to meet someone in the Dunkeldi camp." She leaned toward him and whispered. "And I think Tyg was in on the whole thing."

Now Brion stared. All of his doubts and misgivings returned with a vengeance.

Brion shook his head. "What do we do? Looks like we're betrayed at every turn.

"I don't know," Finola said. "But I think we should be very careful who we trust. Neahl seemed to think that the Duke of Saylen would help us, but even *he* wasn't so sure. Hayden could have been going to him just as easily as to the Dunkeldi."

Brion nodded. "You're right. Hayden and Jaxon cut off our escape so that we would be driven right into the trap they had set for us in the rocks. I knew it was all wrong. I sensed it. Tyg might have killed Jaxon to keep him quiet."

Finola shrugged. "Funny how you can sit on the edge of a great grassland and feel like the whole world is against you."

"Looks like it is," Brion said.

Brion fought the bitter sleep that gnawed at his eyes as the gray of dawn peaked over the mountains and struggled to penetrate the gray haze. The steady drizzle had slipped from the sky as soon as he assumed the watch. Brion had packed his bow away in its oiled, leather bag to protect it and his string from the moisture. He felt vulnerable without it, but a wet string would reduce the cast of his bow.

He had agreed with Tyg to let the women sleep, so Tyg had awakened him for the last watch. During the long hours of darkness while he sat hunched over under the twisted juniper breathing in the sharp scents of the cedar and wet heather, he struggled with the despair and the guilt. Brion had tried to keep from thinking about Neahl and Seamus. He had been pushing the sorrow away, but it was getting more difficult.

Against his better judgment, he had let Seamus come with them.

From what Finola told him about that first fight, Seamus had fought hard and well, but he was too inexperienced, too untrained. Now his body lay under a pile of stones that the wolves would soon disturb.

And worst of all was Neahl. If Brion had pushed through the night or risen before dawn, he could have arrived in time to save Neahl from Jaxon's treachery. Neahl. His friend. His mentor. His protector. When his parents had been murdered, Neahl had been there to sustain him with his strength and determination. Neahl had molded him into a warrior despite Brion's laziness and immaturity. Neahl had willingly sacrificed himself to allow Brion to escape with Finola and Brigid after their daring raid at the Great Keldi. Neahl had crossed the heathland to bring him word of Cluny's treachery, and he had died trying to rescue Brigid for a second time. Without Neahl, Brion wouldn't even be alive to witness this coming dawn.

The ache forced the tears from his eyes, and he wept. He wept for them all—for Rosland and Weyland and Seamus, for Airic and Neahl. He would never hear their voices, see their faces, or feel their friendship and love again. They were gone from the world, and all that was left were the memories and the emotions that had become a part of him. Those at least would persist until he died.

As the gray-black of night brightened to the silvery-gray of morning, the drizzle ceased and the mist rolled in to replace it. Brion's thoughts strayed to the Duke, his real father. What would the Duke say when he saw his son? Would he recognize him? Would he treat him like just another pawn on his gameboard? Brion couldn't suppress the curiosity to know what the Duke looked like and the fear that the Duke would simply send him packing—or worse, kill him.

Brigid stirred, shook Finola, and the two of them rose from the cover of the little shelter Tyg and Brion had constructed for the ladies and came to sit beside Brion. They advanced on him as if this had been planned.

Brigid held up Rosland's diary.

"I'd almost forgotten it," Brion said.

"Well, I haven't," Brigid said. Her brow furrowed in annoyance. Brion tried to understand why his comment had offended her. He guessed it was just that she was worried about Emyr.

"I've been reading it," Brigid said, "whenever I got a chance. Most of it is just the normal stuff you would expect, but there are several passages that you need to hear."

"Okay." Brion shifted his back against the juniper and settled in. He was grateful for the company and the chance to escape his gloomy thoughts. "Let's hear them."

Brigid opened the diary as Finola clasped Brion's hand and settled in beside him. Her hand was warm, calloused, and reassuring.

Brigid began. "In May of 782, she wrote: 'Weyland has gone back to the Heath Wars with Neahl. Neahl's lust for revenge consumes him. How much blood will be enough?' Then in September of the same year she wrote, 'I'm with child. Perhaps now Weyland will settle down and give up his hatred of the Salassani.'"

"Sounds like Neahl and Weyland had the same ideas about the Salassani," Finola said.

"Papa, uh, Weyland never talked much about it," Brion said. "But Neahl told me that Redmond thought they were being foolish and bloodthirsty."

"Sounds like Redmond was right," Finola said.

Brigid glared at Brion.

"What?" he said. Why was Brigid being so moody? It wasn't like her.

"You should call Weyland 'Father,' not some duke. Papa and Momma loved you. They gave you everything, including their lives."

Brion sat in shock for a moment before the anger boiled up in his throat.

"You don't think I know that?" he said. "Why do you think I've been trying so hard to keep you alive and to keep my promise to Papa?" He paused as Brigid bowed her head in silence. "I just don't know what to believe anymore," he said.

Finola adjusted her cloak, and Brigid flipped through the pages of the diary.

"Anyway," Brigid said, without looking at Brion, "seven months later in 783, Momma wrote, 'I wish we had never worked for the Duke of Saylen. He has forced Weyland away on some new secret mission. The midwife says I can expect the child in a few weeks. What if something goes wrong and Weyland is not here? I wish Momma had not been hanged at Dunfermine. I wish she were here.'"

"Whoa, wait a minute," Brion said. "Momma and Papa both worked for the Duke? What would he have them do?"

Finola scoffed. "That's what caught your attention? Did you notice that she said her mother had been hanged?"

"Well, yeah, but—"

"It doesn't matter," Brigid cut in. "We don't know the answer to either question."

"Men," Finola said. "They have a habit of leaving us when we need them most." She cast Brion an annoyed glance.

"Hang on—" Brion tried to defend himself.

"Not now," Brigid interrupted. "Let me finish."

When Finola gave Brion her devilish grin, and Brion shook his head in resignation. Brigid continued.

"In May of the same year she wrote, 'My poor child. My poor, beautiful, redheaded baby. He came forth with the cord wrapped around his neck and so pitifully small. He won't eat, and his skin has turned yellow. The midwife says I should prepare for the worst. How can I live with this pain? Where is Weyland when I need him?'"

Brion studied a line of ants, while Brigid and Finola sniffled. Water dripped from Brion's hood. Brion didn't have red hair. He had never had red hair. Even Cluny had said that Brion didn't look like Weyland.

"Then," Brigid continued with a quavering voice, "at the beginning of June, Momma wrote, 'The Duke has given Weyland permission to return and has promised to reward him. I can see the disappointment in Weyland's eyes. He won't look at me.'"

Finola clicked her tongue. "Like it was her fault the baby was sickly," she said.

"I don't think he blamed her," Brion said. "It wouldn't make any sense."

Brigid ignored them and continued. "Then two weeks later she says, 'The Duke has come. How could he ask me to give him my child? My own flesh and blood. I will not. I cannot. We have given him too much already.'"

"What?" Brion said in surprise.

"It's obvious," Brigid said. "The Duke wanted her to give him her son so he could swap him for the prince."

"But people would know," Brion said.

"Not if both babies had red hair," Finola said, "and if only a few people had seen the prince."

Betrayal

"But—"

"Just listen," Brigid interrupted. "There's more. Here's an entry from the end of June. 'My heart is broken. My poor child has died, and Weyland has taken his little body to the Duke. What if they find out what we have done? How can I live with this pain?'"

"She didn't give them her child?" Finola breathed as she covered her mouth with her hand.

"She did," Brigid said. "Or she was forced to."

"But her baby was dead," Brion said.

"Maybe all they needed was a body." Brigid closed her mouth into a tight, thin line. The horror of the thought turned Brion's stomach and tightened his chest. The Duke had forced them to give up their own dead child so he could save the prince. Brion kicked at a clump of wet grass. He wasn't sure he wanted to hear anymore.

But Brigid continued. "The beginning of July she says, 'Weyland has returned with a baby boy. At first, I could not hold the child, but my heart aches with love to give. Then the baby smiled up at me with those soft, brown eyes, and I could not deny him. My heart yearns for someone to love, and my arms ache to hold my son. I will raise him as my own even though I know they will come for him someday.'"

Brigid glanced up at Brion. "You must have been born in May or June about the same time as Father's and Mother's son."

Brion swallowed the knot in his throat, but couldn't speak. He had never imagined how painful the experience must have been for Weyland and Rosland.

Brigid continued. "In September of 783, she wrote, 'Weyland has returned from the war with a crippled arm. I knew something like this would happen. I begged him not to go. How will he care for his family now?'"

"That's the same time Redmond left," Brion said. "Emyr must have been born around then."

Brigid bowed her head to the little book and continued. "Then in November of the same year, Momma wrote, 'He visited yesterday, coming on his great horse dressed in his fancy, blue cloak. I kept the baby close to me all day. Weyland was shaken by his visit. He wouldn't say, but I think the Duke has threatened him. As if we haven't sacrificed enough for him and his intrigues.'"

Brion nodded to Brigid. "That must have been when the Duke gave him the ring and the papers."

"There's more," Brigid said. "In December, Momma wrote, 'Someone is hunting us. The Duke has ordered us to leave. He has a place where he says we will be safe. Brion is crawling and getting into everything, and another child is coming. I am terrified. I can't do it again.'"

"Then Redmond was right," Brion said.

"About what?" Finola asked.

"When he first came back to the island," Brion said, "he told us that he had left so that Lara and her family wouldn't be chased by assassins. Maybe that's why they are all still alive."

Brigid coughed and wiped at a tear that trickled down her cheek. Brion put a reassuring hand on her arm. She flipped a bunch of pages toward the end of the book and continued reading in a quavering voice.

"In July 784, Momma wrote, 'Weyland says that I cannot keep my book. I convinced him not to burn it but to put it in the grave where my baby should have been. I love little Brion, but I cannot help but wonder what they have done with my baby's little body. I placed a purple tulip in the grave as a reminder of where he has gone.'"

"I knew it was tulip," Finola said.

Brigid sniffled and wiped at her eyes. Finola reached over and patted her hand. Brion stared into the distance, trying to sort through the rush of emotions. How does one accept that he was abandoned by his real father who had forced a grieving mother to sacrifice her child's body for some rich men's quarrel?

"So that's how the prince escaped," Brion said. "They switched babies and probably gave Momma's dead baby to the rebels."

"That's disgusting," Finola said. "I can't believe they even asked it of her." She pulled her hand away from Brion's and brushed some damp hair from her cheek.

"But Papa did it anyway," Brigid said as she stared down at the pages that stirred in the morning breeze. "Why would he do it?"

"Maybe," Brion said, "he had no choice."

They sat in silence, wrapped in the darkness of their own thoughts as the dawn crept into the world. Brion picked up a twig and began twirling it.

"Anyway," Brigid finally said. "I thought you should know."

"I don't know what to think," Brion said.

"Well, this doesn't prove that you're the Duke's son," Finola said. "Rosland didn't say."

"It seems obvious," Brion said.

"But it isn't proof."

"If the Duke is your father, then who is your mother?" Finola asked.

Brion glanced up at her. "And why would she be outside of Wexford in the midwife's cave?" he asked. His hand drifted up to clutch at the little ring that still hung around his neck.

"And," Finola added, "why would the Duke give you to Weyland and Rosland? Was he just trying to repay them for giving up their child, or was he trying to use them again somehow?"

Brion shook his head. "Life used to be a lot simpler," he said.

Brigid closed the book and held it to her chest. "I can't imagine what she must have gone through," she said.

"Is there anything else?" Brion asked.

Brigid shook her head. "That's about it. But there's something I still don't understand."

Brion waited for her to continue.

"Why a tulip?" she said.

"What?"

"The tulip we found in the grave," Brigid said. "Why a single tulip?"

Brion had completely forgotten about the tulip and couldn't see why it mattered.

"I mean," Brigid continued, "if she was going to put flowers in the grave with her journal, why would she pick a purple tulip and nothing else?"

"She said it was a reminder of where he had gone," Finola said. "Maybe it has something to do with the prince."

"Don't ladies say there's some kind of language of love around flowers?" Brion asked.

Both young women glared at him.

"Well, don't they?" Brion persisted. "Maybe she was trying to send some kind of message with it."

Brigid shook her head. "I never heard of a purple tulip meaning anything."

"Okay," Brion said. "Now, what do we do?"

"You're going to have to go to the Duke one way or the other," Finola said. "Maybe he will tell you the rest."

"Maybe he has been the one trying to have us killed," Brion said.

Neither of the girls replied because they all knew that that was as likely as any of the other possible scenarios.

The sounds of Tyg and Lara beginning to stir ended their little conference. But the shadow of Rosland's diary clung to Brion all day. He kept remembering Neahl's words: "To the nobility, we are nothing more than animals." Rosland's diary seemed to prove his point.

"I want the truth," Brion said. He handed Hayden a bowl of warm broth and some jerky as the rest of the group readied for another day's journey.

Hayden gazed up at him from under the cowl of his cloak. Brion resisted the urge to punch Hayden in the face. He had never liked Hayden and, now that he was convinced Hayden had had a hand in Neahl's death, he couldn't stand the sight of him. Still, he needed Hayden to talk. So he untied Hayden's hands and watched as he ate.

Hayden swallowed. "Will you believe the truth?" he asked.

Brion shrugged. "Will you speak it?"

"Look," Hayden said, "it's more complicated than you think."

"Things usually are."

Hayden pinched his lips tight and surveyed Brion as if deciding what to do. "All right," he said. "But you're not going to like it."

Brion waited.

"I was sent to protect you."

Brion opened his mouth to protest the obvious lie, when Tyg appeared behind Hayden and pressed a knife to his throat.

"Convince me," Tyg said.

Brion lunged forward, certain that Tyg was going to silence Hayden the way he had silenced Jaxon. He slipped in the mud and fell to his knees. But he needn't have worried.

"Let him speak," Tyg said.

Brion scrambled to his feet and stared at Tyg. He didn't understand. He wanted to trust Tyg, but he couldn't let his desperation to trust cloud his judgment. Hayden had gone rigid as the cold steel pressed against his throat.

"You're crazy," he said to Tyg.

"Not the kind of thing you want to say to a guy who has seen his friend die after you sold us out to the Dunkeldi," Tyg said.

"I didn't sell out anyone," Hayden protested.

"You screamed at them to kill us," Tyg said.

Hayden sneered. "You're hearing isn't very good then," he said. "I was screaming at you to kill *him*."

When Hayden saw that Brion wasn't convinced, he continued.

"After that first raid, I suspected that Jaxon had been the one to give us away, so I kept a close watch on him. I was on the ridge watching for the Dunkeldi, when I saw Jaxon ride up to them. I slipped down to see what he was doing, but he saw me."

"Where is Emyr?" Brion asked.

"I don't know. I ran to warn you that Jaxon had betrayed us. After he found out that Brigid had been captured, he left me behind so that he could catch up with the Taurini. I followed him to where you found us."

"Why would he go after the Taurini and Brigid?" Brion asked.

"I think he figured that you would follow them. I'm sure he hoped to kill you before I could find you and warn you."

Tyg raised a questioning eyebrow at Brion, who nodded. Tyg removed the knife from Hayden's throat. Hayden reach up a hand to massage the thin, red line the knife had made.

"What do you mean that you were sent to protect me?" Brion asked.

Hayden smirked. "I belong to a group that wants to restore the old royal family to the throne. We believe you have the key to finding him."

"Me? Why me?" Brion asked. It seemed that everyone knew more about him than he knew about himself. It was galling.

"Because the Duke has kept you in hiding all these years," Hayden said.

Tyg cocked his head sideways in interest.

"What are you suggesting?" Brion said.

"It has been rumored for years that the Duke rescued the last prince."

"What has that got to do with me?"

Hayden shrugged. "Weyland was the Duke's favorite."

Brion stared at him. "You think I'm the prince?" It was preposterous. It couldn't be true. But Rosland's diary had said that Weyland took a dead baby away and came back with Brion. She had also said that someone would be coming to take him away someday. Could this be the real secret?

Hayden shrugged again. "There aren't many other alternatives."

Tyg smiled at Brion. "This trip is getting more interesting all the time," he said.

Brion glared at him before turning back to Hayden. Then he sat on a rock and studied him.

"Then why have you been challenging me at every turn?" he demanded.

Hayden shrugged. "I had orders to test you. To see what you were made of."

Now Brion really wanted to kick him in the teeth. This arrogant noble had done everything he could to make Brion's life miserable for weeks. He had flirted with Finola and shown disdain for everyone else in the party.

"I'm not the prince," Brion said.

Hayden shifted. "It seems to me that you don't know who you are."

Brion chose to ignore the comment. "Cluny said the King sent you," Brion said.

Hayden snorted. "Kings can be manipulated just like anyone else."

"Why would you commit treason against the King?"

Hayden's lips lifted in a sneer. "Geric isn't a bad king, but he's a failure as a father. His son is a grasping monster with no conscience and dreams of an island empire. He will destroy Coll."

"Brion!" Brigid waved at him. "Someone is coming."

"I'm not finished with you," Brion said as he rose to his feet. He motioned for Tyg to retie Hayden's hands, before striding into the bunch of junipers surrounding their camp. Brion struggled with the desperate frustration that Weyland hadn't explained this whole mess to him before he had been murdered. If he had, Brion's life since then would have been so much easier.

Betrayal

Brion crouched behind the clump of juniper as the lone rider approached. Brion's little party had climbed out of the valley of the Leetwater and worked their way into the southwestern foothills of the Aveen. Rocky outcrops speckled vast grasslands; bunches of heather and stands of juniper spread out before him. Brion had expected to come upon Dunkeldi patrols and thought this man might be a Dunkeldi courier. He hadn't yet had time to consider how they might get around the Dunkeldi and Taurini that surrounded Dunfermine and into the Duke's camp. And he had no idea how the Duke would receive them.

Brion sensed Tyg's presence before he appeared beside him. Tyg crouched by his side, and Brion was surprised to feel that same sense of strength he had often felt with Neahl and Redmond. But Brion was afraid to let the feeling last because he knew that Tyg might betray him at any moment.

"That's no Dunkeldi," Tyg said.

"Looks like a nobleman," Brion said. He hadn't seen that many noblemen, but the man's clothes and weapons were much too fine for a Dunkeldi courier. His horse's legs and sides were splattered with mud.

"He's either a fool or he knows he's secure," Tyg said.

"Either way, it's no good for us," Brion said.

As the man came between the rock and the stand of juniper, Brion stood. The man whipped his sword from its sheath and wheeled his horse to face the threat. But when he saw the longbow trained on him with a broadhead glinting in the late-morning light, he snapped the sword back into its sheath.

"Who are you?" Brion demanded.

"Cedrick of Saylen," the man replied. He gazed up at Brion with the air of a man confident in his own ability and certain that he was in no danger. Brion didn't know if it was bravado or if he really believed he was safe alone in the heathland.

"The Duke's son?" Brion asked.

"The same."

Brion lowered his bow. It took him a moment to realize that he was looking at his half-brother. "What are you doing up here?"

Cedrick cocked his head. "Looking for you, I think."

Brion watched him.

"That is, if you are Brion of Wexford. I have a message for you from the Duke himself."

"Don't trust him," Tyg whispered.

Brion glanced at Tyg and stepped out of the trees, but kept an arrow on the string and a healthy distance from the reach of the man's blade.

"What's your message?"

"I was told you'd be up the Leetwater."

"We were, but things have changed."

"So I see. May I?" He gestured as if to dismount.

Brion nodded. "Might as well."

Tyg stepped out of hiding, and Cedrick glanced at him.

"Ah, Tyg, isn't it? I believe we met once before."

Tyg nodded, but didn't speak.

Cedrick searched the hill where Brion was standing.

"Where's the rest of your company?"

Brion shrugged as Cedrick brushed the mud from a boulder, sat down, and pulled off his gloves.

"I see. Well, I can't blame you. My father sent me to find you because he has information you may need, and he seeks your assistance in a rather delicate matter."

Brion waited.

"I guess I'll start with the bad news," Cedrick continued, "though I have a feeling you may already know." He paused again, but Brion waited.

"Cluny, the High Sheriff of Mailag had Lara's entire family arrested shortly after you left."

"What?" Brion blurted.

A smile curved at the edge of Cedrick's lips. "I guess you didn't know. Well, Cluny seemed to think that Redmond would be more pliable with his sweetheart's family in prison should his order to have you all killed fail."

When Brion showed no response to this statement, Cedrick nodded. "But you already knew that you had been betrayed. Did Neahl find you then?"

"How . . .I mean . . .you have news of Neahl?"

Cedrick raised a knowing eyebrow. "He did find you, and he's dead, isn't he?"

Brion hesitated and nodded. A rock landed in his stomach again. He didn't like thinking about Neahl—not when he needed to focus.

Cedrick glanced at Tyg. "I need to speak to you alone, Brion. I mean no offense Tyg, but my orders are clear."

Tyg scowled. "Somehow," he said, "when you people mean no offense, you always seem to give it."

"I'm sorry," Cedrick said. "I must insist."

Tyg glanced at Brion. "I'll be watching him," he whispered and stomped away.

Cedrick's gaze followed him. "He's the most skilled man alive with blades," he said.

"What's your message?" Brion asked, not trying to hide his impatience.

Cedrick surveyed Brion for a moment. Brion noted how Cedrick's dark eyes watched him as if he were trying to read Brion's thoughts. Cedrick was a handsome man with short, light-brown hair. Brion wondered if the Duke and his son looked alike.

"I knew Weyland," Cedrick said. "I was very young, but I saw him fight. He was a great warrior."

Brion nodded.

Cedrick wiped at the mud on his pant leg with his glove. "He saved the King's life and my father's life. Did he ever tell you?

"No."

"Did he tell you how he came to own his farm?"

"What has this got to do with—"

"Everything," Cedrick interrupted.

Brion scowled as Cedrick continued.

"My father made sure that Weyland received it in payment for a sensitive and important service."

"I don't know what you're talking about." Brion needed to keep Cedrick from guessing how much he did know. There was something about Cedrick that made Brion uneasy. He felt himself drawn to him, but unwilling to trust him. Maybe he was becoming just as paranoid as Tyg.

"I see," Cedrick said. "Then let me tell you, but you must give me your word as a man and as a warrior that you will not share what I will tell you with anyone. Only the Duke can tell you with whom you may share it."

Brion hesitated, then nodded. "Okay," he said, even though he knew he had already told the others about this, and he fully intended to keep them informed. Neahl had warned him to trust his friends, and he wasn't about to let himself be manipulated by a stranger whose trustworthiness was questionable.

"Good," Cedrick said. He spread his gloves out on his leg. "Weyland had certain papers written in Salassani and a ring that the Duke must retrieve. Your father's cabin has been searched, and they were not found."

"*You* searched my cabin?" Brion narrowed his eyes. Had Cedrick been the one that had exhumed his parents and left their bodies desecrated? Hot anger filled his chest, and he resisted the urge to shoot Cedrick with the arrow he still had on the string of his bow.

Cedrick shrugged. "We had no choice. You weren't there to ask permission. My father only found out that Weyland was dead a few weeks ago, and now things are moving quickly. He must have those papers."

"Why?" Brion thought he knew the answer, but he wanted to hear why Cedrick wanted them.

"I'm not at liberty to tell you that. But . . ." Cedrick paused. "You have them, don't you? Have you read them?"

Brion's anger flared. This man presumed much, and he had an uncanny ability to read Brion's thoughts. Brion was about to answer when Cedrick grinned.

"Oh, you don't know how to read, do you?" Cedrick seemed to delight in Brion's supposed inferiority.

Brion almost protested, but it occurred to him that it might be useful to let Cedrick think he couldn't read.

"Let us say," Brion said, "that I know where they are."

Cedrick considered him. "The Duke, my father, would be very much in your debt if you could find your way to take them to him. You may deliver them directly into his own hands if you wish."

Brion considered. "All right," he said. "You can camp with us tonight. I'll let you know my decision in the morning."

A cry and the clatter of rocks on the bluff broke into their conversation. Then the galloping of hooves reached their ears. Brion sprinted toward the knoll where he had left Brigid, Finola, and Lara. When he crested it, he found Brigid flying on horseback down the hill toward two riders galloping in their direction with a spare horse and a couple pack horses trailing behind them. Brigid's red hair flew out like a cape caught upon the wind. Finola and Lara galloped behind her. Their horses' hooves tore the earth up in great chunks as they flew over the heathland.

Chapter 17
The Duke

ara struggled to maintain her dignity as a mature woman. The sight of Redmond and Emyr riding toward them through the heather and scattered junipers had torn a strangled cry of relief and joy from her throat. She had followed Brigid in her mad dash through the heather and had joined her in her tear-filled embraces of the men she loved. She remembered the time Redmond had looked at her the way Emyr now looked at Brigid. Was it foolish of her to long for the warmth of a budding romance at her age? Probably.

Now she sat beside the glowing fire as the sun sank behind the rolling hills of the broad heathland, wanting to be close to Redmond and Emyr but afraid to appear like a lovesick child or an over-protective mother.

She had treated the wound in Redmond's thigh and wrapped Emyr's ribs. Lara didn't know how he had withstood the pain of cracked or broken ribs while riding. She had been fighting the urge to hover around them and tend to their every need. But they wouldn't want her to baby them, and she didn't want to embarrass herself. She sat with her hands in her lap, trying to broadcast a sense of calm that she did not feel.

They had gathered around the small fire, breathing in the pungent scent of burning juniper and pine as the twilight shadowed the foothills of the Aveen Mountains. A warm, summer breeze ruffled through the bunches of heather. They sat on boulders and the trunk of a fallen juniper. Emyr and Redmond had questioned Brion about Cedrick and wondered why Hayden was tied to a nearby tree. Brion just shook his head, apparently unwilling to answer.

Redmond scanned the group anxiously—the confusion plain on his face. "I don't understand," he said. "We found Jaxon's unburied body and a stone grave, but the rest of you are all here. We've been imagining the worst."

When no one looked him in the eye, he demanded that Brion tell him what had happened.

Brion glanced to where Cedrick lounged by the fire, trying to look disinterested in the entire affair.

"Would you give us a minute to talk in private?" Brion said to Cedrick.

Cedrick nodded, but Lara noted the flash of annoyance that crossed his face before he could conceal it.

After Cedrick moved off to tend to his horse, Brion kicked at the still-damp ground and shook his head. "You tell us what happened to you first," he said.

Lara understood that Brion was avoiding the question of Neahl's death as long as he could, and she worried how Redmond would take it. Redmond had no reason to conclude that the stone grave hid Neahl's body. He still thought Neahl was fighting over in the Laro Forest.

"They were waiting for us," Redmond said. "When Jaxon and I came around the northern end of the valley, an entire squad of them came at us. But Jaxon disappeared and left me alone."

"Hayden disappeared on me, too," Emyr said. "I didn't see him again until I saw Jaxon galloping after him. I knew something was wrong. So I rode to warn Father because he was closer to me than you were, thinking that we could come back together. But I found him encircled by a dozen Dunkeldi."

"It was hard fighting," Redmond said, "until we managed to break away." Redmond's hand drifted to the bandage on his leg. "We fled north until darkness fell and then circled back around to make our way back to where we left you. We found evidence that the Dunkeldi had captured someone wearing Taurini boots, by the tracks. He had been spying on your position from the looks of it. And then we came across Lara's horse."

Redmond glanced at Brion. "I take it the ambush did not go well."

Brion looked up for the first time. "No," he said.

Redmond waited for him to continue, but Brion didn't say anything else.

"You want to tell me who you buried up in the pass?" Redmond asked.

Brion dropped his gaze again and kicked at the dirt. "Neahl," Brion said in a barely audible whisper.

Lara had always thought that Neahl was pigheaded and impulsive, and she bitterly resented his role in driving Redmond from the island. But she couldn't stop the tears leaking from her eyes as the devastation spread over Redmond's face. His entire body seemed to crumple inward as if some monster were sucking the life out of him.

No one spoke for several, long moments. Emyr picked up a stick and began snapping it into little pieces. Brigid and Finola sniffled. Brion studied Redmond's face as if he expected to read the blame written there that he had already cast upon himself. Redmond blinked rapidly and swallowed several times before he could say anything.

"How?" he choked.

Brion cast a furtive glance at Cedrick who brushed his horse on the other side of the camp. Lara had seen Cedrick riding around Dunfermine over the years, and she had heard the gossip that he was more of a libertine than his father, from whom he had become estranged. And now he came to them alone with a message from his father? Lara didn't trust him. She may not know all the plots nobles spun behind closed doors, but she knew enough from personal experience to convince her that Cedrick was playing a double game.

Lara leaned over to Emyr. "I don't think we should be too open with Cedrick around," she whispered. "He may not look like he's listening, but he is."

Emyr glanced at Cedrick and nodded.

Brion explained how the Taurini had captured Brigid and how they had pursued them only to find that Neahl had already rescued her and was fighting for his life.

"It was Jaxon," Brion said.

A hardness came into Redmond's face to replace the devastation. Lara had seen it before. Redmond was a kind man, but he could be very dangerous when he had that look in his eyes.

"You didn't expect me to let him live, did you?" Tyg said. Redmond glanced at Tyg as if he were deciding how to handle him. Lara braced herself, afraid that Redmond might lunge up and skewer the man with his sword.

"But why was Neahl here?" Redmond asked.

"Cluny," Brion said. "Neahl found out that Cluny had signed the order to have us killed and came to warn us."

Redmond stared at Brion for a moment and then nodded.

"What of Hayden?" Emyr asked as he gazed over the fire to where Hayden sat tied to a juniper.

"We're still trying to work that out," Brion said. "But he denies any involvement."

Redmond passed a hand over his forehead, and Lara fought the desire to wrap her arms around him to comfort him.

Emyr touched Redmond's arm and gestured toward Cedrick. Redmond studied Cedrick for a moment.

"We'll talk more about this later," Redmond said. Brion nodded, and Lara understood that he meant alone without any potentially unfriendly ears lurking nearby. "Have you decided what you're going to do?"

"Actually, we should talk about that, too," Brion said.

Brion waited until the camp was quiet and everyone appeared to be asleep except for Emyr, who had volunteered for the first watch. Brion awoke Redmond and the two of them sat beside Emyr in the shadow of a boulder some distance from the camp.

Brion started without any preamble.

"Do either of you know anything about this Cedrick of Saylen?"

Emyr and Redmond shook their heads.

"He was just a child when I left," Redmond said.

"He told me that Cluny has taken Lara's family prisoners," Brion said.

Redmond and Emyr scowled.

"He thinks he can control you better if he threatens them."

Redmond shook his head. "Cluny is not the man he once was," he said. "And I am going to see that he pays." Redmond picked up a rock and began squeezing it as he shifted it from hand to hand.

Brion agreed with the sentiment, but there wasn't anything they could do for Lara's family at the moment. "Should we tell the ladies?" Brion asked.

Redmond considered. "Probably not. There's nothing we can do now." Redmond glanced at Emyr for his opinion, and Emyr nodded. Brion accepted their decision and continued.

"Cedrick says the Duke wants the papers and the ring, and that I'm to tell no one." He shrugged. "You already know."

"Did he say why?" Redmond asked.

"No. He hinted that it had something to do with Weyland's secret."

"He didn't say what that secret was, did he?" Emyr asked.

"Oh, I almost forgot to tell you," Brion said. "We know what it was."

Brion explained what they had discovered in Rosland's diary.

"His own child?" Emyr said after Brion finished.

"Yes, but there's more." Brion then explained that Hayden suggested that Brion was the true prince, but Hayden didn't seem to know about the midwife and her story that Brion was the son of the Duke of Saylen.

"No wonder the entire kingdom seems to be after you," Redmond said. "If the King thinks you might be the heir to the throne, he would need to make sure you were dead. But if they believe you are the Duke's son, you can't help but get mixed up in his intrigues, whatever they are."

"And," Brion said, "it might explain why that slave gave me the little eagle at the Great Keldi. What if he is the prince? Should I tell Cedrick?"

Redmond dropped the rock and placed his boot on it. "I wouldn't be too anxious to tell him anything until we understand what he wants," he said. "We should trust no one."

"That's what Neahl said before he died," Brion said.

Redmond scowled.

"The slave you're talking about," Emyr asked, "is the young man who ran me down when you were escaping with Brigid, isn't he?"

Brion grinned and nodded. "Sorry about that."

Emyr waved the apology away. "I know of him," he said. "He had a reputation as a gifted fighter. His master employed him in the fighting rings. It's rumored that he has never been defeated."

"You think he's the real King of Coll?" Brion asked.

Emyr shrugged. "I think somebody thinks he is, and I can only think of two reasons why they might want to find him now." He paused. "To kill him or to bring him back and make him king."

"But . . ." Brion began. The enormity of what Weyland had done all those years ago overwhelmed him. Here he was barely eighteen years old fighting for his life, and only now was he beginning to understand why. Where would he be now if Neahl and Redmond hadn't trained him? What would have happened if Neahl and Redmond hadn't taken him into the heathland? How many more assassins would he have faced?

Brion shook his head. Could his situation get any worse? He glanced back at the camp, wondering how much Cedrick knew or suspected and realizing that he had been foolish to let the man remain with them.

"By the King's long, shaggy beard," he cursed.

Emyr smiled. "What kind of curse is that?" he said.

Brion ignored him. "What are we going to do?" he asked.

"Before we decide on that," Redmond said, "I want to know about Jaxon."

So, Brion told him all that he knew or suspected.

"Jaxon must have been working for Cluny," Brion said. "Cluny signed the death sentence."

"He did," Redmond said. "But, for all we know, it was the King himself who ordered it, or some faction at court, or even the Duke of Saylen. So Jaxon was probably working for someone else. Now tell me what Hayden told you."

Brion picked a blade of grass and began twirling it around his finger. He explained his conversation with Hayden and how he had claimed that he had been sent to protect Brion, because some secret group in Chullish believed that Brion might be the lost prince.

"Do you think we can trust him?" Brion asked.

Redmond raised an eyebrow. "No, I don't. But unless you're willing to execute him, you have few options."

"We could send him away," Brion suggested.

"You could, but then you wouldn't be able to watch him," Redmond replied.

"What about Tyg?"

Redmond considered. "If he wanted to kill you, I think you would be dead already."

Brion nodded. "I think you're right. So what now? Do I go with

Cedrick?"

Redmond and Emyr exchanged glances.

"Do you have any choice?" Redmond said. "Neahl thought you should find the Duke. I can't see how you're going to untangle this mess until you can speak to the source of it all."

"But what if he is the one trying to kill us?" Brion adjusted his seat to avoid the rock that poked him in the backside.

Redmond shrugged. "As long as you have the papers and the ring, I don't think he'll kill you."

Brion sighed. "All right. But we need to watch each other's backs. I still don't understand why the Taurini were taking Brigid toward Dunfermine, and we don't know who Jaxon was working for." Brion stood. "I'm glad you two are back," he said.

"You didn't make it easy to find you." Redmond gave a sad smile that reminded Brion how much had changed. Redmond had always been the less serious and more lighthearted brother. He had always been quick to laugh and to tease.

"Well, we had to keep you two in practice," Brion said, trying not to let his own bitterness show. "We can't have you going soft, now can we?"

Brion squinted into the light of the setting sun as Cedrick approached the Dunkeldi sentry. He kept an arrow on the string of his bow ready to shoot Cedrick if Cedrick betrayed him. It had taken them four days' steady travel through the foothills of the Aveen mountains out onto the grassy plain around Dunfermine before they reached the Dunkeldi lines, and they had found no way around them. If they were going to reach the Duke, they would have to pass through the Dunkeldi army. Brion did not relish the prospect. After everything that had happened, a Dunkeldi army was the last place he wanted to be. And he couldn't see how the son of the Duke, the commander of the opposing army, could just stroll into the Dunkeldi camp and survive. But it didn't look like they had much of a choice.

Brion suppressed the uneasy feeling that he was walking into a trap. Lara had pulled him aside before they left and told him not to trust Cedrick. But what choice did he have? He had to meet the

Duke. He had to speak with him. Brion wished for the thousandth time that his companions were with him. But he had left the women with Redmond, Emyr, and Tyg and had come on alone with Cedrick. He would have felt more confident with his friends by his side.

"You can't leave me behind," Finola had said.

"Finola," Brion began.

"Don't 'Finola' me," she snapped. "You can't go in alone."

"I don't have a choice. We have to know what the Duke is up to."

"It could be a trap."

"Which is why you can't come with me."

Finola had scowled.

"You'll be here to help me if anything goes wrong," Brion said.

"Not if you're dead." Finola had choked on the last word.

Brion had checked to make sure no one could hear them before embracing Finola. "We have a plan. He won't kill me—not if he wants his papers and that ring. We have it all worked out." He had kissed her gently and followed Cedrick toward Dunfermine.

The words had sounded so smart and crafty in the early morning light with the blue haze drifting over the heather. But now, crouched down in the gathering gloom, they seemed empty. The truth was that if the Duke wanted him dead, there wasn't much Brion could do to stop him. Not when the Duke commanded an entire army.

Cedrick gave the signal, and Brion kicked Misty into a walk; but he didn't take the arrow off his string. He wondered again how Cedrick expected to ride right through the Dunkeldi lines. Why would they let him do it—unless he was a traitor?

The sentry simply turned a blind eye as Brion rode past him. Cedrick kept a leisurely pace as they entered the Dunkeldi encampment. Heads turned their way, but no one seemed to take much interest in them. Once again, Brion doubted the wisdom of their plan.

They rode on into the night, passing through the camp and out past the Dunkeldi sentries. The fires of the Duke's army flickered in the distance and danced on the shadowed ramparts of the city. Misty picked her way amid the corpses of men and horses that littered the grassland between the two armies. From the little Brion could see under the rising moon and from the stench that assailed his nostrils, the battle for Dunfermine had been fierce. But the Duke's army had not yet been driven back into the city.

Cedrick reined his mount to a stop and shifted in the saddle to face Brion.

"We're nearing my father's lines," he said. "The sentry will expect each of us to give a different watchword. After I give the first answer, he will ask you where the gray geese fly. You will reply that they fly to the King's table to be baked in his pies."

"Really?" Brion asked. "What kind of password is that?"

Cedrick chuckled. "Making them silly makes them easier to remember." He gestured to the bow Brion held in his hands. "You will not want to look like you intend to fight," he said.

Brion dropped the arrow back into his quiver and slipped the bow over his head. The string pulled tight against his chest.

The sentry challenged them, and Cedrick gave his reply. Then Brion gave his response and the sentry let them pass.

It's too easy, Brion thought. *This man should not be able to simply ride through both the Dunkeldi and Alamani armies.* Brion tipped his head back to feel the handle of the knife that Tyg had strapped to his back. The knife sat at the base of his neck just below the collar of his tunic.

"Just in case," Tyg had said, and Brion felt strangely reassured that it was there.

Brion scanned the faces that peered up at them in the flickering light of the fires. These men looked tired, scared—maybe even trapped. The camp reeked of human and animal waste that mingled unpleasantly with the clouds of smoke from the fires to sting Brion's eyes and nostrils. Rows of cone-shaped tents fanned out around him. It was a large encampment, but Brion didn't know if it would be enough to stop the Dunkeldi this time.

Goose bumps rippled up Brion's arm and that familiar tingle tickled his stomach. He dropped a hand to the hilt of his sword. A bowstring slapped, and he flattened himself against Misty's back as the arrow zipped over his head. Then everything around him burst into commotion.

Cedrick shouted and whirled his horse to face the rush of men. His horse reared, and his sword flashed in the firelight. Metal clashed on metal. Men shouted. Brion didn't have time to watch Cedrick or to shrug his own bow from off his back. He had to find that archer. He slid to Misty's side clinging to her with one hand in her mane and his knee pinched tight against the pommel of his saddle. He slashed his way through the men that opposed him as he kicked Misty in the direction from which the arrow had come. Misty neighed and bit and kicked as they cleared a path through their attackers. A man perched on top of a wagon with his bow drawn.

Brion cursed. He couldn't reach him in time. The archer had a clear shot, and Brion could see him aim directly at him. The man jerked and released the string. His arrow slapped into the ground at Misty's feet. Then the man revolved in slow motion as he fell to the ground. A knife protruded from his throat. Brion jerked his head around to see who had thrown the knife, but in the chaos of the attack, he couldn't find him.

Another man ran at him, swinging a battle-axe. Misty sidestepped, and Brion deflected the blow and sliced through the man's tunic. The man fell to his knees. Brion whirled Misty in search of Cedrick, when a voice boomed over the fray.

"Enough!"

The attackers paused and faced a large man sitting on the back of a black horse. A large group of soldiers dressed in blue tunics pressed in behind him. Someone stepped toward Brion again, but the man's second command stopped him.

"I said enough!"

Cedrick kicked his horse through the crowd.

"Father," he said.

Brion's breath caught in his throat. The Duke? His father? He pulled himself upright in his saddle and stared at the Duke and Cedrick. He didn't know what he had expected or how he was supposed to feel. But he hadn't expected to feel confused.

The Duke kicked his horse toward Brion and studied him for a moment. Brion tried to see what he looked like, but the shadows cast by the dancing fires obscured the Duke's face. The Duke was a large man with a commanding presence.

"What is going on here?" he demanded.

"I think we would call it an assassination attempt, Father."

The Duke examined the men who stood with naked swords and knives in their hands.

"Explain," he said.

A tall man stepped forward and knelt.

"My Lord," he said. "Your son has brought the traitor who caused this war into our camp."

This statement gave Brion pause. How would anyone know who he was?

The Duke considered the man for a moment. "Arrest them all," he said with a sweep of his arm towards the men who had been attacking Brion and Cedrick.

A howl of protest arose from the men. The Duke's blue-clad soldiers worked their way through the crowd to disarm the attackers and bind their hands behind their backs.

"Follow me," the Duke said to Brion and Cedrick.

Brion kept his sword ready, but fell in behind the Duke. They rode deep into the camp until they came to a large tent with tassels hanging from the corners and the Duke's blue standard snapping in the breeze. The standard displayed the stag in the teardrop shield that was the Duke's personal coat of arms. The Duke dismounted and gestured for Brion to follow him into the tent.

Brion dismounted, patted Misty, pulled his saddlebags over his shoulder, and followed the Duke. He glanced up at Cedrick, who simply watched him as he pushed the flap aside. Brion ducked low to clear the longbow strung across his chest of the tent flap as he stepped inside. He had no intention of leaving it outside where it could be tampered with.

The Duke stood beside a large fire grate where a fire burned. Lamps blazed in metal brackets at regular intervals. A rich, pungent aroma filled the tent, far more pleasant than the stench of the army camp. The furnishings were sparse but fine. Brion had never seen anything like it. A deep, red carpet filled the center of the tent and several dark, wooden chairs and a bed piled high in expensive furs lined the walls. A huge table sat to one side, with a map spread across it.

"You're a hard man to find," the Duke said as he shrugged off his cloak. In the light of the torches, Brion could see that he was a powerful man with broad shoulders and an angular jaw. His hair was thinning, but it was the same, sandy-brown as Brion's. He might have been several years older than Neahl and Weyland, but he wasn't an old man as Brion had imagined him.

Brion said nothing as the Duke examined him.

Betrayal

"I was sorry to hear about Weyland," the Duke said. "He was a good man."

An unexpected anger boiled up in Brion's chest, hot and furious. This man's intrigues had caused Weyland's and Rosland's deaths. They had caused Brigid and Finola to be enslaved. They had caused Seamus to be killed and Neahl to be murdered by his own friend. They had robbed Brion of almost everything he had loved.

"What do you want?" Brion said. He dropped the saddlebag to his feet. The Duke's gaze followed it to the ground as if he suspected that the ring and the documents he sought were in it. Then the Duke raised his eyes to study Brion.

"You know what I need," he said.

"I didn't bring them with me."

"You would have been a fool to do so," the Duke said. "But this isn't only about the signet ring and the papers anymore." The Duke sat and gestured for Brion to sit. Brion remained standing. The Duke raised an eyebrow.

"You look remarkably like your mother," he said.

The statement surprised Brion. He had never considered that possibility.

"You don't know who I am, do you?" the Duke said.

"I know that you abandoned my mother to die in childbirth."

The Duke shook his head. "I should have sent for you earlier," he said. "But I couldn't."

"I wouldn't have come."

The Duke eyed him for a long moment as if considering.

"I didn't abandon her," he said. "She ran away." The Duke pulled off his gloves and draped them over the back of the chair next to him. He turned his back to Brion as if he didn't want Brion to see his face.

"She was a Carpentini servant. We were young and in love." He turned to study Brion's face as if he hoped to find understanding or forgiveness in Brion's expression.

"I couldn't marry her," he said. "I was already married." A pained expression slipped across his face. "When I asked her to stay with me anyway, she ran. I searched for her for months. By the time I found her, she was dying in an old midwife's cave outside of Wexford."

The emotion in the Duke's face surprised Brion. After Neahl's warning about the nobility and his murder by a nobleman's orders, Brion had thought he knew all he needed to know about them. But this man seemed to be genuinely saddened by his servant's death. Brion's hand strayed to the tiny ring he still wore beneath his shirt. The midwife had told him that it had been his mother's.

"Did you murder the midwife?" Brion said. He hadn't considered how dangerous that question might be before blurting it out. But the surprise and concern on the Duke's face told him that the Duke hadn't done it.

"Was she murdered?"

Brion nodded. "I found her body when I went looking for answers."

The Duke cursed and lunged to his feet. He began pacing. His agitation made Brion think that there was more to his tale about the midwife and his Carpentini servant than the Duke was telling him. Why would the murder of a mere midwife so upset him?

"These are dangerous times, Brion," the Duke said. "Your mother..." He paused. "I need your help."

"And why should I help you?"

The Duke stopped pacing and faced Brion. "Because you are the son of the only woman I ever loved. And because only by helping me can you hope to survive the coup that is now in motion."

A lump suddenly formed in Brion's throat. The Duke had loved his mother. It hadn't been a simple nobleman's infatuation with a commoner. But Brion couldn't focus on that right now. The Duke had just admitted that he was planning a coup. Neahl had been right.

"How do I know you aren't the one who has been trying to kill me?" Brion asked.

The Duke nodded in approval and sniffed.

"I like your boldness," he said. "But I have risked everything to save you."

"What?" That didn't make any sense to Brion. It seemed that Weyland and Rosland had taken all the risks.

The Duke passed a hand over his head. "The chances are that we will never meet again, and there are things that you must understand."

"What?" Brion blurted again. "That you abandoned your own

family?"

The Duke scowled. "I did what had to be done to save the heir to the throne. If I hadn't joined the coup, I would have been executed like the rest of them, and the prince would have died. But I saved him."

"You forced Rosland to give up her own child for the prince." Brion tried not to shout, but the anger and frustration he had been controlling for weeks threatened to burst out of him.

The Duke stepped back and sat down as if surprised that Brion should know this. "How did you find out?"

"Rosland kept a diary," he said. "I found it in the empty grave where her child should have been buried."

The Duke nodded, but his brow furrowed, and Brion thought he wasn't going to explain. When the Duke spoke, he averted his eyes.

"Rosland had worked for me before," he said. "She and Weyland rescued the princess just before the first coup."

Brion stared. Weyland and Rosland had been spies for the Duke? He couldn't believe it. "A princess?" he asked.

The Duke nodded. "I had her smuggled out of Chullish, but she was followed to Brechin. Weyland and Rosland had to fight their way free of the city before my agents could get her safely away. I thought if I could save her, I could either forestall the coup or use her to restore the royal family when she came of age." The Duke glanced up at Brion. "But she died of the fever a few weeks after the rescue, so I had to come up with another plan."

Brion slipped the bow over his head and sat down. The leather chair creaked under his weight. Neahl had been right about nobles and their intrigues. And here Brion was up to his neck in such a tangled mess that he didn't think he would ever be able to unravel it. Brion had half-decided just to leave before the Duke could drag him in any deeper, when the Duke spoke again.

"Rosland's child was dead already," the Duke said. "At least his death could save another. But when I discovered that you were alive, I risked everything to see that you had a good home with a man who could train you to survive."

"Risked?"

The Duke leaned forward and rested his hands on his knees. "If they discovered that you lived and that Weyland's baby had been exchanged for the prince, the entire plan would have come undone."

Brion shook his head in disbelief. "Looks like they did find out," Brion said. "Why else would they have tried to kill all of us?"

"Yes. Well, now your only hope is to find the prince and bring him back."

"Why?"

"Because we are going to execute a coup within a coup."

"You mean someone else is planning a coup?"

The Duke nodded. "Yes, but we are going to use the turmoil they cause to restore the Hassani line to the throne."

Brion considered. Then he drew the little golden eagle the slave had given him from his pocket and held it out to the Duke. "Someone said to give this to you."

The Duke picked up the eagle and examined it. A grin spread across his face, and he closed his fist around the eagle.

"You've already met him then?"

Brion nodded. "Once. He saved my life."

"I knew I had picked the right man," the Duke said. "Will you go find him?"

"Do you plan to kill him?"

The Duke stood and stepped toward Brion. He raised his fist as if to strike.

"Don't insult me, boy. I've just told you that I saved his life. Why would I want him dead? I will see him on the throne of Coll, or I will die trying."

"Who has been trying to kill me then?" Brion asked. He shifted in his seat so he could rise quickly if he needed to. "The Salassani knew we were coming for the girls. King Tristan himself was waiting for us. An assassin tried to shoot me. The entire Dunkeldi army is hunting me, and I was attacked again here tonight. The Dunkeldi seem well-informed of my every move. If you're not behind it, then who is?"

The Duke stared at Brion for a long moment before he shook his head.

"I heard about Tristan," the Duke said. "Nicely done, by the way. He deserves a comeuppance." The Duke paused. "You're a survivor, Brion. I can see that." The Duke began pacing again when Brion made no response.

Betrayal

"I don't know who's after you," the Duke said. "The obvious answer is the King or his son. They have the most to gain by silencing you and me. The only reason I'm not dead yet is because they haven't found the prince or the papers. When they do, I won't last long."

"All right," Brion said. "But what do I do when I find him?"

The Duke stopped and picked up a stone weight from the table with the map. "Bring him to me," he said. "But if I am already . . . uh . . .gone, take him to Chullish. Hayden will know where to go."

"Hayden?" Brion blurted.

The Duke surveyed Brion. "Why do you say his name like that? Has he been killed?"

"No. But Jaxon murdered Neahl."

The Duke pursued his lips. "I heard that Cluny was after him. That's why I sent Hayden with you."

"*You* sent Hayden?"

The Duke raised his eyebrows. "Don't like him much, eh? He has that effect on people."

"I thought he was betraying us to the Dunkeldi."

The Duke shook his head. "Not Hayden."

"Why not?"

"Because the King's son raped Hayden's mother and then whipped his father to death when he complained. Hayden will never serve Geric or his son."

"He never said."

"No. He wouldn't, would he?"

Brion considered the Duke. "Are you aware that Cedrick can walk right through the Dunkeldi camp?"

The Duke put the stone back on the table and leaned against it. "He is resourceful," the Duke said.

"How do you know he isn't a traitor?"

The Duke's expression darkened for a moment, and Brion thought that he had gone too far.

"He is my eldest son," the Duke said. "I am his father."

After all he had seen, Brion didn't think that meant a great deal. But he didn't say anything.

The Duke sat back down.

"Well," the Duke said. "You should leave tonight."

"Tonight?"

"After what just happened, I don't think it would be wise for you to remain in the camp."

"How did those men know who I was, and why did they blame me for starting the war?"

The Duke gave a gruff laugh. "Redmond and Neahl aren't hard to describe," he said. "Neither is a red-headed beauty wandering the heathland. The coup leaders needed a war and someone to blame it on. You and Neahl gave them a convenient excuse."

"Why would they want a war?"

"Because wars provide cover for royal deaths without the uncomfortable problems of simple murder."

"But King Tristan wanted a war, too," Brion said.

"Yes, and you gave him a good excuse as well, didn't you?" The Duke shook his head. "I believe he has labeled you an assassin and put a price on your head."

Brion shook his head. "I didn't know it was him."

"It doesn't matter," the Duke said. "You won't be safe until Coll is safe. And the kingdom won't be secure until the prince has returned to claim the throne."

"All right," Brion said. "But what about the papers and the ring?"

The Duke stood and paced around the edge of the red carpet with his hands behind his back. He stopped by the table with the maps on it. He ran his finger along the edge. "You've kept them safe. Give them to the prince when you find him. He'll need the signet ring."

"Okay." Brion stood to leave. He wanted to ask more questions, but the Duke seemed anxious to send him on his way, and Brion wanted to get out of the camp before any more trouble found him. He suppressed a sudden pang of sorrow. He had spent a considerable amount of time over the last few weeks imagining this meeting, wondering how the Duke would respond to him. Instead of declarations of parental love, the Duke had been all business. It hurt somehow.

"Where do I find this prince?" Brion asked.

"Cedrick's tent is next to mine," the Duke said. "Tell him that I have ordered you both to leave immediately. You will find three packhorses loaded with supplies behind Cedrick's tent. The prince was last seen near Comrie."

"He was at the Great Keldi," Brion said.

The Duke nodded. "He's been moving south. My last two messengers were murdered."

"That's nice," Brion said. "So I just have to ride into a thousand square miles of heathland that happen to be crawling with Dunkeldi and Taurini who all want my head and try and come out alive?"

"You've done it twice already," the Duke said.

Brion bowed his head. "I had Neahl," he said. Brion knew that without his friends, he never would have survived in the heathland.

"There is no one else," the Duke said. "You are all the prince has."

Brion snapped his head up in surprise. Those were almost the exact words that Weyland had said to him with his last breath. And Brion had promised Weyland that he wouldn't abandon them. At the time, he had thought Weyland meant Rosland and Brigid. But now he knew that he was speaking of the prince and the Duke. Something hardened inside Brion. He could not ignore Weyland's last request.

"I'll find a way," Brion said.

The Duke handed him the golden eagle. "Take this," he said. "It will give you safe passage when you get to Chullish."

"Thanks," Brion said. Their gazes met, and Brion struggled to know what to say. He wanted to ask about his mother and to understand this crafty man who stared at him. Brion wanted to trust him, but Neahl's warning not to trust anyone—especially any noble—seemed to ring in his ears. So he turned to leave.

"Brion," the Duke said. Brion faced him. But the Duke didn't say anything for a moment. He seemed to be struggling with himself. "Don't tell Cedrick that you still have the papers and the ring. Let him believe you gave them to me for now."

Brion nodded. So the Duke didn't trust his own son. Lara had been a good judge of character. Cedrick had known all about Weyland's secret. He had been able to move freely through a Dunkeldi camp. Cedrick had had Brion's home searched. What else had Cedrick been doing?

"And," the Duke continued as he shifted his stance uncomfortably. "I'm proud of the man you've become, Brion. I'm sorry I was never there for you."

Brion blinked at the sudden stinging in his eyes.

"I had a good father," he said.

"I know," the Duke said. "That's why I selected him and Rosland."

Chapter 18
Secrets and Saviors

hodri ground his teeth to keep the scream from tearing from his throat as the red-hot iron melted the skin on his chest. The acrid smell of his own burning flesh choked him. He jerked against the cords that bound him. It had been at least four days since he awoke to find himself staked to the ground. He had been beaten, starved, and now branded. Darkness swam before his eyes, swirling with the flickering light of the torches and hooded figures that loomed over him.

"Where are they going?"

Rhodri blinked with heavy eyelids. He tried to focus his mind on Finn, but his mind wouldn't stay still. It roamed through his past, casting up images of Finn teaching him to fight, of the old woman helping him memorize the history of Coll, the thin, slave girl with whom he had shared his first kiss, and of the men he had defeated in the fighting ring.

The scream escaped his throat as another red-hot iron jerked him back to the real world of searing pain and agony.

"I don't think he knows anything." It was a voice that Rhodri hadn't heard before. "He might be telling the truth."

Someone cursed and kicked Rhodri in the side.

"Prince Tomas will be here in a few days," the voice said. "Let *him* decide what to do with our prisoner."

Lara glanced around wondering where Tyg had gone. Redmond had set off in search of a good spot to await Brion's return. He had left Emyr to guard the women and Hayden, who was still tied to a juniper. There had been no time to continue questioning him. Tyg had a habit of disappearing without a sound only to reappear when no one expected him. Lara thought he might have gone with Redmond.

By Tyg's own account, he had no reason to remain with them. Neahl and Jaxon were both dead. The company no longer harassed the Dunkeldi. Tyg had kept his end of the bargain and could have left at any time. But he had stayed.

She had seen the way Tyg watched Brion and the girls, but she couldn't figure out what it meant. She was a good judge of character, and, unless she was wrong, Tyg was mostly bluster. He wasn't the cold-hearted assassin he claimed to be. Nor was he the disinterested sot he appeared. There was more to him. And now he had disappeared without a word. Lara couldn't decide if he had finally abandoned them.

"Lara?" Finola's voice broke into her thoughts.

"Yes?" Lara said. She had grown close to these two young women in the last few weeks. They had become something like daughters to her. It hadn't taken her long to see why men like Emyr and Brion would be drawn to them. Not only were they beautiful, they each exuded an inner strength and confidence. Lara imagined that it grew from the dangers they had been forced to overcome.

"Do you know anything about the Duke of Saylen and Weyland?" Finola asked.

Lara shook her head. "Not much," she said. "After Comrie was destroyed, I was in a village on the other side of the Aveen Mountains in Carpentini lands, and most of the fighting in the last war took place around Chullish and the Laro Forest."

Finola furrowed her brow in disappointment. Lara hesitated to say more. She didn't know if she dared tell them all that she knew.

"The Duke has a reputation for being crafty," she said, "and his son is, well, arrogant and selfish. I've seen him mistreat the townsfolk in Dunfermine on more than one occasion. People whisper that he isn't entirely sane."

"And now Brion is off alone with him?" Finola said.

Lara nodded.

"What about Weyland?" Brigid said.

"Weyland was intensely loyal to the Duke," Lara said. "One time, when Redmond challenged Weyland's blind faith in the Duke, he and

Weyland nearly came to blows. I don't think Rosland liked the Duke much, though."

"I wonder why," Finola said in an exaggerated tone that suggested she knew very well indeed.

Lara didn't understand the statement, so she continued. "Rosland seemed afraid of him. But after Redmond left the island, I only saw her once. By then, I had lost Emyr."

"Do you think the Duke can be trusted?" Brigid asked.

Lara considered. "I think Neahl and Redmond were correct about nobles," she said. "I know for a fact that they will betray any of us if it suits their needs."

"How . . ." Finola's question died on her lips as Redmond rode into camp.

"Time to go," Redmond said.

Lara sighed, grateful for the interruption. She had said too much. Her secrets could be dangerous for the wrong ears.

"Shh." Redmond held a finger to his lips.

Lara lay prostrate in the dirt, peeking underneath the twisted branches of an old, heather bush. Redmond lay next to her. She hadn't realized how much she relied on him for strength and confidence in the face this constant uncertainty. She wanted to throw away all the hurt and distrust, but it was too deep, too profound. Emyr, Finola, and Brigid lay next to them as they spied on a party of Dunkeldi picking their way up the narrow canyon. Lara couldn't see them in the darkness, but the clip of their horses' shod hooves and the jangle of their bridles penetrated the night.

Redmond had insisted that they leave the campsite after Brion had departed with Cedrick for his meeting with the Duke of Saylen. They had set up a fake camp with a fire burning before dusk and circled around to watch the camp from the little rise where they now hid.

Loose stones tumbled behind them. Redmond and Emyr rolled away and came up with weapons in their hands. Lara thought that maybe Tyg had finally returned, but Hayden crouched in the darkness, grinning at them. The ragged ends of the rope that had bound him dangled from his wrists.

"I got curious," he said.

Betrayal

"Get down and shut up," Redmond said.

Lara wondered why Redmond didn't insist on tying Hayden up again. She glanced over at Brigid and Finola, who were both glaring. When Hayden crawled up beside them, both girls backed down the hill away from him and crawled to another vantage point. Lara scooted down the hill to sit by a boulder. There wasn't anything to see, and she was getting dirt and stickers down her shirt.

She kept her gaze on Redmond's back. She had been trying to work out what was bothering him. He hadn't spoken much to her since he and Emyr had returned. She knew that he mourned the loss of the brother he had loved and admired. But there was something else. It might be that he resented the extra responsibility of her and the girls. Maybe he resented her presence. It could also be that he was worried about Brion.

Lara remembered well how Redmond had followed Neahl around as a child, insisting that he could do anything Neahl could do. Redmond had worshiped Neahl. Perhaps that is why, when Neahl had boasted that he would kill Redmond for abandoning them, Redmond had left the island. She hadn't considered before how much that must have hurt a young man whose only dream had been to please his brother.

But Redmond had also been gentler than Neahl. He had always constrained Neahl in his darker moods. And he had been brave and noble. When the Salassani attacked Comrie, Redmond had not scampered into the heather, like many of the men. He had picked up a wooden staff and fought his way to Lara's home. He had pulled her from the burning cabin and carried her to safety under his secret hiding place beneath the rock by the lake.

Lara shivered at the memory. She could still smell the acrid, greasy aroma of burning flesh. Her father and sister had escaped the fire and the Salassani. The rest had perished. She had curled up under the rock with Redmond's arms around her and waited for death.

Wasn't that what they were waiting for now? With all the Salassani tribes hunting them and even the nobles of Coll, what chance did they have? Maybe she should have remained behind with her family. What had made her think a spinster like herself could withstand the rigors of warfare? That was the problem. She hadn't thought. She had followed her heart, and she knew that she would follow it again if she had the choice.

Redmond and the others crawled away from the crest of the hill and gathered around Lara.

"They're hunting us," Redmond said. "They knew where we camped. It's time to leave."

"I'd like to knock a few Dunkeldi heads," Hayden said. He gave the wicked smile that Lara assumed he meant to be disarming.

Redmond examined him. "Be my guest," he said. "But we're moving on. Don't follow us."

Hayden stared. "What? You're leaving me to the Dunkeldi?"

Lara was surprised to see the anger on Redmond's face. He slipped a knife from its sheath. He held it up so Hayden could see it.

"I'm not playing games with useless nobles or their pawns," Redmond said. "I don't care about your coup or your kings. You understand?"

Hayden gaped. "But you're Alamani."

"So was Neahl, and an Alamani noble's dog killed him."

"But—"

"We don't have time for this," Redmond interrupted. "If you're staying to die, get out of here and get on with it. If not, shut up and get on your horse."

"You still think I betrayed you."

Redmond whipped the knife up to Hayden's throat.

"If I thought that you had sold us to the Dunkeldi, you would be dead. So don't give me any excuses."

Redmond sheathed his knife, took Lara's hand, and led her to her horse. He helped her up and then mounted himself. Hayden stood watching them before he mounted his own horse.

Lara found that she had to blink back the tears. Redmond was hurting and his pain was making him more dangerous, more unpredictable. Redmond glanced at her, and a momentary expression of sadness swept across his face. Then he reined his horse around and led them deeper into the canyon.

Brion stepped out into the cool night air and gazed up at the stars that twinkled overhead. If it hadn't been for the reek of the camp all around him, it might have been a beautiful night. Why did he feel that he had missed something important in his first, and probably last, conversation with his father? He had expected something more, something deeper. But a peculiar emptiness filled his chest. It's not that he expected to experience some overwhelming love for the man he had never known. He just expected something more than this emptiness.

Brion strode over to where Misty cropped the grass. He hadn't unsaddled her and brushed her as he usually did, but he didn't have time now.

"How are you holding up, old girl?" he said as he stroked her muzzle.

Misty raised her head and nuzzled his cheek. He dropped his saddlebags over her rump and secured them in place. He patted her again.

"I'm sorry to do this to you," he said. "But we have to ride again."

He pulled the bow over his head and hung it from Misty's saddle horn when a strangled cry came from Cedrick's tent. Brion glanced at the guards in front of the Duke's tent, but they either hadn't heard it or chose to ignore it, which seemed odd. If someone was attacking the Duke's son, surely they would move to protect him. But they didn't stir. So Brion sprinted the few paces to Cedrick's tent and threw the flap aside.

"No, please."

The words brought Brion to a halt. Cedrick loomed over a girl about Brigid's age who was cowering in a corner of the tent. She clutched at the torn edge of her shirt. Brion stared in confusion as Cedrick whirled to face him. Cedrick held a knife in his hand.

"What are you doing?" Brion demanded.

"Get out," Cedrick said.

"The Duke says we have to leave tonight," Brion said. "Now."

"I said get out." Cedrick advanced on Brion. Behind him, the girl looked on in wide-eyed terror.

Brion held up his hands. "Let's just go."

Cedrick lunged, and Brion caught the smell of alcohol. Cedrick had been drinking.

Brion jumped out of the way of the slashing blade and then closed the distance before Cedrick could swing the blade for a return strike. Brion caught the arm and drove his knee up into Cedrick's stomach.

As Cedrick bent over with an explosion of air from his lungs, Brion swung his leg over Cedrick's arm, kicked him in the face with his heel, and dropped his weight on Cedrick's arm.

The rage inside him made him want to cripple Cedrick for life, but his better judgment told him to be more careful. He used enough pressure on the shoulder to make sure it would cause Cedrick some pain for a few weeks, but not enough to tear it loose.

Cedrick groaned as Brion released the hold. Brion took three quick strides to the cowering girl, grabbed her elbow, and hurried her out of the entrance.

"Get out of here," he said. After watching her slender form disappear into the darkness, he glanced down at Cedrick where he groveled in pain on the carpet, clutching at his shoulder. Brion's gaze drifted to Cedrick's boots, and he stared at them as if he were seeing them for the first time. He had seen that fancy stitch somewhere before, pressed into the wet earth.

Brion hurried to Misty's side, grabbed up his bow, and leapt onto Misty's back. He rode around the tent in search of the three pack-horses the Duke had promised. A man dressed as richly as the Duke, with a bold shock of white hair running over his ear stood holding the horses' reins. Brion surveyed him, remembering the man with the stripe of white hair that had talked to Weyland on the road so many months ago. This must have been the same man, and he worked for the Duke.

The horses were piled high with bundles of supplies, including dozens of arrows, for which Brion was grateful. He had worried about his dwindling supply. The man handed the reins to Brion with a nod. Brion accepted them, tied the horses in a chain, and rode into the darkness. He wanted to question the man about what he had said to Weyland, but now was not the time. Brion chanced one last glance over his shoulder to find the Duke standing in the shadows of his tent, watching Brion ride away.

Brion paused at the edge of the encampment. There was no way he could pass the sentries unnoticed with three packhorses in tow. He dismounted and tied the line of packhorses to Misty's saddle, patted her once, and then crouched low, ghosting toward the nearest sentry. Brion waited until the man moved on to survey a different place in the line before slipping past him to disappear into the heather.

When he was well-past the sentry, he gave a low whistle. Moments later, Misty trotted into the ring of light cast by the sentry's fire with the other three horses in tow. The sentry ran toward them with a shout, but stopped when he realized that he couldn't catch them. Brion hoped that he would assume they were some stray horses that had escaped their tether when he didn't see a rider. Misty approached Brion with a soft whinny, and Brion stroked her muzzle.

"You're an amazing horse," he said. Then he climbed into the saddle and headed toward the Dunkeldi lines. That army would not be so easy to avoid.

Brion swung far to the east, hoping to avoid the army all together. But he kept coming upon a well-positioned line of double pickets whose intent seemed to be to close off Dunfermine from any outside communication.

Brion rubbed his eyes and stretched as the gray line of dawn began to expand across the eastern horizon. He knelt in the shadow of a gnarled old juniper, studying the nearest sentries. If he didn't get through the line before daylight, he would be trapped between the two armies.

"Follow me." Tyg's voice breathed in his ear, and Brion jerked so violently that his hand missed its attempt to draw his sword.

Tyg waved him on and disappeared into the heather.

Brion cursed. "One of these days," he said. But he didn't have time to make idle threats. Tyg was fast-approaching the two sentries. Brion retrieved the horses and pulled Misty after him until he could peer over the little rise. He kept his bow ready with an arrow nocked on the string in case Tyg stirred up any trouble.

But Tyg was standing where the two sentries had stood as if he were waiting for Brion. Their bodies lay crumpled amid the grass. When Brion's head appeared over the rise, Tyg disappeared again, this time in the direction of the next picket.

"He's crazy," Brion whispered. "He's completely crazy." Still he couldn't afford to lose the chance Tyg had given him. He jumped onto Misty's back and kicked her into a gallop. The other horses followed.

Tyg was waiting for him as he galloped through the gap Tyg had created in the line. Brion reached an arm down and dragged Tyg onto Misty's back behind him. A Dunkeldi rider appeared in front of them, but Brion shot him from his horse and kicked Misty into a gallop again.

"You're full of surprises," Brion said to Tyg.

"And you should learn to listen," Tyg said.

"That only works if the person makes a sound," Brion replied.

"You're welcome," Tyg said.

"Thanks. I'm going after the lost prince."

"So I heard."

Brion craned his head around to stare at Tyg. "You know that you are the most frightening person I have ever met?"

Tyg grinned. "Better stay on your best behavior then," he said.

Chapter 19
Stranger in the Rocks

"I have sent my son to his death," the Duke said. He sat at his writing desk, staring at the short missive that had arrived from Chullish. Pain and despair flashed across the Duke's face. "What have I done?"

Killian examined the Duke with a discerning eye. The Duke rarely removed his armor anymore, and he had Killian prepare all of his food. The Duke's face and posture sagged under the heavy strain he had endured for weeks now. Dunfermine was surrounded, and no aid could be sent. It was only a matter of time before the city fell and the Duke fell with it. His plans to restore the throne to the Hassani line would have to succeed or fail without him.

"You've done what you must," Killian said.

Killian suppressed the pang of regret. The Duke had been a bright-eyed, exuberant child, anxious to please. He had become a curious and contemplative teenager who wanted to reform the monarchy and modernize the Kingdom of Coll. Then his father died, and he was confronted with a war and a coup before he had even reached manhood. That he had survived at all was a testament to his skill and determination. Now it seemed as if things were spinning beyond his control, and he was grasping at every possible thread to salvage the goal for which he had lived and worked ceaselessly for most of his life.

"That's no excuse," the Duke said. "I should have anticipated this."

"Things may yet work out, My Lord," Killian said.

The Duke raised his gaze to study Killian. "I think it's time," the Duke said. "Bring me my lawyer. We will have to prepare yet one more plan. If everything else fails, perhaps we may yet save my family and its claims to the Crown."

Killian understood. The Duke meant to sacrifice all that he had left to restore his family to the throne. But Killian no longer believed it could be done.

"You need to leave the island now before it's too late." Brion had never seen Redmond so agitated. "I can take you into the southland. I have friends there."

Brion and Tyg had found Redmond and the others waiting for them by a waterfall deep in the canyons of the southern Aveen Mountains. The dell where they camped was filled with rich grass for the horses and a thick grove of birch and cedar to conceal them. Redmond hadn't said a word as Brion told them about his meeting with the Duke. Then without any warning, he had lunged to his feet, paced around, and then stopped in front of Brion, demanding that he leave the island.

"But what about the prince?" Brion asked.

Redmond's gloved hands balled into fists. "No prince ever cared two coppers for me, and Damian has probably been trying to kill us for eight months."

"Neahl would—"

"Neahl is dead!" Redmond interrupted. The scars on his cheeks burned white as his face reddened. "And he told you to get out of Coll as soon as you had informed the Duke. You've done that. Let's get out of here before any more of us die so some useless, scabby noble can sit on a throne and order people around."

Brion sat stunned. He had never seen Redmond this angry. Redmond had always been the levelheaded one, the voice of reason when Neahl was feeling reckless. Redmond's gaze rested on Lara for an instant, and Brion understood. Redmond couldn't lose Lara and Emyr. Not after losing Neahl and Weyland.

Brion shook his head. "I can't. Not yet."

"You don't owe them anything," Redmond said. "If the Duke really is your father—"

"Wait. What?" Hayden stood up. He searched their faces. "What do you mean the Duke is his father?"

Brion gazed at Hayden. It didn't matter how hard he tried, he couldn't like him—even though he now knew that Hayden hadn't betrayed them.

"I'm the illegitimate son of the Duke of Saylen," Brion said. "He told me that he sent you to protect me."

Hayden stared. "But I thought he sent me because you were the prince."

"Sorry to disappoint you," Brion said.

Hayden dropped onto the ground. "I don't believe it. I thought all of this talk about going to get the prince was just a front to keep me guessing. But you're serious." Hayden picked up a twig and snapped it. "If I'd known that, I wouldn't have wasted my time."

"Poor baby," Finola snapped.

"No one's stopping you from leaving," Brion said to Hayden. "You're right," he said to Redmond's back. "I don't owe them anything."

Redmond turned to face Brion with guarded anticipation.

"But I do owe Weyland and Rosland," Brion said. "Weyland begged me with his last breath not to abandon the prince and the Duke. I promised him I wouldn't."

"Brion—" Redmond began.

"I'll keep that promise," Brion cut in. "I owe them that much."

Redmond sat down beside Lara. "This is a mistake," he said.

Lara watched him with wide eyes. Those two knew something they weren't telling Brion. He knew it.

"And," Brion continued, "I owe it to myself. I'm going to find Cluny and anyone else who is responsible for Neahl's death, and I'm going to kill them."

No one spoke, but everyone watched Brion. Tyg slid a knife from its sheath and beamed at them. "Now that is a cause worth fighting for," he said.

Redmond smiled, despite his misgivings.

"Then," Brion said to Redmond, "we can go south, and you can show me those horseback archers that you say are so good."

"So we're going back then?" Finola said.

Brion studied his little band. How could he ask any of them to sacrifice themselves to fulfill a promise he had made?

"I won't make any of you go with me," he said, "But I have to do this. I leave tomorrow morning."

Brion rose to tend to Misty and to care for his equipment. He needed to leave them all to decide what they would do. His decision was made. But despite his insistence that he wouldn't force them to go, he knew full well that by insisting to go himself, he left them little choice. His friends wouldn't abandon him.

Brigid followed him down to the creek where he filled his waterskins.

"Is this going to change everything?" Brigid's green eyes were earnest and her brow wrinkled. The falls at the head of the little canyon gave off a quiet roar that dampened sound in the dell.

"What are you talking about?" Brion asked.

"There's no doubt now," she said. "You are the Duke's son."

Brion paused before setting the waterskin on the bank and rising to face Brigid. He had been so wrapped up in his own doubts and fears about the Duke that he hadn't stopped to consider what this would mean to Brigid. And he had also forgotten that she wasn't yet seventeen. She was only a year and a few months younger than he was, but few girls her age had endured so much.

Brion stepped toward her. "I'm sorry," he said.

Brigid's eyes widened in surprise. "You are going to let it change things," she accused. She pushed away from him, but he grabbed her hand and pulled her back.

"Wait a minute," he said. "You're getting as hot-headed as Finola."

A tear slid down Brigid's cheek.

"Hang on," Brion said. He pulled her into a hug. "I don't know what this is going to mean," he said. "But one thing can't ever change." He held her at arm's length to look into her eyes. "When I met the Duke, I just felt empty, you know? I thought I would feel . . . I don't know—*something*. But I just felt empty. You will always be my sister. No one can replace you or Papa or Momma."

Brigid nodded and sniffed. She wiped at the tears.

"Don't let them change you," she said. "You're all the family I have left."

Brion pulled her into another hug. "I'll always be here," he said. But he didn't know if he could keep that promise. He didn't know if he could keep any of them alive—especially not now that they would be heading north, back into the foothills crawling with Dunkeldi and Taurini warriors.

Betrayal

"He's alone." Brion said. He and Emyr crouched beside a boulder on a ridge watching a lone figure work his way down a narrow ravine. The valley floor was strewn with boulders and bunches of junipers and brambles that liked the lower, dryer elevations. The game trail the man followed wound its tortuous way over the rugged floor of the valley.

They had taken the shorter, more difficult route up and over the ridges of the mountains toward Comrie through the tall pines. Though it probably took them longer, it kept them out of the path of Dunkeldi patrols. Brion and Emyr had started scouting the hills above Comrie for any sign of the prince when they found the old man's trail and followed it for several miles.

"Something is wrong with him," Emyr said. The man was using a stick and moving slowly, meandering as if he were lost or searching for something. One arm dangled useless at his side.

"Could be a trap." Brion said this more for his own benefit than for Emyr's. He needed to stay focused on finding the prince, not roaming the foothills helping lost travelers.

"He could be a Carpentini who survived a Dunkeldi ambush," Emyr suggested. Most Carpentini and Salassani had refused to join King Tristan of the Dunkeldi in his war and Tristan allowed his men to prey upon them whenever they had the chance.

Brion considered. "Should we check it out?" Brion said.

"I was hoping you'd ask," Emyr said.

They swung wide to get in front of the man and wait for him. But, after two hours, the man still had not appeared.

"You don't think he climbed out of the valley?" Emyr said.

Brion shook his head. "He could barely walk."

They crawled out of their cover and began working their way carefully up the canyon. Brion remained in the shadow of the trees where possible and hurried across open spaces to crouch behind a boulder or a bush. He kept his gaze moving, scanning the ridgeline and the ground in front of him. He listened to the normal sounds of the heathland, searching for any sound that didn't belong.

Emyr, who had taken the other side of the valley, caught his attention and pointed to the valley floor where a pool of water created a sudden patch of vibrant green against the more subdued greens and browns of the heathland. A form lay half-in and half-out of the water.

Alert to the possibility that someone had killed the old man, Brion dropped behind a juniper to watch and wait. He found no sign of a struggle or of anyone passing in or out of the valley. A shadow passed overhead, and Brion glanced up to see a turkey vulture circling lazily on the wind high above them. Convinced that the man was alone, Brion signaled for Emyr to cover him as he approached.

For a moment, it appeared that the man had fallen into the pool of water and drowned, but, when Brion came closer, he found that the man's face rested on a stone that stood a few inches above the water as if he had lain down to sleep. Brion bent to examine the man. He had an injury on his head that leaked yellow pus, and he smelled as if he had already died and was rotting. Brion pinched his nose against the stench. The man was alive. His back rose and fell.

Brion reached with the tip of his bow and poked the man in the ribs. The man groaned. Brion poked him again. The man's eyes flickered open. When his gaze focused on Brion, he gave a strangled cry and tried to struggle to his feet. He fell into the pool of water and dunked his head. He tried to push himself upright with his one good arm, but his hand sank into the mud, and his head submerged again.

Brion sprang forward, collared the man, and yanked him free of the water. The man came up sputtering and coughing. Brion set him down and waited until the coughing subsided.

"Who are you?" Brion asked in Salassani.

The man eyed him. "That depends," he mumbled. The man had gray hair and blue eyes. Wrinkles sagged around the sockets, but his cheeks were gaunt. He had a hunted look about him, like a rabbit cowering in the bushes, knowing it has been seen but afraid to move. The man clearly wasn't bred to live in the wild heathland. He was soft and refined.

"Okay. What are you doing up here by yourself?"

"That also depends." The man was starting to get his wits back again.

"Depends on what?"

"Who you are."

Brion pursed his lips. "Who I am depends on who you are," he said.

The man watched him. His eyes narrowed.

"You're not Dunkeldi," the man said, "or Salassani."

"No. Well . . . not really." Brion now knew that his mother was Carpentini, but this hardly seemed like the time or place to worry about that little detail.

"Whom do you serve?" the man asked.

Brion sat on the ground in front of the man. This old man had more than a casual interest in who he was.

"Well, at the moment, I serve myself," Brion said.

The man considered him. Now that Brion examined this stranger more closely, he realized that he wasn't Carpentini or Dunkeldi. He wore Taurini square-toed boots, but his accent was strange. The only weapon the man appeared to be carrying was a small knife in a sheath at his hip. A breeze blew through the valley, and Brion caught the awful stench again.

"Are you sick?" Brion asked.

The man blinked as sadness and despair crept into his expression.

"I'm dying," he said.

"Can I help you?"

"There's no point."

Brion waved a hand at Emyr to come. As Emyr approached, his face tightened as the stench reached his nostrils. Emyr knelt next to him and gave Brion a questioning glance.

"My name is Brion. And this is Emyr," Brion said. "We can help you."

"If you're not Salassani, why are you so far north of the Kingdom of Coll, and why do you speak Salassani?" the man asked.

"We're looking for someone." Brion tried to sound disinterested, but the man cocked his head in sudden interest.

"Whom?" he said.

"Um, I'm not sure I should tell you that."

"Did the Duke send you?" The man's eyes were wide and expectant.

Brion exchanged a quick glance with Emyr, who raised his eyebrows.

"Why would you ask that?" Emyr said.

"Because I'm waiting for the Duke's men to find me."

Brion nodded and glanced at Emyr. "That's very interesting," he said.

"He's here," the man said.

"Who?"

"The one you're looking for." Brion was surprised to see tears brimming in the old man's eyes. "They have him," he said. "The Dunkeldi have him at Comrie."

The foul stench smote Lara's nostrils, forcing the bile into her throat. She had never, in all her experience, smelled anything so revolting. She tied a strip of cloth around her face to fend off the smell that rose up from the man Brion and Emyr had carried into camp. The cloth didn't help much, but at least it took the edge off.

They had made a small encampment high up on a spur of the Aveen Mountains that overlooked Comrie Lake. From there, they could make out the tents of the Dunkeldi army in the hazy distance.

The man looked to be at least sixty years old. His clothes were torn and stained. He had an injury on his head, and his right arm lay limp and useless on the ground. His cheeks were gaunt as if he had had little to eat. But his bright, blue eyes were alert. He surveyed each them carefully as they peered down at him.

Lara and Emyr bent over him to examine his wounds. Emyr slipped a knife under the bandages on the man's arm to cut them away. The man cried out and jerked against Brion's restraining hands. Redmond knelt to help Brion hold him. Emyr peeled the bandages away to reveal a black, oozing wound. The arm was red and swollen. Red streaks crawled up onto his shoulder. The stench penetrated Lara's cloth. She bent to the side and struggled not to vomit, before turning back to see Emyr and Redmond sharing a knowing glance. Emyr shook his head.

"I told you," the man said. "I'm dying."

"That's a sword wound," Redmond said. "What happened?"

"We were attacked by a band of Alamani and Dunkeldi up north of Comrie," he said. "They killed the entire Carpentini band we were with. Only Rhodri and I escaped."

"Rhodri?"

The man eyed them for a moment, and then he seemed to come

to a decision.

"I'm Finn," he said. "I was Lord Chamberlain to King Edward Hassani before the coup."

That statement caught everyone's attention. Hayden stood up and strode over to peer down at Finn. Tyg stopped twirling his knife and stared. Brigid and Finola exchanged wide-eyed glances. Lara studied the man more closely. She had not expected this.

"Did you know his father, Karl?" she blurted.

Finn turned his penetrating, blue eyes on her and furrowed his brow. Lara regretted her impetuous words. How could she explain that question without telling them everything she knew?

"I did," Finn said. "He was not the King his son Edward was, but he enjoyed a successful reign."

Lara glanced up at Redmond, beseeching him to rescue her. Redmond didn't understand until she bobbed her head at him. Comprehension blossomed on his face. He rushed to change the subject.

"So Rhodri is the prince?" Redmond asked.

Lara sighed in relief. She should have kept her silence. Secrets like the one she held about her father were dangerous at any time. But, during a time of war and instability, they were worse. People over-reacted.

"Yes," Finn said.

Lara followed Redmond's gaze to the crowd of tents far below them, perched on the edge of the shimmering, blue lake.

"And the Dunkeldi have him?" Emyr asked.

"Yes," Finn said again.

"That might explain the Taurini they captured," Emyr said. "We saw his tracks, but we didn't have time to follow them."

Brion studied Lara curiously. Her reaction to Finn was odd. He had never seen her so agitated for no apparent reason. She seemed upset that she had asked about King Karl—even though it seemed like a harmless question. And the way Redmond had rushed to change the subject meant that the two of them shared some secret. Brion gave a mental shrug. He guessed that two people with as much history between them as Redmond and Lara were bound to have secrets.

"There are a lot of Dunkeldi down there," Finola said. "You're not just going to walk in and get him out."

Redmond nodded to Brion and Emyr. They stood and walked with him a few paces from camp. Redmond signaled Tyg to join them.

"No more secrets," Hayden called after him. Redmond paused, glanced at Brion, who nodded. Hayden joined them.

"That arm has to come off," Emyr said. "Or he's going to die."

"He's already half dead," Hayden said.

"We don't have a saw," Redmond said.

"I do." Tyg raised his hand as if he were excited by the prospect.

Redmond appraised Tyg. "I'm not going to ask why you have a saw."

"You never know," Tyg said with a grin.

Redmond nodded. "Okay, but we'll worry about that in a minute. If they have the prince, they must know who he is. He's probably already dead."

"We have to be sure," Hayden said. The defiant, arrogant way Hayden had of sneering at them made Brion want to punch the look off his face.

"Let's see what Finn can tell us and scout around a bit," Brion said.

Redmond scowled. Brion knew what he was thinking.

"I don't want to die rescuing a dead prince any more than you do," Brion said.

"This won't be like last time," Redmond said. "These men are ready for war. We have no pass to slow them down."

"But this is the land that bred you," Brion said. "You know it better than any of them."

Redmond bowed his head. "We only go in if we have positive proof that the prince is there and that he's alive," he said.

"Agreed," Brion said.

Tyg crouched in the shadows of the tent. The sun had long since fallen behind the peaks of the Aveen Mountains that towered over him, casting the valley in the gray quiet of twilight. He had left the others to the grotesque work of amputating Finn's arm. He had seen enough of that sort of thing, and they had all agreed that he was the most likely candidate to enter the Dunkeldi camp and survive. After all, moving unnoticed was his profession. It had become second nature to him.

The aroma of cooking food and wood smoke drifted among the tents. The camp hadn't been here long enough to take on the peculiar overpowering reek that all army encampments developed. But it was getting there. The glow of lamps shone through the tent fabric, casting long shadows of men moving about. A few hours' listening to the conversations of men lounging around fires as they ate their evening meals had given Tyg a good idea of where the prisoner was being held. When the young man wearing the purple cloak came riding in shouting orders, Tyg had followed him to the tent.

The tent was erected off to the side of the encampment near the lake. Guards stood at the entrance, so Tyg circled around back and hunkered down beside the pile of boxes and bags, making himself as much a part of the shadows as possible. The young man who had been screaming orders entered the tent, speaking so loudly his voice carried over the racket of the camp.

"You people are fools." The voice was high-pitched and sounded young. Tyg raised an eyebrow. Were the Dunkeldi employing children?

"Forgive me, My Lord," another man said. "We were not informed."

"That's no excuse," the young man said. Then there was a thump. "You." Someone groaned. "Who is your contact?"

"I told them. I'm a Taurini slave." This voice also sounded young, but it was low, dry, and raspy.

There was another thump and a groan.

"Taurini slaves aren't branded with the coat of arms of the deposed kings of Coll." The young man with the high-pitched voice seemed to be working himself up.

"I don't know what you're talking about."

A resounding slap rang out. "Don't lie to me. I know who you are. Where is Finn? He's out there, isn't he?"

There was a pause and a shuffle of feet.

"Take a patrol to where you found him and search the area. If you find the old man, bring him here." The heavy canvas of the tent flap snapped open, and the sound of hurrying footsteps retreated into the camp.

"Well, lost prince," the young man said, "if you won't talk, you're of no use to me." There was another pause. "I think we'll use the gallows tomorrow. That's a proper execution for a runaway slave."

The tent shuttered again as the flap was thrown back. Tyg waited until the nighttime hum of the camp swallowed the sounds of the retreating men before he yanked up two tent stakes and wiggled under the canvas into the deeper darkness inside. The stench of human waste and burned flesh filled his nostrils as he waited for his eyes to adjust. The tent was empty except for a man staked spread-eagle to the ground.

Tyg crept up to him and placed a hand over his mouth. The man stiffened.

"Rhodri?" Tyg whispered into his ear.

The man nodded.

"We found Finn. We'll get you out of here." Tyg lifted his hand from Rhodri's mouth.

"Who are you?" Rhodri whispered.

"The Duke sent us."

"Tristan knows about you," Rhodri said. "He sent his son to kill you. He's in the camp now."

"I know. We'll take care of it," Tyg said. "Drink this."

"What is it?"

"It's a healing tea. It'll help you regain your strength." Tyg placed his waterskin to Rhodri's mouth and let him drink as much as he would take.

"Are you seriously injured?" Tyg asked

Rhodri shook his head. "But I've been staked for days. I don't know how well I can run."

"We need to build up your strength a bit if we can." Tyg broke off pieces of dried meat and Finola's biscuits and fed them to Rhodri. While Rhodri ate, Tyg talked.

"Sleep as much as you can tonight. If they decide to execute you before we come, do anything you can to stall them."

"How many are with you?" Rhodri asked after swallowing some jerky.

"Five men, three women."

"Women?"

Tyg smiled to himself. Rhodri had never seen the fire in Finola's eyes as she fought like a wildcat or the cold, steady way Brigid aimed and released arrows from her bow.

"Don't underestimate them just because they're women," he said. "They can be very handy."

Tyg continued feeding Rhodri until the slap of approaching footfalls drew near.

"We'll come for you later," he whispered. He wiggled under the tent back out into the night. He replaced the stakes and ghosted through the shadows until he once again stood under an old, twisted, beech tree looking down on the fires of the Dunkeldi camp.

"Looks like we're going in tonight," Tyg said.

Chapter 20
To Rescue a King

Tomorrow? They're hanging him tomorrow?" Brion dropped the leather strap he had been oiling and stared at Tyg. He had hoped they had a few days at least. How could they extract a wounded man from a camp of watchful Dunkeldi with no more than a few hours to prepare?

"Could be a bluff," Tyg said. He sat down and reached for one of the hot biscuits Finola had flipped out of the coals of the fire.

"But you don't think it is?" Emyr asked.

Tyg shrugged and bit into the biscuit. He talked around the mouthful while he chewed. "I think if you want your prince alive, you had better get him tonight."

"All right," Redmond said. He set his mug down in the dirt and scanned them. "Who here can swim?" he asked.

Hayden and Emyr were the only ones to raise their hands. Redmond regarded Brion in some surprise.

"What?" Brion said. "You and Neahl never taught me."

"That was a large oversight," Redmond said. He gazed over their heads for a few moments as if remembering. "I once met some warriors who trained to swim in mail shirts," he said.

"They must have liked to clean rust off their mail," Hayden said.

"Since none of us have mail shirts," Finola said, "we probably don't need to worry about that." She picked one of her biscuits from the ashes, dusted it, and took a bite.

Redmond ignored them. "Any chance one of you can handle a boat?" he said to Hayden and Emyr.

Emyr nodded, but Hayden shook his head. "It wasn't necessary for the pages at court," he said.

Betrayal

"I can," Tyg said as he reached to fill his bowl with stew.

Redmond frowned at him. "You can't swim, but you can handle a boat?"

Tyg grinned. "If you can handle a boat, you don't need to know how to swim," he said.

Brion laughed. "Can't argue with that logic, Redmond," he said.

Redmond raised an eyebrow at Brion. A sideways smile played at the corner of Redmond's mouth, but he suppressed it. Lara covered her mouth with her hand and turned away so Redmond couldn't see.

"Okay," Redmond said. "We go in on foot then. If we can't go out the way we came in, then we take the boats. Brion, are the snares in the valley ready?"

"Not all of them. But I did get a few in place."

"Ladies, your job is to guard Finn and to be ready to ride. Hayden you're the bait."

"Very nice," Hayden said. "You wouldn't be planning to run off and leave me with several hundred Dunkeldi hot on my tail, would you?"

Redmond gazed at him. "We're not traitors, but don't tempt me," he said. "How's your leg?"

Hayden glanced at Finola. "Better," he said.

"You know your way through the valley?"

Hayden nodded.

"You know where the snares are set?"

Hayden nodded again.

"Emyr," Redmond said, "you might be recognized in the camp."

"But I speak better Salassani than any of you," he protested.

Annoyance flashed across Redmond's face. Brion understood what Redmond was doing. He was making sure that Emyr and Lara were as safe as he could make them under the circumstances.

"We can't risk someone recognizing you," Redmond said.

Emyr scowled, but held his tongue.

Tyg twirled his spoon between his fingers like he did his knives and plunged it into the stew.

"Well, I'm ready for some action," Hayden said. "Beats being tied to a tree day and night."

"You might change your mind," Redmond said. "Your job is to wait until we slip past you, confuse our trail, and then draw off any pursuers into the valley and into the snares."

Hayden smiled. "Sounds like fun."

Brion watched Tyg's barrel shape disappear into the darkness as he slipped ahead of Brion and Redmond to clear a path through the Dunkeldi sentries. The waters of Comrie Lake shimmered in the moonlight. The large, Dunkeldi horse herd milled about their pickets near the lake. The camp had long since fallen into the quiet murmur of sleep. Redmond glanced at Brion. The light of the fires burning in the Dunkeldi camp danced in his eyes.

"If I don't make it out," Redmond began.

"What?" Brion peered at him through the darkness. There was an earnestness to Redmond's gaze that made Brion uncomfortable.

"We know any of us could die in this rescue," Redmond said. "If I die, promise me that you will see that Lara is cared for."

"You're not going to—"

"Promise me."

"Of course," Brion said.

Redmond fidgeted. "And," he said, "when you leave Coll, cross over to the city of Aradel. There's an apothecary near the center of the city next to the cooper's shop. The owner is an old friend of mine. I promised him I would come back and help him with a little problem. He'll be a friend to you. You can trust him."

Before Brion could press Redmond to explain, Tyg reappeared and motioned for them to follow. Redmond had never said much about his time in the southland, and Brion was curious about this friend. But now was not the time to ask him about it. Redmond's words left a sinking feeling in Brion's stomach. He couldn't lose Redmond, too. Not after Neahl and Seamus.

Voices filtered through the forest of tents, carried on the smoke of the cooking fires that burned everywhere. A few of those tents glowed with the internal light of lamps and candles. The lingering aroma of cooked food and burning wood mingled with the smell of sweating horses and men and the dry, dusty odor of the heather. The night air was heavy with dew, and the camp was quiet.

Brion breathed this air in deeply, trying to still his nerves. He hadn't been this jumpy since the night he had strolled into the encampment at the Great Keldi to rescue Brigid. Redmond's morbid premonition only made it worse. He and Redmond followed Tyg's silent form into the darkness. Brion marveled again at how the stocky, barrel-chested man could creep so quietly. Tyg drifted from shadow to shadow, never making a sound.

Tyg stopped at a small tent and bent to yank up several stakes. The tent sagged in on itself. Tyg crawled under, and they followed.

Brion's stomach revolted at the stench inside, and he had to suppress a gag. By the time he reached the form on the ground, Tyg had already cut Rhodri's bonds and was helping him to sit up.

Redmond slipped through the darkness to guard the entrance.

"Can you walk?" Tyg whispered.

Rhodri wobbled where he sat and tried to crawl to his feet before he sat back, breathing hard.

"Give me a bit," he said.

Brion crouched beside him and handed him his waterskin. Rhodri tried to drink deeply, but Brion snatched the skin away. "Small sips," he whispered. He didn't want Rhodri drinking too much and getting sick. Then with Tyg and Brion each on an arm, Rhodri struggled to his feet.

"They haven't fed me much," he said as his feet shuffled the dirt.

"Be quiet," the guard outside the tent snapped. They all froze. Brion glanced over at Redmond. He could barely make out his form in the darkness. He waved them on. Brion crawled under the tent first to make sure the area was clear. Then Rhodri wiggled through. His foot caught one of the cords and the tent shook.

The tent flap jerked open. "I told you—" The voice was cut off with a gurgle.

Brion dragged Rhodri free of the tent, desperate to get clear. Tyg and Redmond scrambled out after him. Tyg shoved the stakes back into the ground, and Brion and Redmond half-carried, half-dragged Rhodri into the shadows of the next tent as he stumbled along with them. Rhodri was a large, muscular, young man, and Brion knew they wouldn't be able to carry him far.

"He's not going to make it to our horses," Brion whispered.

Redmond nodded. "Wait here." He handed Rhodri's arm to Tyg and disappeared. He angled toward the horse herd, and Brion understood what he intended. They could borrow a few Dunkeldi ponies to carry them out of the camp.

"Well now," a high-pitched, youthful voice cut through the darkness, speaking in Alamani. Brion spun to find a man dressed in a mail shirt standing with his hands on his hips, a dark cloak draped over his shoulders. Five Dunkeldi men dressed in matching uniforms of red and gold stood beside him. Two had their short, recurve bows drawn. The sharpened broadheads glinted in the light of the campfires.

Brion drew his sword and straightened. Maybe Redmond had been wrong. Maybe it was Brion who would die tonight. He wished they hadn't left their own bows in camp. Redmond had argued that the longbows would have given them away since no Dunkeldi used them.

"I thought you might come tonight," the man said. "Spies are mostly useless, but occasionally they get things right."

Brion watched and waited. Tyg slipped a knife into each hand. Brion swallowed. How could this man know who he was? And how could he have known they would try to rescue Rhodri tonight?

"Is Cedrick with you?"

Brion blinked. He was talking about Cedrick of Saylen. Why would he have expected Cedrick? When they didn't answer, the man stepped closer to them to get a better look.

"Oh, I see," he said. "Cedrick didn't send you." Then he smiled. "You're the *real* rescue party," he laughed. "You really thought you were saving the prince? Cedrick has messed up this time." Then he gestured to the men behind him.

"Kill them," he said. "Leave the lost prince alive."

The guards with the bows loosed their strings. Brion let go of Rhodri and leapt to the side, slashing his sword at the arrow. He cut it in two, but the broadhead sliced a shallow cut along his shoulder. Tyg had ducked and rolled to avoid the arrow aimed at him. He came up with a knife in his hand.

"Wait," the arrogant stranger said. He held up his hand and cocked his head to one side as if considering. "I have a better idea." The guards paused, but did not lower their weapons.

A self-satisfied grin spread across the young man's face. "Let's just have a bit fun," he said. "I'll send Cedrick a little present—a lost prince ought to make his life more interesting. We'll see how he likes this new problem."

Then he whirled away and waved at the guards to follow him. "Take the prince away, if you can," he called over his shoulder to Brion and Tyg as the guards retreated. "I won't interfere, but I can't promise the same from Captain Moran. He's a little annoyed that you've killed so many of his men."

Brion stared in confused anger for a moment until Tyg punched his leg from where he knelt beside Rhodri.

"Get him up," Tyg whispered.

Brion sheathed his sword, swung Rhodri's arm over his shoulder, and wrapped his own arm around Rhodri's waist to support him. He and Tyg began moving toward the horses again. Rhodri stumbled between them. They hadn't made it far when the sound of pounding hooves reached them. But it wasn't one or two horses. It sounded like the entire herd was galloping into camp. Someone shouted, and Redmond was beside them astride a Dunkeldi pony.

"Get him up behind me," Redmond said.

Redmond reached down to lift Rhodri up as Brion and Tyg pushed him from below. A hollow thump sounded and Redmond reeled in the saddle. Someone yelled. Rhodri fell on top of Brion as Redmond's horse reared and galloped after the horses that were stampeding through the camp. Redmond slipped from its back and crashed to the ground. Brion untangled himself from Rhodri in time to see Redmond stagger to his feet and wave at them to follow him.

"To the boats," Redmond said.

Brion and Tyg dragged Rhodri to his feet and struggled through the flood of panicked horses and men. An arrow zipped past Brion's head, and he ducked. Tyg dropped Rhodri's arm, gave Brion one meaningful glance and turned back. Brion knew he was going after the archer, so Brion did his best to drag Rhodri along behind Redmond. But Redmond wasn't doing well at all. He kept stumbling and weaving like he was drunk. Brion didn't understand what was wrong with him. A fall from a horse shouldn't affect him that much.

As they neared the lake, a sentry appeared in front of them. "What's going on?" he said in Salassani. They stopped. The man eyed them and then drew his sword. Brion expected Redmond to deal with the man, but he stood there as if he were in a trance. The man began shouting for help, so Brion let go of Rhodri and drew his own sword. He rushed the man. After a short exchange, Brion penetrated his guard and drove his blade through the man's heart. He kicked it free and spun to find that Redmond and Rhodri were gone.

"Redmond," he called. A sudden terror nearly strangled him. Where could they have gone? Why hadn't they waited? Had they been captured? He ran back the way they had come only to meet Tyg hurrying toward him.

"Where are they?" Brion said.

Tyg scowled at him. "You lost them?"

"I had to fight a guard, and they just disappeared."

Tyg cursed. They ran back to where the guard's body lay. Brion bent to search for tracks, but the ground had been so thoroughly trampled that he couldn't make anything of it.

Tyg let him search for a few minutes and then grabbed his shoulder. He yanked Brion around toward the lake and raced into the darkness. Now that Brion remembered that Redmond had been taking them to the boats, this seemed like the best place to look for them. But when they arrived at the lakeside, Redmond and Rhodri weren't there. Brion spun back to stare into the chaos of the encampment. He would go back for them. He couldn't leave them. A shout rang out and then more followed. Someone with a torch rushed in their direction.

"They've found them." Brion sprang toward the commotion.

"Brion," Tyg shouted, heedless of the danger of drawing attention to themselves. Brion stopped. Tyg was dragging a boat out into the water. "Get in," he said.

"What are you doing?" Brion demanded. The desperation choked him. "We can't leave them."

"We have no choice," Tyg said. "If they didn't get away, we'll come back for them. We're no good to anyone dead."

Brion hesitated. Had Redmond chosen this place to die? Is that why he had asked Brion to care of Lara? Is that why he had refused to fight the sentry? Had he chosen to end it all in Comrie, the village of his childhood, the place where his path as a warrior had begun? To join his brother in death?

"Now, Brion!" Tyg's voice was angry.

Brion ground his teeth and then leapt into the boat with Tyg, fighting the horrible, gut-wrenching feeling that he had just failed Redmond and left him to die.

Lara huddled next to the boulder, peering down into the ravine where Hayden was supposed to lead the Dunkeldi that pursued him. The sliver of moon hovered above them, casting its pale light over the boulders that littered the valley floor. Emyr shifted beside her. Brigid and Finola crouched behind another boulder where Finn lay beside them. Occasionally he groaned, and Finola placed her hand over his mouth to quiet him. He had been in state of delirium ever since they had amputated his arm. The smell of rotting had mostly gone away, but she didn't think Finn would live more than a few days.

The men were late. Hayden should have ridden through the valley long ago. That familiar tickling feeling wiggled its way around in her belly. Something had happened to Redmond. She knew it.

Maybe he had known that this rescue would go badly for him. Maybe that was why he had argued against it. She asked herself again why she had come with them into the heathland. She told herself that it was because she couldn't bear to lose her child again—even though deep down she knew it had always been about Redmond.

In the weeks of scurrying about the heathland playing hide-and-seek with the Dunkeldi and whoever else was hunting them, Redmond had remained aloof as if he were afraid of getting too close. Had she been so off-putting? Was he afraid of offending her, or had he been disappointed in her? After all, she was no fighter like Finola and Brigid. She was no longer the slender, young girl he had known. Beside Brigid and Finola, Lara must have looked like a dried up old prune. The years of sorrow had etched lines in her face and made it hard for her to trust.

Emyr stirred. A ray of moonlight lay across his face.

"I've never heard you talk about my grandmother," he said.

Lara was grateful for the distraction. "She was a character," she said. "Every man in Comrie was afraid of her big, wooden spoon. She carried it around with her, and, if anyone gave her grief, she would rap them over the knuckles or across the head with it." Lara hadn't talked about her mother in years. The sudden rush of memories made her blink against the sting in her eyes.

"She was an herbalist, and sometimes she delivered babies," she said. "Papa adored her. He never recovered after the raid. We pulled her corpse from the still-smoldering cabin."

Lara stopped and swallowed.

"I'm sorry," Emyr said.

Lara waved a hand him. "It happened a long time ago," she said.

"Where did they come from," Emyr asked. "I mean, before they settled in Comrie?"

Lara turned her gaze back to the valley. "Momma had been born in a village south of Chullish, but her papa moved north when she was a child. Papa…" Lara paused. "He was born somewhere in the south, I don't really know where."

"Were his family cobblers?"

Lara shook her head and gave a little laugh. "No, his mother was, well, she worked for a wealthy family."

Emyr bent closer to peer at her. "What do you mean?" he said.

Lara shrugged. "That's all I know," she said.

Something fluttered at the far end of the valley. Emyr jerked his head around and raised a finger to his lips. Lara breathed a sigh of relief as Emyr crawled to the edge of the ridge.

Lara watched the lone horseman work his way up the valley. He trailed three riderless horses behind him. Hayden passed below them. He didn't look at them, but kept riding until he disappeared around the bend. Lara understood that he was laying a false trail in case the Dunkeldi were following.

But her heart sank. The horses weren't supposed to be riderless. She glanced around to see Brigid and Finola exchange worried glances. Emyr crawled back to her. He didn't say anything, but his lips pinched tight with worry.

Lara wondered if maybe Hayden had revealed their plans to the Dunkeldi and simply left his post without drawing the Dunkeldi after him. But that wouldn't make any sense. Why would he come back this way, knowing that Emyr would be watching? Why would he bring their horses with him? Maybe Redmond had taken the boats.

They waited until the blush of dawn pushed back the darkness. Lara had dozed off and on until Emyr motioned for them to leave the ridge.

"What now?" Finola said as they gathered around their horses. Finola had that determined expression on her face. Lara wondered if Brion understood how much this girl loved him.

"They might have taken the boats," Brigid said. She stepped over to Emyr and lifted his hand as if trying to draw strength from him.

Emyr considered. "I thought of that, but if they had made a clean get away, they should have been here by now. Let's go back to the base camp. If they aren't back by noon, we'll go after them."

Lara tried to suppress the nagging doubt, but her gut told her that Redmond was in trouble. That he was still in Comrie.

"He's in trouble," she said. Emyr glanced around at her. "I don't think we should wait," she said. How could she explain that she knew that if they didn't do something soon Redmond would die?

Emyr sighed. "Okay, but let's check the base camp first."

"I thought you knew how to handle a boat," Brion said. He sat on a boulder on the far side of the lake, wringing the water from his clothes. The sun hadn't yet risen into the sky. Brion shivered.

Tyg scowled at him as he dumped out his own boot. "You're alive, aren't you?"

"Barely," Brion replied. "You paddled in circles all night and then you ran us right into that rock."

"The current caught me."

"Current? We're on a lake. There is no current."

Since neither of them could swim, the only reason they were still alive was that the rock had been close enough to shore that they could wade out.

"Stop complaining," Tyg said. "We've got to find the others."

"We need to go back for Redmond," Brion said. "They were probably captured."

"You don't know that," Tyg said. "He could be waiting for us back at camp."

Brion did know it. All the way across the lake, he had pondered why Redmond had acted so strangely. Only when he remembered the thump had he realized that Redmond had been hit by the arrow. It must have been a dangerous wound. There was no way Redmond and Rhodri could have made it to Hayden and the horses on their own. Redmond might even have bled to death already.

"We should have stayed," Brion said.

"And fight five hundred Dunkeldi by ourselves?" Tyg replied.

Brion pulled out his sword and his knives and wiped them as dry as he could get them on the grass and leaves. Then he pulled out the little vial of oil he always carried and wiped on a layer of oil with is finger. He couldn't afford to let his blades rust.

"Redmond wouldn't have left us behind," he said as he finished wiping his blades.

"You can thank me later for saving your life," Tyg said. "Let's get going."

Tyg stalked off up the rise without waiting for Brion. Brion finished wringing out his shirt, pulled it on, and sloshed up the hill in his wet boots. He would go back for Redmond, and, if the Dunkeldi had killed him, Brion would take his revenge.

Tyg and Brion found the others waiting at the base camp. No one had seen Redmond or Rhodri, though the Dunkeldi patrols were out in force. They spent the rest of the day evading patrols. By late afternoon, they had climbed high up the foothills above the lake from where they could look down on the Dunkeldi camp.

"How are we going to find them?" Brion asked.

"I know where they are." Lara sat with her hands in her lap as she often did, staring at the ground. When no one spoke, she raised her head.

"He would go there if he was in trouble," she said.

"Where?" Brion asked.

"The rock."

Brion understood. Redmond had told him about a large rock by the lake where a few people could hide. He had forgotten about it.

"But that's right in the camp," he said.

Lara nodded. "We hid there when the Salassani attacked Comrie. He saved my life."

"What are you talking about?" Hayden said.

"There's a large cavity under a rock beside the lake," Lara said. "It's well-hidden."

"Can we get to it by boat?" Tyg asked.

"Oh no," Brion said. "I'm not getting in a boat with you again."

"You *could* use the boats," Lara said, "but there was a trail that crossed the Leetwater and came out of the trees about a hundred paces from the rock."

"It's risky," Hayden said.

"Do you want your prince or not?" Tyg said.

"We have to do it," Emyr said. "Can you draw a map so we can find it?"

"I'm going with you." Lara stared at Emyr, daring him to contradict her.

Emyr shook his head. "No."

"We're going too," Brigid said.

"Wait a minute," Brion said.

"Don't use that tone on us," Finola said.

"You three didn't do so well on your own," Hayden said. "Let them come."

Brion paused to study Hayden. His arrogant disdain for the ladies had turned to respect. But Brion wasn't going to allow Brigid and Finola into that camp.

"Not into the Dunkeldi camp," Brion said. "Brigid and Finola would stand out."

"We can go around to the other side and cause a distraction," Hayden said, "while you three go in to get them."

Brion didn't like the idea of sending Hayden alone with the girls, but he couldn't take them into the camp either. He glanced at Emyr, but he shook his head.

"He's my father. I'm going in for him."

"Tyg?" Brion said.

Tyg glanced around at Finola and Brigid. He winked at them.

"Looks like we get to have some fun, ladies," Tyg said. Then he paused, and his expression grew serious. "You all need to understand that we aren't going to get another chance at this."

Chapter 21
Under the Stone

ara paused at the line of trees and knelt behind a large birch tree to look out over the open ground in front of her. The slanting light of the fading sun danced on the waters of the lake and filtered through the columns of wood smoke that rose in lazy spirals into the air.

They had left Finn and their extra horses and baggage well hidden in a copse of trees deep in the foothills. If they survived the night, they would return for them.

Lara had led Brion and Emyr down the overgrown paths, now used only by wild animals. In her childhood, those paths had led up to the high pastures where she had spent many happy hours watching over the village's herd of sheep and goats. Long-forgotten memories had come rushing back to her as they descended into the valley. They had crossed the Leetwater at the wading place where the children of Comrie had splashed and played on hot, summer days. The familiar blackberry patches on the hillsides were denser and more tangled as they bent under the weight of their fruit.

Now she knelt, gazing out over the valley of her youth. Tents had been erected amid the burned-out remains of her home. The faces of those who had lived and died in the violent inferno danced in her memory. There were so many.

Lara had never believed that she would return to this place of death—the place where most of her family and friends had perished and where Redmond had first professed his love for her. The great rock rose up from a pile of boulders left over from some ancient upheaval of land that jutted out over the lake.

Heather and chokecherry bushes clustered amid the boulders, and a lone beech tree stabbed toward the sky in defiance of the solid stone. Beyond the rock, a line of boats had been pulled up on the shore, and, beyond those, the tents of the camp stood stark and white in the evening twilight.

"What if he's not there?" Brion whispered in her ear.

"He will be," she said.

Brion placed a hand on her shoulder and pointed to a group of Taurini who appeared to be patrolling the edge of the encampment. Together they crawled back into a dense patch of mahogany shrubs and lay flat on the ground to await the coming darkness.

The moon had not yet risen when Brion and Emyr brought up the horses they had concealed by the Leetwater. Lara climbed into the saddle and pulled a hood over her blonde hair so she wouldn't stand out. She waited for Brion to give her the nod before she kicked her horse into a walk, trying to appear as if they belonged. They hadn't gone far when Brion's horse, Misty, gave a quiet snort. Brion reined her to a stop and placed an arrow on the string of his bow. He waved at them to continue.

Fear rippled through Lara's chest and crept into her throat as something rustled in the undergrowth behind them. She craned her neck around as her horse kept walking. A white face appeared and then another. Brion drew and loosed. Someone cried out. Brion shot another arrow so fast she barely saw him move.

"Go," he said. "Run."

Lara kicked her horse into a gallop, terrified that they were going to die before she could even see Redmond's face again. They pounded over the hundred paces between the tree line and the pile of boulders and slid to a stop. Brion and Emyr vaulted from their saddles and splashed out into the lake, searching for the entrance Lara had told them about. Lara clambered down with much less dexterity and hurried to join them. The last time she had come to this stone was with Redmond the day the Salassani had destroyed their village.

"Over here," Lara said. She fell to her hands and knees in the water and crawled under the overhang. She blinked at the darkness, but couldn't see anything.

"Redmond?" she whispered.

"Lara?" His voice was tired, but it sent a thrill up her spine. He was alive!

"I came for you," she said. The tears sprang to her eyes. A hand reached out to touch her face.

"I love you," she whispered. She didn't know why she said it now when haste was their first priority. Perhaps it came from a deep-seated fear that she would not be able to say it at all if she waited much longer.

Someone tugged on her clothing. "Are they there?" It was Emyr's voice.

"We need to go," Lara said to Redmond.

"I'll need help," Redmond said.

Lara backed out and let Emyr crawl in. He came out, dragging Rhodri, who struggled to find his feet in the slippery mud of the bank. Redmond followed, crawling out without using his left arm, which he held close to his chest. He grabbed Lara's hand as he clambered to his feet. Brion helped Emyr lift Rhodri into the saddle.

Redmond gazed at Lara for a moment before pulling her to him in a tight one armed embrace.

"I love you too," he whispered and kissed the top of her head.

She squeezed him back briefly before they splashed to the horses. She climbed up and helped Redmond up behind her. He wrapped his good arm around her waist, and she was conscious of the weight she had put on around her middle in the years of Redmond's absence.

Shouts and cries came from the encampment.

Brion slapped the flank of Lara's horse, and they all galloped back toward the dark line of trees. More cries came from the camp, and Lara craned her head around to see a golden glow rising up on the far side of the camp. Tyg and Hayden must have been successful. Shadows separated from the encampment and bobbed in their direction. Emyr galloped past her with Rhodri in the saddle in front of him to lead the way. Brion fell behind them with his longbow in his hands to cover their escape.

Flames licked at the cluster of wagons and baggage. Tyg gave a satisfied grunt as the orange tongues of fire whipped and curled higher into the sky. Arrows arced through the flickering light as men ran to put out the fire. Finola and Brigid shot arrow after arrow from the cover of the blind that Tyg had built to shelter them from view. Hayden sat astride his horse in the shadows waiting for Tyg to give the order to ride. Tyg had worked his way into the camp alone to start the fires. When Hayden had offered to join him, Tyg had smirked.

"You look like a pampered noble, boy," he had said. "You wouldn't make it ten steps without arousing curiosity."

"What? And you look like a Dunkeldi?" Hayden had said.

"No," Tyg said, "I look like a man of no account."

Hayden had stared at him. "Be my guest," he had said with a wave of his hand toward the camp.

Tyg understood that the secret to not being seen was to be unremarkable, ordinary. No one worried about a barrel of a man who looked like he spent all of his time at the table or the jug. Appearances mattered, and Tyg was skilled at manipulating people's desire to see him as non-threatening.

Half a dozen Dunkeldi sprawled around the blaze or writhed in agony before anyone seemed to notice that arrows were falling in the camp. When an officer deduced the direction of the attack and rounded up some men to check it out, Tyg signaled for Hayden to expose himself.

No doubt the Dunkeldi officer wondered why the sentries hadn't raised the alarm, but Tyg didn't leave sentries alive when he found them.

Hayden saluted the girls, reined his horse into an open space where he could be seen, and shot an arrow from a short Salassani bow into the camp. Even Tyg could see that the boy had no idea how to handle the weapon, but the arrow flew into the camp and narrowly missed a man riding next to the officer. When the men shouted and gestured in his direction, Hayden flung the bow into the bushes and kicked his horse into a gallop. Tyg watched him pause inside the line of birch and willow until a group of men found their horses and gave pursuit. Hayden disappeared into the darkness.

"There goes the bait," Tyg muttered. "I hope that gives the others enough time."

He signaled for Brigid and Finola to mount their horses. As he climbed into his saddle, a sound made him spin back to stare at the encampment. A large party on horseback rode past the inferno, heading straight for them.

"Time to go," Tyg called.

"Guess they took the wrong bait," Finola said.

"Looks like it," Tyg said. "Ride hard."

Brigid swiveled in the saddle and loosed two arrows into the massed bunch of riders. Two horses fell, which caused considerable confusion as men and horses tried to avoid the flailing feet. Several horses tripped, but the main body came on.

"No time for heroics," Tyg called. "Ride! Ride!"

Tyg knew they had the advantage of a dark night, but the moon would soon rise, and they needed to be far ahead by then. He had taken the precaution of rigging a snare of his own, and he directed the girls toward it.

"Watch the line," he called.

Brigid and Finola ducked low, clinging to their horses' necks as they passed between the trees where Tyg had stretched the thin wire. Tyg followed them before he drew his sword and reined his horse around. "Keep riding," he shouted. "Turn south along the wash and head for the outcrop."

"Tyg, no!" Finola yelled.

Lara struggled to keep Emyr in sight as he wove his way amid the boulders and the mixed woodland of birch, oak, and beech trees that littered the hills surrounding the Leetwater. Redmond clutched at her desperately with his right arm, and, more than once, she had to reach back to steady him. When they dropped down a hill into a copse of trees, Redmond simply tumbled from the horse's back.

"Emyr!" Lara cried out as she reined her horse around. She leapt from the saddle and knelt beside Redmond. She reached her arms around him to lift his head into her lap. Her hands found him covered in something warm and sticky. Emyr dropped beside her. Rhodri remained on his horse, watching them.

"He's injured," Lara said as she showed him a hand that was smeared with blood.

"My shoulder," Redmond said.

Emyr peeled the clothes away to find the broken shaft of an arrow poking up several inches. The arrow had entered from the top and passed down just inside the collarbone. Emyr felt around Redmond's back and glanced up at Lara. The grim expression on his face told her that the wound was serious.

"I'm going to have to push it through," Emyr said.

Redmond blinked and nodded.

Lara held Redmond's head steady in her lap and Redmond gazed into her eyes. The expression on his face twisted her insides into a knot. He expected to die. His hand found hers.

"Do it," Redmond said.

Emyr shoved the shaft into the wound with a sudden jerk. Redmond stiffened and groaned. His hand squeezed Lara's so hard she thought he might break it. Emyr reached behind Redmond and drew out the shaft.

"There's no time to clean it properly," he said. "But I'll do the best I can."

Just then, Brion galloped into the clearing and reined Misty to a stop.

"What's the matter?" he said.

"Redmond took an arrow in the shoulder last night," Emyr said. "He's too weak to ride."

Brion jumped down beside them to peer at Redmond as Emyr rinsed the wounds with water and sprinkled his red powder on them.

"Why didn't you say your injury was so serious?"

Redmond tried to smile. "There was no time," he said.

"That's what Neahl said," Brion replied, "and it nearly killed him."

"He can't go on tonight," Lara said.

Brion gazed at her, but she could tell by his expression that he would insist that they go on.

"Leave me," Redmond said.

"Not happening," Brion said.

"I'm slowing you down."

Brion glanced up at Emyr who shook his head.

"We'll tie you to the saddle," Brion said.

They heaved Redmond into the saddle in front of Lara and tied him to it.

"Can you keep riding?" Brion asked Rhodri. Rhodri nodded, so Brion mounted and they rode on into the night.

Another long hour of ducking under branches and scrambling over broken hillsides brought them to the rocky outcrop where they had agreed to meet the others, but the place was empty. Brion dismounted to study the ground.

"No one has been here," he said.

"They'll come," Emyr said. But his furrowed brow revealed his concern. Then the sound of pounding hooves reached them. Emyr and Brion waved Lara back into the shadows of the trees.

In a few moments, Hayden galloped into view, his long hair flying out behind him. He angled toward the outcrop as Brion and Emyr stepped out of the shadows.

"It worked," Hayden yelled, "better than we expected."

"Where are the others?" Brion shouted.

"Coming a different way. No time to explain." Hayden sped past them. "Better hide."

Just then, a band of Dunkeldi pounded up the trail in hot pursuit. Emyr and Brion melted back into the shadows, as the Dunkeldi flew past them, heedless of everything but their fleeing prey.

"He's a lunatic," Emyr said.

"He did seem to be enjoying himself," Brion replied.

"What now?" Lara asked.

The girls and Tyg were out there alone. It seemed like everything they planned went wrong.

"We wait," Brion said.

Tyg ignored Finola's cry and waved her away. If he let these men follow them, none of them would make it out of the heathland alive. The first dozen riders plowed headlong into the thin wire and were jerked free of their saddles. They tumbled into the men coming behind them. Tyg kicked his horse into the confused body of screaming men and neighing horses, slashing about him with the sword. Five or six more men fell before they realized what was happening.

But Tyg disengaged, turned tail, and galloped away. They would now be less eager in their pursuit, and he had thinned their ranks almost in half. Tyg hadn't had the time or the creativity that Brion had. But he still had one more trick up his sleeve. He raced his horse toward the steep embankment that fell twenty feet into a rocky wash.

In the darkness, the rugged landscape became a featureless blur. But Tyg had been careful to note the jagged trunk of a long-dead juniper that sat on the edge of the cutaway where it dropped down at a more gradual angle. When the tree materialized out of the darkness in front of him, Tyg reined his horse to a trot, eased it over the side and down into the wash.

As he expected, the first riders pelted over the edge and plummeted to the ground twenty feet below. Men and horses screamed in terror and agony amid the sickening crunch of bones and the crash of bodies that filled the air. Tyg chanced a glance behind him and cursed. Several riders had avoided the fall and were angling down the embankment toward him. That was his last trick. Now all he could do was race to escape them. But his horse was tiring, and the men began to close the distance.

Tyg wheeled his mount south along the floor of the wash, seeking to gain a bit of distance before he swung back west toward the encampment. He had no desire to die this night, but he would not lead these men to his friends. It had been many years since Tyg had belonged to anything worthwhile. Not since the wars had he done more than ply his bloody craft to keep beer in his belly and knives in his sheaths. What was he good for?

When Neahl offered him the opportunity to do something other than kill—to protect a promising young man—he had jumped at the opportunity. Then the two, pretty, young girls had worked their way into his affections when he thought those affections had withered and died long ago. He used to be so careful, so calculating. He was becoming reckless.

The men pressed close behind him. The beat of their horses' hooves pushed him on. He leaned low over his horse's neck and urged it forward, but he could feel the weariness in its stride. He would have to stand and fight.

The buzz and whine of arrows flew past his head. But they were flying in the wrong direction. He glanced up to see Finola and Brigid silhouetted on a small rise off to his left. One of his pursuers fell as two more arrows zipped over Tyg's head. Tyg's pursuers broke off their pursuit of him and galloped toward the girls.

"No," Tyg said. He wheeled his horse and gave chase. The three remaining Dunkeldi outdistanced him. Brigid and Finola disappeared as the men urged their horses up the rise. He would be too late. He couldn't reach them in time. Why hadn't they run?

Brigid's scream split the air.

Chapter 22
Of Silk and Herbs

espite his words, Brion couldn't wait and had gone off in search of Tyg, Brigid, and Finola. Lara wasn't about to sit around while Redmond took an infection—not when she could do something about it.

"He needs tending," she said to Emyr.

Emyr glanced up at her and nodded. "We may have to ride at any moment," he said.

"He might not live at all if we don't treat that wound," Lara said.

"We can't build a fire," Emyr said.

"We don't need a fire. We need moldy bread and yarrow."

"Bread?"

"Yes, and yarrow. Do you know it?"

Emyr nodded.

"I wish we had some aloe," Lara said.

"I have some," Emyr said. "In my bag."

He retrieved a leather satchel from his saddlebags and extracted a small wooden box.

"It's a salve," he said.

Lara took it and rummaged in the pack until she found a moldy biscuit. She set them down beside Redmond and stepped off into the darkness, bent low in search of the low-lying yarrow plants. She had seen them among the heather and knew they were about, but locating them in the dark would be a challenge.

Emyr followed her. "Don't go far," he said.

Within fifteen minutes, they had collected a supply of yarrow, and Lara knelt beside Redmond. She removed the bandages, cleaned the entrance and exit wounds with clear water again and then chewed the yarrow leaves while rubbing the moldiest part of the biscuit over both wounds.

"How does this work?" Emyr asked.

Lara shrugged and talked around the wad of yarrow in her mouth. "It just does, better than anything else."

"Mold?"

"Yes. Trust me."

As she worked the sticky, aloe salve into the wounds, Redmond kept his gaze steady on her face. He made no sign that he was in pain. With the aloe applied, she packed the wounds with the chewed yarrow and reapplied the bandages.

"We'll sew them up later," she said. "We need to let them drain first."

Redmond reached up to brush aside the hair that had fallen into Lara's eyes. He let his fingers rest against her cheek.

"I missed you," he said. "I never stopped loving you."

Lara swallowed the knot that rose in her throat. She blinked and nodded. She bent and kissed his forehead before going to see to Rhodri.

Rhodri leaned back against the cool boulder watching the tender care with which Lara treated Redmond's wounds. He was grateful for their rescue, but he could not suppress the guilt that they had sacrificed so much for him. They didn't even know him. For all they knew, he could be a scoundrel, and yet, they had risked their lives to pluck him from the heart of the Dunkeldi encampment. They were more than bold. They were brazen.

"How are you feeling?" Lara said as she approached him.

"Like I've been trampled by a horse," he said. He meant it to sound lighthearted, but the words seemed lame and insensitive when they left his lips. He bowed his head.

"Let me see." She bent to peer at his bare chest. The blackened wounds where the brands had seared his flesh were filled with dirt and oozed a clear liquid.

"We had best treat this now," she said, "or you're sure to take an infection."

Rhodri nodded. He was acutely aware that he reeked of filth having lain in his own urine and excrement for days. The water from the lake had washed some of it away, but it still clung to his clothing. He couldn't keep the embarrassment from burning his cheeks. So he laid his head back against the stone and tried to ignore the pain as she poured water onto the wounds and scrubbed them with a cloth.

"I'm sorry about the smell," he said.

"I've smelled worse," Lara said. "Looks like they were drawing a picture on your chest."

Rhodri raised his head. "I think they were enjoying themselves."

"It looks like a boar."

"What?"

Lara glanced at his face. "It's crude, but it's a boar."

Rhodri laid his head back. So they had branded him with the symbol of the family that had murdered his parents and seized their throne—adding insult to injury.

Lara worked on in silence. The cool aloe salve she applied eased the pain. When she finished, she sat back and surveyed him.

"You have a cut by your eye. Are you hurt anywhere else?"

Rhodri grimaced at the stabbing pain in his ribs as he tried to take a deep breath.

"I think they bruised or cracked my ribs," he said. "But they don't seem broken."

Lara nodded and massaged the aloe salve into his bruises. Then she retrieved a clean change of clothes from Emyr's saddlebags and turned her back while he struggled into them.

"You'll be needing some boots," she said.

"There's an extra pair in my bags," Redmond said.

Lara pulled them from Redmond's saddlebags and brought water and food for them both.

"Thank you," Rhodri said. "You're a good woman."

Lara nodded her thanks.

"I'm sorry for your trouble," he said. "And I thank you all."

"Thank Finn," Emyr said, "for telling us where you were."

"Finn? Where is he?" Rhodri tried to rise, but the pain in his side and the weakness in his legs convinced him to remain seated.

"He's safe, for now," Emyr said. "He's well-hidden back at our base camp. But he may yet have a brush with death."

"What do you mean?"

Betrayal

Emyr glanced at Lara and Redmond. Rhodri couldn't tell if Emyr looked guilty or just concerned.

"We had to take his arm off," Emyr said. "It was rancid. He would already be dead if we hadn't done it."

Rhodri passed a hand over his head. "I should have been there for him," he said.

"He'll be glad to see you," Emyr said.

Rhodri gazed at Emyr. "I know you," he said.

Emyr smiled. "Last time I saw you," he said, "you ran me over."

"Sorry about that," Rhodri said. "I was trying to help."

"I know," Emyr said.

Rhodri glanced at Redmond. "Aren't you the two I saw down by that ambush?" Emyr glanced at Rhodri's new boots.

"Were you wearing Taurini boots?" he asked.

Rhodri nodded.

"Then it probably was," Emyr said.

They sat in silence for a long while.

"I hope your friends are all right," Rhodri said.

No one spoke as they all peered into the darkness as if expecting them to materialize from out of the night.

The clatter of horse hooves brought them all to their feet. Redmond staggered to his horse, while Emyr nocked an arrow and faded into the shadows. It wasn't one horse, like they had expected. It sounded like an entire Dunkeldi patrol.

Tyg galloped over the rise, heedless of the danger. Any other time, he would have dismounted and crept over the hill. But he had to reach the girls. He couldn't bear the thought of losing them, when he was supposed be their protector. He crested the rise to find one man holding Brigid while Finola struggled with a second. The third raised his bow for a hurried shot. An arrow plunged into side of Tyg's belly just above his belt before he could avoid it. Tyg grunted but kept riding. He drew his sword. One swipe killed the bowman. His next stroke cut into the man who held Finola. Tyg's sword jerked from his hand. He wheeled his horse around to find the man who had held Brigid with a long knife at her throat.

"It's over," the man said in Salassani. "You're done for."

The man's face gleamed with sweat in the light of the newly risen moon as he peered defiantly over Brigid's head. Tyg swayed in the saddle. He could feel the arrow stabbing his belly. Brigid watched him with wide, frightened eyes.

Finola brandished a blade in her hand and stepped toward the man. "Let her go," she demanded.

Tyg blinked. The fire in his belly made it hard to breath. He slipped a knife into his hand. The man saw the movement.

"You don't want to play . . ." the man began.

Tyg's arm flashed and a blade blossomed in the man's eye. He grunted and stumbled backwards. Brigid twisted from his grasp and punched him in the throat. But she needn't have wasted her effort. The man tumbled backward without a sound. Both girls stood there, shaking and panting as they peered down at his body.

Tyg swayed in the saddle again.

Brigid was the first to tear her gaze from the man's still form. She rushed to Tyg's side and helped him slip from his horse's back. The horse stood blowing and trembling as Brigid laid Tyg on the ground. The fletchings on the arrow shaft quivered with each rattling breath.

"At least I've finally done something worthwhile," Tyg breathed.

"Still here?" Hayden said as he approached the outcrop with a line of horses strung out behind him. Finn slumped over his saddle as his horse followed Hayden around the outcrop. Lara had just finished treating Rhodri's wounds, and she stepped away from him as he struggled to his feet and stumbled to Finn's horse. He helped Finn down and the two embraced. Lara hadn't decided what she thought of Rhodri until she witnessed the tenderness with which he greeted Finn. The boy was loyal and caring.

"My boy," Finn mumbled. "You're safe."

Rhodri helped him sit with his back to a rock.

"I'm sorry," Rhodri said. "I never meant to abandon you."

Finn patted him on the back but appeared to be struggling to speak.

Rhodri glanced at the folded sleeve where Finn's arm had been.

"Are you all right?"

Finn nodded. "Better than I was." But Rhodri's gaze passed over

Finn's sickly pallor and sunken cheeks.

"You need rest," Rhodri said.

Hayden dismounted and pulled the horses over to tie them to the birch trees. He looked around.

"Where are the others?"

Emyr glanced at him and shook his head. Lara tried to suppress the nervous anxiety. They were all worried. Tyg was a skilled man, but he was only one man. The girls were daring and brave, but they were still so young.

Hayden scowled. "But I drew the Dunkeldi off," he said. "They were supposed to swing east and then south. They should have been here by now." He glanced at Redmond, who had taken his seat by the beech tree again. "What happened? Where's Brion?"

"Brion went after Tyg and the girls," Emyr explained.

"I should go look for them, then," Hayden said.

"Stay here," Redmond replied. "If they can be found, Brion will find them."

Lara glanced at Redmond. He was still pale, but that fire hadn't left his eyes. He didn't trust Hayden, and now Lara realized that he might even blame him for Neahl's death.

Hayden stopped pacing and glared at Redmond. "You know," he said. "I just managed to lose a dozen Dunkeldi and retrieve Finn and the supplies all by my little self. I think it's time you started giving me credit."

"I have started," Redmond said, "or I wouldn't have let you be the decoy."

Hayden spun and stared into the darkness. Lara smiled to herself. The selfish boy was having a hard time accepting authority from an old warrior with no status and no title. But she hoped that Redmond didn't push him too far.

"What do we do?" Brigid said as she cradled Tyg's head in her lap. The moon had risen overhead, casting a thin light into the depression where their horses cropped the grass. The dead men lay where they had fallen.

Tyg blinked up at the girls. He had never had a child. But if he could have chosen his own children, he would have picked these two.

191

"Brion said never to pull an arrow out because it could do more damage," Finola said.

"But pushing it through could be worse," Brigid said.

Tyg had seen many men die from arrow wounds to the torso. Those who had been hit in the belly often died slow, lingering deaths. But this wasn't the first time he had been seriously injured in his violent life. Tyg reached up and laid a hand on Brigid's arm. Tears slipped from her eyes.

"Cut away my outer shirt," Tyg said.

Finola bent and slipped her blade under the shirt. She sliced it open. Brigid peeled it away.

"You see the silk undershirt?" Tyg asked.

They nodded.

"Grab the silk on either side of the arrow and pull on the silk."

Finola scowled in confusion. "Why?"

"Just do it."

Brigid's hands trembled as she tugged gently on the silk.

"Pull harder," Tyg said as he braced himself for the stab of pain.

Brigid's gaze flicked to his face. Her brow creased, but she did as he said.

Tyg sucked in his breath and ground his teeth as the arrow shaft turned, backing itself out of the wound.

Finola gave a quiet gasp. Brigid kept pulling until the arrow fell out and rolled to the dirt. A gush of warm blood spilled down his side. Tyg could feel Brigid fingering the silk.

"It didn't even tear," she said.

"Amazing material isn't it?" he said.

"But I don't understand," Finola said.

"It's a trick I learned from an old renegade from the east," Tyg explained. "The silk is so tough it carries into the wound with an arrow rather than getting cut. Makes arrow wounds to the body less dangerous."

Finola sat back in wonder, while Brigid pulled the silk undershirt up to expose the wound.

"It doesn't always work," Tyg said, "but it helps to have several inches of body fat." He tried to smile. "My beer belly is good for catching arrows."

Tears still glistened on Brigid's cheeks. "I thought you were going die."

"There's no guarantee," Tyg said. "But I'm not that easy to kill." Tyg raised a hand to wipe a tear from Brigid's cheek. A surge of warmth filled his chest. The beautiful child had actually been afraid for him.

Finola grabbed a satchel from her saddlebags and began treating Tyg's wounds.

"Lara's been teaching me," she said as Tyg gave her a questioning glance.

"She says that men are never very good at taking care of themselves."

Misty's hooves splashed in the shallow creek bed as Brion led his exhausted party as far from Comrie as he could. He knew they had stirred up a hornet's nest, and he wanted to get far beyond their reach. So much had changed in the dark hours before the pale glow of morning touched the rocky outcrop where the company had awaited Brion's return. Brion would long remember the horror of finding Finola and Brigid covered in blood and the relief at finding them unhurt. He wondered if they would ever be safe again.

He still couldn't understand how Tyg could take an arrow to the stomach and still seem so unaffected. Brion could only the imagine the terror the girls must of felt as they had struggled to reach the meeting place with a man who should have been mortally wounded. Brion had found them exhausted and desperate, huddled in the shadows of the trees. Tyg had changed, too. He had dropped his harsh exterior and watched Brigid and Finola with something akin to fatherly devotion.

Brion had also noted the tenderness in Lara's face as she treated Redmond's wounds and massaged his shoulder to keep it loose. They seemed to communicate without speaking. Hayden had said nothing when Brion had staggered into camp with Tyg and the girls. His sarcasm had apparently been silenced by the arrival of Rhodri—the lost prince he had come to protect.

But Brion's mind remained uneasy. He couldn't escape the feeling that he was still being manipulated to pursue someone else's agenda. Who was the arrogant stranger they had met in the camp? He seemed to know all about them. He had said, "you're the *real* rescue party." That could only mean that he had expected a fake rescue party and that he expected Cedrick to be in it. If he had known who Rhodri was, why had he let Rhodri go? Clearly, the arrogant stranger and Cedrick had schemes of their own.

The stranger had only added yet another layer to the already complicated cast of personalities and alliances that Brion was struggling to understand. How many more surprises would he uncover before this was over? And how many more of them would have to die as pawns in the games of the nobility?

Brion tried to understand what had driven Weyland to join the Duke in his secret intrigues and even to sacrifice his own son's body to save a prince he'd never know. At least Brion understood Neahl's drive for revenge and his sense of manhood. Redmond was driven by loyalty to his family and friends—even though he didn't care about or believe in the political intrigues that swirled around them.

Brion looked over the open heathland and wondered what drove him. Was he becoming like Neahl, or was he more like Redmond? He had been so sure that if he could find the Duke and fulfill his promise to Weyland everything else would make sense. But after losing Neahl and nearly losing Redmond and Tyg, Brion wasn't so sure anymore. Maybe he should take Brigid and Finola and leave the island for good—let Rhodri fend for himself.

Late that afternoon, a flock of ravens appeared over the horizon, looping and swirling as they followed a band of horsemen. Brion didn't wait to see who they were. He reined Misty around and galloped back to warn the others. Emyr returned a moment after Brion did, and Brion led them to a valley enclosed in a circle of boulders with a stand of scrub oak hugging the bank of a stream. The group dismounted and tried to disappear into the oaks, while Brion and Emyr ran back to confuse their trail.

Emyr and Brion took up posts at either end of the oak stand while the rest huddled in silence until they were sure the riders had passed them.

"No point in moving on today," Brion said. "We all need rest. This is as good a spot as any."

They settled in to camp as the shadows lengthened. Finola found Brion as he filled their waterskins at the creek.

"How are you holding up?" Brion asked. He stood and pulled her into an embrace.

"I'm all right," Finola said in his ear. "But Finn isn't good. His arm is starting to smell again."

Brion pushed her away. "Does Rhodri know?"

Finola nodded. "He's sitting by him now. You can't miss it."

"How about the others?" Brion said.

Finola sighed. "Tyg swears that he can't even feel the wound anymore, but he's lying."

Brion sniffed. "Of course he is," he said.

Finola continued. "Rhodri seems okay. Lara was tending to him. Redmond can't use his arm much, and he's got some pus discharging out the back. Lara says she wants it to clear up before she stitches it closed."

"I don't know what to do," Brion said. "We've got to get out of the heathland. With three of us seriously injured and one dying, we're vulnerable. They need time to heal." He peered over Finola's head at the weary group.

Finola nodded her understanding.

"I am not sure we can even reach the Duke," Brion said, "and we don't know what kind of reception we will get if we have to go to Chullish. I don't think Rhodri, Finn, or Hayden have told us everything they know."

Finola nodded again and bent to pick up the waterskins. "Time to ask them then," she said.

So Brion gathered his band together under the gently rustling leaves of the gnarled oaks while the horses cropped the grass nearby.

"We have to make some decisions," Brion said. "Like I promised before, everyone will have a say." He contemplated each of them. Weariness and lingering fear showed in their faces and postures. Their clothes were stained and torn. Dirt and grime smeared their faces. They had all endured so much in the last few weeks. But they all watched him expectantly. "Finn, Rhodri," he said, "we need to know everything you can tell us about your plans."

Rhodri glanced at Finn, who nodded. Then he shifted in his seat and pulled his shirt away from his chest as if it were bothering him.

"The Duke sent word at the beginning of the summer," Rhodri began, "that he would be sending someone to fetch us. We were to join a group of Carpentini at the Great Keldi and come south with them to the area around Comrie. We were to wait for his messengers there. But they never came. Then the Carpentini were slaughtered by a raiding party that seemed to know we would be there." Rhodri glanced at Finn. "That's where Finn was wounded. I was out hunting, and they missed me."

"Who were you supposed to meet?" Brion asked.

Rhodri shrugged. "We weren't told."

"What was supposed to happen after that?"

Rhodri glanced at Finn. Finn stirred. When he spoke was voice was thin and shaky.

"The Duke has been building an underground movement among the nobles and the military leaders who are discontented with Geric and his son. We were supposed to take Rhodri to the Duke, and he would give us the rest of the details. That's all I know."

"Well?" Brion said to Hayden.

Hayden blinked. "All right," he said. "I'm not one of the leaders, so I don't know any details. But the Duke has a network that has infiltrated the palace. I was one of his contacts. You need to understand that Damian, the King's son, has visions of grandeur. He thinks Geric is a weak king, and he wants a full-scale invasion of the heathland. He wants to unite the entire island under his rule and enslave the Salassani tribes."

"Are you suggesting that he's planning a coup against his own father?" Redmond asked.

Hayden nodded. "He's behind this drive to war."

"So Neahl was right," Brigid said.

"We heard that he was providing information to King Tristan," Rhodri said.

"He was," Hayden said. He turned to face Brion. "He informed King Tristan that you would be going to rescue Brigid and Finola."

"That explains why Tristan was waiting for us that night," Brion said.

Rhodri nodded. "He had someone watching you, but you slipped past them. I tried to warn you," he said.

"You did," Brion said, "but somehow, you never got around to telling me what was going on."

Rhodri shrugged. "I tried," he said. He glanced at Emyr. "No hard feelings?"

Brion remembered how Rhodri had plowed over Emyr during the chaotic rescue at the Great Keldi to make sure that Brion and Brigid could get away.

"You did what you had to do," Emyr said.

"What plot were you talking about?" Brion asked.

"The plot to start a war," Rhodri said.

Finola glanced around at them. "So there are a couple of things I don't understand," she said. "If you are the lost prince, how do you expect anyone to believe you? And how exactly are you going to take back the throne without an army?"

Rhodri glanced at Finn, who had closed his eyes. Finn didn't move, so Rhodri held up his right hand to show her the brand of the eagle.

Finola shook her head. "Anyone can get a brand on their hand," she said.

Brion was surprised to see the doubt slip across Rhodri's face. Brion almost didn't believe he had seen it. If the lost prince doubted who he was, no one would believe him.

"The documents," Finn said. "The documents and the ring prove it, and I'll vouch for him. I was the King's chamberlain. I took the child, and I have been with him all these years."

"What documents?" Hayden asked. Brion hesitated and then explained how Weyland had given him the royal signet ring before he died and how Brion had found the papers explaining that the prince had been sold into slavery.

Hayden grinned. "I heard Geric searched high and low for that ring."

"Okay," Finola said. "You might be able to convince people, but you still don't have an army."

"We will have," Hayden said. "That's what we've been doing all these years."

"But," Brigid cut in, "we are being invaded by the Dunkeldi. Doesn't seem like a good time to be starting a civil war."

"Damian is already planning a civil war," Hayden said. "We need to organize a coup against his coup."

"You've got to be joking," Finola said. "You expect us to take Rhodri to the Duke, and you can't even tell us exactly how you plan to orchestrate this coup within a coup?"

Hayden shrugged. "That was never my problem," he said.

"You do know how to get him into Chullish, if we have to go there, don't you?" Finola said.

Hayden considered and shook his head. "We'll figure that out when we come to it."

"Might be too late," Brigid said.

"I can get you in," Tyg said.

Everyone watched him. "What?" he said. "I haven't spent my life sneaking around without picking up some useful information."

"Good," Brion said. "We'll talk about that later. But I have another question. Who was the man that let us go in the Dunkeldi camp?"

"King Tristan's son, Tomas," Rhodri said.

This surprised Brion, but, upon reflection, he realized that Tristan would benefit from having a lost prince show up right in the middle of a war. If he could get the nobility of Coll to fight amongst themselves, Coll would be easy pickings.

"But he seemed to be expecting Cedrick," Brion said, "and he said he was sending you as a present to Cedrick. What did he mean?"

Rhodri shrugged. "I don't know. Maybe he just assumed that the Duke would send his son on such an important mission."

Brion frowned. He hadn't forgotten the signals he had picked up from the Duke that he didn't trust his oldest son.

"The Duke intended for Cedrick to come with me," Brion said. "But the sot was drunk and more interested in a young girl than in obeying his father's wishes."

Cedrick was certainly playing a double game. How else would Tomas, the son of Coll's most ardent enemy, know that Cedrick would be sent to rescue the prince? But why? What could he gain? If Rhodri managed to seize the throne, Cedrick would be in the line of succession. But if Damian seized the throne, he would be out of luck. He had everything to gain and nothing to lose by seeing Rhodri assume the throne.

"Tomas also mentioned spies," Tyg said. "Spies that told him we would be coming for you."

Rhodri shrugged again. "If Geric's son knows I'm alive, he would do anything to stop me."

"Unless Damian wants you to go to Coll," Lara said. They all waited for her to continue. She sat quietly beside Redmond, watching them with interest. "If you show up and try to claim the throne, you give Damian an excuse to seize it for himself while his father is away."

Hayden whistled. "You should have been a politician."

"Any woman would do a better job," Lara said.

This statement was so unlike anything Brion had ever heard Lara say that he simply stared at her. Hayden had also been shocked into silence. But Tyg and Redmond started chuckling. Lara glared at them. Finola and Brigid exchanged glances.

Redmond held up his hand in surrender as Lara turned on him. "You're right," he said. "It's just Brion's expression when you said that."

"It's true," Finola said.

Brion saw that Finola and Brigid were preparing for an argument, so he waved his hands at them trying to head off the debate. "Not now," he said.

Finola spun on him and glared, but she let him steer the conversation in another direction.

Brion hurried on. "We have the very real problem of taking Rhodri to the Duke," Brion said. "The Dunkeldi have Dunfermine surrounded."

Just then, Misty gave her soft, purring sound and shuffled her feet. Someone was out there.

Chapter 23
The Wolves of War

ara watched as Brion lifted his bow and slipped an arrow onto the string. Tyg handed Rhodri a knife, while everyone else prepared for the worst. But nothing seemed to stir. The entire heathland had grown quiet. The gurgling of the stream was magnified in the stillness. Brion and Emyr slipped into the shadows of the oaks in opposite directions.

A wavering howl lifted into the night. It was answered by another and then another. The horses shifted and tugged at their hobbles. Goose bumps erupted all over Lara's body. She shivered.

"They smell the blood," Redmond whispered. He glanced at Finn, and Lara understood that he also meant Finn's gangrenous flesh. "They're probably haunting the edges of the armies."

"Will they attack us?" Lara asked.

"Don't know," Redmond said. "I would prefer that we had a fire."

The howling and yipping continued for a long while before it died away, and the night grew quiet except for the nervous shuffling of the horses and the gurgle of the stream.

The agitated horses told Lara that the wolves were still out there, hunting. Lara reached over to take Redmond's hand. She was careful not to jar his arm. Redmond had drawn his sword and held it in his right hand.

"I think Brion was surprised that you have political ideas," Redmond said.

Lara shrugged. "Why is it that young people always think we old fogeys haven't experienced anymore of life than they have?"

"He should have heard you when you were his age," Redmond said.

Lara smirked. She had said a lot of crazy things when she was young and the kingdom was in turmoil—not the least of which was her open annoyance at the nobility for always expecting the humble folk to fight their wars and receive none of the benefit from it. She couldn't forgive them for what they had done to her father.

"As I remember," Lara said, "we both thought the government should be chosen by the people."

"You should try that argument out on Brion," Redmond said. "See how he responds."

A bow thrummed. A wolf yelped and snarled. Pandemonium erupted all around them. Another wolf yelped, and the shadows of bounding, snarling wolves leapt around them, dancing in and out of the trees. A shiver ran up Lara's spine.

Redmond shoved her behind him as a wolf bounded into their little circle. Tyg threw a knife that buried itself in the wolf's shoulder. Redmond raised the sword as the wolf came right at them. But it sprang to one side of them, apparently more intent on getting away than in attacking them. Several wolves crashed through the oak trees.

A wolf snapped at the flanks of Brion's horse, but she kicked it in the head, sending it rolling amid the leaves. It leapt up as two arrows appeared in its side. It yelped and growled and sprinted into the darkness. Brigid and Finola nocked arrows on the strings of their bows and exchanged a satisfied glance.

They waited, listening to the quiet.

"Emyr is curious about his grandparents," Lara whispered in Redmond's ear.

Redmond glanced around at her. "What did you tell him?"

"Not much, but he wanted to know about my father."

Redmond pursed his lips. "It's only natural, I suppose."

"We can't hide it from him," Lara said. "Why should we?"

"We're not hiding it," Redmond said. "But now just isn't the time. Let's wait until this is all over."

"That might be too late," Lara said. She knew very well that one, or both, of them might be dead by then. "He deserves to know."

"Well, they weren't very hungry," Tyg said as Brion and Emyr walked back into their camp.

"Not hungry enough to tackle prey that bites back anyway," Rhodri said.

Hundreds of fires blinked in the darkness like stars fallen to the earth. Brion lay on a knoll northwest of Mailag overlooking the wide crescent of fires spread out on the plain. They had traveled by night and hid during the day for more than a week in an attempt to avoid Dunkeldi patrols. Their pace had been slow and careful. Brion couldn't afford any more confrontations or injuries with two of his most skilled fighters wounded.

Then there was Finn. Despite everything they could do, he was failing. The gangrene had spread up his shoulder and into his neck. It was only a matter of time. Rhodri had taken to riding behind Finn so he could hold him up in the saddle. They had avoided all well-worn trails and angled toward Dunfermine, hoping that they might get word of the Duke and his army when they had come across this mixed Dunkeldi and Bracari army encamped in the valley before them. It was moving east toward Mailag.

"This doesn't look good," Hayden whispered in Brion's ear.

"Maybe Dunfermine has already fallen," Brion replied.

"We should go straight to Chullish," Hayden said.

"But we need the Duke."

"If Dunfermine has fallen, he won't be there," Hayden said.

"Then we need to find out where he is."

Brion scooted back off the knoll, climbed into Misty's saddle, and rode back to where the rest of their band waited. Hayden followed.

Brion knew something was wrong the moment he found them, huddled in a circle beside the horse Finn had been riding. Brion dismounted and hurried up to them. They parted to let him enter their circle.

Rhodri knelt beside Finn's frail body. The stench of the gangrene reached Brion's nostrils. He had to force himself not to plug his nose. Finn's eyes were closed, and Rhodri bent over him, holding Finn's hand in his.

"I'm sorry," Rhodri said.

Finn's eyes fluttered open. "Listen to me," Finn murmured. "Behind the altar in the Temple of the Ancients." Finn paused and blinked. "Push the eagle's eye. The King's sword is there."

"My father's sword?" Rhodri said in some surprise.

Finn's head rolled back and forth as if he were delirious. "No, the King's sword."

"I don't understand," Rhodri said.

"You will need the King's sword."

"Finn, do you mean Geric?"

"No. The King."

Finn was becoming agitated, and his mind was wandering. Rhodri glanced up at Brion, and the doubt Brion had seen on his face once before had returned.

"Where is Dustin?" Finn mumbled.

"Who?" Rhodri said.

"The Duke, my boy. The Duke." Finn blinked again. "Weyland has the baby." Finn grabbed Rhodri's hand. His eyes bulged. He pulled himself up toward Rhodri. "Nurse, can you revive him? You must. Or all is lost."

Finn lay back panting and closed his eyes. "The prince," he whispered. "I tried."

Finn's breathing slowed and his eyes fluttered open again. They focused on Rhodri.

"My boy," he said. "I'm sorry. Please forgive me."

"There is nothing to forgive," Rhodri said.

Finn gave him a weak smile. "I did what I thought was best."

Those are the words Weyland had used that night he had tried to explain to Brion what he had done. Doubt crept into Brion's mind. What had happened all those long years ago? Just when he thought he understood, some new bit of information surfaced to confuse everything. Either Finn was raving in his fever, or he was remembering something that disturbed him—something he had wanted to keep secret. Brion didn't know which.

Lara bent to wipe Finn's head with a damp cloth. Finn kept his gaze on Rhodri.

"Avenge them, my boy," he said. "They deserve to die."

He reached out to take Rhodri's hand and closed his eyes. Rhodri bent over the hand. Finn let out a long, shuttering sigh and lay still.

Rhodri's emotions churned, raw and angry, as he stared down at Finn's hastily constructed grave. He had lost his guardian, his mentor, his friend. All his life, he had trusted Finn, admired him. Finn had taught him how to read and to write. Had trained him in all the lineages of the noble families in Coll and instructed him in politics and economics. He had seen that Rhodri knew how to manage a farm and work both wood and metal. He had hired the best Taurini and Salassani fighters to train Rhodri to fight, and, when he had turned sixteen, he had sent Rhodri into the fighting rings to make sure he had real, practical experience in combat. It had been risky. Many men did not survive the rings. But Rhodri had. He had never been defeated, if you didn't count his first fight and the ambush where the Dunkeldi had taken him near Comrie.

Finn's last words had left Rhodri torn and confused. He hadn't forgotten that Finn had warned him about the sickly boy that had also been branded and who might still be alive. But, in his rantings, Finn had made it sound as if the sickly child was the one that had survived. Finn had also refused to say that Rhodri was the King's son and insisted that he would need the King's sword. And why had Finn apologized?

Rhodri wanted to believe that he had been apologizing for dying before the task was finished, but he couldn't be certain. Rhodri stole a glance at Brion who also stood quietly staring at the grave. Hayden stood next to Brion with a curious expression on his face. Hayden had been quiet after Finn had died, and he kept sending furtive glances at Brion. Did he believe that Brion was the prince?

In his final rantings, Finn may have let slip the truth of Rhodri's heritage. But now Finn was dead. The only man now alive who knew what had happened all those years ago was Dustin, the Duke of Saylen. Rhodri needed to speak to the Duke before they reached Chullish. How could he seize a throne if he was uncertain that it belonged to him?

Tyg stepped up to Rhodri and placed a hand on his shoulder. "Let him go, lad," he said as he nodded toward the pile of stones. Rhodri blinked the tears from his eyes and mounted his horse.

They rode on well into the morning, circling west to avoid the army encamped on the plain. It seemed obvious that this army was marching on Mailag, and Rhodri knew that they needed to get word to the Duke and find out what he needed them to do.

Rhodri considered simply wheeling his horse around and heading back into the heathland. At least he understood how to be a Taurini. No one there would expect him to shoulder the responsibility of an entire kingdom. He could go back to the farm he and Finn had managed all those years high up on Kemp Moor.

But even as he thought it, he felt the lure of the throne. He had lived his entire life in hiding, working with his hands, assuming the role of a slave, bowing and serving, all while he knew he should have been living in luxury, being pampered in some palace.

Finn had taken Rhodri to the Dunkeldi port city of Ballach once to see the royal palace there. Rhodri had marveled at the high, stone walls and round towers. A nobleman had ridden past them on a huge warhorse, wearing a mail shirt that glinted in the morning light with a bejeweled sword swinging at his side. And Rhodri had wondered what it would be like to ride through a city where all the townsfolk gaped at you in awe and made way for your passing.

He had always been taught it was his due and his duty to reclaim this life from the men who had stolen it from him and murdered his family. And he had wanted to do it. But what if he was no better than they had been? What if he was an impostor who had been tricked into pursuing another man's vendetta? Would he take the throne anyway? Finn had always insisted that Rhodri was the heir. If he was, Rhodri had a responsibility to avenge his murdered family.

"Doesn't look like a war party," Hayden said. He, Brion, and Emyr surveyed the road that snaked along beside the river like a pale shadow of the river itself. The dark ribbon of water cut its way through the prairie toward Mailag. It had taken them three nights of careful scouting to work their way around the army to the river valley. Now they watched several wagons pulled by mules and men laboring along the road. Women and children straggled out behind the wagons.

"They could be from Dunfermine," Emyr suggested.

"But how would they have escaped the siege?" Brion asked.

"There's only one way to find out," Hayden said. He mounted his horse. "Ask them." He kicked his horse up over the hill.

"Hayden," Brion called. But Hayden ignored him. Brion glanced at Emyr. "Do we follow him?" he asked.

Emyr shrugged. "He might get himself killed."

"Sometimes, I'm not sure I would mind," Brion said.

They mounted and rode after him.

As soon as the travelers discovered the riders bearing down upon them, the wagons lurched to a stop. Men and women yelled. Children scampered to the safety of the wagons. Several men with bows appeared. Others wielded axes and shovels.

Brion signaled Emyr and Hayden to stop on their side of the river. He raised his hands in the air. "We mean you no harm," he shouted.

"We've heard that before," a gruff voice shouted back. "Stay where you are." The man who appeared to be the spokesman was a tall, muscular man with a full beard. Brion noted that he spoke with the strong accent of the northern Oban Plain.

"We seek news of Dunfermine," Brion called.

Silence greeted his words as the people shifted and spoke among themselves.

"Who are you?" the spokesman called back.

"We're from Wexford. We're looking for the Duke of Saylen and his army."

"There is no army," the man said.

Brion cast Emyr a concerned glance. "What do you mean?" he asked.

"The Dunkeldi and Taurini overran the city three days ago."

"And the Duke?" Brion blurted the words.

"Dead," the man said.

Brion sat in stunned silence.

"How?" Hayden asked.

The man shrugged. "How would I know? Word is he was murdered by his own son."

Brion's world shifted underneath him for the third time. A strange hole expanded in his chest. It wasn't the horrible, crippling grief he had experienced when Weyland and Rosland had been murdered, or when he had watched Neahl die. It was something different. Something he couldn't explain. But it left him cold, uncertain, and frightened.

Brion realized that Emyr and Hayden were watching him. He didn't want them to see that he was shaken.

"And the city?" Brion asked.

The man shook his head. "They swarmed in like locusts. Most

didn't escape."

"But you did," Emyr said.

The man shifted nervously. A few of the others exchanged glances.

"They bribed their way out," Hayden said.

"It was that or die," the man replied.

"If you're thinking of going to Mailag," Brion said, "don't waste your time. The Dunkeldi are encircling the city already."

This caused a commotion as everyone started talking at once. This question had clearly been a source of contention among them. But Brion was weary of the conversation. He wheeled Misty around and headed back up the hill. The man called something after him. But Brion ignored him. He had far larger problems to worry about.

"That settles it," Hayden said. "We have no choice but to head for Chullish."

They stood with their horses' reins in their hands, debating their next move. Brion sighed. He knew Hayden would push to go to Chullish, but he still wasn't certain that was the best course.

Redmond stirred. "If the Duke has been murdered, then we have to assume that Geric knows about his treason and will therefore be hunting for us." He glanced at Rhodri. "Before we go any further, we all need to decide if we want to attempt a coup." He surveyed them. "Some, or all, of us could get killed."

"Feels like they've been trying to kill us for a while already," Brion said.

"Feels like *everyone* has been trying to kill us," Finola said. "How many more assassins are chasing us right now without our knowing it?"

Redmond nodded to her in acknowledgment. "Except for Hayden and Rhodri, none of us began this venture intending to become embroiled in a coup. And we need to consider the possible consequences."

"Dethrone a tyrant," Hayden said.

"Geric is not a tyrant," Redmond replied. "He seized the throne by foul means, but he has been a tolerable king."

"His son is a beast," Hayden spat the words out, "and he plans a coup against his own father."

"The last coup left a lot of people dead," Redmond said, "and the only ones to benefit were the nobility."

Hayden stepped toward Redmond. "Why don't you just admit it," Hayden sneered. "You're a coward."

Redmond blinked at him impassively, then dropped his horse's reins and stepped up to Hayden. "I'll give you one chance to retract that statement," Redmond said. Lara reached over and tried to grab Redmond's hand, but Redmond pulled away. Cold anger flashed across Redmond's face, and Brion knew that Hayden had gone too far. If he was smart, he would back down.

"Look you two—" Brion began but Redmond raised a hand to silence him. In that moment, he looked like Neahl. Calm, but dangerous.

Hayden stared at him, his face flushed and defiant.

"That's why you ran away before isn't it?" Hayden said. "That's why you left your brother and friend to die."

Redmond's kick caught Hayden in the stomach. Hayden doubled over with a grunt and rush of air. Redmond grabbed Hayden's head with his good hand and brought his knee into Hayden's face. As Hayden staggered backwards, Redmond caught him by the throat and shook him. His lips lifted in a snarl.

"Next time, I will kill you outright," Redmond said.

Hayden's hand drifted toward his knife. The cry of warning froze in Brion's throat as the blade flashed, but, even with his bad arm, Redmond was too quick. Hayden's knife ripped through Redmond's shirt in a slice that might have disemboweled him. But Redmond had jumped back just in time. He kicked Hayden in the groin, caught the hand with the knife and used it to throw Hayden to the ground. Redmond wrenched the knife from Hayden's hands and knelt on Hayden's chest, pressing hard. Hayden struggled until Redmond pushed Hayden's own knife against his throat.

"Redmond." Lara whispered. "No."

Redmond glanced at her then stood abruptly. He threw the knife away. "Get out," he said.

Hayden struggled to his feet. Blood dripped from his nose and he held a hand to his ribs. He cast a glance at Finola and then at Brion, before hobbling to his horse. He mounted and rode away without another word.

As Hayden disappeared over the rise, Tyg stirred. "I'm not sure that was a good idea," he said.

Redmond glared at him.

"I mean, you shouldn't have let him live," Tyg said. When all three ladies opened their mouths in shock, he continued. "He knows we have the prince, and he has reason to hate us now. That's a dangerous combination. It's always better to clean up little messes like that."

"And he was our only contact in Chullish," Rhodri said.

"Well, I'm glad to be rid of him," Finola said. "He always gave me the creeps."

"Can I say something?" Lara asked. Everyone waited for her to speak.

"Redmond is right," she said. "We don't owe the nobility anything. And as much as I think most of us admired Weyland, we don't have to be bound by his choices either. It's even possible that he was wrong." The way she said this made Brion consider her words more carefully.

Lara continued. "Hayden may be arrogant and deceitful and a ladies' man, but I've watched him. He's driven by some powerful motive. I imagine it's probably selfish, but he could still be a useful ally or a dangerous enemy. Cedrick is the type of man who wants power, and he's patient enough to lay complicated plans and wait for them to unfold."

Brion noted that Redmond was not surprised by any of this conversation and that made him curious.

"It's clear to me," Lara continued, "that this war was no accident. Someone in Coll and someone among the Dunkeldi manipulated us to justify this war and has tried to silence us. The way I see it, we have two choices."

Lara glanced around the circle. "We can walk away and let the chips fall where they may. Or we can try to do something about it."

When she saw how Brion and the girls stared at her, the color rose in her cheeks. "I'm sorry," she said.

"What for?" Brion said.

"I know I'm an outsider to your group, so I've kept my peace, but . . . well."

"You're no outsider," Finola said.

"You have as much right as any of us to have an opinion," Brion said.

"I've been waiting for Lara to speak her mind," Brigid said.

Brion gave her a puzzled glance.

"Men don't know anything," Brigid said with a disdainful flip of her head. "Just because a woman is quiet and careful doesn't mean she can't think."

"I never said . . ." Brion began, but he was cut off by Redmond's burst of laughter.

"You're finally meeting the real Lara," he said.

Brion shouldn't have been surprised. Redmond wasn't the kind of man to fall for nothing but a pretty face.

"Well?" Lara said. "Do we run, or do we continue?"

"I haven't been to Chullish in a while," Tyg said. "Might be a nice vacation after scampering like a scared rabbit through the heather."

Chapter 24
Of Fear and Friends

t's huge," Brion said as he gaped at the stone walls surrounding the city of Chullish.

He stood amid the waving prairie grass on a rise south of the city. It had taken them over a week to reach Chullish because they had swung south out onto the Oban Plain in the hopes of avoiding any unfriendly scouting parties. The plain had been abandoned, the villages left empty and desolate. It reminded Brion of the heathland with its isolated ruins of villages, hamlets, and towers. Neahl and Redmond had told him how the southern heathland had been scoured of Salassani a generation before by King Geric. Now it had happened to the Oban Plain out of fear of the Dunkeldi invasion.

It had been more than two weeks since Redmond and Tyg had been injured and both were healing well. Lara had finally stitched Redmond's wounds closed, and he had been working the shoulder to try to get his motion and strength back. They had seen nothing of Hayden since he left them. Brion wondered if he had made it to Chullish alone. Still, it was a relief to be rid of his smirks and snide comments.

Now Brion gaped at the sprawling city that rose up on a hill above the River Tilt. The Laro Forest crept up to the other side of the city, held at bay by a network of irrigated fields. Two, round towers soared above the gates to at least eighty feet in height, and the walls were probably sixty feet high. The slanting light of the afternoon sun gleamed off the plastered walls and shimmered on the waters of the river. Battlements stretched out to either side of the towers. Arrow slits pierced the towers and parapets to allow archers cover

211

when firing on an enemy below. The top of the battlements had been built out so that it overlooked the wall, allowing defenders to drop missiles on any attackers. But the city was not yet under siege. The Dunkeldi were still preoccupied with Mailag and Brechin.

Fires burned along the ramparts where soldiers paced back and forth. The smoke from thousands of cooking fires lingered over the city like a dark rain cloud. A series of long, wooden piers poked out into the river where hundreds of ships were tied to stout beams or anchored to the bottom. Brion had never seen anything like it. Mailag was a toy castle compared to Chullish.

Brion turned to Redmond. Emyr and Rhodri stood next to him.

"Somehow," he said, "you and Neahl never got around to telling me that places like this even existed."

"You wouldn't have believed us," Redmond said. He shrugged. "Chullish is small compared to some of the cities in the southland." Redmond nudged Brion. "I thought we got over this paralysis at the sight of a few people back at the Great Keldi," he said.

Brion glared at him. "I'm not going to be crippled by the city of Chullish," Brion said.

"At least this time," Redmond said, "you won't need to wander around gawking at the wares."

"Neahl would probably have blindfolded me and left me alone in there to find my way out again, and he probably would have thought it was funny," Brion said.

Redmond gave Brion a sad smile. "I miss him, too," he said.

"The entrance is over here," Tyg said.

Brion jumped. He had been staring at the walls again, trying not to think of Neahl. "I'm never going to get used to you sneaking up on me," he said.

"That's the idea," Tyg said.

They followed Tyg back to the huge, stone monument in a valley that hid it from the view of the city walls. The women waited for them with the horses. Six, large stones stood on end as if some giant hand had driven them into the earth so that they angled in towards each other. Another massive stone rested on top. The monoliths stood in the patch of rocky ground surrounded by tall, waving prairie grass. Beyond the patch of grass lay barley fields whose heads of grain were beginning to yellow as the time of harvest approached.

"What is this place?" Brigid asked.

"It was built by the ancients," Tyg said.

"The Salassani call them dolmens," Rhodri said. "They're said to be entrances to the underworld."

Emyr nodded. "Most Salassani won't go near them," he added. "They're supposed to be places of great power, like the Keldi."

"They used to be burial mounds where chiefs were laid to rest," Redmond said. "Earth was piled up over the stones. There are dozens of them further south by Whit-horn and over on the continent."

"I don't know about this," Finola said. "Do we really have to go into a creepy tomb?"

Tyg laughed and led the horses down a narrow aisle created by two lines of upright stones to the entrance. They followed him in and found the interior to be surprisingly spacious, though their horses filled most of that space.

"Welcome to the underworld," Tyg said. He pointed to a large, hollow basin on one side where rainwater apparently collected. "We can leave the horses here with enough grass to keep them comfortable for a few days until we can figure out how to get them into the city."

They hobbled the horses and staked them so they could reach the water, but not wander off. The men cut grass while the women unsaddled and brushed the horses. Soon they had a sizable pile of grass stacked against one wall.

"So," Finola said, "where's your entrance?"

"Beneath your feet," Tyg said.

He stepped to the side of the chamber opposite the horses and bent to scrape the dirt away from two rusted, iron handles set in stone. The earth had filled the space around the handles, and he had to dig with his fingers to clear enough dirt away so that he could get a hand underneath. Tyg grasped the handles and pulled, but he winced and straightened, clutching at his arrow wound. "I guess I'll let one of you young lads lift it," he said.

Emyr grasped the handles and dragged the stone lid free. They all peered into the black hole.

"I don't think I'm going to like this," Finola said.

"Is there a bottom?" Brigid said.

Tyg laughed at them. "Would I lead you into a dangerous place?"

he asked.

"Do you want us to answer that question?" Finola said.

"The tunnel is cut through the rock," Tyg said, "and passes under the river into the city. The problem is that we have to wait until nightfall to come out, because it opens where we could be seen."

"You're joking," Finola said.

"That doesn't sound like a good idea," Brion said.

"If you would like to brave the gates or try to climb the walls, I'll be happy to watch," Tyg said.

"The walls are looking a lot more appealing," Brion said as they dropped into the black pit and began working their way down a narrow passage. The air was thick and moist, filled with the sharp scent of mold and mildew. Their makeshift torches pushed feebly against the blackness, spitting and sputtering, as they cast dancing shadows off the clammy walls.

"At least it's cool down here," Rhodri said.

The walls dripped water, and the ceiling had been supported by large, wooden beams. The passage was so narrow that they had to walk single file.

Tyg paused and bent to inspect something before moving on. When Brion passed the same place, he found a stark white skull staring up at him. The rest of the skeleton had been scattered about. Someone had died alone in the terrible darkness of the passage.

Finola grabbed for Brion's hand. She was trembling. "This is definitely one of the creepiest things we've ever done," Finola said.

Brion tried to distract her. "You're not scared of a little skeleton are you?"

Finola ignored him.

"Oh, I'd forgotten how you used to cry if you had to crawl in to the tiny oven to clean it." he said. "I thought you had outgrown your fear of small, dark places."

"Shut up," Finola said.

"You should have seen Lara when she was your age," Redmond said. "She screamed every time she saw a little mouse."

"Sounds like a perfectly logically response to me," Brigid said.

"Yes," Redmond said, "but she always threw something at them.

Whatever was in her hands."

"I think that's enough," Lara said.

"I want to hear it," Emyr said.

Redmond laughed. "One time she threw a paring knife at a mouse and nailed it to the ground."

"Atta girl," Finola said.

"Yeah, well it was funny to watch unless you were in the way," Redmond said.

"Two can play at this game," Lara said. "How many of you knew that big, tough Redmond is scared of butterflies?"

"Nah," Brion said.

"Somehow you don't seem so dangerous to me anymore," Finola said.

"I'm not scared of them," Redmond said. "I just don't like them landing on me."

"Do you still shriek like a stuck pig?" Lara asked.

"All right, Emyr," Brigid said. "What's your weakness?"

"I don't have any," Emyr said.

"Uh huh. Spit it out."

"Okay, I don't much like snakes."

"Well, I can't tease you about that," Brigid said. "Only a fool wouldn't be afraid of snakes. They can kill you, after all."

"How about you, Rhodri?" Brion said.

"Up north," Rhodri said, "they have this spider that is white and hairy. One crawled over my face once when I was little."

"Okay, no talking about spiders down here," Finola said. She edged closer to Brion. He glanced up at rafters overhead and wondered if any spider would bother spinning a web down here. What could they hope to catch?

"I know what Brion is afraid of," Brigid said.

"Don't—" Brion said.

Brigid cut him off. "Feathers" she said.

"Okay, that's worse than being afraid of butterflies," Finola said.

"Tyg?" Brion said. "Your turn."

"Don't try to change the subject," Brigid said. "Tell them how you used to cry when Momma plucked the chickens and the feathers floated around in the air."

"Tyg," Brion insisted again. "Your turn."

But Tyg didn't say anything. Their footsteps and breathing echoed in the stillness. Their boots scraped against the stone floor.

"Tyg's not afraid of anything," Brigid said.

"Tyg?" Brion said again, trying to look ahead to see if Tyg was still there. His round shape slipped through the darkness ahead of them.

"Dying alone," Tyg said.

The frivolity of the lighthearted teasing melted out of them. Tyg's father had died alone with a knife in his back. No one spoke as they descended down into the darkness and worked their way back up the incline towards Chullish. Dark thoughts of the possibility of their own impending death seemed to chase them through the tunnel.

"We're here," Tyg said at last. "You young'uns get up there and move that door. Just nudge it aside, in case someone's in there."

Emyr climbed the ladder and slid the trap door aside. Dim light and fresh air that smelled of apples washed over them. They clambered out to find themselves in a tiny room crowded with barrels and boxes. They dropped the torches to the floor of the tunnel and let them hiss out before Emyr slid the lid back into place. It was dark in the confined space, but compared to the impenetrable blackness of the tunnel, it almost felt like daylight.

"So where are we?" Brigid asked.

"The palace," Tyg said.

"You're joking," Finola said.

"You might have mentioned that," Brion said.

"Didn't seem necessary," Tyg said. "Let's go." Tyg pushed the door ajar and peered out the crack for a moment before waving them on. "We're on the ground floor near the back gate," he said.

"The gate will be watched," Redmond said.

Tyg ignored him and slipped out the door.

"He's going to get us all killed," Lara said.

"Maybe," Emyr said.

"Watch my toes." Finola pushed Brion aside.

"Sorry," he said.

Brion waited for the rest of the company to fall in behind Tyg as he led them down the hallway. He slipped his knife from its sheath—just in case.

Tyg stopped them before a tall, wooden door. "Wait here," he whispered.

Betrayal

Brion slipped up to the door and peeked through the crack.

"What's he doing?" he whispered to Redmond who also held an eye to the crack above Brion.

Brion watched Tyg stride up to the guard posted at the door as if he belonged there. Brion couldn't understand why Tyg, the assassin, would be so bold, and he didn't think it wise to announce their arrival with a dead body by the back gate of the palace.

The man started when Tyg approached. His sword was half-drawn before he smiled in recognition and strode the few steps between them and embraced Tyg. The two slapped each other on the back and exchanged words before Tyg waved them to come.

Brion shook his head. "It doesn't seem like he should be able to do that," he said as they all hurried into the cool, night air.

"Tyg is a genius," Finola said.

The man stepped quickly to the gate, unlocked it, and let them pass through without speaking a word to them or looking at them. He kept his gaze downcast as if he didn't want to see what they looked like. Then he closed and locked the gate with a sharp, metallic click. They hurried into the shadows of the streets.

The further they moved from the palace, the more crowded the city became. Makeshift tents and shelters had been tossed up in every possible corner or open space. Ragged people huddled in groups, talking in whispers. Still forms lay crumpled on the steps of buildings and along the walls where they struggled to steal a few moments' sleep. The reek of human filth became stronger and stronger.

"Refugees," Brion thought as he caught glimpses of the upturned faces that were tight with worry and fear.

Tyg ignored the crowd of people and kept walking until he stopped before a wooden shack in a back alley whose roof had collapsed in on one side. He waved at them to enter.

When Brion ducked under the sagging roof, the stench of urine and waste filled his nostrils. Wooden boxes and piles of trash littered the floor.

"What is this?" he asked.

"It's a place to hide until we can find a better one," Tyg said.

"I vote we find a better one right now," Finola said as she wrinkled her nose.

Tyg laughed. "This will be character-building for a bunch of spoiled country folk who are used to all the fresh air they can find. We can wait here until dawn."

The pale light of morning was beginning to slip in through the cracks when the quiet slap of bare feet on stone startled them into wakefulness. Knives appeared in hands as they peered toward the door.

A face poked in through the doorway. But it wasn't a man's face. A small child blinked and stepped into the shack. She stared at them. Long, dark hair framed her face, and she wore a red dress that hung below her knees.

The girl held out her hand. "Do you have the birdie," she said.

"Uh," Brion glanced at the others.

"The golden birdie," the girl said.

"Oh," Brion pulled from his pocket the little, golden eagle Rhodri had given him back at the Keldi—the one the Duke had said would give them safe passage. He handed it to her.

She inspected it and smiled. "They're waiting you," she said.

No one spoke for a long minute until Finola knelt in front of the child. "What's your name," she said.

"Margaret. They told me to come get you."

"Who told you, Margaret?"

"The man with the big beard."

"You don't know his name?"

Margaret shook her head. "He's my papa's friend."

"Who's your papa?"

"He told me not to tell you."

Finola glanced over her shoulder at the others. Brion knew that she was annoyed that these men would use a child as their messenger.

Redmond stepped forward. "Could you wait for us outside for just a minute, Margaret?" he asked.

Margaret nodded and left.

"Explain what's going on," Redmond said to Tyg.

Tyg shrugged. "I told you you should have killed him."

This statement gave Redmond pause. "Hayden?" he said.

Tyg nodded. "He's obviously made it here before us."

Redmond surveyed the group. "Do we go?" he asked.

"If you want to see this little coup through," Tyg said, "you don't have much of a choice."

"The Duke said the eagle was our safe passage," Brion said.

"Could it be worse than this place?" Finola said.

"I think we must go," Lara said. Everyone else nodded their assent, and Redmond stepped out the door.

"Lead on, little one," he said.

Brion noted the strangeness of their procession through the city streets. Every head turned as they passed to stare at the line of hardened warriors and travel-worn women, still filthy from their journey, carrying bows and wearing swords that trooped behind a tiny, barefoot child in a red dress.

Brion tried not to gawk at the strangeness of so many buildings built of stone. Most of Mailag's buildings had been wooden and were more widely spaced. These buildings were piled so closely on top of one another that they formed a continuous wall. Some had elegant balconies or twisted pillars of stone framing their doorways. But most were more humble. They passed into a section of the city where the buildings were smaller, and some used nothing more than a piece of hide stretched across the opening to act as a door. The stench of human and animal refuse assaulted Brion's nostrils. It was so overpowering that he couldn't smell anything else.

Brion had thought that learning his way around the heathland had been a challenge, but he was already hopelessly lost in the labyrinth of buildings. All the buildings looked the same.

Eventually, Margaret stopped in a dark alleyway right under the battlements. The soldiers' boots scraped the stone as they paced overhead. Margaret gave a rhythmic tap on the door and waited. A tall, muscular man with a beard that hung to his black belt pulled the door open. Margaret handed him the golden eagle. He waved them inside without a word.

The furnishings of the room into which they crowded were fine, which contrasted sharply with the run-down exterior of the building. A group of men sat in a semi-circle. They all wore mail and had swords at their sides. They appeared to be important men. If they weren't, they certainly believed they were. All of the men stood as Margaret led the party into the room.

Margaret padded over to stand beside a balding man who held a wine glass in his hands. He bent and kissed Margaret on the cheek before stepping towards them.

"Welcome, friends," he said. "You may call me Zach."

"Is that your name?" Redmond asked.

The man ignored the question. He waved a hand at the other men. "We expected you sooner."

"Why would you expect us?" Redmond said.

"Let's just say that we had word."

Rhodri sensed the excitement in the air as the men examined each member of their group. Eventually everyone's gaze settled on Rhodri and an eager anticipation rushed through them. Several of them fidgeted and kept glancing in his direction. Finn's teaching had been thorough, and Rhodri knew he would know who these men were once he heard their names. Three of them, including the bald man who addressed them, appeared to be about as old as Finn, maybe a few years younger. But the third couldn't be much older than Rhodri was—maybe in his mid- to late-twenties.

The bald one kept speaking. "Thank you for bringing us the prince," he said. He glanced at Rhodri's hand. "May I?" he asked.

Rhodri held up his hand to show them the eagle brand. The men nodded.

"Where is your guardian?" the young man demanded. He had light, blonde hair as fine as silk and a steady, confident way of carrying himself.

Rhodri gazed at him without expression. "Finn is dead," he said.

The young man stepped forward in shock and dismay. "How? We heard he was with you."

Rhodri considered him. Why hadn't Hayden told them that Finn was dead? This seemed an odd thing to intentionally leave out. But the other men did not seem surprised by this news.

"We were betrayed," Rhodri said. "He died from injuries he received from traitor Alamani while we were camped with the Carpentini."

Zach waved to the young man, who sat down but remained agitated.

"Let me introduce the rest of our party," Zach said. He indicated a round man with dark hair streaked with gray. "This is Victor, Baron of Whit-horn, commander of the forces that hold Chullish."

Rhodri nodded. He had heard of him. Finn told him that Victor's family had lost most of its land in the coup because its support of the coup had been lukewarm. They were also one of the oldest noble families with ties to the Crown, and they had long despised the new nobility.

Zach gestured to the tall man with the full beard. "This is Liam. He is our strategist with contacts inside the King's personal escort." Liam bowed.

Rhodri knew that Liam's father had not supported the coup, and that Liam had been close friends of King Edward before he was murdered.

Zach gestured to the young man. "This is Master Owen. He serves as our director of communications." Owen rose again and bowed. Rhodri didn't know much about Owen. Finn had mentioned him, but that was all.

"And I am Zach," he continued with a bow. "I am in charge of provisioning, and my men guard the palace and the temple."

Rhodri considered him. Zach was the one that had lost his entire family in the coup because they had chosen to fight to protect the Crown. Finn's education might finally become useful.

"What are your plans?" Redmond asked Zach.

"You'll forgive me," Zach said, "if I don't give you the details of our plans. We have already risked much by bringing you here."

"And you'll forgive me," Redmond said, "for insisting that you at least tell us what role you expect us to play. We have risked *everything*, including our lives, by coming here. Even more so than you."

The men all exchanged glances until Liam nodded. "You're free to leave, if you don't wish to assist us," he said.

"What I wish to know is what my assistance might entail," Redmond replied.

A knock sounded at the door. Liam approached the door and peered through a spy hole.

Hayden stormed in when Liam lifted the latch. "They're here..." he began and then froze. His face flushed, and he raised his arm to point at Brion.

"That's him," Hayden said.

For a moment, Rhodri thought that Hayden was saying that Brion was the real prince. But Hayden continued. "He murdered the Duke."

The words hung in the air for a moment before the men stepped forward as one and drew their weapons. Redmond, Emyr, and Tyg jumped to cover Brion. Rhodri joined them. Finola and Brigid whipped arrows from their quivers and placed them on their bows. Lara backed up to get out of the way.

Brion sneered. "So you really are as stupid as I always thought you were," Brion said.

Hayden advanced to join the other men. "The night the Duke was murdered," Hayden said, "Brion was seen leaving his tent. And then he was seen fleeing the camp with stolen horses."

"You've been talking to Cedrick, haven't you?" Brion said.

Hayden's gaze shifted, and Rhodri figured that Brion had guessed correctly.

"The Duke gave me those horses," Brion said, "and he watched me ride away."

"Lord Cedrick says that you lie," Hayden said. "You attacked them both and injured Cedrick before you killed the Duke."

Brion scoffed and shook his head. "Of course Cedrick told you that," Brion said. "He attacked me because I stopped him from raping a young girl. I let him live, which appears to have been a mistake. When I left the camp, the Duke was standing by his tent watching me ride away with the horses he had given to me."

"You expect us to take the word of a peasant over Lord Cedrick?" Hayden said.

"I don't care what you think," Brion said. "But it seems clear to me that our trust in all of you has been misplaced." Brion glanced back at Rhodri. "We're wasting our time here."

"We should take him to Cedrick for judgment," Hayden said.

Tyg glanced over at Redmond and raised his eyebrows in an "I told you so" gesture.

"That might be difficult," Redmond said.

Liam stepped between the two groups and sheathed his sword. He raised his hands in a submissive gesture. "We shouldn't be fighting amongst ourselves," he said. "We all want the same thing."

"You haven't convinced me of that," Redmond said.

Liam ignored the comment. "Why don't you tell us what happened?"

"I just did," Brion said. He glared at Hayden. "Why would I murder my own father?"

This statement sent a ripple of confusion among the lords.

"What is this?" Victor asked.

Hayden dismissed Brion with a wave. "He's been telling this lie since he came back from the Duke's camp. He doesn't have any proof."

"Well," Owen said with a gesture of his hand. "Do you have proof?"

"Some might think Cedrick's lies are proof enough," Emyr said.

"I was in the camp," Tyg said. "I heard the Duke tell Brion that he was Brion's father.

"This is pointless," Owen said. He and sat down. "Everyone knows the Duke was free with his affections as a young man. If Cedrick wants to argue about whether Brion is the Duke's son or not, that's his affair." When Hayden glared at him, Owen continued. "I'm sorry the Duke was murdered, but I'm finding it difficult to believe these people are responsible. They would hardly risk their lives to bring us the prince if they had killed the Duke. And that's our concern. We only have a few days before Damian springs his trap."

"Agreed," Liam said.

Hayden scowled. The others nodded their assent.

Rhodri struggled with his own inner turmoil. Did he still want to go through with this? Did he have the right? Did it matter?

He glanced around at the two groups in the room. One wealthy, confident, eager for revenge. The other dirty, trail-worn, eager to do the right thing but desperate to keep each other alive. To which group did he belong? Rhodri knew that he should be taking charge of the situation, ordering people around, forcing them to come to terms, but he didn't have the heart. How could he assert an authority he was no longer convinced he had?

Lara had become so accustomed to the quiet murmur of the heathland at night that the sharp noises of the besieged city rang in her ears. The pleasant, sweet aroma of the heather and the lingering sharpness of the juniper had been replaced by the moldy smell of a disused room and the pungent stink of human filth. It was just as well that she couldn't sleep. She needed to speak to Redmond alone.

After the confrontation had been averted, the men had agreed to give them space to rest as they prepared their intrigues. The group had refused separate rooms, preferring the security of each other's company.

Lara waited in her bedroll until Brion awoke Redmond to take his turn at the watch. They had all crammed into this tiny room on the first floor. Guards had been posted at the door and in the street outside the windows, ostensibly to keep them safe. But they all knew the guards were there to keep them contained, controlled.

Redmond stood at the window, studying the street while he massaged his bad shoulder. Lara had stitched up the wound after it had stopped oozing pus, and she was no longer worried about it. It would heal—if Redmond let it alone long enough. Redmond may never be free of discomfort, but he wouldn't be crippled either.

Once Brion's breathing became regular and she was certain that he was asleep, she rolled free of her blankets and padded on bare feet to where Redmond stood staring out the window. She slid up beside him and slipped her arm around his waist. He smiled down at her and draped his arm about her shoulders, pulling her tight.

"Has your life been like this for all these years?" Lara asked.

"Like what?" Redmond said.

"Constantly running, fighting to stay alive, never knowing who to trust?"

"Pretty much. I came home to find some peace."

"That didn't work out," Lara said.

Redmond sniffed. "Not really."

"I wasn't sure we would make it this far," Lara whispered.

"Me neither," Redmond said. He gazed back out the window.

"I'm worried," Lara said.

Redmond glanced back at her. "Emyr?" he said.

"All of them," she said. "I feel like there's something boiling under the surface, and I keep waiting to get scalded."

Redmond nodded. "That's one way to put it," he said. "But Finn's last words have been bothering me the most. From what Brion told me about Rosland's diary, the Duke switched Weyland's dead son for the prince. But in his delirium, Finn seemed confused about Rhodri.

And from the expression on Rhodri's face, he didn't seem so certain himself. What could it mean?"

Lara shifted uncomfortably. "You know that there is more than one claimant to this throne," she said. Redmond stared at her, but she could see that he refused to understand her meaning.

"The Duke of Saylen and Damian both have claims," Redmond said.

"You know that's not what I mean," Lara said.

Redmond shook his head. "He has no claim. Illegitimate children take no place in the line of succession. And after what they did to him . . ." Redmond trailed off.

"Should we tell them?" Lara said.

Redmond scowled. "What good would it do? I don't care who takes the throne so long as they rule justly and leave me and my family alone." Redmond pulled Lara close to him again. She smiled up at him despite her worries and fears. She had not missed the fact that he had used the phrase "my family."

She reached up to kiss him. How many times had she dreamed of being in his arms again? How many times had she longed for his strong embrace? Here he was again after so many lonely years filled with self-doubt and regret. After a long moment, they pulled apart.

"When this is all over," Redmond said. "I'll go wherever you want to go. I'll be whatever you want me to be."

"I only ever wanted you to be yourself," Lara whispered.

They sat together until it was time to change the watch. Lara retreated to her blankets, but she couldn't rest. The others had a right to know. It may not change anything, but they should know.

Chapter 25
Blood and Iron

Brion awoke to the sounds of commotion in the house as the others gathered at the door.

"What is it?" he said as he rose and drew his sword. He had been waiting for something to go wrong. Hayden hadn't been cowed. He would try something else.

"Someone started banging on the front door," Rhodri said. He had been on watch.

"Better see what it is," Tyg said.

They all scrambled out into the hallway to meet Liam striding towards them.

"The King is dead," he said without any preamble. His face was solemn. "We have already set our plans in motion. We strike today. We need to know where you all stand."

"What happened?" Lara asked.

"His guards withdrew at the height of battle and left him alone on the field," Liam said.

"His own guards?" Finola asked.

Liam shrugged. "Damian was never subtle," he said.

They all looked to Rhodri. Rhodri hesitated. He shifted his feet and bowed his head. His fingers played with the hilt of his sword. The silence grew long. Brion exchanged glances with Redmond. Was Rhodri going to back down?

Rhodri nodded. "What do you need me to do?" he said.

Liam scanned them all, waiting for the rest of them to respond. Brion glanced at Redmond and Emyr and then at the ladies. They all seemed to be waiting to see what he would do. Redmond was right that this could get them all killed, but, if they turned back now, then everything they had done in the last month would have been wasted. Neahl and Seamus and Finn would have died for nothing. Weyland and Rosland would have died for nothing.

Brion glanced at Brigid and Finola again. The tension rose in his chest. This was the moment of decision. Would he keep his promise to Weyland?

"I say we see this through," he said.

Everyone else agreed.

Liam grinned. "I was hoping you would," he said. "Damian is preparing to proclaim himself king tonight. The King's army is retreating toward Chullish. We could be besieged as early as this evening."

Brion relaxed. Now that the decision was made and their course was set, he felt calm, as if he had known all along that it would come to this.

"Do you happen to have a plan to break a siege?" Brion asked.

"We have a plan for everything," Liam said. "But first we need to put the rightful king on the throne."

"Damian may have something to say about that," Redmond said.

"I'm sure he will," Liam said, "but we have the advantage."

"How is that?" Tyg asked.

Liam opened his mouth to respond when more banging came on the door. They followed Liam down to the large room where they had first met the conspirators.

Brion found Cedrick and Cluny standing side by side. Brion registered the surprise on both men's faces as the group filed in. They had not expected them to be there. They hadn't expected them to be alive.

A sudden rage burned in Brion's chest. Before he realized what he was doing, his sword was out and he was rushing Cluny. Nothing else mattered in the world but to feel his blade pass through Cluny's heart. He hadn't taken three steps before someone grabbed him from behind.

"Not here. Not now," Emyr whispered in his ear. Brion jerked free of Emyr's grasp and stood breathing heavily, staring at the man who had signed Neahl's death warrant.

Cluny gave them his characteristic condescending smirk, but wouldn't meet Brion's gaze.

Cedrick sneered at him. "Not satisfied with killing my father?" he said.

"You know who the real murderer is," Brion said. "You want a second try? This time there's no young girl begging for mercy to distract you."

"I'll deal with you later," Cedrick said. He gestured toward Rhodri. "Welcome to Chullish, my prince," Cedrick said. Brion noted the narrowing of Cedrick's eyes. He was not happy to find Rhodri here. He had had other plans. "I'm pleased that they managed to bring you safely here."

"Are you?" Rhodri said.

Cedrick glanced at Zach who had been watching from where he stood by the window. "Is everything in order?"

"Yes, My Lord," Zach said. Brion noted the confusion on Zach's face. He was surprised by Cedrick's attitude. "We move at the coronation as planned."

"Are the proofs in hand?" Cedrick asked.

Zach glanced at Rhodri, who nodded.

"We have the ring," Rhodri said.

"And the papers?"

"Yes."

"Good. What are you going to do with them?" Cedrick said, motioning to Brion and his group.

Liam spoke up. "Do with them? They've agreed to help. We could use their swords."

Cedrick scowled.

"Do you doubt them?" Owen asked. "They risked their lives to bring the prince safely here."

"I doubt anyone associated with my father's murder," Cedrick said.

"You must be suffering from considerable self-doubt then," Brion said.

Cedrick's hand slipped to the hilt of his sword. Brion stood, waiting, hoping. All he needed was an excuse.

"We're wasting time," Cluny said. "These people won't give us any trouble." Brion glanced at Lara and Finola. He knew that Cluny was referring to Lara's family and Finola's parents. He hadn't told them about it, and now he realized that it had been a mistake. To hear it from Cluny would only make it worse for them.

"Where are they?" Redmond said.

Cluny raised his eyebrows. "I was starting to think you were going to let the boy do all the talking," he said.

"Who are you talking about?" Owen asked.

"Just a little security measure in case Redmond got out of hand," Cluny said.

Redmond stepped forward, but stopped himself. When he spoke his tone was quiet and dangerous. "The next time I see you Cluny, you're a dead man." Redmond said.

Cluny leered. "It would be a pity to have to kill all of those cute, little children," he said.

"What's he talking about?" Owen asked again.

"He's holding Lara's family and Finola's parents hostage," Tyg said.

Lara gasped and Finola's face paled. But they didn't say anything. Brion reached out and touched Finola's arm. He wanted to tell her that they would be all right, but after what Cluny and Cedrick had done, for all he knew they were already dead.

Cluny appeared to be relishing the pain he was causing. Brion had never trusted the man, and now he knew why. He was crafty and conniving. He had manipulated them into venturing into the heathland when he knew the Dunkeldi were preparing for war. He had used them as bait to draw in the Dunkeldi. Then he had sent them to be killed either by the Dunkeldi or his own assassins and had kidnapped innocent people who trusted him.

"Where are they?" Redmond asked again.

"They were in Mailag before it fell," Cluny said. "I think my people got them out." He paused and glanced at Lara. "The old man didn't make it," he said.

Redmond visibly restrained himself as Lara covered her face with her hands. The muscles worked in Redmond's jaw. His eyes were hard. But he glanced back when he heard Lara crying quietly. Emyr placed an arm around her shoulder and drew her close.

Owen stared at them. "These people are our allies," he said. "What are you two playing at?"

"We must be careful who we choose as friends," Cedrick said. "Keep me informed." Then he and Cluny left, letting the door bang closed behind them.

Redmond enfolded Lara in his arms and began whispering in her ear. Owen strode over to the other conspiracy leaders and began a heated discussion with them. Brion put an arm around Finola's waist.

"We'll find them," he said.

Finola nodded. "Promise me one thing," she said. Brion nodded.

"Kill Cluny before he hurts anyone else." Finola's brow furrowed and unshed tears played in her eyes.

Twice now, her parents had suffered because of Brion. How could Finola still trust him?

Brion embraced Finola, but out of the corner of his eye, he saw the guard by the door casually lift the bar that had fallen into place when Cedrick and Cluny had stormed out. Brion paused. He pulled himself free of Finola.

"Hey!" he said to the guard, when the door burst open. Men dressed in the royal red and purple liveries rushed into the room.

"Surrender to the King," one of the men shouted.

Tyg was the first to respond. Two blades twirled through the air, flashing in the golden light that streamed in through the doorway. Two men fell.

Zach and Liam sprang into action. They grabbed Rhodri and dragged him out of the room. "Let's go," Owen called to them and followed Zach and Liam with his sword in hand.

"Get out!" Brion yelled as he pushed Finola behind him. Emyr was already shoving Lara and Brigid through the door. He stood beside Brion as the soldiers rushed them. Redmond, Brion, Tyg, and Emyr met the first rush, but more soldiers poured in through door. A tall man wearing chain mail strode in and shouted over the clamber of battle.

"Stop," he bellowed.

The soldiers disengaged and backed up, leaving the four men panting. Several soldiers lay on the floor, writhing in pain. A few no longer stirred. Blood stained the floorboards. The tall man surveyed them.

"Let's have no more senseless waste of life," he said. "Surrender now, and I'll personally guarantee that your friends are spared."

Brion had no intention of surrendering. He glanced at the others. They were all prepared to fight. But he knew that if they all remained in the room to fight they would eventually be overwhelmed. He couldn't bear the thought. He motioned for the others to get behind him so they could make it to the back door.

"Someone needs to go with the women folk," Brion said. "They're alone. Go."

Redmond gestured to Emyr and Tyg. They hesitated and then backed out the door.

"Take them," the tall man yelled.

The second rush of soldiers spent itself on the Brion's and Redmond's swords. Men lay on the floor now slick with blood. The reek of gore filled the air. As the men withdrew to prepare for another assault, Brion glanced at Redmond. He was bleeding from a few superficial wounds and held his left arm close. The injury still bothered him, and it might cost him his life.

Brion couldn't bear to lose Redmond—not after Neahl. "Get out," Brion said. "I'll hold the door long enough for you to get away."

Redmond glared at him.

"I'll be right behind you. Hurry before they have the entire building surrounded."

"No heroics," Redmond said. "As soon as I'm through the door, you follow."

Brion nodded. Redmond slipped past him and the men rushed him. Brion kicked the door closed and threw the bolt into place. The movement nearly cost him his life as three soldiers bore down upon him. Brion wounded one of them and parried the attack of the second, sliced through a third and wounded a fourth before one got inside the reach of his sword and delivered a terrible blow from a wooden club to Brion's head. The shock rattled his teeth and sent pain lancing through his skull. Another blow sent him reeling into the wall. As his vision faded, he heard the tall man shouting orders.

"Keep him alive," he cried. "The Duke wants him alive."

Brion awoke to the pulsing pain of a raging headache. A moment of confusion was followed by terrifying clarity. He lay curled on his side in a tiny cage. His face pressed against the cold, metal bars. The air was stale and stank of human filth and burning coal. Brion tried to stretch his cramped muscles, but the cage was too small. He swallowed the panic and tried to remember how he came to be here. The last words he remembered were "the Duke wants him alive."

Brion jerked about in sudden rage at Cedrick's treachery, but that earned him new bruises. Brion craned his head around to see if any of his friends were here with him. Narrow slits in the upper walls let in slender rays of light that left the room in a perpetual gray twilight. Tables, chains, fire pits, cages, and instruments of torture filled the room. The other cages sat empty. Maybe Brion's reckless attempt to save his friends hadn't been wasted.

A big, black rat scuttled past his head, and Brion flinched. He wouldn't normally have worried about rats, but, curled up in the tiny cage, he knew full well that he wouldn't be able to stop them if they decided to dine on his flesh. And maybe that was the point after all.

He had been right about Cedrick. He was playing a double game. Cedrick knew that Brion had ridden out of the camp and that the Duke had intended for Cedrick to go with him. But the Duke had also doubted Cedrick's loyalty. The fact that the Dunkeldi prince had been expecting Cedrick up at Comrie also suggested that Cedrick had been involved in the various plots to start the war and to have Brion and his friends killed. It seemed obvious as Brion lay in the fetal position against the cold, damp floor of his cage that Cedrick had murdered his own father.

After Brion had humiliated him, Cedrick must have seized the opportunity to kill the Duke and blame it on Brion. Brion would seem doubly guilty, sneaking out of the camp with horses laden with supplies. Had Cedrick killed the Duke that very night or later during the final battle for Dunfermine?

Why would he keep Brion alive now? Why had Cedrick gone through the charade of appearing to be interested in placing Rhodri on the throne only to send soldiers to arrest them in the name of the King? Cedrick had clearly betrayed them to Damian. And Cedrick knew all of the conspirators and their plans.

The jangle of metal reached Brion's ears. Brion stiffened and then tried to wiggle around so he could see the entrance. He managed to get to where he could peer over his knee to the ironbound door just visible in the gloom. Metal scraped on metal. His blood raced. He was helpless. Trapped.

The hinges growled as the door scraped open. The blaze of torches smote Brion's eyes and made them water. By the time he had blinked the tears from his eyes, he found a tall, muscular man with blonde hair and a sharp, hawk nose, staring down at him. The man smiled, and a chill swept through Brion. The rich clothing and jewel-encrusted sword hilt told Brion that he was looking up at Damian, King Geric's son. Cedrick had kept him alive to offer him as a trophy to Damian.

"We meet at last," Damian said. "I've been hunting you all summer." His voice had a pleasant tone to it, but the way he smiled as he talked made him seem more menacing.

"You're quite the sly fox," Damian continued. "You escaped my assassins, so I sent the Dunkeldi after you, and you evaded them. Not once, but several times. If you were blessed with nine lives, I think you've about used them up by now, don't you?"

Damian licked his lips and paced around Brion's cage like a wildcat inspecting its prey. Brion watched the booted feet. So Cluny had been working for Damian all along. It had been Damian and Cluny who had sent the assassins, but it had been Cedrick who had ransacked his home and ripped Weyland and Rosland from their graves. Cedrick had also killed the midwife. If Cluny was working for Damian, why had Cluny been with Cedrick?

"There is one thing I want to know," Damian said. "Why did you kill the Duke? I mean, why kill him and then keep trying to put his puppet on my throne?" He stopped in front of Brion and bent down so he could peer into his face.

"I didn't kill him," Brion croaked. He hadn't realized how dry his throat was until he tried to speak.

Damian raised his eyebrows.

"Cedrick," Brion said.

"What?"

Brion tried to swallow. "Cedrick did it," he said again.

Damian stood. "Interesting," he said. He stepped up to one of the guards and whispered something to him. The guard nodded, bowed, and hurried out the door.

"So the Duke convinced you that this Rhodri is the true heir to my throne?"

"Doesn't matter," Brion said.

"I fail to see why it doesn't matter," Damian said, "and why you would risk your life for something that doesn't matter."

"Anyone would be better than a man who murdered his own father so he could enslave an entire people," Brion said.

Damian laughed. "So you've heard the rumors too, have you? Well, let me set your mind at ease. My father's appeasement of the Dunkeldi, the Hallstat, and the Rosythians has left this kingdom vulnerable. The armies sweeping into our land prove it. My father quit governing after the last Heath War, and he turned his back on those who loved him."

Brion stared up at Damian through the bars of his cage. He could make out an expression of bitter sadness on Damian's face.

"Sometimes," Damian continued, "we have to set aside our personal feelings and do what is best for our people."

At first, Brion thought that Damian was mocking him, but Damian was serious. He actually believed that killing his father and seizing the throne was the right thing to do.

"You're both usurpers who betrayed the real king," Brion said.

Damian stared at him for a moment and then knelt beside Brion's cage.

"What do you know about any of this?" Damian said. "You've only been told the lies of men like the Duke and the ignorant prattlings of commoners. You're in way over your head, farm boy. But let me help you understand what is going to happen now."

Damian stood and began pacing again. "There will be one king in Coll. I will have your friends soon enough, and together, you will burn as traitors in the public square. That sounds like a fair reward for treason and regicide, don't you think?

"Regicide?"

"Well," Damian said, "everyone knows how you started a war, murdered your father the Duke, and infiltrated the army so you could murder the King while he fought bravely for his people."

"You can't—"

"I can do whatever I like," Damian said. "Now, enough small talk. You are going to tell me where our little lost prince has gone. And I am going to have fun convincing you that you should."

Chapter 26
The Duke's Man

ara felt small and useless as Emyr sat next to Brigid on one of the wooden boxes and draped an arm around her shoulders. Sobs racked Brigid's body. Her face was buried in her hands.

"I'm sorry," Brigid mumbled. "It's just too much."

Lara put a reassuring hand on Finola's knee, but Finola wouldn't look at her. She stared at the ground between her feet with her lips pinched tight.

Redmond stood over them, blinking down at Brigid. He worked his jaw, fighting to control his emotions. It was odd how someone could age and mature so much and still retain the little habits of childhood.

"I don't know where they've taken him," Redmond said. "He said he would follow me, but he locked himself in the room with them. I couldn't get through."

The morning light slanted through the cracks in the walls of the little hovel where they had taken refuge. The stench of human filth filled the air, but Lara took no notice. Her heart ached. It ached for Brigid and Brion and Finola, but especially for her poor father who had died while being imprisoned by the nobility that had scorned him. She knew it was possible that none of them would survive the next few days. They were being hunted in a city they did not know by men who would have no scruples about killing them. Brion's capture meant that none of them would leave until all hope was lost at recovering him alive. She didn't know what had happened to Rhodri. He had apparently been whisked away by the men who wanted to put him on the throne.

"He's all the family I have left," Brigid said. She raised her tearstained face to blink at Emyr.

Finola stared at Brigid. Her face was pale and grim. Lara didn't know what she was thinking, but she knew how she would have felt if Redmond had been captured.

"We'll find him," Emyr said.

"I'm sick of all the killing," Brigid moaned.

No one replied to that statement because they all knew there would be a lot more killing before they escaped this city. Redmond stepped over to Lara and put a hand on her shoulder. She glanced up at him and saw the despair and fear in his eyes. Redmond was worried.

"I'm sorry," Redmond said.

Lara nodded and held him.

"What will I do if they kill him?" Brigid said.

"I will take care of you," Emyr said.

Lara hoped they would survive long enough to let Emyr do just that.

Tyg followed the old man as he wound his way through the crowd of refugees that clogged the streets. The man wore simple trousers and a leather jerkin, but he seemed unaccustomed to such clothing. And the man seemed familiar. Tyg had seen him somewhere before. The black hair with the white streak over his left ear was not common. So Tyg followed him until he could remember where he had seen him.

Tyg had left the others to contemplate their next move while he had gone out to listen to the rumors that circulated in the city. He had learned long ago that people had a way of knowing what happened behind closed doors. It often paid to listen. Given their circumstances, it was probably the only tool they had left if they wanted to find Brion and Rhodri. At least it was better than sitting around the urine-soaked hovel, guessing.

The old man stopped at each vendor, spoke with them briefly, and then moved on. Curious, Tyg slipped up behind him to overhear his conversations.

"A young warrior with a longbow," he was saying.

The merchant laughed. "Look around friend," he said. "There's plenty of those to choose from."

"He would have been accompanied by a young, redheaded girl."

The vendor shook his head. "You're fishing for a small fish in a big pond," he said and waved the man away.

When the old man moved on up the street, Tyg fell into step behind him.

"Follow me," Tyg whispered in his ear.

The man jumped and spun. But Tyg shook his head and motioned for him to follow. He led the man back to the alley before turning to face the him. The man glanced around and clasped his hands in front of him.

"I know your man," Tyg said. Now, looking the man full in the face, Tyg remembered where he had seen him. The old man had left the Duke's tent just before Brion had entered.

"Where is he?" the old man said.

Tyg considered. This man could be working for Cedrick. But if he was, why didn't he know that Brion had been taken?

"That depends on why you want to see him," Tyg said.

"Are you his friend?" the man asked.

"You could say that."

"Then you should take me to him."

"I'm still waiting for you to answer to my question," Tyg said.

The old man studied the streets again and seemed to come to a decision.

"I am Killian, the Duke's steward."

Tyg nodded but waited for him to continue.

"I have the Duke's will," Killian said.

"And you're not taking it to Cedrick?" Tyg asked.

Killian shook his head. "Cedrick would kill me if he knew I were here. Please take me to Brion."

Tyg nodded. "Follow me," he said and led him to the shack where the other's were hiding.

Killian wrinkled his nose at the smell of their hovel and pulled a handkerchief from his pocket. The red silk contrasted sharply with the plain, leather jerkin he wore. Tyg smiled. The man had no idea how to blend in. Killian scanned the inhabitants with the red silk pressed tightly over his mouth and nose.

Tyg introduced the group while they all surveyed Killian expectantly. Tyg could see that Brigid had been crying and that Finola was angry and scared. They all sat bunched together on the boxes and piles of wood that filled the hovel.

"Where's Brion?" Killian said from beneath his handkerchief.

"He was taken by Damian's men this morning," Tyg said.

Killian bowed his head. "Then I am too late."

"For what?" Finola asked. Finola had been tight-lipped since the morning's events, and Tyg knew that the revelation that her parents were imprisoned, combined with the Brion's capture, had unnerved the girl. Tyg had almost come to believe that nothing could really frighten this fiery, young woman who had fought so bravely in the face of such grave dangers. It made him feel foolish that he had begun to think of Finola and Brigid as something more than the young women that they were—something more like warriors and daughters.

Killian didn't respond to Finola's question, so Tyg did. He gestured to Killian. "He says he has the Duke's will," he said.

Killian raised his head and dropped the handkerchief from his nose and mouth.

"What harm can it do now?" he said. Then he withdrew an oiled, leather pouch from the inner pocket of his jerkin and handed it to Redmond.

"You will find that the Duke has legitimized Brion and named him his sole heir to his estates and titles." They sat in stunned silence, so Killian continued. "You will understand, of course, that this places him in the line of succession for the throne."

Finola stirred. "Seems like you're forgetting Cedrick," she said.

Killian's face wore a somber expression. "I think not," he said. "The Duke has disowned him and stripped him of any claim to his title or lands."

"Why?" Brigid asked. "Why would he disown Cedrick?"

Killian sighed and slipped the silk kerchief back into his pocket. "The Duke has known for some time that Cedrick has been working against him. Cedrick arranged to have Weyland and his entire family killed." Killian glanced at Brigid. "I'm sorry, child," he said.

"Why didn't the Duke tell this to Brion?" Redmond asked.

"The Duke wasn't certain at that time."

"At that time?" Emyr said. "The Duke was killed the night Brion left."

Killian shook his head. "Cedrick has been spreading that rumor," he said. His face grew grim. "I saw Cedrick murder the Duke the night before Dunfermine fell."

Redmond stirred. "The Duke was an accomplished warrior," he said.

"Yes," Killian said. "But, in the end, he could not bring himself to slay his own son."

"You mean he let Cedrick kill him?" Tyg asked.

Killian nodded. "Once Cedrick understood that the Duke did not have the signet ring and the papers and he was assured the Brion did, he had no more use for his father."

"So Cedrick just wanted to cast the blame on Brion?" Finola said.

Killian nodded. "Cedrick has been seeking out information about Brion. When the Duke discovered that he had murdered the midwife at Wexford, he knew he had to act."

Brigid and Finola frowned and exchanged glances.

"This would explain why Damian wanted him, as well," Lara said.

"Yes," Killian said. "Cedrick had been working with Damian to destabilize Coll and to cause a new heath war. But Cedrick really wants the throne."

"So the Duke has tried to deny him the throne by disinheriting him," Lara said.

"You know," Tyg said. "That makes three coups by my count."

"Indeed," Killian said.

Finola stood up to peer between a crack in the boards. "I can't see how any of this matters right now," she said. "If no one but us knows about the will, there's nothing to stop Cedrick from taking the throne."

"The truth always matters, young lady," Killian said.

"Not if people refuse to accept it," Lara said. Redmond cast her an annoyed glance, but Tyg couldn't fathom why. Lara had been much more vocal about her political views since Redmond's rescue, and Tyg wondered if this hadn't become a source of tension between them.

"What do you suggest that we do?" Emyr asked.

Killian shrugged. "Find Brion and save him, if you can. If Rhodri fails to take the throne, Brion will need to do so."

Finola glared at Killian. It seemed clear to Tyg that Finola did not much like the idea of Brion becoming king.

"Finding him is a bit of a problem right now," Finola said.

"Oh," Tyg said. "Did I forget to tell you? I know where he is."

Brigid came to their feet.

"Spit it out," Finola demanded.

Tyg smiled, enjoying their suspense. "In the dungeon beneath the palace."

"How do you know?" Redmond asked.

"You all seem to keep forgetting what I do for a living," Tyg said.

Killian pulled out his silk handkerchief again, but this time he wiped it across his forehead. "I must be going," he said.

"Where?" Tyg asked.

"I have other messages to deliver." He paused and then he stepped up to Lara and handed her a small, folded letter. It was sealed with red wax that bore the Duke's seal.

"The Duke asked me to deliver this to your hand only, My Lady," Killian said.

Lara's brow wrinkled in confusion and shook her head. "I'm no lady," she said.

Killian raised his eyebrows as if he disagreed, but he didn't argue. "The Duke said that you would know best what to do with this letter."

Then Killian handed Redmond a gold ring. "Keep this and the will safe for me. If Cedrick finds me with either, he will take them."

Redmond nodded and accepted the packet and ring with obvious distaste. Tyg couldn't understand why Redmond had such a hatred for the nobility. It made sense that he would hate Cedrick and Cluny and maybe even Damian, but why all nobles? Tyg had no answers as he watched Killian bow and take his leave.

"They captured Brion," Hayden said.

Rhodri gazed at him not trying to conceal his distrust. Hayden had been trying to get Brion arrested since they had arrived in Chullish, and now he acted like he was surprised that Damian had captured Brion.

After the attack, the men had rushed Rhodri out of the building and through a network of back alleys until they had lodged him here. He had remembered enough from Finn's maps to know that he was close to the palace. He had assumed that the others were making their way behind him until he had found himself alone. The room was small but finely furnished with a bed and silk-covered chairs.

"What about the others?" Rhodri said.

"Don't know." Hayden shook his head. "They got away, but no one has seen them. Zach sent men out to look for them."

Rhodri considered Hayden, trying to decide if Hayden had sold them out to Damian.

"What?" Hayden said. Then he gave Rhodri his characteristic smirk. "You think I betrayed them?"

Rhodri raised his eyebrows.

"I didn't do it," Hayden said. "I should have. That fool nearly cost us everything. And to think I thought he was the prince. He convinced us all that the Duke is his father just so he could kill him."

"Brion didn't kill him," Rhodri said.

"That's what he says."

"That's what Tyg says, and he was there." Rhodri resisted the urge to slam Hayden into the wall.

"Tyg is his pet bulldog," Hayden said. "He'd say anything to protect Brion."

"Sounds to me like you're jealous of Brion," Rhodri said.

Hayden spat in disgust. "I've spent my entire life trying to find you, organizing and planning, buying people off so you could take this throne, and all you care about is a spoiled boy who murdered his father."

That did it. Rhodri stepped toward Hayden. "It's time you explained to me what this is all about." Rhodri said. "Because I'm not going into the palace with some unstable, immature, palace brat."

Hayden's hand drifted toward his sword, and he stepped backward. Rhodri raised his eyebrows. "Are you really threatening your prince, your soon-to-be king?"

Hayden paused. "I . . ." He backed up another step. "I'm sorry," he said.

"Because," Rhodri continued, "if you are, things are about to get real ugly." Rhodri half-hoped that Hayden would draw his sword. He was itching for a fight. He wanted to do something, anything.

"No, I . . ." Hayden's face reddened.

"I'll consider accepting your apology," Rhodri said, "while you tell me why you hate Damian and Brion so much."

Hayden hesitated and then sat on a trunk that was pushed against the wall.

"My father was a master swordsman who worked for King Geric," he began. "I wasn't a noble, but my father's position at court meant I was allowed to become a page. I made the mistake of besting Damian in a sword fight once. He beat me with an iron poker and swore that, when his father finally decided to die and he was made king, he would watch while they cut my fingers off one by one."

"Sounds like a nice fellow," Rhodri said.

Hayden continued. "My mother died when I was young, and my father's second wife was raped by the prince. When my father complained, they whipped him to death. My stepmother never recovered from the rape. Damian had beaten her around the head so much that she couldn't talk anymore. She just sits in a chair and slobbers and mumbles."

Hayden stood up and began pacing. His hand played nervously with his belt. "When the brotherhood asked me to spy for them, I jumped at the chance." He stopped and faced Rhodri. "Before this is through, I'll even the score."

Rhodri nodded. "I'm okay with that. But what about Brion?"

Hayden blew out his air in disgust. "I took all that risk to protect him from Jaxon because I thought he was the prince. And what did I get for it? He never trusted me, and that Redmond fellow kept insulting me at every opportunity. Then Redmond kept trying to convince them all to leave everything as it was—to let Damian take the throne. After everything we did."

"Let's get one thing straight," Rhodri said. It was a struggle to keep his voice calm. "I am the prince, and those people are my friends. If you want to have any part in this coup and the court I create after it, you will put this bitterness behind you right now. If you can't," Rhodri pointed to the door, "there's the door."

Hayden stiffened as a war of emotions passed across his face. Then he bowed his head. "I want to see Damian dead," he said.

"Then this is the end of it," Rhodri said.

Hayden pinched his lips tight. A momentary expression of defiance slipped across his face. Then he nodded.

"Good," Rhodri said. "Now let's go get the sword. I believe we only have an hour."

Hayden nodded and led him out the door. They worked their way back through the crowded city and into the palace. The guard didn't challenge Hayden, and Rhodri soon found himself entering the tall doors of the Temple of the Ancients.

Rhodri paused in the shadow of the doorway. Hayden strode toward the altar before he realized he was no longer being followed. He glanced back and then strode up to Rhodri.

"What are you doing?" Hayden whispered.

Rhodri ignored him for the moment. The great hall of the Temple to the Ancients stretched out in front of him. The ceiling rose up in a giant, arched dome with stained glass windows that were lit with the brilliant light of the early afternoon sun. Rhodri had never seen anything like it, though Finn had described it to him.

At the other end of the hall on a raised dais sat the gilded altar. Rhodri had read about it in Finn's books. It was a place of power. A place where every king to rule Coll had been anointed with the blood of a lamb. It was inside the huge stone circle the ancients had erected on the flat-topped hill overlooking the river where the city of Chullish now stood. The stones of the circle had been incorporated into the walls of the temple complex. This was the place where the King's sword lay hidden. The symbol of royal authority. Did he have the right to take it?

"We don't have much time," Hayden whispered again.

Rhodri steadied himself and stepped out into the temple. The thud of his boots echoed in the hall that had been constructed to amplify its acoustic properties. A man speaking in a normal voice could be heard by anyone in the hall, or so Finn had told him.

In a few minutes, Rhodri knelt behind the altar, peering at the eagle with the outstretched wings that formed the back of the altar. He hesitated. If he took the sword, he would be committing himself to a pursuit of the throne. But what choice did he have, if he was going to save his friends and end this war?

He pressed the eye of the eagle. It slipped in and a latch released. Rhodri slid the door aside. There in the shadows of the enclosure lay the royal sword of Coll. A tiny, deep-purple tulip had been set in the pommel.

"I don't believe it," Hayden said. "The tulip was the King's personal symbol."

Rhodri ignored him. This was the sword of his father. He lifted the sword and its sheath gently out from the alcove. When he reached to close the door, he spied something that had been hidden by the sword. He picked it up. It was several pieces of paper folded and sealed together.

"You there," a voice rang out in the empty hall. Rhodri started and peered over the altar to find two guards striding toward them. "What are you doing?"

"This way," Hayden hissed, grabbing at Rhodri's tunic. Rhodri closed the door and sprinted after Hayden.

Brion had long since given up trying to relieve the pain. He simply endured because there was nothing else to do. He felt grateful that he hadn't known anything about the conspirator's plans or where his friends had gone because he wasn't sure he could have kept the information from Damian. The torture had been careful and thorough. Every square inch of Brion's body ached. His ribs were definitely bruised, and he had at least one broken finger.

He kept his eyes closed and tried to find some place deep within where he could hide from the sharp pain, the tight hunger, and the raging thirst. He tried to lick his lips, but his dry tongue was caked with blood and so swollen that it didn't work properly. He worked his jaw around, hoping it hadn't been broken, too.

Brion struggled against the despair. After all they had been through, he was going to die in a dungeon. His friends had all been compromised. Brigid and Finola would soon be prisoners again, if they hadn't already been captured. And there was nothing he could do to protect them—not locked up in a tiny cage like a pig waiting to be slaughtered.

The dungeon door scraped open again and a draft of damp air swept into the chamber. Brion tried to open his eyes. It took real effort. Through the slits of his swollen eyelids, he saw them drag a lifeless form into the room and drape it over the stone slab. A torch blazed in a bracket beside the open door, adding to the thin rays of light that slipped through the slits in the ceiling.

"The old man couldn't take it," one of the guards said.

"I have a feeling we're going to be doing a lot more of this," the other said.

"That's none of our concern."

"I don't like it," the second voice said. "We've done a boy, two women and this old man just today, and what did any of them know?"

Brion's heart sank. Two women? They couldn't mean Brigid and Finola. He tried to get a better view of the man on the table. He couldn't tell if it was Redmond or not. Redmond couldn't really be called an old man. But Zach could. What if they had all been captured?

"I don't think it had anything to do with them knowing something," the first voice said. "The Lord Prince likes to play."

"If he paid more attention to—"

"Quiet," the other guard interrupted. "You want this to be us? Keep your mouth shut."

Brion's despair wrung his insides like they were being twisted on a stick. He couldn't stand thinking about what these men might have done to Finola and Brigid.

The guards swung the man up so that he was lying on his back on the slab. His arms and legs flopped around as they settled him there. The guards left without any more ceremony, but their argument continued as they closed the door. Silence and shadow descended upon him again. Brion closed his eyes. It was over. There was no way he could escape his cage, and, if the others had already been caught, what was there left to fight for?

A shuffling sound broke into his dark thoughts. He opened his eyes to squint at the man on the stone slab. A ray of light sliced across his body. Brion thought he saw the body move. He adjusted his position and tried to open his eyes wider.

The figure slid to one side and slipped to the ground with a grunt. Then he raised his head and dragged himself toward Brion's cage. A chill ran through Brion. He had heard stories of the dead returning to suck the blood of the living in a vain attempt to heal their ravaged bodies.

This man had seemed dead a few moments before, and now he

was clawing his way toward Brion's cage. Brion wriggled around so he could see better. His body cried out in agony. He tried to think what he could do to keep the man from sucking his blood.

The dragging stopped.

"Brion?" The man's voice was weak.

Brion started. "Who are you?" Brion tried to speak, but the words came out garbled. His tongue was dry and swollen, and the muscles in his jaw were stiff and sore.

He swallowed and tried again, but the man didn't wait for him to speak.

"The Duke sent me," the man said. He dragged himself closer. "If Rhodri fails, you must seize the throne."

Brion could see the blood dripping from a terrible gash in the man's scalp. He wondered for a moment if the man had been knocked out of his wits. What could he mean, the Duke sent him? Brion considered pointing out that he was locked up in a cage and so could hardly do anything about the throne, but figured that would be a waste of breath.

"What?" Brion croaked.

"He legitimized you," the man said. His breathing was ragged as he struggled to speak. "He made you the heir of his lands and titles. If Rhodri is killed, you are next in line to the throne once Damian is dead."

Brion tried to get his brain to understand what the man was saying. He had never even considered that the Duke of Saylen still had a claim to the throne.

"What about Cedrick?" he said.

The man blinked as if he were trying to remain focused. He sucked in a ragged breath.

"He is no longer the Duke's son. He has been disinherited." The man took another long, shuttering breath. "You must get out of here. Damian knows about Rhodri. The Duke feared he would fail, and so he sent you to take the throne if he did."

"I'm no king," Brion said.

The man blinked and the determination that had been driving him seemed to melt away. "You're all the Duke has left," he said. He slumped to the ground with a quiet moan. His bleeding head rested on his outstretched arm.

"Who are you?" Brion said again.

"I am Killian, the Duke's servant," Killian mumbled. "Your friends will come for you. This is our last chance. If we fail now, the line of the Hassani is ended."

"Have you seen them?" Brion said. He wasn't worried about the line of Hassani so much as he was the safety of his friends.

"Yes. They know." Killian's words slurred together. His breath gurgled in his throat.

A sudden rush of frustration overwhelmed Brion. He shoved against the bars that kept him curled up like a defeated animal. He kicked at the door in impotent fury. The cage rattled, and his body protested. He gave up and lay still, breathing hard, grimacing at the raw pain his flailing had caused. What was he going to do? He had never felt so helpless in his entire life—not even when he had first looked down on the bodies of Weyland and Rosland. At least then he knew he could avenge them.

"There is one more thing," Killian said. He raised his head. "A secret." Something gurgled in his throat. "Your mother is still alive." He choked on the words.

Brion's chest constricted. "What?" Brion grabbed at the cage, trying to pull himself closer to Killian. Had he heard him correctly? His real mother? The one the Duke had loved?

"The midwife said she was dead," Brion said. The Duke had told him the same thing.

"She lied for him," Killian said. "The Duke hid her among the Carpentini."

Killian's body jerked and spasmed under a fit of coughing that left him wheezing and gasping for air. He struggled to raise his head again but failed. He let it rest on his arm while he kept his gaze on Brion.

"Cedrick knows," he whispered. "Save her." Killian groaned. "A cottage between boulders . . . Aveen . . . Elsie . . ." He breathed out the last word and lay still.

The burning in Brion's chest exploded into rage. He kicked against the cage again and again. So many secrets. So many lies. Tears slipped from his eyes.

"Where is she?" he croaked at the dead man. "Where is she?" He wanted to scream the words, but his voice failed him. "Please," he whispered.

Killian didn't move. His body lay crumpled on the cold, stone floor as the rats approached to sniff at him.

Tyg crouched in the shadows of the palace wall as the gray of evening descended over the city. Rhodri had been safely delivered, though if he was still safe Tyg did not know. Rhodri's fate was no longer Tyg's concern. But if he could save Brion for the girls, he would do it. He glanced back at Finola, Brigid, Emyr, and Redmond. Lara was watching the front gates of the palace where they had planned to meet. Redmond had insisted that she not enter the dungeons with them.

They waited in silence. Their faces were grim. They all knew that they could die, trapped in the palace or the dungeons in the middle of a coup. But they all went willingly. That was what had first puzzled Tyg about this group. They worried more about the safety of their friends than about their own skins. Tyg couldn't remember the last time he had met anyone like them. He smiled to himself. Was he becoming one of them?

The back door cracked open as he had expected. He had carefully cultivated the relationships that let him move about unseen and unnoticed in the Kingdom of Coll. Without them, he would have died years ago.

Tyg rose up and slipped inside the walls of the palace. The others followed. Tyg led them past the Temple of the Ancients that loomed large in the growing dusk. The flames of hundreds of torches burst from the vaulted doorway and made the stained glass windows glow from within in a rainbow of color.

Tyg avoided the small groups of well-dressed men and women that were filing through the doors. He marveled that anyone would take the time to pretty themselves up for a coronation on the eve of an assault on their city. It seemed to him they had bigger problems to worry about; but, then again, he wasn't a noble.

Tyg circled around behind the large, square tower of the keep, seeking the back entrance to the dungeons. He signaled for the rest of them to stay behind while he slipped forward to dispatch the guard.

Betrayal

How many times had he done this? How long would he keep doing it? Killing had become so mechanical to him. It was so easy when you didn't stop to consider that you had just snuffed out a unique life that could never be replaced. Tyg couldn't count the lives he had ended. But their shadows haunted him, every one of them, forming a vast parade of macabre dead, clamoring for the life he could not restore. Some of them had deserved to die, but the others . . . Tyg pushed the dreary thoughts aside. He couldn't afford to be distracted—not now. He lifted the guard's keys from his dead body, unlocked the ironbound door, and slipped into the dark stairwell. He dragged the body inside, waited for the rest to crowd in, pushed the door closed, and locked it.

Tyg breathed in the familiar, musty air. He knew the dungeons well. More than one job had taken him into the damp, stone corridors because some noble had wanted an inmate silenced. The smell of human suffering filled the gloom. So many had come here to suffer and die.

The prison was constructed in the shape of a flower. A long corridor led down to the central guard room that permitted access to a semi-circular hallway off of which several corridors looped around like the petals of a flower. Single cells populated the corridors with a large, torture chamber at the heart of the flower so that the sounds of its suffering victims could echo throughout the entire prison.

Tyg approached the central guard room and motioned for the others to wait. He crept up to the door, expecting to hear the normal chatter of guards passing their time playing cards. But when he peered in through the narrow slit that served as a window, he found the room empty. This puzzled him. It had never happened in his experience.

Perhaps the guards had gone to the coronation. Tyg tried the keys and found the one that fit. He led the group inside as he hurried to inspect the semi-circular chamber on the other side of the guard room through the spy hole. No one was there. Suspicion played at the back of his mind. Something was wrong.

The door behind him slammed shut with a bang that echoed in the chamber. Tyg spun. Emyr pushed against the door, but it was blocked. Someone laughed a long, echoing laugh of triumph. Tyg spun back to the spy hole and found a pair of eyes staring back at him with an expression of satisfaction.

Tyg tried the keys in the door. None of them worked.

"I told them you would come like bees to the honey," a voice said.

"Cluny?" Redmond strode to the door and shoved Tyg aside. "You cowardly scoundrel," he snarled. "Come in here, and let's test your skill with that long sword."

Cluny clicked his tongue. "You never could see the larger picture, Redmond," he said. "You and Neahl, so brave, so noble. Wasting your time on little people while kingdoms hung in the balance. Unlike you, I seize opportunities when they come my way. I don't snivel over crippled brothers and chase old maids about."

Redmond whipped his sword from its scabbard and drove it through the spy hole. Cluny gave a cry. Redmond pulled his sword back through the hole. The tip was stained with blood.

Cluny's face appeared at the hole again. Blood trickled from a deep gash on his cheek. He sneered at Redmond.

"I'll repay that in kind and then some," he said. "For now, sit and rot while Brion and Rhodri die."

Chapter 27
A Crown of Thorns

hodri stared dumbstruck at the pages he had pulled from the little space inside the altar where he had found the royal sword of the Hassani. He stood in a tiny room in the Temple of the Ancients where he awaited the summons to enter the great hall. He was moments away from the event for which he had spent his entire life preparing, and now his stomach churned and his chest burned with the fire of shame and despair. He had believed that he was the last prince of the house of Hassani. He had trained and studied and suffered and labored for this day, when he could return in triumph and reclaim the throne of his fathers.

Why now? Why would the Duke wait until he had reclaimed the sword to tell him that it had all been a lie? The papers had been neatly placed beneath the sword so that he had almost missed them.

Rhodri read over the letter again. It had been penned in Salassani script.

"If you are reading this letter," it said, "then you have retrieved the sword and the day of your ascension is near. I have done you a great wrong, and I cannot rest without giving you the chance to choose your own path. I would have you take the path I have laid for you because I believe it is for the good of this people. But I will not compel you without first telling you the truth of your parentage.

"I stood by and watched as my entire family was slaughtered. But I didn't do it to save my own life. I did it because I understood that it was the only chance I had to save the line of my fathers. I tried to save the princess first, but she died of illness soon after. So when the new prince was born, I plotted to spirit him away before the assassins could find him. But I failed. The child was sickly and doomed

251

not to live more than a few months. Still, I could not allow the usurpers to retain the throne they had stolen.

"In my desperation, I turned to Weyland and his newborn babe. Both he and the prince had red hair. They were roughly the same age. When I visited Weyland and his wife and I looked down on their healthy, robust child, I knew what I had to do. I contrived to smear a translucent and odorless cream on the child's hand, which was made of a rare and expensive poison that simulates death.

"When the child appeared to cease his breathing and his heart ceased its beating, Weyland brought me the child as I had instructed. He believed that his dead child would be used to save the life of the prince. But I switched the two spirited away the already dead prince even as Geric slaughtered my family. I concealed his body in his grandfather's tomb. Then I sent Finn, the King's steward, with Weyland's son into the heathland and spread the rumor that the prince had escaped.

"You may wonder why I have not sought to place my own son on the throne. At first, I feared discovery. We were closely watched. Then as my son got older, I realized that he craved power and would not make an honorable king. So I have continued with my plans, knowing that I was disinheriting the family I had sought to save.

"You are Weyland's and Rosland's son, but I have made you a prince. I beg you, for the good of this kingdom and in the name of a vengeance long overdue, to seize this throne and rule as a just king. I have given my life to this one task. Please, do not fail me."

The letter ended with no signature, but a drop of green wax held the seal of the Duke of Saylen.

Rhodri wiped at the sting of bitter tears. This explained why the Duke had sent his son Brion to live with Weyland and Rosland. He was replacing the son the Duke had torn from them through deceit. Rhodri had had parents who loved him and might have raised him if the Duke had not interfered. He also had a sister, who, right now, was in grave danger.

What was Rhodri to do? The pieces on the gameboard were already in motion. People had already sacrificed their lives because they believed in him. More would die tonight. If they knew that he was an impostor, would they still want him as their king?

Rhodri pulled from his pocket the signet ring that Redmond had given to him earlier. He had two of the three symbols of the King—the sword and the ring. All he lacked was the crown, but did he have the right?

He did not. He knew he did not. He was nothing more than an impostor come to take the throne away from another impostor. They were like little boys fighting over toys in the play yard.

But Geric had already been murdered. Damian was about to claim the crown, and, if Hayden was right, he was about to unleash a bloodbath on the Alamani and the Salassani alike. Did Rhodri dare walk away?

Rhodri wiped at the last of the tears. He had no choice. He would take the throne if he could to save his friends—to save the people of Coll and the Taurini among whom he had lived for so long. He consoled himself that he could always abdicate in favor of someone else once he had brought this crisis under control.

A knock sounded at the door. It was time. Rhodri slipped the pages into his pocket. There would be time later to decide what to do about Brigid and the others.

A thud and a shout from the corridor brought Tyg to his feet. He had finally given up trying to force the lock when he realized that the door was barred from the outside. Scuffling and another thud was followed by the soft patter of bare feet and the jangle of keys at the door. They all drew their weapons as the door creaked open. The little girl, Margaret, who had first led them to the conspirators stood before them. Finola gasped and ran to the child.

She bent to hug her, but the child held up her hand and shook her head. "You have to go now," she said. "He is down there," she said pointing. "You will need these." She handed a set of keys to Finola.

"Where are the guards?" Emyr asked.

A guilty expression slipped across the girl's face, and she glanced down at a black glove she wore on her left hand. It had little hooks like claws and seemed to be covered in some kind of translucent grease.

"It makes them sleep," she said.

Tyg knew what it was. He had used it often enough himself. It was a rare poison from the bladder of a fish that swam in the warm waters to the south. The bladder yielded a toxin that, when introduced into the blood stream, rapidly produced a coma-like state that would last for some hours. In very high doses, it killed. Tyg poked his head outside the door and found two guards lying in crumpled heaps against the wall.

Margaret waved at them to hurry. "Go," she said. "It's about to begin."

Rhodri strode into the crowd, pretending that he belonged there. He experienced an odd mixture of fulfillment, terror, and guilt. It required a lot more than a ring and sword to make a king. Even with those symbols of royal power hidden beneath his cloak, he could never forget that he was a fraud. The long, dark cloak concealed the purple one he wore underneath. It also covered the hilt of the sword of the Hassani kings that thumped against his leg as he walked. The murmur of voices was so loud that he couldn't even hear his boots slapping the paved stone floor. He glanced up at the dark, stained glass windows and around at the balconies where guards stood. Indeed, the hall was filled with armed guards at every entrance and all around the crowd of spectators.

The smell of perfumes and sweat mingled with the musty dampness of the great hall and the sharp stench of burning torches. Zach had assured Rhodri that the assassins were in place. Their forces were prepared to seize the palace. They already occupied the walls of the city. Nothing could possibly go wrong. Then why did the sweat trickle down Rhodri's back? Why did his knees feel weak?

Hayden grabbed his arm to pull him to a stop and indicated the guards forcing the crowd apart to form an aisle on either side of the hall. A trumpet rang out and was joined by others, making the hall echo with a triumphant marching tune. Damian entered, flanked by guards in royal purple. He wore a brilliant, purple silk robe edged with fine, white fur. Jewels glittered on his fingers, and a long sword swung at his side.

He strolled along slowly, giving the crowd time to recognize their new king. A child made a scene by pushing her way to the front of the crowd only to be slapped back by a big, burly man. Damian stopped. He spoke sharply to the guards who dragged the man away.

Then he knelt to the child, kissed her forehead, took her hand in his, and walked with her to the front of the hall.

If he was faking it, he was a very good actor.

"He knows," Hayden whispered in Rhodri's ear.

Rhodri glanced at him, then back to Damian and understood. He was using the girl as a shield. The assassins wouldn't attack him so long as they might hit the child.

Damian mounted the steps of the dais, kissed the child again, and made her stand in front of him. At that moment, a shout rang out in the hall. Damian flinched and his guards rushed to cover him.

"The city is under attack," the voice called again.

A moment of silence gave way to tumult. Damian hesitated, then reached for the crown. Several of the guards crumpled to the ground around him with arrows protruding from their bodies. Damian dropped the crown and drew his sword as Rhodri, Hayden, and the rest of the conspirators rushed the dais. Damian and his guards fell back, outnumbered and confined by the throbbing crowd of terrified spectators. Several more of Damian's guards fell to the archer assassins, but, apparently, none of them could get a clear shot at Damian.

Rhodri raised the sword of the Kings of Coll and entered the battle for his kingdom. Damian's guard held as Damian pushed his way to the back of the dais toward the door that led to the back hallway. Rhodri rushed to follow him, but Zach grabbed Rhodri and dragged him back to the altar.

"Take it now," he yelled over the noise. "Proclaim yourself king." He shoved the crown into Rhodri's hand but Rhodri could only stare at it, uncertain. He thought he had made up his mind, but now that he faced the moment, he found that he had not. Zach snatched it away from him and shoved it onto Rhodri's head. A sharp pain stabbed into Rhodri's scalp as the crown settled on his brow. But he didn't have time to consider it as Zach swept off Rhodri's black cloak, raised the hand with the sword in it and bellowed over the uproar.

"Behold your king!" he cried. "Behold your king!" His voice boomed in the great hall. The hall grew quiet.

"Rhodri, son of Edward, the lost prince of the Hassani, has returned to claim his throne."

Silence filled the hall.

"Impostor," someone shouted.

Zach snatched the sword from Rhodri's hand and held it aloft. "He bears the lost signet of his father and the sword of the kings of Coll."

Rhodri tried to focus on what Zach was saying, but his vision swam and a sharp pain began to spread in his gut. Rhodri swayed on his feet. Something was wrong.

Someone made his way toward him through the crowd. They parted like water before the prow of a ship. Rhodri recognized him. It was Cedrick.

Cedrick climbed the steps of the dais with a handful of men.

"I challenge your claim to the throne," he bellowed so that everyone in the hall could hear.

Brion jerked his cage every time a rat came close to Killian's body. He couldn't stand to lay there and watch them devour him. Another rat approached.

"Hey!" Brion shouted as loud as he could. He kicked the cage again. But the rat turned his beady eyes on him and stepped closer to Killian.

The light of day had faded from the cracks that lit the dungeon, but his eyes had become used to the lingering gray twilight. Killian's clothing twitched and jerked as more rats advanced on his body. Brion shivered at the thought of listening to them feed all night in the utter blackness of the dungeon. It made the bile rise in his throat.

"Hey!" he yelled again.

The door of the dungeon burst open and a crowd of armed men rushed in. The rats scattered.

"It's over," Brion thought. *"They've come to kill me."*

But he was blinking at Finola's face, lit by the flare of torches. Someone played with the lock on his cage.

"Finola?" he said.

Finola pushed a hand through the bars and laid it on his cheek. It was cold, and strong, and reassuring.

"Are you okay?" she asked.

Brion tried to nod. "My mother," he said. "The Duke."

"We know about the Duke," Finola said.

Someone bent over the body on the floor. "It's Killian," Emyr said.

Relief bubbled up inside Brion, filling his throat with a knot so big he couldn't speak. They had come for him—his friends, the only people left in the world who cared about him.

"He said he had another message to deliver," Brigid said.

"He gave himself up so he could reach Brion," Emyr said. "Brave fool."

"The keys don't work," Tyg said.

"Get the hammer," Redmond said.

"I can pick it," Tyg said.

"We don't have time." Redmond loomed over Brion and slammed the hammer into the lock. The cage shuddered with the violence of the impact. Two more strikes and it burst open. Emyr and Tyg reached in to drag Brion from the cage. They tried to set him on his feet, but he couldn't stand. He gasped in pain, and they carried him to the stone slab. Tyg massaged the muscles of Brion's legs , checking for broken bones, while Emyr poured water into his mouth. Finola and Brigid gathered around searching his body for any wounds.

"You've looked better," Redmond said.

"Thanks," Brion said. He peered at Redmond from his swollen eyes. "Good thing I had you and Neahl to teach me how to take a beating," he said.

Redmond's smile slackened. "I'm sorry, Brion. I never should have left you."

Brion shook his head. If Redmond hadn't slipped out the door when he did, he probably would have been dead already.

"It could have been worse," Finola said.

Brion stared up at her, trying to decide if she was joking.

"Well," Finola continued, "let's just say it's a good thing they didn't know about the feathers."

"Nice," Brion said. "How can you make fun of me right now?"

"It's either that or cry," Finola said.

Brion touched her cheek. "I'm sorry," he said.

Then he remembered what Killian had told him.

"Cedrick is going to try to take the throne," he blurted.

"Probably," Redmond said. "So we need to get you on your feet."

"I don't know what's broken," Brion said. He raised his hands. One finger on his left hand was bent at an awkward angle. Finola and Brigid both gasped. Emyr shouldered them aside, grasped Brion's hand, and yanked the finger back into place.

"Ow!" Brion howled. "You could have warned me."

Emyr shook his head. "It's always better this way," he said.

With all of them working on him at the same time, they soon had Brion bandaged up as best they could. His broken finger had been tied tightly to the one next to it to give it support. His ribs had been rubbed with salve and bandaged. Redmond had rubbed the same salve around his swollen eyes.

While they worked, Brion surveyed his friends with relief. So Damian hadn't captured them. But . . .

"Where's Lara?" Brion asked, suddenly terrified that she had been one of the women Damian's men had tortured.

"She's watching the front door for us," Redmond said.

"Then she's safe?" Brion asked.

"Safer than we are," Finola said.

"Try again," Tyg said. Brion swung his legs over the table and put his weight on his feet. Everything ached, but his knees didn't give out this time. He tried a few unsteady steps.

"Not too fast," Redmond said. "Let's get more water in you and some food. We need you to be able to stand on your own because we're going to have to fight our way out of here."

"That should be fun," Brion said. He sipped some water and nibbled on a piece of bread as they told him how they had escaped, how Killian had found them, and how Rhodri was fighting to seize the throne.

At first, Brion's stomach rebelled at the water and bread, but it stayed down, and soon he had emptied the waterskin and eaten a piece of bread and a piece of jerky, though the jerky made his jaw ache. Tyg took the time to secure another knife behind Brion's back at the nape of his neck. Damian had taken his last one.

"Just in case," Tyg said.

"We need to move," Redmond said.

Finola and Brigid supported Brion as they hurried through the door and into the corridor. Tyg led the way with a blazing torch. Redmond was close behind him. Emyr took up the rear behind Brion, Finola, and Brigid.

Tyg and Redmond cleared the way of any remaining guards as they ascended. Brion forced Finola and Brigid to stop while he retrieved a sword from one of the fallen soldiers.

"You can barely walk," Finola said.

"I'll still need it," Brion replied.

They came out into a narrow courtyard that separated the palace from the Temple of the Ancients and crowded around the door, uncertain which path they should take. The cries and clashes of battle rang from the Temple. Bleeding men huddled against walls or lay crumpled where they had fallen. An open doorway revealed men struggling, swords flashing.

"Is there a way around this?" Redmond asked.

"This way," Tyg said. He led them along the wall of the keep toward the palace. Someone ran along the upper balcony above them, paused, and drew a bow.

"Tyg!" Brion yelled.

Chapter 28
Arrows of Fate

edrick stood before Rhodri and Zach, defiant and proud. "What are you doing?" Zach whispered.

Cedrick sneered at him. "Fixing the mistake my father made," he said.

Zach gasped at the same time as several other people on the dais. Rhodri glanced around to see the leaders of the conspiracy swaying on their feet. Men stood beside them clutching bloody knives in their hands.

"What have you done?" Zach whispered as blood gurgled past his lips. He sank to his knees.

The struggle on the dais paused as everyone stood in shock to watch Liam, Zach, and several of their guards collapse to lay in expanding pools of blood.

Rhodri raised his sword to strike Cedrick down, but the sword had become so heavy. He blinked again and tried to keep from crumpling over at the pain that raged in his chest. It was spreading to his stomach.

Cedrick sneered at him. "You didn't really believe that Damian or I would just let you walk in here and take what doesn't belong to you, did you?" he said.

Rhodri couldn't fight the agony anymore. He bent over and groaned. The pain burned like molten lead had been poured down his throat. His muscles convulsed, and he fell to his knees.

Cedrick lifted the crown off Rhodri's his head. Rhodri peered up at him through the fog of pain. Cedrick examined the crown, yanked something from it, and then placed it on his own head.

"Pitiful," Cedrick said to Rhodri. "Your plans were always pitiful."

Betrayal

Then he raised his hands to the crowd as his men on the stage attacked the remaining conspirators. Damian's guards also counter-attacked, and the conspirators fell before them.

Rhodri finally understood. He had been so foolish. Cedrick had pretended to work for both Damian and the conspirators, when all along he had been working for himself. And now Rhodri had been poisoned. The crown had poisoned him. How ironic. The crown he had been trained from childhood to desire and to seek. The crown that was supposed to be his birthright had become his assassin. Then he remembered Brion. He had to find them and warn them before it was too late. Rhodri dragged himself to his hands and knees, fighting the rending agony that coursed through his body and crawled toward the door Damian had used to escape.

Tyg slid to a stop as Brion's cry rang out in the courtyard. He glanced up. A man wearing a purple robe with white fur trim was bending a bow in their direction. Tyg glanced back and saw that Brion was his target. And Brion was staring up at the archer, holding a sword loosely in his right hand as Brigid and Finola tried to hurry him on. Brion stumbled. Finola swung around in front of Brion, dropping her bow as she tried to help him to his feet. Brion struggled to shove her aside. His eyes fixed on the archer. Desperate terror spread across Brion's face as he realized that Finola stood between him and death. The archer released the string. Tyg lunged.

The arrow drove through Tyg's ribs with a terrible crack and searing pain. It buried itself up the fletchings before he slammed into Finola and sent her flying into the wall. He landed on his side and slid a few feet before he came to a stop. The arrow snapped underneath him as his gaze focused on the man fleeing along the balcony. Redmond snatched up Finola's bow, yanked an arrow from Brigid's quiver, drew, and shot. The man in purple stumbled into the balcony railing and then pitched over the side. Tyg heard the crunch of his landing.

Finola bent over Tyg. Warm tears dropped onto his face. Her gaze searched his body. But Tyg knew his silk undershirt would do him no good now. He could feel his life's blood filling his lungs. Breathing became difficult and painful.

"Tyg," Finola whispered. Her lips trembled.

Brigid appeared beside her. Her beautiful, red hair framed her lovely face.

"You saved me again," Finola said.

Tyg swallowed. "Well, at least I've done something worthwhile in my wretched life," he said. He choked on the blood in his lungs.

Emyr knelt beside him and fumbled with his shirt. The point of the arrow had carried the silk undershirt through the wound. Emyr cut it away and dragged the broken shaft the rest of the way though the wound.

Tyg grabbed his hands. "Don't waist your time on me, son," he said. "Get them out of here."

"Tyg," Brigid and Finola said together.

Tyg brushed at Finola's tears. "You were like a daughter to me," he said. "Both of you."

Brigid bent and kissed his forehead.

Tyg choked again. The warm blood gurgled in his mouth and spilled down his cheeks. "Go," he gasped.

He blinked, and a silver light hovered before his eyes. Someone shook his body. Voices called from far away. The silver light shimmered and faded. *"Goodbye,"* Tyg thought as the darkness swept in to smother the light.

Brion stared at Tyg's still form. Tyg had taken the arrow meant for him. This time the assassins had found a mark. Brion knelt beside Tyg's body as Redmond hurried away to examine the man in the purple cape that lay crumpled on the stone.

Redmond hurried back to them. "It was Damian," he said. He dragged Brion to his feet. "Let's go."

But Brigid and Finola ignored him. Emyr glanced up at Redmond and then gently lifted Brigid to her feet. Then he lifted Finola. Both girls sobbed as they grabbed up their bows and followed Emyr to the door Tyg had indicated. Once inside, they found the hallway empty save for the single crumpled form draped in a bright purple cloak. His auburn hair spilled out on the floor. Redmond paused.

"Rhodri?" Brigid ran to him and lifted his head into her lap. "Rhodri?" she said again. "Not you, too."

The rest of them gathered around. Rhodri's eyes blinked open, his body twitched and jerked. A black froth collected at the sides of his mouth.

"Brion," he stammered.

Brion knelt beside him. Rhodri pulled the royal signet ring from his finger and shoved it into Brion's hands.

"You," Rhodri said, "are king now."

Brion shook his head. "No," he said.

"I was never the prince." Rhodri's body shuttered from a violent spasm. "Weyland," he gasped, "was my father."

Brion's heart dropped into the pit of his stomach. Was Rhodri confused? Brigid let out a quiet sob as she stroked Rhodri's hair. Brion stared in bewilderment. It couldn't be true.

"Cedrick double-crossed us," Rhodri said again. "He took the crown and the sword."

"Where is he?" Brion said as rage burst through his pain.

Rhodri blinked at them. "The crown was poisoned. They're all dead."

"Who is dead?" Finola asked.

"Zach, Liam, the others. All dead."

"We have to get out of here," Redmond said. "Now!" His voice was laced with urgency and fear.

"Take the papers," Rhodri. "In my pocket. They explain everything."

Emyr bent to pick Rhodri up, but Rhodri pushed him away.

"I'm sorry I failed you," he said.

"Don't," Brigid sobbed.

Emyr hauled Rhodri over his shoulder, and Brion stumbled along behind them as they made their way down the hallway. Brion tried to focus on what was happening. Everything was falling apart, and Cedrick would be left holding the crown.

A door slammed open behind them. Brion glanced around to see Cedrick stride into the hallway wearing the golden crown on his head, clutching a bloodstained sword in his hand. Cluny was at his side and a small group of soldiers trailed behind them. Rage surged up inside Brion as Cedrick paused, apparently surprised to see them.

"Take them," Cedrick commanded.

The soldiers rushed forward. Two fell with arrows in their chests from Finola's and Brigid's bows before the men were among them. Emyr let Rhodri slide to the ground out of the way and ran to meet the soldiers. Redmond was beside him. The soldiers were swept away in their fury, leaving Cedrick and Cluny looking on.

Cedrick swished his sword through the air. Brion noted the purple tulip inlaid in the pommel. It confused him. Was it some symbol the kingship he hadn't known about? If so, why would Rosland bury a tulip where her baby should have been?

Emyr launched himself at Cedrick, who deflected Emyr's attack with practiced ease. Redmond hurtled toward Cluny with a savage growl. Cluny kept him at bay with his long sword while Brion watched, wanting to help, but unable to decide who to attack first and not wanting to get in his friends' way. He was still so weak and awkward.

Cluny's arrogant sneer decided him. Emyr could handle Cedrick. But Cluny had ordered Neahl killed. Cluny had betrayed them from the beginning. Here was Brion's chance, and he would not leave this hallway until Cluny was dead.

"Guards!" Cedrick screamed. A note of panic sounded in his voice. Brion took grim satisfaction in it. "Guards!" Cedrick and Emyr disappeared down a side hallway as Emyr pressed him hard.

Cluny and Redmond circled like two great wolves searching for an opening. Brion slipped along the wall, using it for balance. His body rebelled against every step. His hand felt too weak to grip the sword. The knife Tyg had strapped to his back pressed into the base of his neck. All he had to do was get inside the reach of that long sword.

Redmond cast Brion an annoyed glare as Brion worked his way along the wall. But Brion ignored him. Cluny swung the great sword in an arc that would have split Redmond in two, but Redmond wasn't there. Redmond closed the distance in a flash and drove his blade into Cluny's side. Cluny jerked the pommel of his long sword up and smashed it against Redmond's temple. Redmond slumped to the ground. Brion stepped in to deflect Cluny's killing stroke.

But Cluny's sword tore Brion's sword from his hand. Brion stumbled forward to grab Cluny in a bear hug—anything to keep inside the reach of that sword. Cluny's hand closed on Brion's throat while the other dropped his sword to the floor. Cluny's free hand fumbled for his knife. Pressure swelled behind Brion's eyes. Cluny was cutting off his air. Brion released his bear hug, whipped his knife from its sheath behind his neck and drove it into Cluny's eye.

Lara haunted the boarded up stalls and shops that lined the street in front of the palace. Refugees straggled about or clustered in the shadows of buildings—cowering away from the turmoil erupting in the Temple. Lara understood that Redmond and Emyr had wanted to keep her out of harm's way, but the inactivity and the certainty that her family could die without her being able to do anything about it nearly drove her mad. She had been waiting there for over an hour. It shouldn't have taken them this long. The sounds of fighting in the palace and the roar of the army assaulting the walls of the city mingled in the cool shadows like the voices of phantoms on the wind.

People poured out of the Temple of the Ancients, stumbling and trampling each other in their haste to escape the fighting. Lara knew that Rhodri was in there, probably fighting for his throne at that very moment. But why hadn't Redmond appeared?

To find something else to occupy her mind, Lara pulled from her pocket the little folded packet that Killian had given her. She hadn't had time to read it yet, so she retreated to where someone had left a fire burning in an iron grate and bent to read the letter by the light of the flickering flames. It was short.

"You know who he is," it said. "If the others fail, he must assume the throne." The rest of the packet was a complex genealogical chart of the royal line of the Hassani. Each page bore the Duke's signature and seal, stamped in bold red wax.

Lara examined the chart in disbelief. The Duke had known all along. Why hadn't he done something to help her father? All those years of poverty and exile, and now, he wanted her to do him this little favor? Lara began pacing again. This hadn't helped at all. How could the Duke have known? Why would he put her in a position like this?

Here was yet another example of the arrogance of the nobility. How dare the Duke ask her to help the people that had abandoned her grandmother and her father to poverty? People who had driven them as outcasts into the heathland and then refused to help them when the Salassani had destroyed their village and burned their home. She wouldn't do it. She couldn't.

Someone yelled down the street, and Lara crouched in the shadow of the stall. Another group of people began pouring down the steps of the Temple of the Ancients. Steel rang upon steel. Voices cried out in anger and pain. Soldiers dressed in the colors of the royal guard burst from a side street and began launching arrows into the crowd. The fighting had finally spilled out into the streets in earnest.

A small group stumbled down the front steps of the palace. Brigid's fiery hair flashed in the light of torches burning in the sconces along the wall. She drew her bow and loosed. Finola was beside her, propping Brion up. Emyr and Redmond fought side by side, as they were pushed down the steps. They were desperate. Redmond fought like he was drunk. His crisp efficient movements had given way to a frantic struggle to remain alive. She had to do something. But what could she do? She was no warrior.

Lara stuffed the royal genealogies into her pocket and rose to rush toward them. An archer stepped in front of her and drew. To her horror, Lara realized that he was aiming at Redmond. She grabbed up a shovel and swung it with all of her might.

"Redmond!" she screamed as the shovel crashed into the archer's head. The archer dropped to the cobblestones. Lara sprinted toward Redmond. The terror that slipped across Redmond's face as he spun toward her confused her until the pain flashed into her back. She stumbled and fell headlong onto the cobbled street.

Redmond's cry of anguish rang out over the sounds of fighting. Something zipped over her head and someone grunted behind her. She dragged herself to her hands and knees. She had to reach Redmond, but it was suddenly hard to breathe.

Feet slapped the cobblestones. Strong arms lifted her and carried her out of the street to the shadow of a doorway away from the fighting that now surged past them and up into the great hall. She blinked up into Redmond's stricken face. One side of his head was caked in blood.

"Please," Redmond said.

Lara swallowed, trying to understand where the pain was coming from. Emyr's blood-spattered face appeared next to Redmond's.

"I love you," she said to both of them.

Tears dripped from Redmond's chin.

"Please," he said again. "Don't leave me. Not now."

Emyr investigated the wound in Lara's back. When his head appeared next to Redmond's again, she understood the tight lips and frightened gaze.

"Listen," she said. She tugged at the wad of papers she had stuffed into her pocket. Emyr pulled them free for her.

"We have to tell him," she said to Redmond. Redmond nodded.

Lara raised a hand to touch Emyr's cheek. "You are royalty," she said.

Emyr blinked at her in confusion. "My father, Kurk, was the illegitimate son of King Karl," Lara continued. "That's why he survived the coup. The King drove my grandmother out when he discovered she was pregnant with his child. Tell him Redmond."

Redmond blinked. When he spoke, his voice was thick with emotion. "Kurk went to his brother, King Edward," he said, "when his mother was sick, seeking aid. Edward imprisoned him and whipped him. Then he dumped him in the river. But Kurk survived and fled to Comrie."

Lara nodded. "If Rhodri and Brion fail," she said, "the Duke wants you to be king."

Emyr shook his head and glanced back at someone Lara couldn't see.

"No," Emyr said.

"Are the others alive?" Lara asked.

"Damian and Cedrick are dead," Emyr said. "So is Rhodri, but Brion . . ."

Brion now knelt next to Lara. He laid the crown on the cobblestones beside her. Emyr considered it with narrowed eyes and shook his head.

Lara blinked at Emyr. "My son," she said. She reached her hand up to touch Redmond's cheek. "Our son," she whispered. Then she closed her eyes. The pain made it difficult to breathe. The beat of her heart seemed to echo in her ears. The shadows began to envelop her. They called to her.

"Redmond," she whispered. "I love you."

Her heartbeat slowed. It fluttered. She breathed a sigh and quit fighting the pain.

Brion sat stunned, blinking at Lara's still form. The fighting seemed to be dying down around the great hall, and no one paid them any heed where they crouched in the shadows of the doorway. For Brion, the noises of battle faded to a dull roar. In less than fifteen minutes, three of his closest friends had been killed, and he had watched them all die. He found it hard to breathe, hard to think.

Brigid and Finola sobbed quietly beside him. He wanted to reach out to comfort them. But the image of Redmond drooped over Lara's body, cradling her head in his lap while his body shook with violent sobs, seemed to paralyze Brion. Emyr held Lara's hand in his. Tears streamed down his face. Brigid wrapped her arms around Emyr.

Brion's whole world seemed confined to the small spot of dirty, cobblestone street where everyone he loved in the world huddled in sorrow, enfolded in the gathering darkness. Finola shifted closer to him, and he raised an arm to encircle her waist. When she hugged him, the pain in his ribs made him jerk and stiffen. Finola misunderstood the movement and tried to pull away, but Brion held her.

"My ribs," he mumbled. Finola held him more gently, laid her head on his shoulder and wept.

The golden crown lay on the cobblestones next to Emyr. The sword with the purple tulip in the handle lay next to it. Brion suddenly made the connection. The purple tulip must be a symbol of the Hassani kings. The sword Finn had said would help Rhodri claim the throne had the purple tulip. Rosland must have known that the son she believed to be dead had been sent to save the prince. She had left the tulip in the grave so that anyone searching it would know where her child had gone. But if she only could have known that her child had lived and had been substituted for the dead prince, what would she have done? That knowledge would have tormented her.

The royal signet ring bulged in Brion's pocket. Rhodri had handed it to Brion and asked Brion to take the crown. Killian had told him that the Duke had sent him to do it if Rhodri failed. Brion imagined himself as king, sitting in some rich hall dispensing justice. Think of all the good he could, all the power he could wield. He could bring peace to Frei-Ock Isle once and for all. Finola would never have to work again. Brigid would be safe.

For one long and glorious moment, Brion really thought he could do it. But when he considered the long years, trapped in the city away from the enchantment of the open heathland, he knew he couldn't. He had been poor all his life. All he needed were his family and friends and the freedom to roam the lands he had grown to love. He was no king. He was an archer. An archer of the heathland.

Besides, with the rumors Cedrick had been spreading about him killing the Duke and King Geric, half the kingdom would rebel against him anyway. It wouldn't do. For the good of Coll, for all of them, he had to let it go.

Brion swallowed the knot that lurked in his throat and examined Emyr more closely. Emyr *looked* like a king. He was tall and strong. Quiet, but decisive. He had been trained to lead. He had been raised to become the headman of the Salassani.

Brion shifted so he could get the ring out of his pocket. He stretched out his hand to Emyr. Emyr stared at the ring in the palm of Brion's hand. Then he raised his gaze to stare at Brion. Brion nodded, picked up the crown and handed it to Emyr. Emyr didn't stir.

Someone yelled Brion's name, but it seemed so distant. It came again more persistent and was accompanied by the slapping of boots on stone. Brion blinked swollen eyes and turned to watch Hayden and Owen sprinting toward them.

"Where's Rhodri?" Hayden said. He didn't even notice that Lara was dead. This irritated Brion. He fought the desire to reach out and strike Hayden—the arrogant fool.

"Dead," Brion said.

Hayden glanced at Owen. "What do you mean?" Hayden said.

"Damian killed him. The crown was poisoned."

Hayden cursed. "Where's Damian?"

"Dead," Brion said again.

Hayden seemed to see the crown and sword lying on the cobblestones for the first time.

"But Cedrick took the sword. How did you—"

"He's dead too," Brion said.

Hayden straightened. His face blanched. "By the King's great, shaggy beard," he said. "Now, what are we going to do? Zach and

269

Liam and all the others are dead."

"But we've secured the palace and the temple," Owen said. "The city is ours. We have to have a king to put on the throne."

Brion stretched out the ring to Emyr again.

"Uh, what are you . . ." Hayden began, but he fell silent when he understood what Brion was doing.

Emyr glanced at Hayden and Owen.

"Don't you have any other heirs?" Emyr asked.

"No," Hayden said. He glanced at Brion. "Well, unless . . ." he trailed off.

Emyr glanced at Brigid. She lifted her shoulders in a tiny shrug of indecision. Fear played across her tear-streaked face.

Finola handed Owen the folded papers that Lara had given Redmond. Owen's gaze moved over the papers and grew wider as he read.

"Is this true?" he asked.

Emyr shrugged. "The Duke seemed to think it was," he said. "He had his servant, Killian, deliver this to my mother."

Owen handed the papers to Hayden.

"The Duke also legitimized Brion and transferred his lands and titles to him," Finola said. "Redmond has those papers."

Hayden gaped at them in open shock. He exchanged glances with Owen.

"Then we have two potential heirs," Owen said. He swiveled his gaze between Brion and Emyr.

This was Brion's last chance. He could agree to take the throne, and Emyr would let him. The Duke had seen to it that Brion even had a legal claim by inheritance. Brion glanced up at Owen, who stood staring down at them with anticipation and confusion playing across his features.

Brion glanced at Finola. She would make a beautiful queen, but he couldn't do it. Coll needed a man like Emyr.

Brion shook his head.

"I don't want to be king," he said.

All eyes turned on Emyr.

"Are you offering?" Hayden said to Emyr.

Emyr glanced at Brigid again. "Do you want me to do this?" he said.

Owen considered. "If you or Brion don't take it," he said, "then we will be left with a bunch of nobles who will forget all about the Dunkeldi and scramble to take the throne for themselves. Frankly, I don't think Coll will survive if one of you doesn't claim that throne today."

Emyr sighed and looked down at Redmond, who still held Lara's body. Then he glanced at Brigid who watched him with wide, green eyes.

"Will you be my queen?" he asked. "Will you help me?"

Brigid paled. She glanced at Brion and Finola as if seeking their approval. Then she nodded and clasped Emyr's hand.

"All right," Emyr said. "Gather the generals and the loyal nobility to the palace. I will meet them there."

Owen grinned, visibly relieved.

"How many defend the walls?" Emyr asked.

"Four thousand," Owen said. "We have about five hundred in the palace and the temple. There are another five thousand in Laro. We will need to round up Cedrick's and Damian's supporters and order them to defend the city. The Dunkeldi are still attacking the front gate. We have pulled all the men we can from the castle to the walls, but we need to get word out of the city to our reinforcements in Laro Forest."

Emyr considered. He scanned the area. The fighting had nearly ceased. "I'll meet them on the steps of the palace in fifteen minutes," he said.

Owen grinned and hurried off, but Hayden stood staring at them. His jaw worked as if he meant to speak. He hesitated.

"I . . . I'm sorry for the way I've acted," he said. His gaze finally fell on Lara. "And I'm sorry for the way things worked out. I just want you to know that I'll be loyal to you, Emyr, if you'll have me."

Emyr considered Hayden. "You've been arrogant and deceitful," Emyr said. "You were ready to turn us over to Cedrick to be killed."

"Not you," Hayden began. He glanced at Brion.

"All the same," Emyr continued. "You betrayed people who trusted you."

Hayden bowed his head. For the first time, Brion thought he saw all the fight go out of Hayden.

"How do I know that I can trust you now?" Emyr said.

Hayden's head came up. He drew his sword and placed it at Emyr's feet. Then he knelt.

"I swear," Hayden said, "on the grave of my dead father that I will serve you and your heirs faithfully until the end of my days. I can do no more than this."

Emyr considered him for a moment and then lifted his sword and handed it to him. "Good," he said. "We're going to need you."

Hayden smiled. "Thank you, My Lord," he said. He sheathed his sword and hurried after Owen.

Emyr laid a hand on Redmond's arm.

"Father," he said. Redmond raised his head slowly as if he were drunk or asleep. His face was stricken. His eyes swollen.

"We need to move her," Emyr said. Redmond blinked at him.

Emyr bent as if to pick Lara up, but Redmond pushed his hands away. He lifted Lara in his arms, hugged her close, and trudged toward the palace steps. The fighting had ceased, save for a few scattered groups who refused to surrender. Emyr carried the sword in one hand and the crown in the other, which drew the attention of everyone not otherwise occupied. They ascended the stairs, and Redmond laid Lara on the uppermost step.

Brion hobbled up the steps to sit beside Lara. Finola took his hand.

"Why?" she said.

Brion knew that she was curious to know why he hadn't wanted to be king. He placed a hand on his aching ribs.

"Emyr's the better man," he said.

Finola shook her head. "You know that's not true."

"I don't know," Brion replied. He examined the whitewashed walls and the bloody streets of the city. "I couldn't live in a place like this," he said. He looked back to Finola. "Weyland was my real father, no matter who sired me. And I need to smell the scent of the heather on the wind. Not the stench of a city crawling with people." He paused again. "I couldn't be a king."

Finola smiled. Even with tearstains cutting lines through the dirt and grime on her cheeks, she was beautiful.

"I wouldn't want you to be," she said.

"I feel like I've been trampled by a herd of horses," Brion said.

Finola gave a short laugh. "That eye is about the size of an apple," she said.

Betrayal

She gazed past Brion to Redmond and new tears glistened in her eyes.

"How will he survive this?" she asked.

A lump rose in Brion's throat again as he watched Redmond bend over Lara. She had been a strong, quiet woman—the perfect match for Redmond. They had just rediscovered their love after years of empty longing, only to have it snatched from them. How could life be so cruel, so random?

Brion sensed the sudden weight of the past, the accumulated debris of choices and decisions that left a stain on the present. The Duke, his father, had believed he could rewrite the past by changing the future. Redmond had been trapped in a past, filled with the regret of one, fateful decision. Weyland had sacrificed his life and that of his wife and child to pursue an ideal. Neahl had allowed himself to be fooled by his dreams of reclaiming his lost manhood. Tyg had spent his life killing others in an attempt to rid himself of the guilt of not being there to save his father's life. Damian had killed his father, not just for power and wealth, but because he thought his father had become a danger to the stability of the kingdom. Cedrick had murdered his own father so he could be king. Lara had died in a desperate attempt to save the men she loved. Rhodri had died because others had never let him choose his own path. Seamus had died trying to prove he could be more than a tanner's son. And now Emyr and Brigid were giving their lives for the good of the kingdom.

Brion had stepped into the painful clutter of all of those choices, and somehow he had survived when better men had perished. Brion blinked back the tears and squeezed Finola's hand.

"I don't know if I can stand the ache," Finola said. "They shouldn't be dead. It isn't right."

"I know," Brion said.

"At least Tyg didn't die alone," Finola said. She wiped away a tear.

"Yeah," Brion said. But he found little consolation in this. Tyg had died saving Brion's and Finola's life.

Owen returned with the captains and generals, some of whom were dirty and blood stained from battle. Emyr took Brigid's hand and descended a few steps to greet them. Brion found himself struggling with disbelief. Brigid. Little Brigid. The one who used to crawl into his lap and demand that he tell her a story. The one that used to fawn over a useless cow. The one that used to look to him for protection and to tease him about Finola. Now she stood erect and confident in her travel-worn clothes, her red hair trailing down her back. And beside her stood the young man who had torn her from her parents' home after leading a raid upon it and had then abandoned his former life and lands among the Salassani to follow her. How could so much change so quickly?

"My Lords," Owen said. "The house of Hassani has been restored. I give you Emyr son of Redmond and Lara, grandson of Kurk, great grandson of Karl Hassani."

A murmur swept through the men.

"He is not the prince we sought to crown today," Owen continued, "but now that Rhodri is murdered by the hand of Cedrick and both Cedrick and Damian are dead, only two remain with legitimate claims to the throne—Brion of Wexford, son of Dustin, the Duke of Saylen, and Emyr of the house of Hassani. Brion has refused the throne. Will you accept Emyr?

"We will want proof," an older gentleman who wore a blood-stained mail shirt demanded.

Owen raised the papers Lara had given them and gestured for them to gather around. The men studied the papers for some time, each taking a turn to examine them.

"They are signed in the Duke's own hand and sealed with his seal," Owen said.

"Where has he been all these years?" someone asked.

"Living among the Salassani," Owen said.

Men grumbled and some turned hesitant, distrustful looks on Emyr and Brigid.

Just then, Hayden approached with a Dunkeldi man dressed in the dark red royal colors of the Dunkeldi and bowed low to Emyr. Brigid glanced at Emyr. The men parted to give him room.

"Your Majesty," Hayden said.

Emyr twitched at the formal address, and Brigid bowed her head. Brion guessed all of this would take some getting used to.

"King Tristan has sent a messenger," Owen said.

Emyr nodded to the man. The space in front of the palace was lit with many torches that had been placed to provide light for Damian's coronation. Several overturned wagons and merchant's stalls also burned. Bodies littered the street and steps. The faint clash of swords indicated that the fighting still continued somewhere. The stench of the smoke, mixed with the horrible gore of death, filled the air.

The messenger bowed to Emyr, but not as deeply as Hayden had done.

"King Tristan brings you greetings, King Cedrick," he said.

Several people gasped and one young warrior drew his sword. The messenger eyed them in confusion.

"Cedrick is dead," Emyr said. "You are speaking to Emyr, son of Redmond, grandson of Kurk, great grandson of Karl of the line of the Hassani. You will please inform his Majesty, King Tristan, that he will so address me if he wishes to parley."

Brion sat stunned. Emyr hadn't skipped a beat. He had transitioned from rebel-peasant to king in less than fifteen minutes.

The messenger paled visibly and stepped backward. "My message was for Cedrick," he said.

"You will deliver that message to me," Emyr said.

"I . . ." The servant looked around again.

"Your words have already revealed Cedrick's treachery," Emyr said. "What bargain has he struck with Tristan?"

"Uh, he promised King Tristan all of the heathland including most of the Laro Forest, and the cities of Dunfermine and Mailag."

"In exchange for what?"

The servant shuffled his feet and cast his gaze around at the gathering of somber-faced warriors.

"Cedrick wanted a determined attack on Coll, a guarantee that he would be allowed to hold the throne, and the death of the lost prince and one Brion of Wexford and all his kin and associates."

The few in the crowd who knew who Brion was now scrutinized him. Brion knew he looked pitiful, all bruised and swollen, sitting in filthy, bloody clothes on the steps of the palace. But he didn't care.

Redmond stirred and glared at the messenger. Then he surveyed the crowd. Brion didn't know what had roused Redmond from his grief, but it concerned him. Redmond reached for Brigid's discarded bow. Pulled an arrow from the quiver and nocked it. Brion gave him a questioning glance, thinking that Redmond was going to shoot the messenger. He started to shake his head when Redmond spoke in a quiet tone.

"Emyr shouldn't be meeting them in the open," he said. "It's still too dangerous."

Redmond stood abruptly, drew, and released. But he hadn't shot at the messenger. His arrow found a man in Damian's livery who had been concealed behind an overturned wagon. The man's bow clattered on the street as it slipped from his grasp. An arrow skipped harmlessly across the cobblestones.

Emyr glanced at Redmond and nodded to him. Again, Emyr didn't miss a beat.

"Tristan should choose his allies more carefully," Emyr said to the messenger. Several of the captains let their gaze drift to the dying man Redmond had shot.

"Now I have a message for Tristan," Emyr continued. "Listen well. You will tell Tristan that, for the first time in the history of our two kingdoms, a king who has lived among the Salassani sits upon the throne of Coll. He will never get a better opportunity to redress old wrongs. I know what Coll has done to the Salassani tribes, and I know what the Salassani have done to Coll. I am willing to negotiate a reasonable peace, but I will not sit idly by while he slaughters my people. The killing ends immediately, or I will unleash the power of Coll upon him, and I will personally pursue him into the halls of his own palace until the line of the Dunkeldi kings is broken." Emyr paused to let the messenger absorb his words. Then he continued. "Foolish, greedy men sought this war, but I will end it—in peace if I can, in blood if I must. The choice is his."

The messenger hesitated and then bowed his head.

"He has until dawn to withdraw from Chullish and three days to withdraw from the rest of my lands and cities."

"But he has taken Dunfermine and Mailag in fair combat," the messenger said.

"He has taken them because of the treachery of men who sought power at the expense of innocent lives," Emyr growled. "I will yield no cities or lands to which the Dunkeldi do not have a just claim. If he refuses this chance, then he is a fool and unworthy to call himself king."

The messenger stood taller. "Those are strong words," he said "from a man who has ruled less than half an hour."

Betrayal

Hayden drew his sword, but Emyr restrained him with a raised hand.

"They are strong words spoken from a position of strength," Emyr said. "Tristan would do well not to underestimate me or the power of Coll. I know that most of the Salassani and Carpentini have not supported him and the Bracari and Taurini will desert him after a single defeat. He bullied them into joining him in the first place. I also know that he cannot pay the mercenaries who have already been deprived of the port cities they were supposed to ransack, and I know that the Alamani of Coll outnumber him six to one. We fight for our homes and our families. I have lived under Tristan's rule. I know how to break it."

The messenger kept his peace.

"You have until dawn," Emyr said again.

The messenger bowed, and Owen sent him away with an escort. When the man was out of earshot, Emyr addressed the captains and nobles who stood in a wide crescent watching him. Emyr had earned their respect with his handling of Tristan's messenger. Brion could see it in their faces and postures.

Emyr nodded to them. "Captains," he said. "Before I ask you for your reports and recommendations, I want to you to understand something," he glanced at Brigid. "I never sought this throne. I would have happily returned to the heathland."

Emyr glanced back at Lara's body. "We have all paid dearly to return the government of Coll to the line of Hassani. Now I ask you, will you join me?"

There was a brief pause. The men studied each other for a moment before they all raised their swords and gave a shout. Owen knelt and the rest followed.

"Thank you," Emyr said. "Now I need to know the disposition of our forces, our strengths and weaknesses."

Emyr climbed down the steps to join the captains, and Brion quit listening to them. He stretched out on the steps of the palace and laid his head in Finola's lap. Stars glittered faintly overhead. He closed his eyes and sighed. Despite the stiffness, it felt good to be able to lay down in something other than a fetal position. His body enjoyed the respite, but his heart ached. Would he ever be able to escape the pain? Should he ever want to?

Chapter 29
Home Again?

rion and Finola rode over the hill and reined their mounts to a stop. They looked down on the little cottage by the south road. The fields were overgrown with grass. The woods, now turning shades of yellow and red, stretched out in the distance, surrounded by waving prairie grasses. The crisp wind carried the familiar scents of fall.

A strange melancholy filled Brion. It had been more than a month since Tristan had withdrawn his forces from Coll. Emyr and Brigid had wed and busied themselves with the matters of court. Brion and Finola had buried their friends, married, and then escaped the stifling, suffocating city.

"Well, Duke Brion," Finola said. "Your palace awaits."

"Yes, Duchess," Brion said, "but you don't seem to have warned the servants of our arrival."

Finola laughed, but the levity didn't last.

"It's so strange," she said. "How lonely and unfamiliar a place can become."

Brion gazed at his childhood home. The memories rushed around him, inviting him and repelling him. The little valley would seem empty without Weyland, Rosland, and Neahl. Seamus would never come sneaking through the barley to lead Brion away from his work to their favorite fishing hole. Brigid would not be there to fuss over the silly cow. So many had died. So much had changed.

"You know I can't stay here," Brion said.

Finola stroked the neck of her horse. "We could have gone with Redmond into the southland," she said.

Brion shook his head. She had misunderstood him. Killian's broken message about his mother had seared into his memory. She was out there, somewhere. He couldn't simply take up his life again without knowing what had happened to her.

"Redmond blames me," Brion said.

Finola reached out to touch his arm. "No he doesn't," she said. "He's just mourning. Give him time."

"But it is my fault," Brion said. "I refused to let things alone. He warned us that people would die. But I insisted."

"No one forced anybody to go into that city," Finola said. "We all knew the risk."

"Maybe," Brion said. He wasn't convinced.

"Well, if you don't want to go into the southland, we could stay in Chullish with my parents," Finola said. "Emyr would give us an entire wing of the palace."

Brion shuddered. "I would rather go boating with Tyg again."

Finola laughed. "You can still go to the Duke's home in the south," she said. "Owen might need help administering your lands."

"I have to find her, Finola," Brion said. "What if she's waiting for me to find her? What if she's in danger?"

"She could be anywhere, Brion, and the heathland is still crawling with Dunkeldi warriors. We can't just wander in there."

"I know." He gazed at the little vale for a long moment. His mind drifted to the heathland, to Redmond and Neahl and their daring rescue, to the brutally beautiful landscape that had worked itself into his skin.

"Do you remember that waterfall up in the Aldina Mountains?" Brion asked. "The big, beautiful one that looked like lace woven into the moss?"

Finola gave him a puzzled expression. "Of course," she said. "But what has that got to do with—"

"I can't stop thinking about it," Brion interrupted.

"What about it?"

"And do you remember the way the heathland blossomed after every rain storm?"

"Now what are you talking about?" Finola asked.

"It's in my bones, Finola. It's like a disease."

"Brion?"

"No listen. I want to see it again. I want to disappear with you into the heathland and just let it take us where it will. I don't want to have to worry about kingdoms and armies and palaces. I just want to roam and see what's over the next rise. Do you know what I mean?"

Finola smiled that sweet, enchanting smile.

"It beats busting my back in a bakery or suffering the false politeness of the court," she said. "I'm game, so long as you don't try to do any of the cooking."

Brion smiled back at her. The craving to see the heathland in full blossom again mingled with the ache to find his mother until they became one. She was out there, in the heathland, and he would find her.

"Too late in the season to set out now," Finola said. "We best let things settle down for a bit."

Brion kicked Misty into a walk. "True," Brion said, "but I can run you through Neahl's and Redmond's training program until the snow melts. In fact, I would really like to see if you can touch a deer."

Thassani Royal Line

♔Felix = Gwena

Morgan = ♔Edward ≠ Evalyn   Kene = Ann

Albert = Winifred

Ryan = ♔Brianne

Fredrick = Lynette   Luther = Rachel   Lynette   Adelaide = Reynold ≠ Tiana

Christopher   Catherine = ♔Jerome   Keith = Eliana   Dean = Irene

Charles   George = Camille   Felix = Christina

Aleisha = Gilbert   helena = Gilbert   Rebecca = ♔Karl ≠ Eliza

Elise   Edward = Eliza   Peter = Annette

Brianna = Alec   Victoria   Jarod   Shaanan = William   ♔Edward   Anna   Kurk = Sarah

Weyland = Rosland   ♔Geric = Olivia

Jeffrey   Sarah = William   Eryann   Derek = Morwyn   Lara ≠ Redmond

Brigid   Damian

Isabel = Dustin ≠ Elsie   Emyr

Cedrick   ?   Rhodri

ABOUT J.W. ELLIOT

J.W. Elliot is a professional historian, martial artist, canoer, bow builder, knife maker, wood turner, and rock climber. He has a Ph.D. in Latin American and World History. He has lived in Portugal, Brazil, Idaho, Arizona, Oklahoma, and Massachusetts. He writes non-fiction works of history about the Inquisition, Columbus, and Pirates. J.W. Elliot loves to travel and challenge himself in the outdoors.

Connect with J.W. Elliot online at:
www.jwelliot.com/contact-us

Books by J.W. Elliot

Archer of the Heathland Series
Prequel: *Intrigue*
Book I: *Deliverance*
Book II: *Betrayal*
Book III: *Vengeance*
Book IV: *Chronicles*
Book V: *Windemere*
Book VI: *Renegade*

The Miserable Life of Bernie LeBaron
Somewhere in the Mist
Walls of Glass

If you have enjoyed this book, please consider leaving an honest review on Amazon and sharing on your social media sites.

Please sign up for my newsletter where you can get a free short story and more free content at: **www.jwelliot.com**

Thanks for your support!

J.W. Elliiot

Made in the
USA
Lexington, KY